THE WRITINGS OF
LAFCADIO HEARN
Large=Paper Edition

IN SIXTEEN VOLUMES

VOLUME X

SHADOWINGS

AND

A JAPANESE MISCELLANY

BY

LAFCADIO HEARN

BOSTON AND NEW YORK
HOUGHTON MIFFLIN COMPANY
MDCCCCXXII

THE LARGE-PAPER EDITION IS LIMITED TO
SEVEN HUNDRED AND FIFTY COPIES PRINTED
AT THE RIVERSIDE PRESS, CAMBRIDGE, U.S.A.
NUMBER . . . .

CONTENTS

SHADOWINGS

CONTENTS

A JAPANESE MISCELLANY

ILLUSTRATIONS

SHADOWINGS

STORIES FROM STRANGE BOOKS

Il avait vu brûler d'étranges pierres,
Jadis, dans les brasiers de la pensée . . .

EMILE VERHAEREN

SHADOWINGS

. .

THE RECONCILIATION [1]

THERE was a young samurai of Kyōto who had been
reduced to poverty by the ruin of his lord, and found
himself obliged to leave his home, and to take service with the Governor of a distant province. Before
quitting the capital, this samurai divorced his wife
— a good and beautiful woman — under the belief
that he could better obtain promotion by another
alliance. He then married the daughter of a family
of some distinction, and took her with him to the
district whither he had been called.

But it was in the time of the thoughtlessness of
youth, and the sharp experience of want, that the
samurai could not understand the worth of the affection so lightly cast away. His second marriage
did not prove a happy one; the character of his new
wife was hard and selfish; and he soon found every
cause to think with regret of Kyōto days. Then he
discovered that he still loved his first wife — loved
her more than he could ever love the second; and he
began to feel how unjust and how thankless he had

[1] The original story is to be found in the curious volume entitled
Konséki-Monogatari.

3

been. Gradually his repentance deepened into a remorse that left him no peace of mind. Memories of the woman he had wronged — her gentle speech, her smiles, her dainty, pretty ways, her faultless patience — continually haunted him. Sometimes in dreams he saw her at her loom, weaving as when she toiled night and day to help him during the years of their distress: more often he saw her kneeling alone in the desolate little room where he had left her, veiling her tears with her poor worn sleeve. Even in the hours of official duty, his thoughts would wander back to her: then he would ask himself how she was living, what she was doing. Something in his heart assured him that she could not accept another husband, and that she never would refuse to pardon him. And he secretly resolved to seek her out as soon as he could return to Kyōto — then to beg her forgiveness, to take her back, to do everything that a man could do to make atonement. But the years went by.

At last the Governor's official term expired, and the samurai was free. "Now I will go back to my dear one," he vowed to himself. "Ah, what a cruelty — what a folly to have divorced her!" He sent his second wife to her own people (she had given him no children); and hurrying to Kyōto, he went at once to seek his former companion — not allowing himself even the time to change his traveling-garb.

When he reached the street where she used to

4

live, it was late in the night — the night of the tenth
day of the ninth month; — and the city was silent
as a cemetery. But a bright moon made everything
visible; and he found the house without difficulty.
It had a deserted look: tall weeds were growing on
the roof. He knocked at the sliding-doors, and no
one answered. Then, finding that the doors had not
been fastened from within, he pushed them open,
and entered. The front room was matless and empty:
a chilly wind was blowing through crevices in the
planking; and the moon shone through a ragged
break in the wall of the alcove. Other rooms presented a like forlorn condition. The house, to all
seeming, was unoccupied. Nevertheless, the samurai
determined to visit one other apartment at the farther end of the dwelling — a very small room that
had been his wife's favorite resting-place. Approaching the sliding-screen that closed it, he was startled
to perceive a glow within. He pushed the screen
aside, and uttered a cry of joy; for he saw her there
— sewing by the light of a paper-lamp. Her eyes at
the same instant met his own; and with a happy
smile she greeted him — asking only: "When did
you come back to Kyōto? How did you find your
way here to me, through all those black rooms?"
The years had not changed her. Still she seemed as
fair and young as in his fondest memory of her; —
but sweeter than any memory there came to him the
music of her voice, with its trembling of pleased
wonder.

5

Then joyfully he took his place beside her, and told her all: — how deeply he repented his selfishness — how wretched he had been without her — how constantly he had regretted her — how long he had hoped and planned to make amends; — caressing her the while, and asking her forgiveness over and over again. She answered him, with loving gentleness, according to his heart's desire — entreating him to cease all self-reproach. It was wrong, she said, that he should have allowed himself to suffer on her account: she had always felt that she was not worthy to be his wife. She knew that he had separated from her, notwithstanding, only because of poverty; and while he lived with her, he had always been kind; and she had never ceased to pray for his happiness. But even if there had been a reason for speaking of amends, this honorable visit would be ample amends; — what greater happiness than thus to see him again, though it were only for a moment? "Only for a moment!" he answered, with a glad laugh — "say, rather, for the time of seven existences! My loved one, unless you forbid, I am coming back to live with you always — always — always! Nothing shall ever separate us again. Now I have means and friends: we need not fear poverty. To-morrow my goods will be brought here; and my servants will come to wait upon you; and we shall make this house beautiful. . . . To-night," he added, apologetically, "I came thus late — without even changing my dress — only because of the

6

longing I had to see you, and to tell you this." She seemed greatly pleased by these words; and in her turn she told him about all that had happened in Kyōto since the time of his departure — excepting her own sorrows, of which she sweetly refused to speak. They chatted far into the night: then she conducted him to a warmer room, facing south — a room that had been their bridal chamber in former time. "Have you no one in the house to help you?" he asked, as she began to prepare the couch for him. "No," she answered, laughing cheerfully: "I could not afford a servant; — so I have been living all alone." "You will have plenty of servants to-morrow," he said — "good servants — and everything else that you need." They lay down to rest — not to sleep: they had too much to tell each other; — and they talked of the past and the present and the future, until the dawn was gray. Then, involuntarily, the samurai closed his eyes, and slept.

When he awoke, the daylight was streaming through the chinks of the sliding-shutters; and he found himself, to his utter amazement, lying upon the naked boards of a mouldering floor. . . . Had he only dreamed a dream? No: she was there; — she slept. . . . He bent above her — and looked — and shrieked — for the sleeper had no face! . . . Before him, wrapped in its grave-sheet only, lay the corpse of a woman — a corpse so wasted that little remained save the bones, and the long black tangled hair.

. . . .

Slowly — as he stood shuddering and sickening in the sun — the icy horror yielded to a despair so intolerable, a pain so atrocious, that he clutched at the mocking shadow of a doubt. Feigning ignorance of the neighborhood, he ventured to ask his way to the house in which his wife had lived.

"There is no one in that house," said the person questioned. "It used to belong to the wife of a samurai who left the city several years ago. He divorced her in order to marry another woman before he went away; and she fretted a great deal, and so became sick. She had no relatives in Kyōto, and nobody to care for her; and she died in the autumn of the same year — on the tenth day of the ninth month. . . ."

A LEGEND OF FUGEN-BOSATSU [1]

THERE was once a very pious and learned priest, called Shōku Shōnin, who lived in the province of Harima. For many years he meditated daily upon the chapter of Fugen-Bosatsu [the Bodhisattva Samantabhadra] in the Sutra of the Lotus of the Good Law; and he used to pray, every morning and evening, that he might at some time be permitted to behold Fugen-Bosatsu as a living presence, and in the form described in the holy text.[2]

One evening, while he was reciting the Sutra, drowsiness overcame him; and he fell asleep leaning upon his kyōsoku.[3] Then he dreamed; and in his dream a voice told him that, in order to see Fugen-Bosatsu, he must go to the house of a certain courte-

---

[1] From the old story-book, *Jikkun-shō*.

[2] The priest's desire was probably inspired by the promises recorded in the chapter entitled "The Encouragement of Samantabhadra" (see Kern's translation of the Saddharma Pundarîka in the *Sacred Books of the East*, pp. 433-34): "Then the Bodhisattva Mahâsattva Samantabhadra said to the Lord: . . . 'When a preacher who applies himself to this Dharmaparyâya shall take a walk, then, O Lord, will I mount a white elephant with six tusks, and betake myself to the place where that preacher is walking, in order to protect this Dharmaparyâya. And when that preacher, applying himself to this Dharmaparyâya, forgets, be it but a single word or syllable, then will I mount the white elephant with six tusks, and show my face to that preacher, and repeat this entire Dharmaparyâya.'" But these promises refer to "the end of time."

[3] The kyōsoku is a kind of padded arm-rest, or arm-stool, upon which the priest leans one arm while reading. The use of such an arm-rest is not confined, however, to the Buddhist clergy.

9

san, known as the "Yujō-no-Chōja,"[1] who lived in the town of Kanzaki. Immediately upon awakening he resolved to go to Kanzaki; — and, making all possible haste, he reached the town by the evening of the next day.

When he entered the house of the yujō, he found many persons already there assembled — mostly young men of the capital, who had been attracted to Kanzaki by the fame of the woman's beauty. They were feasting and drinking; and the yujō was playing a small hand-drum (tsuzumi), which she used very skillfully, and singing a song. The song which she sang was an old Japanese song about a famous shrine in the town of Murozumi; and the words were these:

> Within the sacred water-tank[2] of Murozumi in Suwō,
> Even though no wind be blowing,
> The surface of the water is always rippling.

The sweetness of the voice filled everybody with surprise and delight. As the priest, who had taken a place apart, listened and wondered, the girl suddenly fixed her eyes upon him; and in the same instant he saw her form change into the form of Fugen-Bosatsu, emitting from her brow a beam of light that seemed to pierce beyond the limits of the universe, and riding

---

[1] A yujō, in old days, was a singing-girl as well as a courtesan. The term "Yujō-no-Chōja," in this case, would mean simply "the first (or best) of yujō."

[2] Mitarai (or mitarashi) is the name especially given to the water-tanks, or water-fonts — of stone or bronze — placed before Shintō shrines in order that the worshiper may purify his lips and hands before making prayer. Buddhist tanks are not so named.

a snow-white elephant with six tusks. And still she sang — but the song also was now transformed; and the words came thus to the ears of the priest:

On the Vast Sea of Cessation,
Though the Winds of the Six Desires and of the Five Corruptions
    never blow,
Yet the surface of that deep is always covered
With the billowings of Attainment to the Reality-in-Itself.

Dazzled by the divine ray, the priest closed his eyes: but through their lids he still distinctly saw the vision. When he opened them again, it was gone: he saw only the girl with her hand-drum, and heard only the song about the water of Murozumi. But he found that as often as he shut his eyes he could see Fugen-Bosatsu on the six-tusked elephant, and could hear the mystic Song of the Sea of Cessation. The other persons present saw only the yujō: they had not beheld the manifestation.

Then the singer suddenly disappeared from the banquet-room — none could say when or how. From that moment the revelry ceased; and gloom took the place of joy. After having waited and sought for the girl to no purpose, the company dispersed in great sorrow. Last of all, the priest departed, bewildered by the emotions of the evening. But scarcely had he passed beyond the gate, when the yujō appeared before him, and said: "Friend, do not speak yet to any one of what you have seen this night." And with these words she vanished away — leaving the air filled with a delicious fragrance.

STORIES FROM STRANGE BOOKS

The monk by whom the foregoing legend was recorded, comments upon it thus: The condition of a yujō is low and miserable, since she is condemned to serve the lusts of men. Who therefore could imagine that such a woman might be the nirmaṇakaya, or incarnation, of a Bodhisattva. But we must remember that the Buddhas and Bodhisattvas may appear in this world in countless different forms; choosing, for the purpose of their divine compassion, even the most humble or contemptible shapes when such shapes can serve them to lead men into the true path, and to save them from the perils of illusion.

THE SCREEN-MAIDEN [1]

SAYS the old Japanese author, Hakubai-En Rosui: [2]

In Chinese and in Japanese books there are related many stories — both of ancient and of modern times — about pictures that were so beautiful as to exercise a magical influence upon the beholder. And concerning such beautiful pictures — whether pictures of flowers or of birds or of people, painted by famous artists — it is further told that the shapes of the creatures or the persons, therein depicted, would separate themselves from the paper or the silk upon which they had been painted, and would perform various acts; — so that they became, by their own will, really alive. We shall not now repeat any of the stories of this class which have been known to everybody from ancient times. But even in modern times the fame of the pictures painted by Hishigawa Kichibei — "Hishigawa's Portraits" — has become widespread in the land.

He then proceeds to relate the following story about one of the so-called portraits:

There was a young scholar of Kyōto whose name

---

[1] Related in the *Otogi-Hyaku-Monogatari*.

[2] He died in the eighteenth year of Kyōhō (1733). The painter to whom he refers — better known to collectors as Hishigawa Kichibei Moronobu — flourished during the latter part of the seventeenth century. Beginning his career as a dyer's apprentice, he won his reputation as an artist about 1680, when he may be said to have founded the Ukiyo-yé school of illustration. Hishigawa was especially a delineator of what are called "fūryū" ("elegant manners") — the aspects of life among the upper classes of society.

13

was Tokkei. He used to live in the street called Mu-
romachi. One evening, while on his way home after
a visit, his attention was attracted by an old single-
leaf screen (tsuitaté), exposed for sale before the
shop of a dealer in second-hand goods. It was only
a paper-covered screen; but there was painted upon
it the full-length figure of a girl which caught the
young man's fancy. The price asked was very
small: Tokkei bought the screen, and took it home
with him.

When he looked again at the screen, in the solitude
of his own room, the picture seemed to him much
more beautiful than before. Apparently it was a real
likeness — the portrait of a girl fifteen or sixteen
years old; and every little detail in the painting of
the hair, eyes, eyelashes, mouth, had been executed
with a delicacy and a truth beyond praise. The
manajiri [1] seemed "like a lotus-blossom courting
favor"; the lips were "like the smile of a red flower";
the whole young face was inexpressibly sweet. If the
real girl so portrayed had been equally lovely, no
man could have looked upon her without losing his
heart. And Tokkei believed that she must have been
thus lovely; — for the figure seemed alive — ready
to reply to anybody who might speak to it.

Gradually, as he continued to gaze at the picture,

[1] Also written "méjiri" — the exterior canthus of the eye. The Japanese (like the old Greek and the old Arabian poets) have many curious
dainty words and similes to express particular beauties of the hair, eyes,
eyelids, lips, fingers, etc.

he felt himself bewitched by the charm of it. "Can there really have been in this world," he murmured to himself, "so delicious a creature? How gladly would I give my life — nay, a thousand years of life! — to hold her in my arms even for a moment!" (The Japanese author says "for a few seconds.") In short, he became enamoured of the picture — so much enamoured of it as to feel that he never could love any woman except the person whom it represented. Yet that person, if still alive, could no longer resemble the painting: perhaps she had been buried long before he was born!

Day by day, nevertheless, this hopeless passion grew upon him. He could not eat; he could not sleep: neither could he occupy his mind with those studies which had formerly delighted him. He would sit for hours before the picture, talking to it — neglecting or forgetting everything else. And at last he fell sick — so sick that he believed himself going to die.

Now among the friends of Tokkei there was one venerable scholar who knew many strange things about old pictures and about young hearts. This aged scholar, hearing of Tokkei's illness, came to visit him, and saw the screen, and understood what had happened. Then Tokkei, being questioned, confessed everything to his friend, and declared: "If I cannot find such a woman, I shall die."

The old man said:

"That picture was painted by Hishigawa Kichibei — painted from life. The person whom it represented is not now in the world. But it is said that Hishigawa Kichibei painted her mind as well as her form, and that her spirit lives in the picture. So I think that you can win her."

Tokkei half rose from his bed, and stared eagerly at the speaker.

"You must give her a name," the old man continued; — "and you must sit before her picture every day, and keep your thoughts constantly fixed upon her, and call her gently by the name which you have given her, *until she answers you*. . . ."

"Answers me!" exclaimed the lover, in breathless amazement.

"Oh, yes," the adviser responded, "she will certainly answer you. But you must be ready, when she answers you, to present her with what I am going to tell you. . . ."

"I will give her my life!" cried Tokkei.

"No," said the old man; — "you will present her with a cup of wine that has been bought at one hundred different wine-shops. Then will she come out of the screen to accept the wine. After that, probably she herself will tell you what to do."

With these words the old man went away. His advice aroused Tokkei from despair. At once he seated himself before the picture, and called it by the name of a girl (what name the Japanese narrator has forgotten to tell us) over and over again, very tenderly. That day it made no answer, nor the next day, nor the next. But Tokkei did not lose faith or patience; and after many days it suddenly one evening answered to its name:

"Hai!" (Yes.)

Then quickly, quickly, some of the wine from a hundred different wine-shops was poured out, and reverentially presented in a little cup. And the girl stepped from the screen, and walked upon the matting of the room, and knelt to take the cup from Tokkei's hand — asking, with a delicious smile:

"How could you love me so much?"

Says the Japanese narrator: "She was much more beautiful than the picture — beautiful to the tips of her finger-nails — beautiful also in heart and temper — lovelier than anybody else in the world." What answer Tokkei made to her question is not recorded: it will have to be imagined.

"But will you not soon get tired of me?" she asked.

"Never while I live!" he protested.

"And after — ?" she persisted; — for the Japanese bride is not satisfied with love for one lifetime only.

"Let us pledge ourselves to each other," he entreated, "for the time of seven existences."

"If you are ever unkind to me," she said, "I will go back to the screen."

They pledged each other. I suppose that Tokkei was a good boy — for his bride never returned to

17

the screen. The space that she had occupied upon it remained a blank.

Exclaims the Japanese author:
"How very seldom do such things happen in this world!"

THE CORPSE-RIDER [1]

THE body was cold as ice; the heart had long ceased to beat: yet there were no other signs of death. Nobody even spoke of burying the woman. She had died of grief and anger at having been divorced. It would have been useless to bury her — because the last undying wish of a dying person for vengeance can burst asunder any tomb and rift the heaviest graveyard stone. People who lived near the house in which she was lying fled from their homes. They knew that she was only *waiting for the return of the man who had divorced her.*

At the time of her death he was on a journey. When he came back and was told what had happened, terror seized him. "If I can find no help before dark," he thought to himself, "she will tear me to pieces." It was yet only the Hour of the Dragon; [2] but he knew that he had no time to lose.

He went at once to an inyōshi, [3] and begged for succor. The inyōshi knew the story of the dead woman; and he had seen the body. He said to the supplicant: "A very great danger threatens you. I will try to save you. But you must promise to do

---

[1] From the *Konsêki-Monogatari.*

[2] Tatsu no Koku, or the Hour of the Dragon, by old Japanese time, began at about eight o'clock in the morning.

[3] Inyōshi, a professor or master of the science of in-yō — the old Chinese nature-philosophy, based upon the theory of a male and a female principle pervading the universe.

whatever I shall tell you to do. There is only one way by which you can be saved. It is a fearful way. But unless you find the courage to attempt it, she will tear you limb from limb. If you can be brave, come to me again in the evening before sunset." The man shuddered; but he promised to do whatever should be required of him.

At sunset the inyōshi went with him to the house where the body was lying. The inyōshi pushed open the sliding-doors, and told his client to enter. It was rapidly growing dark. "I dare not!" gasped the man, quaking from head to foot; — "I dare not even look at her!" "You will have to do much more than look at her," declared the inyōshi; — "and you promised to obey. Go in!" He forced the trembler into the house and led him to the side of the corpse.

The dead woman was lying on her face. "Now you must get astride upon her," said the inyōshi, "and sit firmly on her back, as if you were riding a horse. . . . Come! — you must do it!" The man shivered so that the inyōshi had to support him — shivered horribly; but he obeyed. "Now take her hair in your hands," commanded the inyōshi — "half in the right hand, half in the left. . . . So! . . . You must grip it like a bridle. Twist your hands in it — both hands — tightly. That is the way! . . . Listen to me! You must stay like that till morning. You will have reason to be afraid in the night —

plenty of reason. But whatever may happen, never let go of her hair. If you let go — even for one second — she will tear you into gobbets!"

The inyōshi then whispered some mysterious words into the ear of the body, and said to its rider: "Now, for my own sake, I must leave you alone with her. . . . Remain as you are! . . . Above all things, remember that you must not let go of her hair." And he went away — closing the doors behind him.

Hour after hour the man sat upon the corpse in black fear; — and the hush of the night deepened and deepened about him till he screamed to break it. Instantly the body sprang beneath him, as to cast him off; and the dead woman cried out loudly, "Oh, how heavy it is! Yet I shall bring that fellow here now!"

Then tall she rose, and leaped to the doors, and flung them open, and rushed into the night — always bearing the weight of the man. But he, shutting his eyes, kept his hands twisted in her long hair — tightly, tightly — though fearing with such a fear that he could not even moan. How far she went, he never knew. He saw nothing: he heard only the sound of her naked feet in the dark — picha-picha, picha-picha — and the hiss of her breathing as she ran.

At last she turned, and ran back into the house, and lay down upon the floor exactly as at first.

Under the man she panted and moaned till the cocks began to crow. Thereafter she lay still.

But the man, with chattering teeth, sat upon her until the inyōshi came at sunrise. "So you did not let go of her hair!" — observed the inyōshi, greatly pleased. "That is well. . . . Now you can stand up." He whispered again into the ear of the corpse, and then said to the man: "You must have passed a fearful night; but nothing else could have saved you. Hereafter you may feel secure from her vengeance."

The conclusion of this story I do not think to be morally satisfying. It is not recorded that the corpse-rider became insane, or that his hair turned white: we are told only that "he worshiped the inyōshi with tears of gratitude." A note appended to the recital is equally disappointing. "It is reported," the Japanese author says, "that a grandchild of the man [who rode the corpse] still survives, and that a grandson of the inyōshi is at this very time living in a village called Otokunoi-mura [probably pronounced Otonoi-mura]."

This village-name does not appear in any Japanese directory of to-day. But the names of many towns and villages have been changed since the foregoing story was written.

THE SYMPATHY OF BENTEN [1]

In Kyōto there is a famous temple called Amadera. Sadazumi Shinnō, the fifth son of the Emperor Seiwa, passed the greater part of his life there as a priest; and the graves of many celebrated persons are to be seen in the temple-grounds.

But the present edifice is not the ancient Amadera. The original temple, after the lapse of ten centuries, fell into such decay that it had to be entirely rebuilt in the fourteenth year of Genroku (1701 A.D.).

A great festival was held to celebrate the rebuilding of the Amadera; and among the thousands of persons who attended that festival there was a young scholar and poet named Hanagaki Baishū. He wandered about the newly laid-out grounds and gardens, delighted by all that he saw, until he reached the place of a spring at which he had often drunk in former times. He was then surprised to find that the soil about the spring had been dug away, so as to form a square pond, and that at one corner of this pond there had been set up a wooden tablet bearing the words "Tanjō-Sui" (Birth-Water).[2] He also saw that a small, but very handsome temple of the

[1] The original story is in the *Otogi-Hyaku-Monogatari*.

[2] The word "tanjō" (birth) should here be understood in its mystical Buddhist meaning of new life or rebirth, rather than in the Western signification of birth.

23

Goddess Benten had been erected beside the pond. While he was looking at this new temple, a sudden gust of wind blew to his feet a tanzaku,[1] on which the following poem had been written:

> Shirushi aréto
> Iwai zo somuru
> Tama hōki,
> Toruté bakari no
> Chigiri narétomo.

This poem — a poem on first love (hatsu koi), composed by the famous Shunrei Kyō — was not unfamiliar to him; but it had been written upon the tanzaku by a female hand, and so exquisitely that he could scarcely believe his eyes. Something in the form of the characters — an indefinite grace — suggested that period of youth between childhood and womanhood; and the pure rich color of the ink seemed to bespeak the purity and goodness of the writer's heart.[2]

Baishū carefully folded up the tanzaku, and took it home with him. When he looked at it again the

---

1 Tanzaku is the name given to the long strips or ribbons of paper, usually colored, upon which poems are written perpendicularly. Poems written upon tanzaku are suspended to trees in flower, to wind-bells, to any beautiful object in which the poet has found an inspiration.

2 It is difficult for the inexperienced European eye to distinguish in Chinese or Japanese writing those characteristics implied by our term "hand" — in the sense of individual style. But the Japanese scholar never forgets the peculiarities of a handwriting once seen; and he can even guess at the approximate age of the writer. Chinese and Japanese authors claim that the color (quality) of the ink used tells something of the character of the writer. As every person grounds or prepares his or her own ink, the deeper and clearer black would at least indicate something of personal carefulness and of the sense of beauty.

writing appeared to him even more wonderful than at first. His knowledge in calligraphy assured him only that the poem had been written by some girl who was very young, very intelligent, and probably very gentle-hearted. But this assurance sufficed to shape within his mind the image of a very charming person; and he soon found himself in love with the unknown. Then his first resolve was to seek out the writer of the verses, and, if possible, make her his wife. . . . Yet how was he to find her? Who was she? Where did she live Certainly he could hope to find her only through the favor of the gods.

But presently it occurred to him that the gods might be very willing to lend their aid. The tanzaku had come to him while he was standing in front of the temple of Benten-Sama; and it was to this divinity in particular that lovers were wont to pray for happy union. This reflection impelled him to beseech the goddess for assistance. He went at once to the temple of Benten-of-the-Birth-Water (Tanjō-sui-no-Benten) in the grounds of the Amadera; and there, with all the fervor of his heart, he made his petition: "O Goddess, pity me! — help me to find where the young person lives who wrote the tanzaku! — vouchsafe me but one chance to meet her — even if only for a moment!" And after having made this prayer, he began to perform a seven days' religious service (nanuka-mairi)[1] in honor of the goddess;

[1] There are many kinds of religious exercises called "mairi." The

vowing at the same time to pass the seventh night in ceaseless worship before her shrine.

Now on the seventh night — the night of his vigil — during the hour when the silence is most deep, he heard at the main gateway of the temple-grounds a voice calling for admittance. Another voice from within answered; the gate was opened; and Baishū saw an old man of majestic appearance approaching with slow steps. This venerable person was clad in robes of ceremony; and he wore upon his snow-white head a black cap (eboshi) of the form indicating high rank. Reaching the little temple of Benten, he knelt down in front of it, as if respectfully awaiting some order. Then the outer door of the temple was opened; the hanging curtain of bamboo behind it, concealing the inner sanctuary, was rolled half-way up; and a chigo[1] came forward — a beautiful boy, with long hair tied back in the ancient manner. He stood at the threshold, and said to the old man in a clear loud voice:

"There is a person here who has been praying for a love-union not suitable to his present condition, and otherwise difficult to bring about. But as the young man is worthy of Our pity, you have been

performer of a nanuka-mairi pledges himself to pray at a certain temple every day for seven days in succession.

[1] The term "chigo" usually means the page of a noble household, especially an Imperial page. The chigo who appears in this story is of course a supernatural being — the court-messenger of the goddess, and her mouthpiece.

26

called to see whether something can be done for him. If there should prove to be any relation between the parties from the period of a former birth, you will introduce them to each other."

On receiving this command, the old man bowed respectfully to the chigo: then, rising, he drew from the pocket of his long left sleeve a crimson cord. One end of this cord he passed round Baishū's body, as if to bind him with it. The other end he put into the flame of one of the temple-lamps; and while the cord was there burning, he waved his hand three times, as if to summon somebody out of the dark.

Immediately, in the direction of the Amadera, a sound of coming steps was heard; and in another moment a girl appeared — a charming girl, fifteen or sixteen years old. She approached gracefully, but very shyly — hiding the lower part of her face with a fan; and she knelt down beside Baishū. The chigo then said to Baishū:

"Recently you have been suffering much heart-pain; and this desperate love of yours has even impaired your health. We could not allow you to remain in so unhappy a condition; and We therefore summoned the Old-Man-under-the-Moon [1] to make you acquainted with the writer of that tanzaku. She is now beside you."

With these words, the chigo retired behind the

---

[1] Gekkawō. This is a poetical appellation for the God of Marriage, more usually known as "Musubi-no-kami." Throughout this story there is an interesting mingling of Shintō and Buddhist ideas.

bamboo curtain. Then the old man went away as he had come; and the young girl followed him. Simultaneously Baishū heard the great bell of the Amadera sounding the hour of dawn. He prostrated himself in thanksgiving before the shrine of Benten-of-the-Birth-Water, and proceeded homeward — feeling as if awakened from some delightful dream — happy at having seen the charming person whom he had so fervently prayed to meet — unhappy also because of the fear that he might never meet her again.

But scarcely had he passed from the gateway into the street, when he saw a young girl walking alone in the same direction that he was going; and, even in the dusk of the dawn, he recognized her at once as the person to whom he had been introduced before the temple of Benten. As he quickened his pace to overtake her, she turned and saluted him with a graceful bow. Then for the first time he ventured to speak to her; and she answered him in a voice of which the sweetness filled his heart with joy. Through the yet silent streets they walked on, chatting happily, till they found themselves before the house where Baishū lived. There he paused — spoke to the girl of his hopes and fears. Smiling, she asked: "Do you not know that I was sent for to become your wife?" And she entered with him.

Becoming his wife, she delighted him beyond expectation by the charm of her mind and heart.

28

Moreover, he found her to be much more accomplished than he had supposed. Besides being able to write so wonderfully, she could paint beautiful pictures; she knew the art of arranging flowers, the art of embroidery, the art of music; she could weave and sew; and she knew everything in regard to the management of a house.

It was in the early autumn that the young people had met; and they lived together in perfect accord until the winter season began. Nothing, during those months, occurred to disturb their peace. Baishū's love for his gentle wife only strengthened with the passing of time. Yet, strangely enough, he remained ignorant of her history — knew nothing about her family. Of such matters she had never spoken; and, as the gods had given her to him, he imagined that it would not be proper to question her. But neither the Old-Man-under-the-Moon nor any one else came — as he had feared — to take her away. Nobody even made any inquiries about her. And the neighbors, for some undiscoverable reason, acted as if totally unaware of her presence.

Baishū wondered at all this. But stranger experiences were awaiting him.

One winter morning he happened to be passing through a somewhat remote quarter of the city, when he heard himself loudly called by name, and saw a man-servant making signs to him from the gateway of a private residence. As Baishū did not know the man's face, and did not have a single acquaintance in that part of Kyōto, he was more than startled by so abrupt a summons. But the servant, coming forward, saluted him with the utmost respect, and said, "My master greatly desires the honor of speaking with you: deign to enter for a moment." After an instant of hesitation, Baishū allowed himself to be conducted to the house. A dignified and richly dressed person, who seemed to be the master, welcomed him at the entrance, and led him to the guest-room. When the courtesies due upon a first meeting had been fully exchanged, the host apologized for the informal manner of his invitation, and said:

"It must have seemed to you very rude of us to call you in such a way. But perhaps you will pardon our impoliteness when I tell you that we acted thus upon what I firmly believe to have been an inspiration from the Goddess Benten. Now permit me to explain.

"I have a daughter, about sixteen years old, who can write rather well,[1] and do other things in the common way: she has the ordinary nature of woman. As we were anxious to make her happy by finding a good husband for her, we prayed the Goddess

[1] As it is the old Japanese rule that parents should speak depreciatingly of their children's accomplishments the phrase "rather well" in this connection would mean, for the visitor, "wonderfully well." For the same reason the expressions "common way" and "ordinary nature," as subsequently used, would imply almost the reverse of the literal meaning.

Benten to help us; and we sent to every temple of Benten in the city a tanzaku written by the girl. Some nights later, the goddess appeared to me in a dream, and said: 'We have heard your prayer, and have already introduced your daughter to the person who is to become her husband. During the coming winter he will visit you.' As I did not understand this assurance that a presentation had been made, I felt some doubt; I thought that the dream might have been only a common dream, signifying nothing. But last night again I saw Benten-Sama in a dream; and she said to me: 'To-morrow the young man, of whom I once spoke to you, will come to this street: then you can call him into your house, and ask him to become the husband of your daughter. He is a good young man; and later in life he will obtain a much higher rank than he now holds.' Then Benten-Sama told me your name, your age, your birthplace, and described your features and dress so exactly that my servant found no difficulty in recognizing you by the indications which I was able to give him."

This explanation bewildered Baishū instead of reassuring him; and his only reply was a formal return of thanks for the honor which the master of the house had spoken of doing him. But when the host invited him to another room, for the purpose of presenting him to the young lady, his embarrassment became extreme. Yet he could not reasonably decline the introduction. He could not bring himself, under such extraordinary circumstances, to announce that he already had a wife — a wife given to him by the Goddess Benten herself; a wife from whom he could not even think of separating. So, in silence and trepidation, he followed his host to the apartment indicated.

Then what was his amazement to discover, when presented to the daughter of the house, that she was the very same person whom he had already taken to wife!

The same — yet not the same.

She to whom he had been introduced by the Old-Man-under-the-Moon, was only the soul of the beloved.

She to whom he was now to be wedded, in her father's house, was the body.

Benten had wrought this miracle for the sake of her worshipers.

The original story breaks off suddenly at this point, leaving several matters unexplained. The ending is rather unsatisfactory. One would like to know something about the mental experiences of the real maiden during the married life of her phantom. One would also like to know what became of the phantom — whether it continued to lead an independent existence; whether it waited patiently for the return of its husband; whether it paid a visit to the real bride. And the book says nothing about these things. But a Japanese friend explains the miracle thus:

"The spirit-bride was really formed out of the tanzaku. So it is possible that the real girl did not know anything about the meeting at the temple of Benten. When she wrote those beautiful characters upon the tanzaku, something of her spirit passed into them. Therefore it was possible to evoke from the writing the double of the writer."

THE GRATITUDE OF THE SAMÉBITO[1]

THERE was a man named Tawaraya Tōtarō, who lived in the Province of Ōmi. His house was situated on the shore of Lake Biwa, not far from the famous temple called Ishiyamadera. He had some property, and lived in comfort; but at the age of twenty-nine he was still unmarried. His greatest ambition was to marry a very beautiful woman; and he had not been able to find a girl to his liking.

One day, as he was passing over the Long Bridge of Séta,[2] he saw a strange being crouching close to the parapet. The body of this being resembled the body of a man, but was black as ink; its face was like the face of a demon; its eyes were green as emeralds; and its beard was like the beard of a dragon. Tōtarō was at first very much startled. But the green eyes looked at him so gently that after a moment's hesitation he ventured to question the creature. Then it answered him, saying: "I am a Samébito [3] — a

[1] The original of this story may be found in the book called *Kibun-Anbaiyoshi.*

[2] The Long Bridge of Séta (Séta-no-Naga-Hashi), famous in Japanese legend, is nearly eight hundred feet in length, and commands a beautiful view. This bridge crosses the waters of the Setagawa near the junction of the stream with Lake Biwa. Ishiyamadera, one of the most picturesque Buddhist temples in Japan, is situated within a short distance from the bridge.

[3] Literally: "a Shark-Person," but in this story the Samébito is a male. The characters for Samébito can also be read Kōjin — which is the usual reading. In dictionaries the word is loosely rendered by "mer-

34

Shark-Man of the sea; and until a short time ago I was in the service of the Eight Great Dragon-Kings [Hachi-Dai-Ryū-Ō] as a subordinate officer in the Dragon-Palace [Ryūgū].[1] But because of a small fault which I committed, I was dismissed from the Dragon-Palace, and also banished from the Sea. Since then I have been wandering about here — unable to get any food, or even a place to lie down. If you can feel any pity for me, do, I beseech you, help me to find a shelter, and let me have something to eat!"

This petition was uttered in so plaintive a tone, and in so humble a manner, that Tōtarō's heart was touched. "Come with me," he said. "There is in my garden a large and deep pond where you may live as long as you wish; and I will give you plenty to eat."

The Samébito followed Tōtarō home, and appeared to be much pleased with the pond.

Thereafter, for nearly half a year, this strange guest dwelt in the pond, and was every day supplied by Tōtarō with such food as sea-creatures like.

[From this point of the original narrative the Shark-Man is referred to, not as a monster, but as a sympathetic Person of the male sex.]

Now, in the seventh month of the same year, there

man" or "mermaid"; but as the above description shows, the Samébito or Kōjin of the Far East is a conception having little in common with the Western idea of a merman or mermaid.

[1] Ryūgū is also the name given to the whole of that fairy-realm beneath the sea which figures in so many Japanese legends.

was a female pilgrimage (nyonin-mōdé) to the great
Buddhist temple called Miidera, in the neighboring
town of Ōtsu; and Tōtarō went to Ōtsu to attend
the festival. Among the multitude of women and
young girls there assembled, he observed a person of
extraordinary beauty. She seemed about sixteen
years old; her face was fair and pure as snow; and
the loveliness of her lips assured the beholder that
their every utterance would sound "as sweet as the
voice of a nightingale singing upon a plum-tree."
Tōtarō fell in love with her at sight. When she left
the temple he followed her at a respectful distance,
and discovered that she and her mother were stay-
ing for a few days at a certain house in the neighboring village of Séta. By questioning some of the
village folk, he was able also to learn that her name
was Tamana; that she was unmarried; and that her
family appeared to be unwilling that she should
marry a man of ordinary rank — for they demanded
as a betrothal-gift a casket containing ten thousand
jewels. [1]

Tōtarō returned home very much dismayed by
this information. The more that he thought about
the strange betrothal-gift demanded by the girl's

[1] Tama in the original. This word "tama" has a multitude of mean-
ings; and as here used it is quite as indefinite as our own terms "jewel,"
"gem," or "precious stone." Indeed, it is more indefinite, for it signifies
also a bead of coral, a ball of crystal, a polished stone attached to a hair-
pin, etc., etc. Later on, however, I venture to render it by "ruby" —
for reasons which need no explanation.

parents, the more he felt that he could never expect to obtain her for his wife. Even supposing that there were as many as ten thousand jewels in the whole country, only a great prince could hope to procure them.

But not even for a single hour could Tōtarō banish from his mind the memory of that beautiful being. It haunted him so that he could neither eat nor sleep; and it seemed to become more and more vivid as the days went by. And at last he became ill — so ill that he could not lift his head from the pillow. Then he sent for a doctor.

The doctor, after having made a careful examination, uttered an exclamation of surprise. "Almost any kind of sickness," he said, "can be cured by proper medical treatment, except the sickness of love. Your ailment is evidently love-sickness. There is no cure for it. In ancient times Rōya-Ō Hakuyo died of that sickness; and you must prepare yourself to die as he died." So saying, the doctor went away, without even giving any medicine to Tōtarō.

About this time the Shark-Man that was living in the garden-pond heard of his master's sickness, and came into the house to wait upon Tōtarō. And he tended him with the utmost affection both by day and by night. But he did not know either the cause or the serious nature of the sickness until nearly a week later, when Tōtarō, thinking himself about to die, uttered these words of farewell:

"I suppose that I have had the pleasure of caring for you thus long, because of some relation that grew up between us in a former state of existence. But now I am very sick indeed, and every day my sickness becomes worse; and my life is like the morning dew which passes away before the setting of the sun. For your sake, therefore, I am troubled in mind. Your existence has depended upon my care; and I fear that there will be no one to care for you and to feed you when I am dead. . . . My poor friend! . . . Alas! our hopes and our wishes are always disappointed in this unhappy world!"

No sooner had Tōtarō spoken these words than the Samébito uttered a strange wild cry of pain, and began to weep bitterly. And as he wept, great tears of blood streamed from his green eyes and rolled down his black cheeks and dripped upon the floor. And, falling, they were blood; but, having fallen, they became hard and bright and beautiful — became jewels of inestimable price, rubies splendid as crimson fire. For when men of the sea weep, their tears become precious stones.

Then Tōtarō, beholding this marvel, was so amazed and overjoyed that his strength returned to him. He sprang from his bed, and began to pick up and to count the tears of the Shark-Man, crying out the while: "My sickness is cured! I shall live! I shall live!"

Therewith, the Shark-Man, greatly astonished, ceased to weep, and asked Tōtarō to explain this wonderful cure; and Tōtarō told him about the young person seen at Miidera, and about the extraordinary marriage-gift demanded by her family. "As I felt sure," added Tōtarō, "that I should never be able to get ten thousand jewels, I supposed that my suit would be hopeless. Then I became very unhappy, and at last fell sick. But now, because of your generous weeping, I have many precious stones; and I think that I shall be able to marry that girl. Only — there are not yet quite enough stones; and I beg that you will be good enough to weep a little more, so as to make up the full number required."

But at this request the Samébito shook his head, and answered in a tone of surprise and of reproach:

"Do you think that I am like a harlot — able to weep whenever I wish? Oh, no! Harlots shed tears in order to deceive men; but creatures of the sea cannot weep without feeling real sorrow. I wept for you because of the true grief that I felt in my heart at the thought that you were going to die. But now I cannot weep for you, because you have told me that your sickness is cured."

"Then what am I to do?" plaintively asked Tōtarō. "Unless I can get ten thousand jewels, I cannot marry the girl!"

The Samébito remained for a little while silent, as if thinking. Then he said:

"Listen! To-day I cannot possibly weep any more. But to-morrow let us go together to the Long

39

Bridge of Séta, taking with us some wine and some fish. We can rest for a time on the bridge; and while we are drinking the wine and eating the fish, I shall gaze in the direction of the Dragon-Palace, and try, by thinking of the happy days that I spent there, to make myself feel homesick — so that I can weep."

Tōtarō joyfully assented.

Next morning the two, taking plenty of wine and fish with them, went to the Séta Bridge, and rested there, and feasted. After having drunk a great deal of wine, the Samébito began to gaze in the direction of the Dragon-Kingdom, and to think about the past. And gradually, under the softening influence of the wine, the memory of happier days filled his heart with sorrow, and the pain of homesickness came upon him, so that he could weep profusely. And the great red tears that he shed fell upon the bridge in a shower of rubies; and Tōtarō gathered them as they fell, and put them into a casket, and counted them until he had counted the full number of ten thousand. Then he uttered a shout of joy.

Almost in the same moment, from far away over the lake, a delightful sound of music was heard; and there appeared in the offing, slowly rising from the waters, like some fabric of cloud, a palace of the color of the setting sun.

At once the Samébito sprang upon the parapet of the bridge, and looked, and laughed for joy. Then, turning to Tōtarō, he said:

THE GRATITUDE OF THE SAMÉBITO

"There must have been a general amnesty proclaimed in the Dragon-Realm; the Kings are calling
me. So now I must bid you farewell. I am happy to
have had one chance of befriending you in return
for your goodness to me."

With these words he leaped from the bridge; and
no man ever saw him again. But Tōtarō presented
the casket of red jewels to the parents of Tamana,
and so obtained her in marriage.

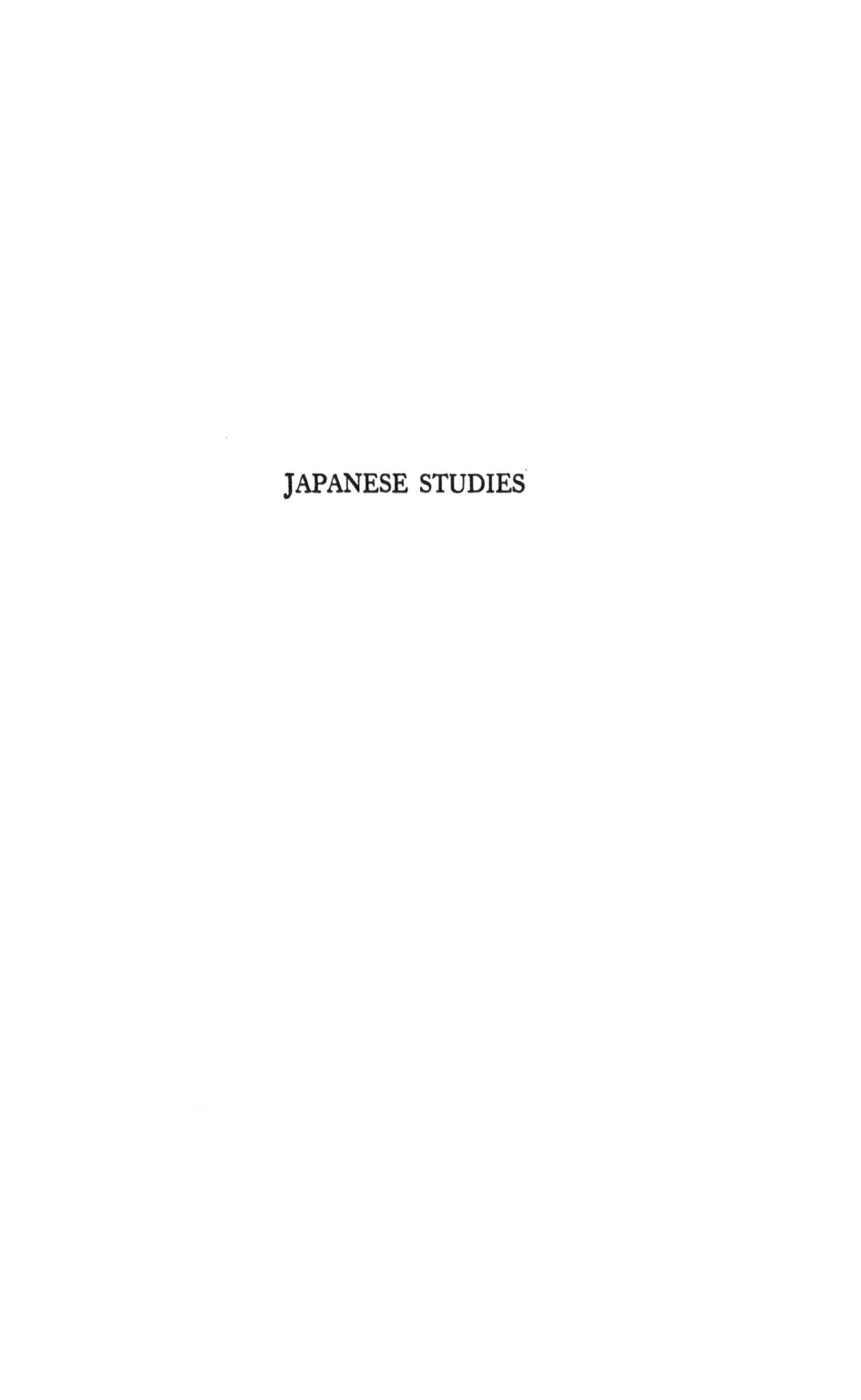

JAPANESE STUDIES

... Life ere long
Came on me in the public ways, and bent
Eyes deeper than of old: Death met I too,
And saw the dawn glow through.
GEORGE MEREDITH

SÉMI
(CICADÆ)

Koë ni mina
Naki-shimōté ya —
Sémi no kara!

Japanese Love-Song

The voice having been all consumed by crying, there remains only the shell of the sémi!

I

A CELEBRATED Chinese scholar, known in Japanese
literature as Riku-Un, wrote the following quaint
account of the Five Virtues of the Cicada:

I. The Cicada has upon its head certain figures or
signs.[1] These represent its [written] characters, style,
literature.

II. It eats nothing belonging to earth, and drinks only
dew. This proves its cleanliness, purity, propriety.

III. It always appears at a certain fixed time. This
proves its fidelity, sincerity, truthfulness.

IV. It will not accept wheat or rice. This proves its
probity, uprightness, honesty.

V. It does not make for itself any nest to live in. This
proves its frugality, thrift, economy.

We might compare this with the beautiful address of Anacreon to the cicada, written twenty-four
hundred years ago: on more than one point the Greek
poet and the Chinese sage are in perfect accord:

[1] The curious markings on the head of one variety of Japanese sémi
are believed to be characters which are names of souls.

45

JAPANESE STUDIES

We deem thee happy, O Cicada, because, having drunk, like a king, only a little dew, thou dost chirrup on the tops of trees. For all things whatsoever that thou seest in the fields are thine, and whatsoever the seasons bring forth. Yet art thou the friend of the tillers of the land — from no one harmfully taking aught. By mortals thou art held in honor as the pleasant harbinger of summer; and the Muses love thee. Phœbus himself loves thee, and has given thee a shrill song. And old age does not consume thee. O thou gifted one — earth-born, song-loving, free from pain, having flesh without blood — thou art nearly equal to the Gods![1]

And we must certainly go back to the old Greek literature in order to find a poetry comparable to that of the Japanese on the subject of musical insects. Perhaps of Greek verses on the cricket, the most beautiful are the lines of Meleager: "O cricket, the soother of slumber . . . weaving the thread of a voice that causes love to wander away!" . . . There are Japanese poems scarcely less delicate in sentiment on the chirruping of night-crickets; and Meleager's promise to reward the little singer with gifts of fresh leek, and with "drops of dew cut up small," sounds strangely Japanese. Then the poem attributed to Anyté, about the little girl Myro making a tomb for her pet cicada and cricket, and weeping because Hades, "hard to be persuaded," had taken her playthings away, represents an experience familiar to Japanese child-life. I suppose that little Myro (how freshly her tears still glisten, after

[1] In this and other citations from the Greek anthology, I have depended upon Burges' translation.

46

seven and twenty centuries!) prepared that "common tomb" for her pets much as the little maid of Nippon would do to-day, putting a small stone on top to serve for a monument. But the wiser Japanese Myro would repeat over the grave a certain Buddhist prayer.

It is especially in their poems upon the cicada that we find the old Greeks confessing their love of insect-melody: witness the lines in the Anthology about the tettix caught in a spider's snare, and "making lament in the thin fetters" until freed by the poet; — and the verses by Leonidas of Tarentum picturing the "unpaid minstrel to wayfaring men" as "sitting upon lofty trees, warmed with the great heat of summer, sipping the dew that is like woman's milk"; — and the dainty fragment of Meleager, beginning:

Thou vocal tettix, drunk with drops of dew, sitting with thy serrated limbs upon the tops of petals, thou givest out the melody of the lyre from thy dusky skin. . . .

Or take the charming address of Evenus to a nightingale:

Thou Attic maiden, honey-fed, hast chirping seized a chirping cicada, and bearest it to thy unfledged young — thou, a twitterer, the twitterer — thou, the winged, the well-winged — thou, a stranger, the stranger — thou, a summer-child, the summer-child! Wilt thou not quickly cast it from thee? For it is not right, it is not just, that those engaged in song should perish by the mouths of those engaged in song.

JAPANESE STUDIES

On the other hand, we find Japanese poets much more inclined to praise the voices of night-crickets than those of sémi. There are countless poems about sémi, but very few which commend their singing. Of course the sémi are very different from the cicadæ known to the Greeks. Some varieties are truly musical; but the majority are astonishingly noisy — so noisy that their stridulation is considered one of the great afflictions of summer. Therefore it were vain to seek among the myriads of Japanese verses on sémi for anything comparable to the lines of Evenus above quoted; indeed, the only Japanese poem that I could find on the subject of a cicada caught by a bird, was the following:

> Ana kanashi!
> Tobi ni toraruru
> Sémi no koë.
>
> RANSETSU

Ah! how piteous the cry of the sémi seized by the kite!

Or "caught by a boy" the poet might equally well have observed — this being a much more frequent cause of the pitiful cry. The lament of Nicias for the tettix would serve as the elegy of many a sémi:

No more shall I delight myself by sending out a sound from my quick-moving wings, because I have fallen into the savage hand of a boy, who seized me unexpectedly, as I was sitting under the green leaves.

Here I may remark that Japanese children usually capture sémi by means of a long slender bamboo tipped with bird-lime (mochi). The sound made by some kinds of sémi when caught is really pitiful — quite as pitiful as the twitter of a terrified bird. One finds it difficult to persuade one's self that the noise is not a *voice* of anguish, in the human sense of the word "voice," but the production of a specialized exterior membrane. Recently, on hearing a captured sémi thus scream, I became convinced in quite a new way that the stridulatory apparatus of certain insects must not be thought of as a kind of musical instrument, but as an organ of speech, and that its utterances are as intimately associated with simple forms of emotion, as are the notes of a bird — the extraordinary difference being that the insect has its vocal chords *outside*. But the insect-world is altogether a world of goblins and fairies: creatures with organs of which we cannot discover the use, and senses of which we cannot imagine the nature; — creatures with myriads of eyes, or with eyes in their backs, or with eyes moving about at the ends of trunks and horns; — creatures with ears in their legs and bellies, or with brains in their waists! If some of them happen to have voices outside of their bodies instead of inside, the fact ought not to surprise anybody.

I have not yet succeeded in finding any Japanese verses alluding to the stridulatory apparatus of sémi — though I think it probable that such verses exist. Certainly the Japanese have been for centuries familiar with the peculiarities of their own singing insects. But I should not now presume to say that their poets are incorrect in speaking of the "voices" of crickets and of cicadæ. The old Greek poets who actually describe insects as producing music with their wings and feet, nevertheless speak of the "voices," the "songs," and the "chirruping" of such creatures — just as the Japanese poets do. For example, Meleager thus addresses the cricket:

O thou that art with shrill wings the self-formed imitation of the lyre, chirrup me something pleasant while beating your vocal wings with your feet! . . .

II

BEFORE speaking further of the poetical literature of sémi, I must attempt a few remarks about the sémi themselves. But the reader need not expect anything entomological. Excepting, perhaps, the butterflies, the insects of Japan are still little known to men of science; and all that I can say about sémi has been learned from inquiry, from personal observation, and from old Japanese books of an interesting but totally unscientific kind. Not only do the authors contradict each other as to the names and characteristics of the best-known sémi; they attach the word sémi to names of insects which are not cicadæ.

The following enumeration of sémi is certainly incomplete; but I believe that it includes the better-known varieties and the best melodists. I must ask the reader, however, to bear in mind that the time of the appearance of certain sémi differs in different parts of Japan; that the same kind of sémi may be called by different names in different provinces; and that these notes have been written in Tōkyō.

I. Haru-Zémi

Various small sémi appear in the spring. But the first of the big sémi to make itself heard is the haru-zémi (spring-sémi), also called uma-zémi (horse-sémi), kuma-zémi (bear-sémi), and other names. It makes a shrill wheezing sound — *ji-i-i-i-i-iiiiiiii* — beginning low, and gradually rising to a pitch of painful intensity. No other cicada is so noisy as the haru-zémi; but the life of the creature appears to end with the season. Probably this is the sémi referred to in an old Japanese poem:

> Hatsu-sémi ya!
> "Koré wa atsui" to
> Iu hi yori.
>
> Taimu

The day after the first day on which we exclaim, "Oh, how hot it is!" the first sémi begins to cry.

II. "Shinné-shinné"

The shinné-shinné — also called yama-zémi, or mountain-sémi; kuma-zémi, or bear-sémi; and ō-sémi, or great sémi — begins to sing as early as May. It is a very large insect. The upper part of the body is almost black, and the belly a silvery-white; the head has curious red markings. The name "shinné-

shinné" is derived from the note of the creature, which resembles a quick continual repetition of the syllables shinné. About Kyōto this sémi is common: it is rarely heard in Tōkyō.

[My first opportunity to examine an ō-sémi was in Shidzuoka. Its utterance is much more complex than the Japanese onomatope implies; I should liken it to the noise of a sewing-machine in full operation. There is double sound: you hear not only the succession of sharp metallic clickings, but also, below these, a slower series of dull clanking tones. The stridulatory organs are light green, looking almost like a pair of tiny green leaves attached to the thorax.]

III. Aburazémi

The aburazémi, or oil-sémi, makes its appearance early in the summer. I am told that it owes its name to the fact that its shrilling resembles the sound of oil or grease frying in a pan. Some writers say that the shrilling resembles the sound of the syllables gacharin-gacharin; but others compare it to the noise of water boiling. The aburazémi begins to chant about sunrise; then a great soft hissing seems to ascend from all the trees. At such an hour, when the foliage of woods and gardens still sparkles with dew, might have been composed the following verse — the only one in my collection relating to the aburazémi:

SÉMI

Ano koë dé
Tsuyu ga inochi ka? —
Aburazémi!

Speaking with that voice, has the dew taken life? — Only the aburazémi!

IV. MUGI-KARI-ZÉMI

The mugi-kari-zémi, or barley-harvest sémi, also called "goshiki-zémi," or five-colored sémi, appears early in the summer. It makes two distinct sounds in different keys, resembling the syllables shi-in, shin — chi-i, chi-i.

V. HIGURASHI, OR "KANA-KANA"

This insect, whose name signifies "day-darkening," is the most remarkable of all the Japanese cicadæ. It is not the finest singer among them; but even as a melodist it ranks second only to the tsuku-tsuku-bōshi. It is the special minstrel of twilight, singing only at dawn and sunset; whereas most of the other sémi make their music only in the full blaze of day, pausing even when rain-clouds obscure the sun. In Tōkyō the higurashi usually appears about the end of June, or the beginning of July. Its wonderful cry — *kana-kana-kana-kana-kana* — beginning always in a very high clear key, and slowly descending, is almost exactly like the sound of a good hand-bell, very quickly rung. It is not a clashing sound, as of violent ringing; it is quick, steady, and of surprising sonority. I believe that a single higurashi can be plainly heard a quarter of a mile away; yet, as the old Japanese poet Yayū observed, "no matter how many higurashi be singing together, we never find them noisy." Though powerful and penetrating as a resonance of metal, the higurashi's call is musical even to the degree of sweetness; and there is a peculiar melancholy in it that accords with the hour of gloaming. But the most astonishing fact in regard to the cry of the higurashi is the individual quality characterizing the note of each insect. No two higurashi sing precisely in the same tone. If you hear a dozen of them singing at once, you will find that the timbre of each voice is recognizably different from every other. Certain notes ring like silver, others vibrate like bronze; and, besides varieties of timbre suggesting bells of various weight and composition, there are even differences in tone, that suggest different *forms* of bell.

I have already said that the name "higurashi" means "day-darkening" — in the sense of twilight, gloaming, dusk; and there are many Japanese verses containing plays on the word — the poets affecting to believe, as in the following example, that the crying of the insect hastens the coming of darkness:

> Higurashi ya!
> Sutétéoitémo
> Kururu hi wo.

O Higurashi! — even if you let it alone, day darkens fast enough!

This, intended to express a melancholy mood, may seem to the Western reader far-fetched. But another little poem – referring to the effect of the sound upon the conscience of an idler — will be appreciated by any one accustomed to hear the higurashi. I may observe, in this connection, that the first clear evening cry of the insect is quite as startling as the sudden ringing of a bell:

> Higurashi ya!
> Kyō no kétai wo
> Omou-toki.
>
> RIKEI

Already, O Higurashi, your call announces the evening!
Alas, for the passing day, with its duties left undone!

VI. "MINMIN"-ZÉMI

The minmin-zémi begins to sing in the Period of Greatest Heat. It is called "min-min" because its note is thought to resemble the syllable "min" repeated over and over again — slowly at first, and very loudly; then more and more quickly and softly, till the utterance dies away in a sort of buzz: "*min — min — min-min-min-minminmin-dzzzzzzz.*" The sound is plaintive, and not unpleasing. It is often compared to the sound of the voice of a priest chanting the sutras.

VII. TSUKU-TSUKU-BŌSHI

On the day immediately following the Festival of the Dead, by the old Japanese calendar [1] (which is incomparably more exact than our Western calendar in regard to nature-changes and manifestations),

---

[1] That is to say, upon the sixteenth day of the seventh month.

begins to sing the tsuku-tsuku-bōshi. This creature may be said to sing like a bird. It is also called "kutsu-kutsu-bōshi," "chōko-chōko-uisu," "tsuku-tsuku-hōshi," "tsuku-tsuku-oïshi" — all onomato-poetic appellations. The sounds of its song have been imitated in different ways by various writers. In Izumo the common version is:

> Tsuku-tsuku-uisu,
> Tsuku-tsuku-uisu,
> Tsuku-tsuku-uisu: —
>   Ui-ōsu
>   Ui-ōsu
>   Ui-ōsu
>   Ui-ōs-s-s-s-s-s-s-su.

Another version runs:

> Tsuku-tsuku-uisu,
> Tsuku-tsuku-uisu,
> Tsuku-tsuku-uisu: —
>   Chi-i yara!
>   Chi-i yara!
>   Chi-i yara!
>   Chi-i, chi, chi, chi, chi, chiii.

But some say that the sound is "Tsukushi-koïshi." There is a legend that in old times a man of Tsukushi (the ancient name of Kyūshū) fell sick and died while far away from home, and that the ghost of him became an autumn cicada, which cries un-ceasingly, "Tsukushi-koïshi! — Tsukushi-koïshi!" (I long for Tsukushi! — I want to see Tsukushi!)

It is a curious fact that the earlier sémi have the

56

harshest and simplest notes. The musical sémi do not appear until summer; and the tsuku-tsuku-bōshi, having the most complex and melodious utterance of all, is one of the latest to mature.

VIII. TSURIGANÉ-SÉMI [1]

The tsurigané-sémi is an autumn cicada. The word "tsurigané" means a suspended bell — especially the big bell of a Buddhist temple. I am somewhat puzzled by the name; for the insect's music really suggests the tones of a Japanese harp, or koto — as good authorities declare. Perhaps the appellation refers not to the boom of the bell, but to those deep, sweet hummings which follow after the peal, wave upon wave.

III

JAPANESE poems on sémi are usually very brief; and my collection chiefly consists of hokku — compositions of seventeen syllables. Most of these hokku relate to the sound made by the sémi — or, rather, to the sensation which the sound produced within the poet's mind. The names attached to the following examples are nearly all names of old-time poets — not the real names, of course, but the gō, or literary names by which artists and men of letters are usually known.

Yokoi Yayū, a Japanese poet of the eighteenth

[1] This sémi appears to be chiefly known in Shikoku.

century, celebrated as a composer of hokku, has left us this naïve record of the feelings with which he heard the chirruping of cicadæ in summer and in autumn:

In the sultry period, feeling oppressed by the greatness of the heat, I made this verse:

> Sémi atsushi
> Matsu kirabaya to
> Omou-madé.

The chirruping of the sémi aggravates the heat until I wish to cut down the pine-tree on which it sings.

But the days passed quickly; and later, when I heard the crying of the sémi grow fainter and fainter in the time of the autumn winds, I began to feel compassion for them, and I made this second verse:

> Shini-nokoré
> Hitotsu bakari wa
> Aki no sémi.

> Now there survives
> But a single one
> Of the sémi of autumn!

Lovers of Pierre Loti (the world's greatest prose-writer) may remember in "Madame Chrysan-thème" a delightful passage about a Japanese house — describing the old dry woodwork as impregnated with sonority by the shrilling crickets of a hundred summers.[1] There is a Japanese poem containing a fancy not altogether dissimilar:

[1] Speaking of his own attempt to make a drawing of the interior, he observes: "Il manque à ce logis dessiné son air frêle et sa sonorité de violon sec. Dans les traits de crayon qui représentent les boiseries, il n'y

SÉMI

Matsu no ki ni
Shimikomu gotoshi
Sémi no koë.

Into the wood of the pine-tree
Seems to soak
The voice of the sémi.

A very large number of Japanese poems about sémi describe the noise of the creatures as an affliction. To fully sympathize with the complaints of the poets, one must have heard certain varieties of Japanese cicadæ in full midsummer chorus; but even by readers without experience of the clamor, the following verses will probably be found suggestive:

Waré hitori
Atsui yō nari —
Sémi no koë!

BUNSŌ

Meseems that only I — I alone among mortals —
Ever suffered such heat! — oh, the noise of the sémi!

Ushiro kara
Tsukamu yō nari —
Sémi no koë.

JOFŪ

Oh, the noise of the sémi! — a pain of invisible seizure —
Clutched in an enemy's grasp — caught by the hair from behind!

Yama no Kami no
Mimi no yamai ka? —
Sémi no koë!

TEIKOKU

a pas la précision minutieuse avec laquelle elles sont ouvragées, ni leur antiquité extrême, ni leur propreté parfaite, *ni les vibrations de cigales qu'elles semblent avoir emmagasinées pendant des centaines d'étés dans leurs fibres desséchées.*"

59

JAPANESE STUDIES

What ails the divinity's ears? — how can the God of the Mountain
Suffer such noise to exist? — oh, the tumult of sémi!

> Soko no nai
> Atsusa ya kumo ni
> Sémi no koë!
>
> SAREN

Fathomless deepens the heat: the ceaseless shrilling of sémi
Mounts, like a hissing of fire, up to the motionless clouds.

> Mizu karété,
> Sémi wo fudan-no
> Taki no koë.
>
> GEN-Ŭ

Water never a drop: the chorus of sémi, incessant,
Mocks the tumultuous hiss — the rush and foaming of rapids.

> Kagéroishi
> Kumo mata satté,
> Sémi no koë.
>
> KITŌ

Gone, the shadowing clouds! — again the shrilling of sémi
Rises and slowly swells — ever increasing the heat!

> Daita ki wa,
> Ha mo ugokasazu —
> Sémi no koë!
>
> KAFŬ

Somewhere fast to the bark he clung; but I cannot see him:
He stirs not even a leaf — oh! the noise of that sémi!

> Tonari kara
> Kono ki nikumu ya!
> Sémi no koë.
>
> GYUKAKU

All because of the sémi that sit and shrill on its branches —
Oh! how this tree of mine is hated now by my neighbor! .

SÉMI

This reminds one of Yayū. We find another poet compassionating a tree frequented by sémi:

> Kazé wa mina
> Sémi ni suwarété,
> Hito-ki kana!
>
> CHŌSUI

Alas! poor solitary tree! — pitiful now your lot — every breath of air having been sucked up by the sémi!

Sometimes the noise of the sémi is described as a moving force:

> Sémi no koë
> Ki-gi ni ugoité,
> Kazé mo nashi!
>
> SŌYŌ

Every tree in the wood quivers with clamor of sémi:
Motion only of noise — never a breath of wind!

> Také ni kité,
> Yuki yori omoshi
> Sémi no koë.
>
> TŌGETSU

More heavy than winter-snow the voices of perching sémi:
See how the bamboos bend under the weight of their song! [1]

> Morogoë ni
> .Yama ya ugokasu,
> Ki-gi no sémi.

All shrilling together, the multitudinous sémi
Make, with their ceaseless clamor, even the mountain move.

> Kusunoki mo
> Ugoku yō nari,
> Sémi no koë.
>
> BAIJAKU

[1] Japanese artists have found many a charming inspiration in the spectacle of bamboos bending under the weight of snow clinging to their tops.

JAPANESE STUDIES

Even the camphor-tree seems to quake with the clamor of sémi!

Sometimes the sound is compared to the noise of boiling water:

Hizakari wa
Niétatsu sémi no
Hayashi kana!

In the hour of heaviest heat, how simmers the forest with sémi!

Niété iru
Mizu bakari nari —
Sémi no koë.

TAIMU

Simmers all the air with sibilation of sémi,
Ceaseless, wearying sense — a sound of perpetual boiling.

Other poets complain especially of the multitude of the noise-makers and the ubiquity of the noise:

Aritaké no
Ki ni hibiki-kéri
Sémi no koë.

How many soever the trees, in each rings the voice of the sémi.

Matsubara wo
Ichi ri wa kitari,
Sémi no koë.

SENGA

Alone I walked for miles into the wood of pine-trees:
Always the one same sémi shrilled its call in my ears.

Occasionally the subject is treated with comic exaggeration:

SÉMI

Naité iru
Ki yori mo futoshi
Sémi no koë.

The voice of the sémi is bigger [thicker] than the tree on
which it sings.

Sugi takashi
Sarédomo sémi no
Amaru koë!

High though the cedar be, the voice of the sémi is incomparably higher!

Koë nagaki
Sémi wa mijikaki
Inochi kana!

How long, alas! the voice and how short the life of the sémi!

Some poets celebrate the negative form of pleasure
following upon the cessation of the sound:

Sémi ni dété,
Hotaru ni modoru —
Suzumi kana!
YAYŪ

When the sémi cease their noise, and the fireflies come out —
oh! how refreshing the hour!

Sémi no tatsu,
Ato suzushisa yo!
Matsu no koë.
BAIJAKU

When the sémi cease their storm, oh, how refreshing the stillness!
Gratefully then resounds the musical speech of the pines.

[Here I may mention, by the way, that there is a
little Japanese song about the matsu no koë, in

63

which the onomatope "zazanza" very well represents the deep humming of the wind in the pine-
needles:

Zazanza!
Hama-matsu no oto wa —
Zazanza,
Zazanza!

Zazanza!
The sound of the pines of the shore —
Zazanza!
Zazanza!]

There are poets, however, who declare that the
feeling produced by the noise of sémi depends altogether upon the nervous condition of the listener:

Mori no sémi
Suzushiki koë ya,
Atsuki koë.

OTSUSHU

Sometimes sultry the sound; sometimes, again, refreshing:
The chant of the forest-sémi accords with the hearer's mood.

Suzushisa mo
Atsusa mo sémi no
Tokoro kana!

FUHAKU

Sometimes we think it cool — the resting-place of the sémi;
— sometimes we think it hot (it is all a matter of fancy).

Suzushii to
Omoéba, suzushi
Sémi no koë.

GINKŌ

If we think it is cool, then the voice of the sémi is cool (that
is, the fancy changes the feeling).

64

SÉMI

In view of the many complaints of Japanese poets about the noisiness of sémi, the reader may be surprised to learn that out of sémi-skins there used to be made in both China and Japan — perhaps upon homœopathic principles — a medicine for the cure of ear-ache!

One poem, nevertheless, proves that sémi-music has its admirers:

> Omoshiroi zo ya,
> Waga-ko no koë wa
> Takai mori-ki no
> Sémi no koë! [1]

Sweet to the ear is the voice of one's own child as the voice of a sémi perched on a tall forest tree.

But such admiration is rare. More frequently the sémi is represented as crying for its nightly repast of dew:

> Sémi wo kiké —
> Ichi-nichi naité
> Yoru no tsuyu.
> KIKAKU

Hear the sémi shrill! So, from earliest dawning,
All the summer day he cries for the dew of night.

---

[1] There is another version of this poem:

> Omoshiroi zo ya,
> Waga-ko no naku wa
> Sembu-ségaki no
> Kyō yori mo!

"More sweetly sounds the crying of one's own child than even the chanting of the sutra in the service for the dead." The Buddhist service alluded to is held to be particularly beautiful.

JAPANESE STUDIES

Yū-tsuyu no
Kuchi ni iru madé
Naku sémi ka?

BAISHITSU

Will the sémi continue to cry till the night-dew fills its mouth?

Occasionally the sémi is mentioned in love-songs of which the following is a fair specimen. It belongs to that class of ditties commonly sung by geisha. Merely as a conceit, I think it pretty, in spite of the factitious pathos; but to Japanese taste it is decidedly vulgar. The allusion to beating implies jealousy:

Nushi ni tatakaré,
Washa matsu no sémi
Sugaritsuki-tsuki
Naku bakari!

Beaten by my jealous lover —
Like the sémi on the pine-tree
I can only cry and cling!

And indeed the following tiny picture is a truer bit of work, according to Japanese art-principles (I do not know the author's name):

Sémi hitotsu
Matsu no yū-hi wo
Kakaé-kéri.

Lo! on the topmost pine, a solitary cicada
Vainly attempts to clasp one last red beam of sun.

IV

PHILOSOPHICAL verses do not form a numerous class of Japanese poems upon sémi; but they possess

an interest altogether exotic. As the metamorphosis
of the butterfly supplied to old Greek thought an
emblem of the soul's ascension, so the natural history of the cicada has furnished Buddhism with
similitudes and parables for the teaching of doctrine.

Man sheds his body only as the sémi sheds its
skin. But each reincarnation obscures the memory
of the previous one: we remember our former existence no more than the sémi remembers the shell
from which it has emerged. Often a sémi may be
found in the act of singing beside its cast-off skin;
therefore a poet has written:

> Waré to waga
> Kara ya tomurō —
> Sémi no koë.
>   YAYŪ

Methinks that sémi sits and sings by his former body —
Chanting the funeral service over his own dead self.

This cast-off skin, or simulacrum — clinging to
bole or branch as in life, and seeming still to stare
with great glazed eyes — has suggested many
things both to profane and to religious poets. In
love-songs it is often likened to a body consumed by
passionate longing. In Buddhist poetry it becomes
a symbol of earthly pomp — the hollow show of
human greatness:

> Yo no naka yo
> Kaëru no hadaka,
> Sémi no kinu!

Naked as frogs and weak we enter this life of trouble;
Shedding our pomps we pass: so sémi quit their skins.

67

But sometimes the poet compares the winged and shrilling sémi to a human ghost, and the broken shell to the body left behind:

Tamashii wa
Ukiyo ni naité,
Sémi no kara.

Here the forsaken shell: above me the voice of the creature
Shrills like the cry of a Soul quitting this world of pain.

Then the great sun-quickened tumult of the cicadæ—landstorm of summer life foredoomed so soon to pass away—is likened by preacher and poet to the tumult of human desire. Even as the sémi rise from earth, and climb to warmth and light, and clamor, and presently again return to dust and silence — so rise and clamor and pass the generations of men:

Yagaté shinu
Keshiki wa miézu,
Sémi no koë.

BASHŌ

Never an intimation in all those voices of sémi
How quickly the hush will come — how speedily all must die.

I wonder whether the thought in this little verse does not interpret something of that summer melancholy which comes to us out of nature's solitudes with the plaint of insect-voices. Unconsciously those millions of millions of tiny beings are preaching the ancient wisdom of the East — the perpetual Sutra of Impermanency.

Yet how few of our modern poets have given heed to the voices of insects!

SÊMI

Perhaps it is only to minds inexorably haunted by the Riddle of Life that Nature can speak to-day, in those thin sweet trillings, as she spake of old to Solomon.

The Wisdom of the East hears all things. And he that obtains it will hear the speech of insects — as Sigurd, tasting the Dragon's Heart, heard suddenly the talking of birds.

JAPANESE FEMALE NAMES

I

By the Japanese a certain kind of girl is called a
Rose-Girl — Bara-Musumé. Perhaps my reader
will think of Tennyson's "queen-rose of the rosebud-
garden of girls," and imagine some analogy between
the Japanese and the English idea of femininity symbolized by the rose. But there is no analogy whatever. The Bara-Musumé is not so called because she
is delicate and sweet, nor because she blushes, nor
because she is rosy; indeed, a rosy face is not admired in Japan. No; she is compared to a rose chiefly
for the reason that a rose has thorns. The man who
tries to pull a Japanese rose is likely to hurt his
fingers. The man who tries to win a Bara-Musumé
is apt to hurt himself much more seriously — even
unto death. It were better, alone and unarmed, to
meet a tiger than to invite the caress of a Rose-
Girl.

Now the appellation of Bara-Musumé — much
more rational as a simile than many of our own floral
comparisons — can seem strange only because it is
not in accord with our poetical usages and emotional
habits. It is one in a thousand possible examples of
the fact that Japanese similes and metaphors are
not of the sort that he who runs may read. And this
fact is particularly well exemplified in the yobina,

or personal names of Japanese women. Because a yobina happens to be identical with the name of some tree, or bird, or flower, it does not follow that the personal appellation conveys to Japanese imagination ideas resembling those which the corresponding English word would convey, under like circumstances, to English imagination. Of the yobina that seem to us especially beautiful in translation, only a small number are bestowed for æsthetic reasons. Nor is it correct to suppose, as many persons still do, that Japanese girls are usually named after flowers, or graceful shrubs, or other beautiful objects. Æsthetic appellations are in use; but the majority of yobina are not æsthetic. Some years ago a young Japanese scholar published an interesting essay upon this subject. He had collected the personal names of about four hundred students of the Higher Normal School for Females — girls from every part of the Empire; and he found on his list only between fifty and sixty names possessing æsthetic quality. But concerning even these he was careful to observe only that they "*caused* an æsthetic sensation" — not that they had been given for æsthetic reasons. Among them were such names as Saki (Cape), Miné (Peak), Kishi (Beach), Hama (Shore), Kuni (Capital) — originally place-names; — Tsuru (Stork), Tazu (Rice-Field Stork), and Chizu (Thousand Storks); — also such appellations as Yoshino (Fertile Field), Orino (Weavers' Field), Shirushi (Proof), and Masago (Sand). Few of these could seem æsthetic to a Western mind; and probably no one of them was originally given for æsthetic reasons. Names containing the character for "Stork" are names having reference to longevity, not to beauty; and a large number of names with the termination "no" (field or plain) are names referring to moral qualities. I doubt whether even fifteen per cent of yobina are really æsthetic. A very much larger proportion are names expressing moral or mental qualities. Tenderness, kindness, deftness, cleverness, are frequently represented by yobina; but appellations implying physical charm, or suggesting æsthetic ideas only, are comparatively uncommon. One reason for the fact may be that very æsthetic names are given to geisha and to jōro, and consequently vulgarized. But the chief reason certainly is that the domestic virtues still occupy in Japanese moral estimate a place not less important than that accorded to religious faith in the life of our own Middle Ages. Not in theory only, but in everyday practice, moral beauty is placed far above physical beauty; and girls are usually selected as wives, not for their good looks, but for their domestic qualities. Among the middle classes a very æsthetic name would not be considered in the best taste; among the poorer classes, it would scarcely be thought respectable. Ladies of rank, on the other hand, are privileged to bear very poetical names; yet the majority of the aristocratic yobina also are moral rather than æsthetic.

JAPANESE FEMALE NAMES

But the first great difficulty in the way of a study of yobina is the difficulty of translating them. A knowledge of spoken Japanese can help you very little indeed. A knowledge of Chinese also is indispensable. The meaning of a name written in kana only — in the Japanese characters — cannot be, in most cases, even guessed at. The Chinese characters of the name can alone explain it. The Japanese essayist, already referred to, found himself obliged to throw out no less than thirty-six names from a list of two hundred and thirteen, simply because these thirty-six, having been recorded only in kana, could not be interpreted. Kana give only the pronunciation; and the pronunciation of a woman's name explains nothing in a majority of cases. Transliterated into Romaji, a yobina may signify two, three, or even half-a-dozen different things. One of the names thrown out of the list was Banka. Banka might signify "Mint" (the plant), which would be a pretty name; but it might also mean "Evening-haze." Yuka, another rejected name, might be an abbreviation of Yukabutsu (precious); but it might just as well mean "a floor." Nochi, a third example, might signify "future"; yet it could also mean "a descendant," and various other things. My reader will be able to find many other homonyms in the lists of names given further on. Ai in Romaji, for instance, may signify either "love" or "indigo-blue"; Chō, "a butterfly," or "superior," or "long"; Ei, either "sagacious" or "blooming";

73

Kei, either "rapture" or "reverence"; Sato, either "native home" or "sugar"; Toshi, either "year" or "arrow-head"; Taka, "tall," "honorable," or "falcon." The chief, and, for the present, insuperable obstacle to the use of Roman letters in writing Japanese, is the prodigious number of homonyms in the language. You need only glance into any good Japanese-English dictionary to understand the gravity of this obstacle. Not to multiply examples, I shall merely observe that there are nineteen words spelled chō; twenty-one spelled ki; twenty-five spelled to or tō; and no less than forty-nine spelled ko or kō.

Yet, as I have already suggested, the real signification of a woman's name cannot be ascertained even from a literal translation made with the help of the Chinese characters. Such a name, for instance, as Kagami (Mirror) really signifies the Pure-Minded, and this not in the Occidental, but in the Confucian sense of the term. Umé (Plum-blossom) is a name referring to wifely devotion and virtue. Matsu (Pine) does not refer, as an appellation, to the beauty of the tree, but to the fact that its evergreen foliage is the emblem of vigorous age. The name Také (Bamboo) is given to a child only because the bamboo has been for centuries a symbol of good-fortune. The name Sen (Wood-Fairy) sounds charmingly to Western fancy; yet it expresses nothing more than the parents' hope of long life for their

74

daughter and her offspring — wood-fairies being supposed to live for thousands of years. . . . Again, many names are of so strange a sort that it is impossible to discover their meaning without questioning either the bearer or the giver; and sometimes all inquiry proves vain, because the original meaning has been long forgotten.

Before attempting to go further into the subject, I shall here offer a translation of the Tōkyō essayist's list of names — rearranged in alphabetical order, without honorific prefixes or suffixes. Although some classes of common names are not represented, the list will serve to show the character of many still popular yobina, and also to illustrate several of the facts to which I have already called attention.

SELECTED NAMES OF STUDENTS AND GRADUATES OF THE
HIGHER NORMAL SCHOOL FOR FEMALES
(1880–1895):

		Number of students so named
Ai	Indigo — the color	1
Ai	Love	1
Akasuké	The Bright Helper	1
Asa	Morning	1
Asa	Shallow [1]	2
Au	Meeting	2
Bun	Composition — in the literary sense [2]	1
Chika	Near [3]	5
Chitosé	A Thousand Years	1

[1] Probably a place-name originally.
[2] Might we not quaintly say, "A Fair Writing"?
[3] Probably in the sense of "near and dear" — but not certainly so.

75

Chiyo	A Thousand Generations	1
Chizu	Thousand Storks	1
Chō	Butterfly	1
Chō	Superior	2
Ei	Clever	1
Ei	Blooming	2
Etsu	Delight	1
Fudé	Writing-Brush	1
Fuji	Fuji — the mountain	1
Fuji	Wistaria-Flower	2
Fuki	Fuki — name of a plant, *Nardosmia japonica*	1
Fuku	Good-Fortune	2
Fumi	Letter [1]	5
Fumino	Letter-Field	1
Fusa	Tassel	3
Gin	Silver	2
Hama	Shore	3
Hana	Blossom	3
Haruë	Spring-Time Bay	1
Hatsu	The First-Born	2
Hidé	Excellent	4
Hidé	Fruitful	.2
Hisano	Long Plain	2
Ichi	Market	4
Iku	Nourishing	3
Iné	Springing Rice	3
Ishi	Stone	1
Ito	Thread	4
Iwa	Rock	1
Jun	The Obedient [2]	1
Kagami	Mirror	3
Kama	Sickle	1
Kamé	Tortoise	2

[1] Fumi signifies here a letter written by a woman only — a letter written according to the rules of feminine epistolary style.

[2] Jun suru means to be obedient unto death. The word jun has a much stronger signification than that which attaches to our word "obedience" in these modern times.

JAPANESE FEMALE NAMES

Kaméyo	Generations-of-the-Tortoise [1]	1
Kan	The Forbearing [2]	11
Kana	Character — in the sense of written character [3]	2
Kané	Bronze	3
Katsu	Victorious	2
Kazashi	Hairpin — or any ornament worn in the hair	1
Kazu	Number — i.e., great number	1
Kei	The Respectful	3
Ken	Humility	1
Kiku	Chrysanthemum	6
Kikuë	Chrysanthemum-Branch	1
Kikuno	Chrysanthemum-Field	1
Kimi	Sovereign	1
Kin	Gold	4
Kinu	Cloth-of-Silk	1
Kishi	Beach	2
Kiyo	Happy Generations	1
Kiyo	Pure	5
Ko	Chime — the sound of a bell	1
Kō	Filial Piety	11
Kō	The Fine	1
Koma	Filly	1
Komé	Cleaned Rice	1
Koto	Koto — the Japanese harp	4
Kuma	Bear	1
Kumi	Braid	1
Kuni	Capital — chief city	1
Kuni	Province	3
Kura	Treasure-House	1
Kurano	Storehouse-Field	1
Kuri	Chestnut	1

[1] The tortoise is supposed to live for a thousand years.

[2] Abbreviation of kannin, "forbearance," "self-control," etc. The name might equally well be translated "Patience."

[3] Kana signifies the Japanese syllabary — the characters with which the language is written. The reader may imagine, if he wishes, that the name signifies the Alpha and Omega of all feminine charm; but I confess that I have not been able to find any satisfactory explanation of it.

77

Kuwa	Mulberry-Tree	1
Masa	Straightforward — upright	3
Masago	Sand	1
Masu	Increase	3
Masuë	Branch-of-Increase	1
Matsu	Pine	2
Matsuë	Pine-Branch	1
Michi	The Way — doctrine	4
Mië	Triple Branch	1
Mikië	Main-Branch	1
Miné	Peak	2
Mitsu	Light	5
Mitsuë	Shining Branch	1
Morië	Service-Bay [1]	1
Naka	The Midmost	4
Nami	Wave	1
Nobu	Fidelity	6
Nobu	The Prolonger [2]	1
Nobuë	Lengthening-Branch	1
Nui	Tapestry — or, Embroidery	1
Orino	Weaving-Field	1
Raku	Pleasure	3
Ren	The Arranger	1
Riku	Land — ground	1
Roku	Emolument	1
Ryō	Dragon	1
Ryū	Lofty	3
Sada	The Chaste	8
Saki	Cape — promontory	1
Saku	Composition [3]	3
Sato	Home — native place	2
Sawa	Marsh	1
Sei	Force	1

[1] The word "service" here refers especially to attendance at meal-time — to the serving of rice, etc.

[2] Perhaps in the hopeful meaning of extending the family-line; but more probably in the signification that a daughter's care prolongs the life of her parents, or of her husband's parents.

[3] Abbreviation of sakubun, a literary composition.

78

JAPANESE FEMALE NAMES

Seki	Barrier — city-gate, toll-gate, etc.	3
Sen	Fairy [1]	3
Setsu	True — tender and true	2
Shidzu	The Calmer	1
Shidzu	Peace	2
Shigë	Twofold	2
Shika	Deer	2
Shikaë	Deer-Inlet	1
Shimé	The Clasp — fastening	1
Shin	Truth	1
Shina	Goods	1
Shina	Virtue	1
Shino	Slender Bamboo	1
Shirushi	The Proof — evidence	1
Shun	The Excellent	1
Sué	The Last	2
Sugi	Cedar — cryptomeria	1
Suté	Forsaken — foundling	1
Suzu	Little Bell	8
Suzu	Tin	1
Suzuë	Branch of Little Bells	1
Taë	Exquisite	1
Taka	Honor	2
Taka	Lofty	9
Také	Bamboo	1
Tama	Jewel	1
Tamaki	Ring	1
Tamé	For-the-Sake-of —	3
Tani	Valley	1
Tazu	Rice-Field-Stork	1
Tetsu	Iron	4
Toku	Virtue	2
Tomé	Stop — cease [2]	1

[1] As a matter of fact, we have no English equivalent for the word "sen," or "sennin" — signifying a being possessing magical powers of all kinds and living for thousands of years. Some authorities consider the belief in sennin of Indian origin, and probably derived from old traditions of the Rishi.

[2] Such a name may signify that the parents resolved, after the birth of the girl, to have no more children.

Tomi	Riches	3
Tomijū	Wealth-and-Longevity	1
Tomo	The Friend	4
Tora	Tiger	1
Toshi	Arrowhead	1
Toyo	Abundance	3
Tsugi	Next — i.e., second in order of birth	2
Tsuna	Bond — rope, or fetter	1
Tsuné	The Constant — or, as we should say, Constance	10
Tsuru	Stork	4
Umé	Plum-Blossom	1
Umégaë	Plum-Tree spray	1
Uméno	Plum-Tree-Field	2
Urano	Shore-Field	1
Ushi	Cow — or, Ox [1]	1
Uta	Poem — or, Song	1
Wakana	Young Na — probably the rape-plant is referred to	1
Yaë	Eightfold	1
Yasu	The Tranquil	1
Yō	The Positive — as opposed to Negative or Feminine in the old Chinese philosophy; — therefore, perhaps, Masculine	1
Yoné	Rice — in the old sense of wealth	4
Yoshi	The Good	1
Yoshino	Good Field	1
Yū	The Valiant	1
Yuri	Lily	1

It will be observed that in the above list the names referring to Constancy, Forbearance, and

---

[1] This extraordinary name is probably to be explained as a reference to date of birth. According to the old Chinese astrology, years, months, days, and hours were all named after the Signs of the Zodiac, and were supposed to have some mystic relation to those signs. I surmise that Miss Ushi was born at the Hour of the Ox, on the Day of the Ox, in the Month of the Ox and the Year of the Ox — "Ushi no Toshi no Ushi no Tsuki no Ushi no Hi no Ushi no Koku."

Filial Piety have the highest numbers attached to them.

II

A FEW of the more important rules in regard to Japanese female names must now be mentioned.

The great majority of these yobina are words of two syllables. Personal names of respectable women, belonging to the middle and lower classes, are nearly always dissyllables — except in cases where the name is lengthened by certain curious suffixes which I shall speak of further on. Formerly a name of three or more syllables indicated that the bearer belonged to a superior class. But, even among the upper classes to-day, female names of only two syllables are in fashion.

Among the people it is customary that a female name of two syllables should be preceded by the honorific "O," and followed by the title "San" — as O-Matsu San, "the Honorable Miss [or Mrs.] Pine"; O-Umé San, "the Honorable Miss Plum-blossom."[1] But if the name happen to have three syllables, the honorific "O" is not used. A woman named Kikuë (Chrysanthemum-Branch) is not addressed as "O-Kikuë San," but only as "Kikuë San."

Before the names of ladies, the honorific "O" is

[1] Under certain conditions of intimacy, both prefix and title are dropped. They are dropped also by the superior in addressing an inferior;—for example, a lady would not address her maid as "O-Yoné San," but merely as "Yoné."

81

no longer used as formerly — even when the name consists of one syllable only. Instead of the prefix, an honorific suffix is appended to the yobina — the suffix "ko." A peasant girl named Tomi would be addressed by her equals as O-Tomi San. But a lady of the same name would be addressed as Tomiko. Mrs. Shimoda, head-teacher of the Peeresses' School, for example, has the beautiful name Uta. She would be addressed by letter as "Shimoda Utako," and would so sign herself in replying; — the family-name, by Japanese custom, always preceding the personal name, instead of being, as with us, placed after it.

This suffix "ko" is written with the Chinese character meaning "child," and must not be confused with the word "ko," written with a different Chinese character, and meaning "little," which so often appears in the names of dancing girls. I should venture to say that this genteel suffix has the value of a caressing diminutive, and that the name Aiko might be fairly well rendered by the "Amoretta" of Spenser's "Faerie Queene." Be this as it may, a Japanese lady named Setsu or Sada would not be addressed in these days as O-Setsu or O-Sada, but as Setsuko or Sadako. On the other hand, if a woman of the people were to sign herself as Setsuko or Sadako, she would certainly be laughed at — since the suffix would give to her appellation the meaning of "the Lady Setsu," or "the Lady Sada."

I have said that the honorific "O" is placed before

the yobina of women of the middle and lower classes. Even the wife of a kurumaya would probably be referred to as the "Honorable Mrs. Such-a-one." But there are very remarkable exceptions to this general rule regarding the prefix "O." In some country-districts the common yobina of two syllables is made a trisyllable by the addition of a peculiar suffix; and before such trisyllabic names the "O" is never placed. For example, the girls of Wakayama, in the Province of Kii, usually have added to their yobina the suffix "ë," [1] signifying "inlet," "bay," "frith" — sometimes "river." Thus we find such names as Namië (Wave-Bay), Tomië (Riches-Bay), Sumië (Dwelling-Bay), Shizuë (Quiet-Bay), Tamaë (Jewel-Bay). Again there is a provincial suffix "no," meaning "field" or "plain," which is attached to the majority of female names in certain districts. Yoshino (Fertile Field), Uméno (Plum-Flower Field), Shizuno (Quiet Field), Urano (Coast Field), Utano (Song Field), are typical names of this class. A girl called Namië or Kikuno is not addressed as "O-Namië San" or "O-Kikuno San," but as "Namië San," "Kikuno San."

"San" (abbreviation of "Sama," a word originally meaning "form," "appearance"), when placed after a female name, corresponds to either our "Miss" or "Mrs." Placed after a man's name it has

---

[1] This suffix must not be confused with the suffix "ë," signifying "branch," which is also attached to many popular names. Without seeing the Chinese character, you cannot decide whether the name Tamaë, for example, means "Jewel-branch" or "Jewel Inlet."

83

at least the value of our "Mr." — perhaps even more. The unabbreviated form "Sama" is placed after the names of high personages of either sex, and after the names of divinities: the Shintō Gods are styled the "Kami-Sama," which might be translated as "the Lords Supreme"; the Bodhisattva Jizō is called "Jizō-Sama," "the Lord Jizō." A lady may also be styled "Sama." A lady called "Ayako," for instance, might very properly be addressed as "Ayako Sama." But when a lady's name, independently of the suffix, consists of more than three syllables, it is customary to drop either the ko or the title. Thus "the Lady Ayamé" would not be spoken of as "Ayaméko Sama," but more euphoniously as "Ayamé Sama,"[1] or as "Ayaméko."

So much having been said as regards the etiquette of prefixes and suffixes, I shall now attempt a classification of female names — beginning with popular yobina. These will be found particularly interesting, because they reflect something of race-feeling in the matter of ethics and æsthetics, and because they serve to illustrate curious facts relating to Japanese custom. The first place I have given to names of purely moral meaning — usually bestowed in the hope that the children will grow up worthy of them. But the lists should in no case be regarded as complete: they are only representative. Furthermore,

---

[1] "Ayamé Sama," however, is rather familiar; and this form cannot be used by a stranger in verbal address, though a letter may be directed with the name so written. As a rule, the ko is the more respectful form.

JAPANESE FEMALE NAMES

I must confess my inability to explain the reason of many names, which proved as much of riddles to Japanese friends as to myself.

NAMES OF VIRTUES AND PROPRIETIES

O-Ai	Love
O-Chië	Intelligence
O-Chū	Loyalty
O-Jin	Tenderness — humanity
O-Jun	Faithful-to-death
O-Kaiyō	Forgiveness — pardon
O-Ken	Wise — in the sense of moral discernment
O-Kō	Filial Piety
O-Masa	Righteous — just
O-Michi	The Way — doctrine
Misao	Honor — wifely fidelity
O-Nao	The Upright — honest
O-Nobu	The Faithful
O-Rei	Propriety — in the old Chinese sense
O-Retsu	Chaste and True
O-Ryō	The Generous — magnanimous
O-Sada	The Chaste
O-Sei	Truth
O-Shin	Faith — in the sense of fidelity, trust
O-Shizu	The Tranquil — calm-souled
O-Setsu	Fidelity — wifely virtue
O-Tamé	For-the-sake-of — a name suggesting unselfishness
O-Tei	The Docile — in the meaning of virtuous obedience
O-Toku	Virtue
O-Tomo	The Friend — especially in the meaning of mate, companion
O-Tsuné	Constancy
O-Yasu	The Amiable — gentle
O-Yoshi	The Good
O-Yoshi	The Respectful

The next list will appear at first sight more hetero-

geneous than it really is. It contains a larger variety
of appellations than the previous list; but nearly all
of the yobina refer to some good quality which the
parents trust that the child will display, or to some
future happiness which they hope that she will
deserve. To the latter category belong such names
of felicitation as Miyo and Masayo.

MISCELLANEOUS NAMES EXPRESSING PERSONAL QUALITIES,
OR PARENTAL HOPES

O-Atsu	The Generous — liberal
O-Chika	Closely Dear
O-Chika	Thousand Rejoicings
O-Chō	The Long — probably in reference to life
O-Dai	Great
O-Den	Transmission — bequest from ancestors, tradition
O-É	Fortunate
O-Ei	Prosperity
O-En	Charm
O-En	Prolongation — of life
O-Etsu	Surpassing
O-Etsu	The Playful — merry, joyous
O-Fuku	Good Luck
O-Gen	Source — spring, fountain
O-Haya	The Quick — light, nimble
O-Hidé	Superior
Hidéyo	Superior Generations
O-Hiro	The Broad
O-Hisa	The Long (?)
Isamu	The Vigorous — spirited, robust
O-Jin	Superexcellent
Kaméyo	Generations-of-the-Tortoise
O-Kané [1]	The Doubly-Accomplished
Kaoru	The Fragrant

[1] From the strange verb kaneru, signifying, to do two things at the
same time.

86

JAPANESE FEMALE NAMES

O-Kata	Worthy Person
O-Katsu	The Victorious
O-Kei	Delight
O-Kei	The Respectful
O-Ken	The Humble
O-Kichi	The Fortunate
O-Kimi	The Sovereign — peerless
O-Kiwa	The Distinguished
O-Kiyo ⎞ Kiyoshi ⎠	The Clear — in the sense of bright, beautiful
O-Kuru	She-who-Comes (?) [1]
O-Maru	The Round — plump
O-Masa	The Genteel
Masayo	Generations-of-the-Just
O-Masu	Increase
O-Mië	Triple Branch
O-Miki	Stem
O-Mio	Triple Cord
O-Mitsu	Abundance
O-Miwa	The Far-seeing
O-Miwa	Three Spokes (?) [2]
O-Miyo	Beautiful Generations
Miyuki [3]	Deep Snow
O-Moto	Origin
O-Naka	Friendship
O-Rai	Trust
O-Raku [4]	Pleasure
O-Sachi	Bliss
O-Sai	The Talented

[1] One is reminded of, "O whistle, and I'll come to you, my lad" — but no Japanese female name could have the implied signification. More probably the reference is to household obedience.

[2] Such is the meaning of the characters. I cannot understand the name. A Buddhist explanation suggests itself, but there are few, if any, Buddhist yobina.

[3] This beautiful name refers to the silence and calm following a heavy snowfall. But, even for the Japanese, it is an æsthetic name also — suggesting both tranquillity and beauty.

[4] The name seems curious, in view of the common proverb, "Raku wa ku no tané" — "Pleasure is the seed of pain."

Sakaë	Prosperity
O-Saku	The Blooming
O-Sei	The Refined — in the sense of clear
O-Sei	Force
O-Sen	Sennin — wood-fairy
O-Shigé	Exuberant
O-Shimé	The Total — summum bonum
O-Shin	The Fresh
O-Shin	Truth
O-Shina	Goods — possessions
Shirushi	Proof — evidence
O-Shizu	The Humble
O-Shō	Truth
O-Shun	Excellence
O-Suki	The Beloved — Aimée
O-Suké	The Helper
O-Sumi	The Refined — in the sense of sifted
O-Suté	The Forsaken — foundling [1]
O-Taë	The Exquisite
O-Taka	The Honorable
O-Taka	The Tall
Takara	Treasure — precious object
O-Tama	Jewel
Tamaë	Jewel-branch
Tokiwa [2]	Eternally Constant

[1] Not necessarily a real foundling. Sometimes the name may be explained by a curious old custom. In a certain family several children in succession die shortly after birth. It is decided, according to traditional usage, that the next child born must be exposed. A girl is the next child born; — she is carried by a servant to some lonely place in the fields, or elsewhere, and left there. Then a peasant, or other person, hired for the occasion (it is necessary that he should be of no kin to the family), promptly appears, pretends to find the babe, and carries it back to the parental home. "See this pretty foundling," he says to the father of the girl — "will you not take care of it?" The child is received, and named "Suté," the foundling. By this innocent artifice, it was formerly (and perhaps in some places is still) supposed that those unseen influences, which had caused the death of the other children, might be thwarted.

[2] Literally: "Everlasting-Rock" — but the ethical meaning is "Con-

JAPANESE FEMALE NAMES

O-Tomi	Riches
O-Toshi	The Deft — skillful
O-Tsuma	The Wife
O-Yori	The Trustworthy
O-Waka	The Young

Place-names, or geographical names, are common; but they are particularly difficult to explain. A child may be called after a place because born there, or because the parental home was there, or because of beliefs belonging to the old Chinese philosophy regarding direction and position, or because of traditional custom, or because of ideas connected with the religion of Shintō.

PLACE-NAMES

O-Fuji	[Mount] Fuji
O-Hama	Coast
O-Ichi	Market — fair
O-Iyo	Iyo — province of Iyo, in Shikoku
O-Kawa (rare)	River
O-Kishi	Beach — shore
O-Kita	North
O-Kiwa	Border
O-Kuni	Province
O-Kyō	Capital — metropolis — Kyōto
O-Machi	Town
Matsuë	Matsuë — chief city of Izumo
O-Mina [1]	South
O-Miné	Peak

---

stancy-everlasting-as-the-Rocks." "Tokiwa" is a name famous both in history and tradition; for it was the name of the mother of Yoshit-suné. Her touching story — and especially the episode of her flight through the deep snow with her boys — has been a source of inspiration to generations of artists.

[1] Abbreviation of Minami.

O-Miya	Temple [Shintō] [1]
O-Mon [2]	Gate
O-Mura	Village
O-Nami [3]	Wave
Naniwa	Naniwa — ancient name of Ōsaka
O-Mishi	West
O-Rin	Park
O-Saki	Cape
O-Sato	Native Place — village; also, home
O-Sawa	Marsh
O-Seki	Toll-Gate — barrier
Shigéki	Thickwood — forest
O-Shima	Island
O-Sono	Flower-garden
O-Taki	Cataract — or Waterfall
O-Tani	Valley
O-Tsuka	Milestone
O-Yama	Mountain

The next list is a curious medley, so far as regards the quality of the yobina comprised in it. Some are really æsthetic and pleasing; others industrial only; while a few might be taken for nicknames of the most disagreeable kind.

NAMES OF OBJECTS AND OF OCCUPATIONS ESPECIALLY
PERTAINING TO WOMEN

Ayako or ⎱ O-Aya [4] ⎰	Damask-pattern

---

[1] I must confess that in classing this name as a place-name, I am only making a guess. It seems to me that the name probably refers to the ichi no miya, or chief Shintō temple of some province.

[2] I fancy that this name, like that of O-Séki, must have originated in the custom of naming children after the place, or neighborhood, where the family lived. But here again, I am guessing.

[3] This classification also is a guess. I could learn nothing about the name, except the curious fact that it is said to be unlucky.

[4] Aya-Nishiki — the famous figured damask brocade of Kyōto — is probably referred to.

JAPANESE FEMALE NAMES

O-Fumi	Woman's Letter
O-Fusa	Tassel
O-Ito	Thread
O-Kama [1]	Rice-Sickle
O-Kama	Caldron
Kazashi	Hairpin
O-Kinu	Cloth-of-Silk
O-Koto	Harp
O-Nabé	Pot — or cooking-vessel
O-Nui	Embroidery
O-Shimé	Clasp — ornamental fastening
O-Somé	The Dyer
O-Taru	Cask — barrel

The following list consists entirely of material nouns used as names. There are several yobina among them of which I cannot find the emblematical meaning. Generally speaking, the yobina which signify precious substances, such as silver and gold, are æsthetic names; and those which signify common hard substances, such as stone, rock, iron, are intended to suggest firmness or strength of character. But the name "Rock" is also sometimes used as a symbol of the wish for long life, or long continuance of the family line. The curious name "Suna" has nothing, however, to do with individual "grit": it is half-moral and half-æsthetic. Fine sand — especially colored sand — is much prized in this fairyland of landscape-gardening, where it is used to cover spaces that must always be kept spotless and

---

[1] O-Kama (Sickle) is a familiar peasant-name. O-Kama (caldron, or iron cooking-pot), and several other ugly names in this list are servants' names. Servants in old time not only trained their children to become servants, but gave them particular names referring to their future labors.

beautiful, and never trodden — except by the gardener.

MATERIAL NOUNS USED AS NAMES

O-Gin	Silver
O-Ishi	Stone
O-Iwa	Rock
O-Kané	Bronze
O-Kazé [1]	Air — perhaps Wind
O-Kin	Gold
O-Ruri [2] } Ruriko }	Emerald — emeraldine?
O-Ryū	Fine Metal
O-Sato	Sugar
O-Seki	Stone
O-Shiwo	Salt
O-Suna	Sand
O-Suzu	Tin
O-Tané	Seed
O-Tetsu	Iron

The following five yobina are æsthetic names — although literally signifying things belonging to intellectual work. Four of them, at least, refer to calligraphy — the matchless calligraphy of the Far East — rather than to anything that we should call "*literary* beauty":

LITERARY NAMES

O-Bun	Composition
O-Fudé	Writing-Brush
O-Fumi	Letter

[1] I cannot find any explanation of this curious name.

[2] The Japanese name does not give the same quality of æsthetic sensation as the name Esmeralda. The ruri is not usually green, but blue; and the term "ruri-iro" (emerald color) commonly signifies a dark violet.

JAPANESE FEMALE NAMES

O-Kaku	Writing
O-Uta	Poem

Names relating to number are very common, but also very interesting. They may be loosely divided into two sub-classes — names indicating the order or the time of birth, and names of felicitation. Such yobina as Ichi, San, Roku, Hachi usually refer to the order of birth; but sometimes they record the date of birth. For example, I know a person called O-Roku, who received this name, not because she was the sixth child born in the family, but because she entered this world upon the sixth day of the sixth month of the sixth Meji. It will be observed that the numbers Two, Five, and Nine are not represented in the list: the mere idea of such names as O-Ni, O-Go, or O-Ku seems to a Japanese absurd. I do not know exactly why — unless it be that they suggest unpleasant puns. The place of O-Ni, is well supplied, however, by the name O-Tsugi (Next), which will be found in a subsequent list. Names signifying numbers ranging from eighty to a thousand, and upward, are names of felicitation. They express the wish that the bearer may live to a prodigious age, or that her posterity may flourish through the centuries.

NUMERALS AND WORDS RELATING TO NUMBER

O-Ichi	One
O-San	Three
O-Mitsu	Three
O-Yotsu	Four

O-Roku	Six
O-Shichi	Seven
O-Hachi	Eight
O-Jū	Ten
O-Iso	Fifty [1]
O-Yaso	Eighty
O-Hyaku	Hundred [2]
O-Yao	Eight Hundred
O-Sen	Thousand
O-Michi	Three Thousand
O-Man	Ten Thousand
O-Chiyo	Thousand Generations
Yachiyo	Eight Thousand Generations
O-Shigé	Twofold
O-Yaë	Eightfold
O-Kazu	Great Number
O-Mina	All
O-Han	Half [3]
O-Iku	How Many? (?)

OTHER NAMES RELATING TO ORDER OF BIRTH

O-Hatsu	Beginning — first-born
O-Tsugi	Next — the second
O-Naka	Midmost
O-Tomé	Stop — cease
O-Sué	Last

Some few of the next group of names are probably æsthetic. But such names are sometimes given only in reference to the time or season of birth; and the

[1] Such a name may record the fact that the girl was a first-born child, and the father fifty years old at the time of her birth.

[2] The "O" before this trisyllable seems contrary to rule; but Hyaku is pronounced almost like a dissyllable.

[3] "Better half?" — the reader may query. But I believe that this name originated in the old custom of taking a single character of the father's name — sometimes also a character of the mother's name — to compose the child's name with. Perhaps in this case the name of the girl's father was HANYémon, or HANbei.

94

reason for any particular yobina of this class is difficult to decide without personal inquiry.

NAMES RELATING TO TIME AND SEASON

O-Haru	Spring
O-Natsu	Summer
O-Aki	Autumn
O-Fuyu	Winter
O-Asa	Morning
O-Chō '	Dawn
O-Yoi	Evening
O-Sayo	Night
O-Ima	Now
O-Toki	Time — opportunity
O-Toshi	Year [of Plenty]

Names of animals — real or mythical — form another class of yobina. A name of this kind generally represents the hope that the child will develop some quality or capacity symbolized by the creature after which it has been called. Names such as "Dragon," "Tiger," "Bear," etc., are intended in most cases to represent moral rather than other qualities. The moral symbolism of the Koi (Carp) is too well-known to require explanation here. The names Kamé and Tsuru refer to longevity. Koma, curious as the fact may seem, is a name of endearment.

NAMES OF BIRDS, FISHES, ANIMALS, ETC.

Chidori	Sanderling
O-Kamé	Tortoise
O-Koi	Carp [1]
O-Koma	Filly — or pony

[1] *Cyprinus carpio.*

95

O-Kuma	Bear
O-Ryō	Dragon
O-Shika	Deer
O-Tai	Bream [1]
O-Taka	Hawk
O-Tako	Cuttlefish (?)
O-Tatsu	Dragon
O-Tora	Tiger
O-Tori	Bird
O-Tsuru	Stork [2]
O-Washi	Eagle

Even yobina which are the names of flowers or fruits, plants or trees, are in most cases names of moral or felicitous, rather than of æsthetic meaning. The plumflower is an emblem of feminine virtue; the chrysanthemum, of longevity; the pine, both of longevity and constancy; the bamboo, of fidelity; the cedar, of moral rectitude; the willow, of docility and gentleness, as well as of physical grace. The symbolism of the lotus and of the cherryflower is probably familiar. But such names as Hana (Blossom) and Ben (Petal) are æsthetic in the true sense; and the Lily remains in Japan, as elsewhere, an emblem of feminine grace.

FLOWER-NAMES

Ayamé	Iris [3]
Azami	Thistle-Flower

[1] *Chrysophris cardinalis.*

[2] Sometimes this name is shortened into O-Tsu. In Tōkyō at the present time it is the custom to drop the honorific "O" before such abbreviations, and to add to the name the suffix "chan" — as in the case of children's names. Thus a young woman may be caressingly addressed as "Tsu-chan" (for O-Tsuru), "Ya-chan" (for O-Yasu), etc.

[3] *Iris setosa,* or *Iris sibrisia.*

JAPANESE FEMALE NAMES

O-Ben	Petal
O-Fuji	Wistaria [1]
O-Hana	Blossom
O-Kiku	Chrysanthemum
O-Ran	Orchid
O-Ren	Lotus
Sakurako	Cherryblossom
O-Umé	Plumflower
O-Yuri	Lily

NAMES OF PLANTS, FRUITS, AND TREES

O-Iné	Rice-in-the-blade
Kaëdé	Maple-leaf
O-Kaya	Rush [2]
O-Kaya	Yew [3]
O-Kuri	Chestnut
O-Kuwa	Mulberry
O-Maki	Fir [4]
O-Mamé	Bean
O-Momo	Peach — the fruit [5]
O-Nara	Oak
O-Ryū	Willow
Sanaë	Sprouting-Rice
O-Sané	Fruit-seed
O-Shino	Slender Bamboo
O-Sugé	Reed [6]
O-Sugi	Cedar [7]
O-Také	Bamboo
O-Tsuta	Ivy [8]

---

[1] *Wistaria chinensis.*

[2] *Imperata arundinacea.*

[3] *Torreya nucifera.*

[4] *Podocarpus chinensis.*

[5] Yet this name may possibly have been written with the wrong character. There is another yobina, "Momo" signifying "hundred" — as in the phrase "momo yo," "for a hundred ages."

[6] *Scirpus maritimus.*

[7] *Cryptomeria japonica.*

[8] *Cissus thunbergii.*

O-Yaë	Double-Blossom [1]
O-Yoné	Rice-in-grain
Wakana	Young Na [2]

Names signifying light or color seem to us the most æsthetic of all yobina; and they probably seem so to the Japanese. Nevertheless the relative purport even of these names cannot be divined at sight. Colors have moral and other values in the old nature-philosophy; and an appellation that to the Western mind suggests only luminosity or beauty may actually refer to moral or social distinction — to the hope that the girl so named will become "illustrious."

NAMES SIGNIFYING BRIGHTNESS

O-Mika	New Moon [3]
O-Mitsu	Light
O-Shimo	Frost
O-Teru	The Shining
O-Tsuki	Moon
O-Tsuya	The Glossy — lustrous
O-Tsuyu	Dew
O-Yuki	Snow

COLOR-NAMES

O-Ai	Indigo
O-Aka	Red
O-Iro	Color
O-Kon	Deep Blue
O-Kuro	Dark — lit., Black

---

[1] A flower-name certainly; but the yaë here is probably an abbreviation of yaë-zakura, the double-flower of a particular species of cherry-tree.

[2] *Brassica chinensis.*

[3] Mika is an abbreviation of Mikazuki, "the moon of the third night" [of the old lunar month].

JAPANESE FEMALE NAMES

Midori [1]	Green
Murasaki [1]	Purple
O-Shiro	White

The following and final group of female names contains several queer puzzles. Japanese girls are sometimes named after the family crest; and heraldry might explain one or two of these yobina. But why a girl should be called a ship, I am not sure of being able to guess. Perhaps some reader may be reminded of Nietzsche's "Little Brig called Angeline":

> Angeline — they call me so —
> Now a ship, one time a maid,
> (Ah, and evermore a maid!)
> Love the steersman, to and fro,
> Turns the wheel so finely made.

But such a fancy would not enter into a Japanese mind. I find, however, in a list of family crests, two varieties of design representing a ship, twenty representing an arrow, and two representing a bow.

NAMES DIFFICULT TO CLASSIFY OR EXPLAIN

O-Fuku [2]	Raiment — clothing
O-Funé	Ship — or Boat

---

[1] Midori and Murasaki, especially the latter, should properly be classed with aristocratic yobina; and both are very rare. I could find neither in the collection of aristocratic names which was made for me from the records of the Peeresses' School; but I discovered a "Midori" in a list of middle-class names. Color-names being remarkably few among yobina, I thought it better in this instance to group the whole of them together, independently of class-distinctions.

[2] Possibly this name belongs to the same class as O-Nui (Embroidery), O-Somé (The Dyer); but I am not sure.

O-Hina [1]	Doll — a paper doll?
O-Kono	This
O-Nao	Still More
O-Nari	Thunder-peal
O-Niho	Palanquin (?)
O-Rai	Thunder
O-Rui	Sort — kind, species
O-Suzu [2]	Little Bell
Suzuë	Branch-of-Little-Bells
O-Tada	The Only
Tamaki	Armlet — bracelet
O-Tami	Folk — common people
O-Toshi	Arrowhead — or barb
O-Tsui	Pair — match
O-Tsuna	Rope — bond
O-Yumi	Bow — weapon

Before passing on to the subject of aristocratic names, I must mention an old rule for Japanese names — a curious rule that might help to account for sundry puzzles in the preceding lists. This rule formerly applied to all personal names — masculine or feminine. It cannot be fully explained in the present paper; for a satisfactory explanation would occupy at least fifty pages. But, stated in the briefest possible way, the rule is that the first or "head-

[1] Probably a name of caress. The word "hina" is applied especially to the little paper dolls made by hand for amusement — representing young ladies with elaborate coiffure; and it is also given to the old-fashioned dolls representing courtly personages in full ceremonial costume. The true doll — doll-baby — is called ningyō.

[2] Perhaps this name is given because of the sweet sound of the suzu — a tiny metal ball, with a little stone or other hard object inside, to make the ringing. It is a pretty Japanese custom to put one of these little suzu in the silk charm-bag (mamori-bukero) which is attached to a child's girdle. The suzu rings with every motion that the child makes — somewhat like one of those tiny bells which we attach to the neck of a pet kitten.

JAPANESE FEMALE NAMES

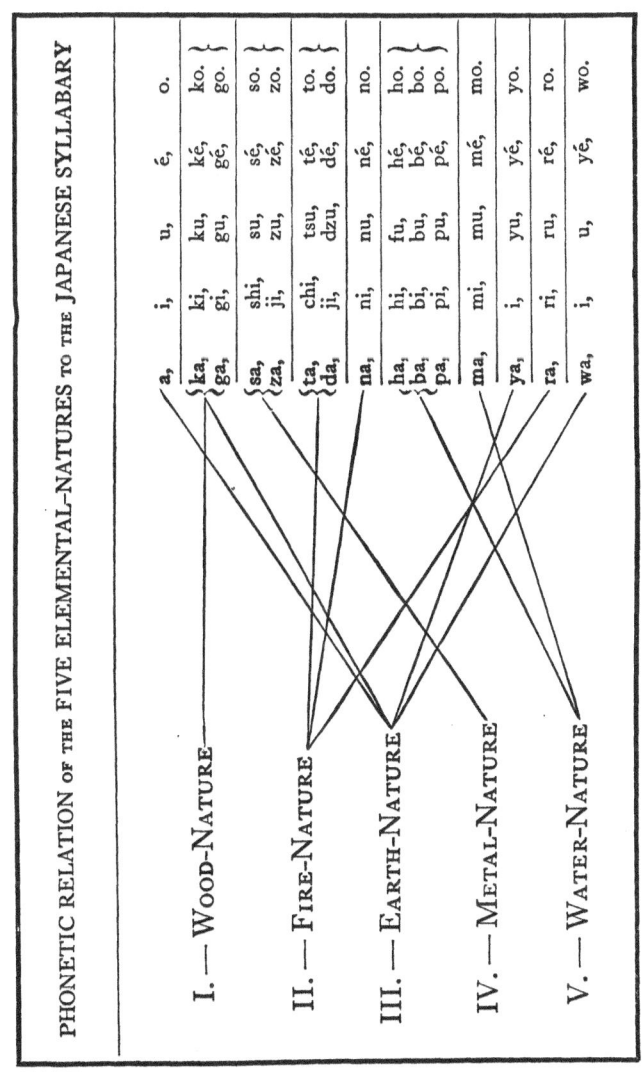

PHONETIC RELATION OF THE FIVE ELEMENTAL-NATURES TO THE JAPANESE SYLLABARY

	a,	i,	u,	é,	o.
	ka,	ki,	ku,	ké,	ko.
	ga,	gi,	gu,	gé,	go.
	sa,	shi,	su,	sé,	so.
	za,	ji,	zu,	zé,	zo.
	ta,	chi,	tsu,	té,	to.
	da,	ji,	dzu,	dé,	do.
	na,	ni,	nu,	né,	no.
	ha,	hi,	fu,	hé,	ho.
	ba,	bi,	bu,	bé,	bo.
	pa,	pi,	pu,	pé,	po.
	ma,	mi,	mu,	mé,	mo.
	ya,	i,	yu,	yé,	yo.
	ra,	ri,	ru,	ré,	ro.
	wa,	i,	u,	yé,	wo.

I. — WOOD-NATURE

II. — FIRE-NATURE

III. — EARTH-NATURE

IV. — METAL-NATURE

V. — WATER-NATURE

character" of a personal name should be made to "accord" (in the Chinese philosophic sense) with the supposed Sei, or astrologically determined nature, of the person to whom the name is given; — the required accordance being decided, not by the meaning, but by the sound of the Chinese written character. Some vague idea of the difficulties of the subject may be obtained from the accompanying table.

III

FOR examples of contemporary aristocratic names I consulted the reports of the Kwazoku-Jogakkō (Peeresses' School), published between the nineteenth and twenty-seventh years of Meiji (1886–95). The Kwazoku-Jogakkō admits other students besides daughters of the nobility; but for present purposes the names of the latter only — to the number of one hundred and forty-seven — have been selected.

It will be observed that names of three or more syllables are rare among these, and also that the modern aristocratic yobina of two syllables, as pronounced and explained, differ little from ordinary yobina. But as written in Chinese they differ greatly from other female names, being in most cases represented by characters of a complex and unfamiliar kind. The use of these more elaborate characters chiefly accounts for the relatively large number of homonyms to be found in the following list:

JAPANESE FEMALE NAMES

Aki-ko	Autumn
Aki-ko	The Clear-Minded
Aki-ko	Dawn
Asa-ko	Fair Morning
Aya-ko	Silk Damask
Chiharu-ko	A Thousand Springs
Chika-ko	Near — close
Chitsuru-ko	A Thousand Storks
Chiyo-ko	A Thousand Generations
Ei-ko	Bell-Chime
Etsu-ko	Delight
Fuji-ko	Wistaria
Fuku-ko	Good-Fortune
Fumi-ko	A Woman's Letter
Fuyō-ko	Lotus-flower
Fuyu-ko	Winter
Hana-ko	Flower
Hana-ko	Fair-Blooming
Haru-ko	The Tranquil
Haru-ko	Spring — the season of flowers
Haru-ko	The Far-Removed — in the sense, perhaps, of superlative
Hatsu-ko	The First-Born
Hidé-ko	Excelling
Hidé-ko	Surpassing
Hiro-ko	Magnanimous — literally: broad, large — in the sense of beneficence
Hiro-ko	Wide-Spreading — with reference to family prosperity
Hisa-ko	Long-Lasting
Hisa-ko	Continuing
Hoshi-ko	Star
Iku-ko	The Quick — in the sense of living
Ima-ko	Now
Iho-ko	Five Hundred — probably a name of felicitation

Ito-ko	Sewing-Thread
Kamé-ko	Tortoise
Kané-ko	Going around (?) [1]
Kané-ko	Bell — the character indicates a large suspended bell
Kata-ko	Condition (?)
Kazu-ko	First
Kazu-ko	Number — a great number
Kazu-ko	The Obedient
Kiyo-ko	The Pure
Kō [2]	Filial Piety
Kō-ko	Stork
Koto	Harp
Kuni-ko	Province
Kuni	Country — in the largest sense
Kyō-ko	Capital — metropolis
Machi	Ten-Thousand Thousand
Makoto	True-Heart
Masa-ko	The Trustworthy — sure
Masa-ko	The Upright
Masu-ko	Increase
Mata-ko	Completely — wholly
Matsu-ko	Pine-tree
Michi-ko	Three Thousand
Miné	Peak
Miné-ko	Mountain-Range
Mitsu-ko	Light — radiance
Miyo-ko	Beautiful Generations
Moto-ko	Origin — source
Naga-ko	Long — probably in reference to time
Naga-ko	Long Life
Nami-ko	Wave
Nao-ko	Correct — upright

[1] It is possible that this name was made simply by taking one character of the father's name. The girl's name otherwise conveys no intelligible meaning.

[2] The suffix "ko" is sometimes dropped for reasons of euphony, and sometimes for reasons of good taste — difficult to explain to readers unfamiliar with the Japanese language — even when the name consists of only one syllable or of two syllables.

JAPANESE FEMALE NAMES

Nyo-ko [1]	Gem-Treasure
Nobu-ko	Faithful
Nobu-ko	Abundance — plenty
Nobu-ko	The Prolonger
Nori-ko	Precept — doctrine
Nui	Embroidery — sewing
Oki	Offing — perhaps originally a place-name [2]
Sada-ko	The Chaste
Sada-ko	The Sure — trustworthy
Sakura-ko	Cherry-Blossom
Sakaë	The Prosperous
Sato-ko	Home
Sato-ko	The Discriminating
Seki-ko	Great
Setsu-ko	The Chaste
Shigé-ko	Flourishing
Shigé-ko	Exuberant — in the sense of rich growth
Shigé-ko	Upgrowing
Shigé-ko	Fragrance
Shiki-ko	Prudence
Shima-ko	Island
Shin-ko	The Fresh — new
Shizu-ko	The Quiet — calm
Shizuë	Quiet River
Sono-ko	Garden
Suë-ko	Last — in the sense of youngest
Suké-ko	The Helper
Sumi-ko	The Clear — spotless, refined
Sumi-ko	The Veritable — real

---

[1] This name is borrowed from the name of the sacred gem Nyoihōju, which figures both in Shintō and in Buddhist legend. The divinity Jizō is usually represented holding in one hand this gem, which is said to have the power of gratifying any desire that its owner can entertain. Perhaps the Nyoihōju may be identified with the Gem-Treasure Veluriya, mentioned in the *Sutra of The Great King of Glory*, chapter I. (See *Sacred Books of the East*, vol. XI.)

[2] A naval officer named Oki told me that his family had originally been settled in the Oki Islands ("Islands of the Offing"). This interesting coincidence suggested to me that the above yobina might have had the same origin.

Sumië-ko	Clear River
Suzu-ko	Tin
Suzu-ko	Little Bell
Suzunë	Sound of Little Bell
Taka-ko	High — lofty, superior
Taka-ko	Filial Piety
Taka-ko	Precious
Také-ko	Bamboo
Taki-ko	Waterfall
Tama-ko	Gem — jewel
Tama-ko	Gem — written with a different character
Tamé-ko	For the Sake of —
Tami-ko	People — folks
Tané-ko	Successful
Tatsu-ko	Attaining
Tatsuru-ko [1]	Many Storks
Tatsuru-ko	Ricefield Stork
Teru-ko	Beaming — luminous
Tetsu-ko	Iron
Toki-ko	Time
Tomé-ko	Cessation
Tomi-ko	Riches
Tomo	Intelligence
Tomo	Knowledge
Tomo-ko	Friendship
Toshi-ko	The Quickly-Perceiving
Toyo-ko	Fruitful
Tsuné	Constancy
Tsuné-ko	Ordinary — usual, common
Tsuné-ko	Ordinary — written with a different character
Tsuné-ko	Faithful — in the sense of wifely fidelity
Tsuru-ko	Stork
Tsuya-ko	The Lustrous — shining, glossy
Umé	Female Hare
Umé-ko	Plum-Blossom
Yachi-ko	Eight Thousand
Yaso-ko	Eighty
Yasoshi-ko	Eighty-four

[1] So written, but probably pronounced as two syllables only.

JAPANESE FEMALE NAMES

Yasu-ko	The Maintainer — supporter
Yasu-ko	The Respectful
Yasu-ko	The Tranquil-Minded
Yoné-ko	Rice
Yori-ko	The Trustful
Yoshi	Eminent — celebrated
Yoshi-ko	Fragrance
Yoshi-ko	The Good — or Gentle
Yoshi-ko	The Lovable
Yoshi-ko	The Lady-like — gentle in the sense of refined
Yoshi-ko	The Joyful
Yoshi-ko	Congratulation
Yoshi-ko	The Happy
Yoshi-ko	Bright and Clear
Yuki-ko	The Lucky
Yuki-ko	Snow
Yuku-ko	Going
Yutaka	Plenty — affluence, superabundance

IV

In the first part of this paper I suggested that the custom of giving very poetical names to geisha and to jorō might partly account for the unpopularity of purely æsthetic yobina. And in the hope of correcting certain foreign misapprehensions, I shall now venture a few remarks about the names of geisha.

Geisha-names — like other classes of names — although full of curious interest, and often in themselves really beautiful, have become hopelessly vulgarized by association with a calling the reverse of respectable. Strictly speaking, they have nothing to do with the subject of the present study — inasmuch as they are not real personal names, but professional appellations only — not yobina, but geimyō.

A large proportion of such names can be distinguished by certain prefixes or suffixes attached to them. They can be known, for example,

(1) By the prefix Waka, signifying "Young"; — as in the names Wakagusa (Young Grass); Wakazuru (Young Stork); Wakamurasaki (Young Purple); Wakakoma (Young Filly).

(2) By the prefix Ko, signifying "Little"; — as in the names, Ko-en (Little Charm); Ko-hana (Little Flower); Kozakura (Little Cherry-Tree).

(3) By the suffix Ryō, signifying "Dragon" (the Ascending Dragon being especially a symbol of success); — as Tama-Ryō (Jewel-Dragon); Hana-Ryō (Flower-Dragon); Kin-Ryō (Golden-Dragon).

(4) By the suffix jî, signifying "to serve," "to administer"; — as in the names Uta-ji, Shinné-ji, Katsu-ji.

(5) By the suffix suké, signifying "help"; — as in the names Tama-suké, Koma-suké.

(6) By the suffix kichi, signifying "luck," "fortune"; — as Uta-kichi (Song-Luck); Tama-kichi (Jewel-Fortune).

(7) By the suffix giku (i.e., kiku), signifying "chrysanthemum"; — as Mitsu-giku (Three-Chrysanthemums); Hina-giku (Doll-Chrysanthemum); Ko-giku (Little Chrysanthemum).

(8) By the suffix tsuru, signifying "stork" (emblem of longevity); — as Koma-tsuru (Filly-Stork); Ko-tsuru (Little Stork); Ito-zuru (Thread-Stork).

These forms will serve for illustration; but there

are others. Geimyō are written, as a general rule, with only two Chinese characters, and are pronounced as three or as four syllables. Geimyō of five syllables are occasionally to be met with; geimyō of only two syllables are rare — at least among names of dancing girls. And these professional appellations have seldom any moral meaning: they signify things relating to longevity, wealth, pleasure, youth, or luck — perhaps especially to luck.

Of late years it became a fashion among certain classes of geisha in the capital to assume real names with the genteel suffix Ko, and even aristocratic yo-bina. In 1889 some of the Tōkyō newspapers demanded legislative measures to check the practice. This incident would seem to afford proof of public feeling upon the subject.

OLD JAPANESE SONGS

THIS New Year's morning I find upon my table two most welcome gifts from a young poet of my literary class. One is a roll of cloth for a new kimono — cloth such as my Western reader never saw. The brown warp is cotton thread; but the woof is soft white paper string, irregularly speckled with black. When closely examined, the black specklings prove to be Chinese and Japanese characters; — for the paper woof is made out of manuscript — manuscript of poems — which has been deftly twisted into fine cord, with the written surface outwards. The general effect of the white, black, and brown in the texture is a warm mouse-gray. In many Izumo homes a similar kind of cloth is manufactured for family use; but this piece was woven especially for me by the mother of my pupil. It will make a most comfortable winter-robe; and when wearing it, I shall be literally clothed with poetry — even as a divinity might be clothed with the sun.

The other gift is poetry also, but poetry in the original state: a wonderful manuscript collection of Japanese songs gathered from unfamiliar sources, and particularly interesting from the fact that nearly all of them are furnished with refrains. There are hundreds of compositions, old and new — including several extraordinary ballads, many dancing-songs, and a surprising variety of love-songs. Neither in sentiment nor in construction do any of these resemble the Japanese poetry of which I have already, in previous books, offered specimens in translation. The forms are, in most cases, curiously irregular; but their irregularity is not without a strange charm of its own.

I am going to offer examples of these compositions — partly because of their unfamiliar emotional quality, and partly because I think that something can be learned from their strange art of construction. The older songs — selected from the antique drama — seem to me particularly worthy of notice. The thought or feeling and its utterance are supremely simple; yet by primitive devices of reiteration and of pause, very remarkable results have been obtained. What strikes me especially noteworthy in the following specimen is the way that the phrase, begun with the third line of the first stanza, and interrupted by a kind of burthen, is repeated and finished in the next stanza. Perhaps the suspension will recall to Western readers the effect of some English ballads with double refrains, or of such quaint forms of French song as the famous —

> Au jardin de mon père —
>   Vole, mon cœur, vole!
> Il y a un pommier doux,
>   Tout doux!

But in the Japanese song the reiteration of the

broken phrase produces a slow dreamy effect as unlike the effect of the French composition as the
movements of a Japanese dance are unlike those of
any Western round:

KANO YUKU WA

(Probably from the eleventh century)

Kano yuku wa,
Kari ka? — kugui ka?
Kari naraba —
   (*Ref.*) Haréya tōtō!
            Haréya tōtō!

Kari nara
Nanori zo sémashi; —
Nao kugui nari-ya! —
   (*Ref.*) Tōtō!

That which yonder flies, —
Wild goose is it? — swan is it?
Wild goose if it be —
            Haréya tōtō!
            Haréya tōtō!

Wild goose if it be,
Its name I soon shall say:
Wild swan if it be — better still!
            Tōtō!

There are many old lyrics in the above form.
Here is another song, of different construction, also
from the old drama: there is no refrain, but there is
the same peculiar suspension of phrase; and the
effect of the quadruple repetition is emotionally
impressive:

OLD JAPANESE SONGS

Isora ga saki ni
Tai tsuru ama mo,
Tai tsuru ama mo —

Wagimoko ga tamé to,
Tai tsuru ama mo,
Tai tsuru ama mo!

Off the Cape of Isora,
Even the fisherman catching tai, [1]
Even the fisherman catching tai —

[Works] for the sake of the woman beloved —
Even the fisherman catching tai,
Even the fisherman catching tai!

But a still more remarkable effect is obtained in the following ancient song by the extraordinary reiteration of an uncompleted phrase, and by a double suspension. I can imagine nothing more purely natural: indeed the realism of these simple utterances has almost the quality of pathos:

AGÉMAKI
(*Old lyrical drama — date uncertain*)
Agémaki [2] wo
Waséda ni yarité ya!
So omou to,
So omou to,

---

[1] *Chrysophris cardinalis*, a kind of sea-bream — generally esteemed the best of Japanese fishes.

[2] It was formerly the custom to shave the heads of boys, leaving only a tuft or lock of hair on either temple. Such a lock was called "agémaki," a word also meaning "tassel"; and eventually the term came to signify a boy or lad. In these songs it is used as a term of endearment — much as an English girl might speak of her sweetheart as "my dear lad," or "my darling boy."

So omou to,
So omou to,
So omou to —

So omou to,
Nani-mo sezushité —
Harubi sura,
Harubi sura,
Harubi sura,
Harubi sura,
Harubi sura!

My darling boy! —
Oh! they have sent him to the rice-fields!
When I think about him —
When I think,
When I think,
When I think,
When I think —

When I think about him!
I— doing nothing at all —
Even on this spring-day,
Even this spring-day,
Even this spring-day,
Even this spring-day,
Even on this spring-day! —

Other forms of repetition and of refrain are furnished in the two following lyrics:

BINDATARA

(Supposed to have been composed as early as the twelfth century)

Bindatara wo
Ayugaséba koso,
Ayugaséba koso,
Aikyō zuitaré!
Yaréko tōtō.
Yaréko tōtō!

OLD JAPANESE SONGS

With loosened hair —
Only because of having tossed it,
Only because of having shaken it —
Oh, sweet she is!
Yaréko tōtō!
Yaréko tōtō!

SAMA WA TENNIN
(Probably from the sixteenth century)

Sama wa tennin!
Soré-soré,
Tontorori!

Otomé no sugata
Kumo no kayoiji
Chirato mita!
Tontorori!

Otomé no sugata
Kumo no kayoiji
Chirato mita!
Tontorori!

My beloved an angel is! [1]
Soré-soré!
Tontorori!

The maiden's form,
In the passing of clouds,
In a glimpse I saw!
Tontorori!

The maiden's form,
In the passage of clouds
In a glimpse I saw !
Tontorori!

My next selection is from a love-song of un-

[1] Literally: "a Tennin"; — that is to say, an inhabitant of the Buddhist heaven. The Tennin are usually represented as beautiful maidens.

certain date, belonging to the Kamakura period
(1186-1332). This fragment is chiefly remarkable
for its Buddhist allusions, and for its very regular
form of stanza:

> Makoto yara,
> Kashima no minato ni
> Miroku no mifuné ga
> Tsuité gozarimōsu.
> > Yono!
> > Sā iyoë, iyoë!
> > Sā iyoë, iyoë!

> Hobashira wa,
> Kogané no hobashira;
> Ho niwa Hokkékyō no
> Go no man-makimono.
> > Sā iyoë, iyoë!
> > Sā iyoë, iyoë!

. . . .

I know not if 't is true
That to the port of Kashima
The august ship of Miroku [1] has come!
> Yono!
> Sā iyoë, iyoë!
> Sā iyoë, iyoë!

As for the mast,
It is a mast of gold; —
The sail is the fifth august roll
Of the Hokkékyō! [2]
> Sā iyoë, iyoë!
> Sā iyoë, iyoë

. . . .

[1] Miroku Bosatsu (Maitrêya Bodhisattva) is the next great Buddha
to come.

[2] Japanese popular name for the Chinese version of the Saddhârma
Pundarîka Sutra. Many of the old Buddhist scriptures were written

OLD JAPANESE SONGS

Otherwise interesting, with its queer refrain, is another song called "Agémaki" — belonging to one of the curious class of lyrical dramas known as "Saibara." This may be found fault with as somewhat "free"; but I cannot think it more open to objection than some of our much-admired Elizabethan songs which were probably produced at about the same time:

AGÉMAKI

(Probably from the sixteenth century)

Agémaki ya!
          Tonton!
Hiro bakari ya —
          Tonton!
Sakarité netarédomo,
Marobi-ainikéri —
          Tonton!
Kayori-ainikéri,
          Tonton!

Oh! my darling boy!
          Tonton!
Though a fathom [1] apart,
          Tonton!
Sleeping separated,
By rolling we came together!
          Tonton!
By slow approaches we came together,
          Tonton!

My next group of selections consists of "local songs" — by which term the collector means songs upon long scrolls, called " makimono " — a name also given to pictures printed upon long rolls of silk or paper.

[1] Literally: "hiro." The hiro is a measure of about five feet English, and is used to measure breadth as well as depth.

peculiar to particular districts or provinces. They are old — though less old than the compositions previously cited; — and their interest is chiefly emotional. But several, it will be observed, have curious refrains. Songs of this sort are sung especially at the village-dances — Bon-odori and Hōnen-odori:

LOVE-SONG
(Province of Echigo)

Hana ka? — chōchō ka?
Chōchō ka? — hana ka?
      Don-don!

Kité wa chira-chira mayowaséru,
Kité wa chira-chira mayowaséru!
      Taichokané!
      Sōkané don-don!

Flower is it? — butterfly is it?
Butterfly or flower?
      Don-don!

When you come thus flickering, I am deluded! —
When you come thus twinkling, I am bewitched!
      Taichokané!
      Sōkané don-don!

LOVE-SONG
(Province of Kii — village of Ogawa)

Koë wa surédomo
Sugata wa miénu —
Fuka-no no kirigirisu!

Though I hear the voice [of the beloved], the form I cannot see — a kirigirisu [1] in the high grass.

---

[1] The kirigirisu is a kind of grasshopper with a very musical note. It is very difficult to see it, even when it is singing close by, for its color is

OLD JAPANESE SONGS

LOVE-SONG
(Province of Mutsu — district of Sugaru)

Washi no kokoro to
Oki kuru funé wa,
Raku ni misétémo,
    Ku ga taënu.

My heart and a ship in the offing — either seems to move with ease; yet in both there is trouble enough.

LOVE-SONG
(Province of Suwō — village of Iséki)

Namida koboshité
Shinku wo kataru,
Kawairashi-sa ga
    Mashimasuru!

As she tells me all the pain of her toil, shedding tears — ever her sweetness seems to increase.

LOVE-SONG
(Province of Suruga — village of Gotemba)

Hana ya, yoku kiké!
Shō aru naraba,
Hito ga fusagu ni
    Nazé hiraku?

O flower, hear me well if thou hast a soul! When any one sorrows as I am sorrowing, why dost thou bloom?

OLD TŌKYŌ SONG

Iya-na o-kata no
Shinsetsu yori ka
Suita o-kata no
    Muri ga yoi.

---

exactly the color of the grass. The song alludes to the happy peasant custom of singing while at work in the fields. .

JAPANESE STUDIES

Better than the kindness of the disliked is the violence of the beloved.

LOVE-SONG
(Province of Iwami)

Kawairashi-sa ya!
Hotaru no mushi wa
Shinobu nawaté ni
     Hi wo tomosu.

Ah, the darling! . . . Ever as I steal along the rice-field-path [to meet my lover], the firefly kindles a light to show me the way.

COMIC SONG
(Province of Shinano)

Ano yama kagé dé
Hikaru wa nanja? —
Tsuki ka, hoshi ka, hotaru no mushi ka?
Tsuki démo naiga;
Hoshi démo naiga; —
Shūto no o-uba no mé ga hikaru —
    (Chorus) Mé ga hikaru!

In the shadow of the mountain
What is it that shines so?
Moon is it, or star? — or is it the firefly-insect?
    Neither is it moon,
    Nor yet star; —
It is the old woman's Eye; — it is the Eye of my
mother-in-law that shines, —
    (Chorus) It is her Eye that shines!

KAËRI-ODORI [1]
(Province of Sanuki)

Oh! the cruelty, the cruelty of my mother-in-law! —
    (Chorus) Oh! the cruelty!

---

[1] I am not sure of the real meaning of the name "Kaëri-Odori" (literally: "turn-dance" or "return-dance").

OLD JAPANESE SONGS

Even tells me to paint a picture on running water!
If ever I paint a picture on running water,
You will count the stars in the night-sky!
　　　　　　Count the stars in the night-sky!

— Come! let us dance the Dance of the Honorable Garden! —
　　　　　　Chan-chan!
　　　　　　Cha-cha!
　　　　　　Yoitomosé,
　　　　　　Yoitomosé!
Who cuts the bamboo at the back of the house? —
　　　　　　(*Chorus*) Who cuts the bamboo? —
My sweet lord's own bamboo, the first he planted —
　　　　　　The first he planted?

— Come! let us dance the Dance of the Honorable Garden! —
　　　　　　Chan-chan!
　　　　　　Cha-cha!
　　　　　　Yoitomosé,
　　　　　　Yoitomosé!

Oh! the cruelty, the cruelty of my mother-in-law! —
　　　　　　Oh! the cruelty!
Tells me to cut and make a hakama [1] out of rock!
If ever I cut and sew a hakama of rock,
Then you will learn to twist the fine sand into thread, —
　　　　　　Twist it into thread.

— Come! let us dance the Dance of the Honorable Garden! —
　　　　　　Chan-chan!
　　　　　　Cha-cha!
　　　　　　Yoitomosé,
　　　　　　Yoitomosé!
　　　　　　Chan-chan-chan!

OTERA-ODORI (TEMPLE-DANCE)
(*Province of Iga, village called Uenomachi*)
Visiting the honorable temple, when I see the august gate,

---

[1] A divided skirt of a peculiar form, worn formerly by men chiefly, to-day worn by female students also.

JAPANESE STUDIES

The august gate I find to be of silver, the panels of gold.
Noble indeed is the gate of the honorable temple —
                                    The honorable temple!

Visiting the honorable temple, when I see the garden,
I see young pinetrees flourishing in the four directions:
On the first little branch of one of the shijūgara [1] has made her
    nest —
                                    Has made her nest.

Visiting the honorable temple, when I see the water-tank,
I see little flowers of many colors set all about it,
Each one having a different color of its own —
                                    A different color.

Visiting the honorable temple, when I see the parlor-room,
I find many kinds of little birds gathered all together,
Each one singing a different song of its own —
                                    A different song.

Visiting the honorable temple, when I see the guest-room,
There I see the priest, with a lamp beside him,
Reading behind a folding-screen — oh, how admirable it is! —
                                    How admirable it is!

Many kinds of popular songs — and especially
the class of songs sung at country-dances — are
composed after a mnemonic plan. The stanzas are
usually ten in number; and the first syllable of each
should correspond in sound to the first syllable of
the numeral placed before the verse. Sometimes
Chinese numerals are used; sometimes Japanese.
But the rule is not always perfectly observed. In
the following example it will be observed that the

---

[1] The Manchurian great tit. It is said to bring good fortune to the
owners of the garden in which it builds a nest — providing that the nest
be not disturbed and that the brood be protected.

correspondence of the first two syllables in the first verse with the first two syllables of the Japanese word for one (hitotsu) is a correspondence of meaning only; — ichi being the Chinese numeral:

SONG OF FISHERMEN
(Province of Shimosa — town of Chōshi) [1]

Hitotsutosé:
>Ichiban buné é tsumi-kondé,
>Kawaguchi oshikomu ō-yagoë.
>>Kono tai-ryō-buné!

Futatsutosé:
>Futaba no oki kara Togawa madé
>Tsuzuité oshikomu ō-yagoë.
>>Kono tai-ryō buné!

Mitsutosé:
>Mina ichidō-ni manéki wo agé,
>Kayowasé-buné no nigiyakasa
>>Kono tai-ryō-buné!

Yotsutosé:
>Yoru-hiru taitémo taki-amaru,
>San-bai itchō no ō-iwashi!
>>Kono tai-ryō-buné!

Itsutsutosé:
>Itsu kité mitémo hoshika-ba ni
>Akima sukima wa sarani nai.
>>Kono tai-ryō-buné!

Mutsutoyé:
>Mutsu kara mutsu madé kasu-wari ga
>Ō-wari ko-wari dé té ni owaré.
>>Kono tai-ryō-buné!

---

[1] Chōshi, a town of some importance, is situated at the mouth of the Tonégawa. It is celebrated for its iwashi-fishery. The iwashi is a fish about the size of the sardine, and is sought chiefly for the sake of its oil. Immense quantities of iwashi are taken off the coast. They are boiled to extract the oil; and the dried residue is sent inland to serve as manure.

Nanatsutosé:
> Natakaki Tonégawa ichi-men ni
> Kasu-ya abura wo tsumi-okuru
> > Kono tai-ryō-buné!

Yatsutosé:
> > Yatébuné no okiai wakashu ga,
> > Ban-shuku soroété miya-mairi.
> > > Kono tai-ryō-buné!

Kokonotsutosé:
> > Kono ura mamoru kawa-guchi no
> > Myōjin riyaku wo arawasuru.
> > > Kono tai-ryō-buné!

Firstly (or "Number One"):
The first ship, filled up with fish, squeezes her way through the river-mouth, with a great shouting.[1]
> O this ship of great fishing! [2]

Secondly:
From the offing of Futaba even to the Togawa,[3] the ships, fast following, press in, with a great shouting.
> O this ship of great fishing!

Thirdly:
When, all together, we hoist our signal-flags, see how fast the cargo-boats come hurrying!
> O this ship of great fishing!

Fourthly:
Night and day though the boiling be, there is still too much to boil — oh, the heaps of iwashi from the three ships together!
> O this ship of great fishing!

---

[1] Ō-yagoë. The chorus-cry or chant of sailors, pulling all together, is called "yagoë."

[2] Tai-ryō buné, literally: "great-fishing," or "great-catching-ship." The adjective refers to the fishing, not to the ship. The real meaning of the refrain is, "this-most-successful-in-fishing of ships."

[3] Perhaps the reference is to a village at the mouth of the river To-gawa — not far from Chōshi on the Tonégawa. The two rivers are united by a canal. But the text leaves it uncertain whether river or village is meant.

Fifthly:
Whenever you go to look at the place where the dried fish are kept,[1] never do you find any room — not even a crevice.
O this ship of great fishing!

Sixthly:
From six to six o'clock is cleaning and washing: the great cutting and the small cutting are more than can be done.
O this ship of great fishing!

Seventhly:
All up and down the famous river Tonégawa we send our loads of oil and fertilizer.
O this ship of great fishing!

Eighthly:
All the young folk, drawing the Yatai-buné [2] with ten thousand rejoicings, visit the shrine of the God.
O this ship of great fishing!

Ninthly:
Augustly protecting all this coast, the Deity of the river-mouth shows to us his divine favor.
O this ship of great fishing!

A stranger example of this mnemonic arrangement is furnished by a children's song, composed at least a hundred years ago. Little girls of Yedo used to sing it while playing ball. You can see the same ball-game being played by girls to-day, in almost any quiet street of Tōkyō. The ball is kept bounding in a nearly perpendicular line by skillful taps of the hand delivered in time to the measure of a song; and

[1] Hoshika-ba: literally: "the hoshika-place" or "hoshika-room." "Hoshika" is the name given to dried fish prepared for use as fertilizer.
[2] Yatai is the name given to the ornamental cars drawn with ropes in a religious procession. Yatai-buné here seems to mean either the model of a boat mounted upon such a car, or a real boat so displayed in a religious procession. I have seen real boats mounted upon festival-cars in a religious procession at Mionoséki.

a good player should be able to sing the song through without missing a stroke. If she misses, she must yield the ball to another player.[1] There are many pretty "ball-play songs"; but this old-fashioned and long-forgotten one is a moral curiosity:

Hitotsu to ya:
    Hito wa kō na hito to iu;
    On wo shiranéba kō naraji.

Futatsu to ya:
    Fuji yori takaki chichi no on;
    Tsuné-ni omouté wasuré-naji.

Mitsu to ya:
    Mizu-umi kaetté asashi to wa,
    Haha no on zo ya omou-beshi.

Yotsu to ya:
    Yoshiya mazushiku kurasu tomo,
    Sugu-naru michi wo maguru-moji.

Itsutsu to ya:
    Itsumo kokoro no kawaranu wo,
    Makoto no hito to omou-beshi.

Mutsu to ya:
    Munashiku tsukihi wo kurashi-naba,
    Nochi no nagéki to shirinu-beshi.

Nanatsu to ya:
    Nasaki wa hito no tamé narodé,
    Waga mi no tamé to omou-beshi.

Yatsu to ya:
    Yaku-nan muryō no wazawai mo
    Kokoro zen nara nogaru-beshi.

---

[1] This is the more common form of the game; but there are many other forms. Sometimes two girls play at once with the same ball — striking it alternately as it bounds.

OLD JAPANESE SONGS

Kokonotsu to ya:
    Kokoro kotoba no sugu-naraba,
    Kami ya Hotoké mo mamoru-beshi.

Tō to ya:
    Tōtoi hito to naru naraba,
    Kōkō mono to iwaru-beshi.

This is the first:
    [Only] a person having filial piety is [worthy to be] called a
        person: [1]
    If one does not know the goodness of parents, one has not
        filial piety.

The second:
    Higher than the [mountain] Fuji is the favor of a father:
    Think of it always; — never forget it.

The third:
    [Compared with a mother's love] the great lake is shallow
        indeed!
    [By this saying] the goodness of a mother should be estimated.

The fourth:
    Even though in poverty we have to pass our days,
    Let us never turn aside from the one straight path.

The fifth:
    The person whose heart never changes with time,
    A true man or woman that person must be deemed.

The sixth:
    If the time [of the present] be spent in vain,
    In the time of the future must sorrow be borne.

---

[1] Literally: "A person having filial piety is called a person." The word "hito" (person), usually indicating either a man or a woman, is often used in the signification of "people" or "Mankind." The full meaning of the sentence is that no unfilial person deserves to be called a human being.

The seventh:
  That a kindness done is not for the sake of others only,
  But also for one's own sake, should well be kept in mind.

The eighth:
  Even the sorrow of numberless misfortunes
  We shall easily escape if the heart be pure.

The ninth:
  If the heart and the speech be kept straight and true,
  The Gods and the Buddhas will surely guard as well.

The tenth:
  In order to become a person held in honor,
  As a filial person one must [first] be known.

The reader may think to himself, "How terribly exigent the training that could require the repetition of moral lessons even in a 'ball-play song'!" True — but it produced perhaps the very sweetest type of woman that this world has ever known.

In some dance-songs the burthen is made by the mere repetition of the last line, or of part of the last line, of each stanza. The following queer ballad exemplifies the practice, and is furthermore remarkable by reason of the curious onomatopoetic choruses introduced at certain passages of the recitative:

KANÉ-MAKI-ODORI-UTA

(" *Bell-wrapping-dance song*." — *Province of Iga* — *Naga district*)

A Yamabushi of Kyōto went to Kumano. There resting in the inn Chōjaya, by the beach of Shirotaka, he saw a little girl three years old; and he petted and hugged her, playfully promising to make her his wife —

(*Chorus*) Playfully promising.

Thereafter that Yamabushi traveled in various provinces; returning only when that girl was thirteen years old. "O my princess, my princess!" he cried to her — "my little princess, pledged to me by promise!" — "O Sir Yamabushi," made she answer — "good Sir Yamabushi, take me with you now! —
"Take me with you now!"

"O soon," he said, "I shall come again; soon I shall come again: then, when I come again, I shall take you with me —
"Take you with me."

Therewith the Yamabushi, escaping from her, quickly, quickly fled away; — with all haste he fled away. Having passed through Tanabé and passed through Minabé, he fled on over the Komatsu moor —
Over the Komatsu moor.

KAKKARA, KAKKARA, KAKKARA, KAKKA! [1]

Therewith the damsel, pursuing, quickly, quickly followed after him; — with all speed she followed after him. Having passed through Tanabé and passed through Minabé, she pursued him over the Komatsu moor —
Over the Komatsu moor.

Then the Yamabushi, fleeing, came as he fled to the river of Amoda, and cried to the boatman of the river of Amoda — "O good boatman, good sir boatman, behind me comes a maid pursuing! — pray do not take her across, good boatman —
"Good sir boatman!"

DEBOKU, DEBOKU, DEBOKU, DENDEN! [2]

Then the damsel, pursuing, came to the river of Amoda and called to the boatman, "Bring hither the boat! — take

---

[1] These syllables, forming a sort of special chorus, are simply onomatopes; intended to represent the sound of sandaled feet running at utmost speed.

[2] These onomatopes, chanted by all the dancers together in chorus, with appropriate gesture, represent the sound of the ferryman's single oar, or scull, working upon its wooden peg. The syllables have no meaning in themselves.

me over in the boat!" — "No, I will not bring the boat; I will not take you over: my boat is forbidden to carry women! —
"Forbidden to carry women!"

"If you do not take me over, I will cross! — if you do not take me over, I will cross! — there is a way to cross the river of Amoda!" Taking off her sandals and holding them aloft, she entered the water, and at once turned into a dragon with twelve horns fully grown —
With twelve horns fully grown.

Then the Yamabushi, fleeing, reached the temple Dōjōji, and cried to the priests of the temple Dōjōji: "O good priests, behind me a damsel comes pursuing! — hide me, I beseech you, good sir priests! —
"Good sir priests!"

Then the priests, after holding consultation, took down from its place the big bell of the temple; and under it they hid him —
Under it they hid him.

Then the dragon-maid, pursuing, followed him to the temple Dōjōji. For a moment she stood in the gate of the temple: she saw that bell, and viewed it with suspicion. She thought: "I must wrap myself about it once." She thought: "I must wrap myself about it twice!" At the third wrapping, the bell was melted, and began to flow like boiling water —
Like boiling water.

So is told the story of the Wrapping of the Bell. Many damsels dwell by the seashore of Japan; — but who among them, like the daughter of the Chōja, will become a dragon? —
Become a dragon?

This is all the Song of the Wrapping of the Bell! — this is all the Song —
All the song! [1]

---

[1] This legend forms the subject of several Japanese dramas, both ancient and modern. The original story is that a Buddhist priest, called Anchin, having rashly excited the affection of a maiden named Kiyo-

OLD JAPANESE SONGS

I shall give only one specimen of the true street-ballad — the kind of ballad commonly sung by wandering samisen-players. It is written in an irregular measure, varying from twelve to sixteen syllables in length; the greater number of lines having thirteen syllables. I do not know the date of its composition; but I am told by aged persons who remember hearing it sung when they were children, that it was popular in the period of Tenpō (1830-43). It is not divided into stanzas; but there are pauses at irregular intervals — marked by the refrain, Yanrei!

O-Kichi-Seiza Kudoki
("*The Ditty of O-Kichi and Seiza*")

Now hear the pitiful story of two that died for love. In Kyōto was the thread-shop of Yoëmon, a merchant known far and near — a man of much wealth. His business prospered; his

---

himé, and being, by reason of his vows, unable to wed her, sought safety from her advances in flight. Kiyohimé, by the violence of her frustrated passion, therewith became transformed into a fiery dragon; and in that shape she pursued the priest to the temple called Dōjōji, in Kumano (modern Kishū), where he tried to hide himself under the great temple-bell. But the dragon coiled herself round the bell, which at once became red-hot, so that the body of the priest was totally consumed.

In this rude ballad Kiyohimé figures only as the daughter of an inn-keeper — the Chōja, or rich man of his village; while the priest Anchin is changed into a Yamabushi. The Yamabushi are, or at least were, wandering priests of the strange sect called Shugendo — itinerant exorcists and diviners, professing both Shinto and Buddhism. Of late years their practices have been prohibited by law; and a real Yamabushi is now seldom to be met with.

The temple Dōjōji is still a famous place of pilgrimage. It is situated not far from Gobō, on the western coast of Kishū. The incident of Anchin and the dragon is said to have occurred in the early part of the tenth century.

life was fortunate. One daughter he had, an only child, by name O-Kichi: at sixteen years she was lovely as a flower. Also he had a clerk in his house, by name Seiza, just in the prime of youth, aged twenty-and-two.

Yanrei!

Now the young man Seiza was handsome; and O-Kichi fell in love with him at sight. And the two were so often together that their secret affection became known; and the matter came to the ears of the parents of O-Kichi; and the parents, hearing of it, felt that such a thing could not be suffered to continue.

Yanrei!

So at last, the mother, having called O-Kichi into a private room, thus spoke to her: "O my daughter, I hear that you have formed a secret relation with the young man Seiza, of our shop. Are you willing to end that relation at once, and not to think any more about that man, O-Kichi? — answer me, O my daughter."

Yanrei!

"O my dear mother," answered O-Kichi, "what is this that you ask me to do? The closeness of the relation between Seiza and me is the closeness of the relation of the ink to the paper that it penetrates. [1] Therefore, whatever may happen, O mother of mine, to separate from Seiza is more than I can bear."

Yanrei!

Then, the father, having called Seiza to the innermost private room, thus spoke to him: "I called you here only to tell you this: You have turned the mind of our daughter away from what is right; and even to hear of such a matter is not to be borne. Pack up your things at once, and go! — to-day is the utmost limit of the time that you remain in this house."

Yanrei!

Now Seiza was a native of Ōsaka. Without saying more than "Yes — yes," he obeyed and went away, returning to his home.

---

[1] Literally: "that affinity as-for, ink-and-paper-soaked-like affinity."

OLD JAPANESE SONGS

There he remained four or five days, thinking only of O-Kichi. And because of his longing for her, he fell sick; and as there was no cure and no hope for him, he died.

Yanrei!

Then one night O-Kichi, in a moment of sleep, saw the face of Seiza close to her pillow — so plainly that she could not tell whether it was real, or only a dream. And rising up, she looked about; but the form of Seiza had vanished.

Yanrei!

Because of this she made up her mind to go at once to the house of Seiza. And, without being seen by any one, she fled from the home of her parents.

Yanrei!

When she came to the ferry at the next village, she did not take the boat, but went round by another road; and making all haste she found her way to the city of Ōsaka. There she asked for the house of Seiza; and she learned that it was in a certain street, the third house from a certain bridge.

Yanrei!

Arriving at last before the home of Seiza, she took off her traveling hat of straw; and seating herself on the threshold of the entrance, she cried out: "Pardon me kindly! — is not this the house of Master Seiza?"

Yanrei!

Then — O the pity of it! — she saw the mother of Seiza, weeping bitterly, and holding in her hand a Buddhist rosary. "O my good young lady," the mother of Seiza asked, "whence have you come; and whom do you want to see?"

Yanrei!

And O-Kichi said: "I am the daughter of the thread-merchant of Kyōto. And I have come all the way here only because of the relation that has long existed between Master Seiza and myself. Therefore, I pray you, kindly permit me to see him."

Yanrei!

133

"Alas!" made answer the mother, weeping, "Seiza, whom you have come so far to see, is dead. To-day is the seventh day from the day on which he died." . . . Hearing these words, O-Kichi herself could only shed tears.

Yanrei!

But after a little while she took her way to the cemetery. And there she found the sotoba [1] erected above the grave of Seiza; and leaning upon it, she wept aloud.

Yanrei!

Then — how fearful a thing is the longing of a person [2] — the grave of Seiza split asunder; and the form of Seiza rose up therefrom and spoke.

Yanrei!

"Ah! is not this O-Kichi that has come? Kind indeed it was to have come to me from so far away! My O-Kichi, do not weep thus. Never again — even though you weep — can we be united in this world. But as you love me truly, I pray you to set some fragrant flowers before my tomb, and to have a Buddhist service said for me upon the anniversary of my death."

Yanrei!

And with these words the form of Seiza vanished. "O wait,

---

[1] A wooden lath, bearing Buddhist texts, planted above graves. For a full account of the sotoba see my *Exotics and Retrospectives*: "The Literature of the Dead." (Vol. ix of this edition.)

[2] In the original: "Hito no omoi wa osoroshi mono yo!" ("How fearful a thing is the thinking of a person!") The word "omoi," used here in the sense of "longing," refers to the weird power of Seiza's dying wish to see his sweetheart. Even after his burial, this longing has the strength to burst open the tomb.

In the old English ballad of "William and Marjorie" (see Child: vol. II, p. 151) there is also a remarkable fancy about the opening and closing of a grave:

> She followed him high, she followed him low,
> Till she came to yon churchyard green;
> *And there the deep grave opened up,*
> And young William he lay down.

wait for me!" cried O-Kichi — "wait one little moment! [1] I cannot let you return alone! — I shall go with you in a little time!"

Yanrei!

Then quickly she went beyond the temple-gate to a moat some four or five chō [2] distant; and having filled her sleeves with small stones, into the deep water she cast her forlorn body.

Yanrei!

And now I shall terminate this brief excursion into unfamiliar song-fields by the citation of two Buddhist pieces. The first is from the famous work "Gempei Seisuiki" ("Account of the Prosperity and Decline of the Houses of Gen and Hei"), probably composed during the latter part of the twelfth, or at the beginning of the thirteenth century. It is written in the measure called "Imayō" — that is to say, in short lines alternately of seven and of five syllables (7, 5; 7, 5; 7, 5, *ad libitum*). The other philosophical composition is from a collection of songs called "Ryūtachi-bushi" ("Ryūtachi Airs"), belonging to the sixteenth century:

I

(*Measure, Imayō*)

Sama mo kokoro mo
Kawaru kana!

---

[1] With this episode compare the close of the English ballad "Sweet William's Ghost" (Child: vol. II, p. 148):
    "O stay, my only true love, stay!"
      The constant Margaret cried:
    Wan grew her cheeks; she closed her een,
      Stretched her soft limbs, and died.

[2] A chō is about one-fifteenth of a mile.

JAPANESE STUDIES

Otsuru namida wa
Taki no mizu:
Myō-hō-rengé no
Iké to nari;
Guzé no funé ni
Sao sashité;
Shizumu waga mi wo
Nosé-tamaë!

Both form and mind —
Lo! how these change!
The falling of tears
Is like the water of a cataract.
Let them become the Pool
Of the Lotus of the Good Law!
Poling thereupon
The Boat of Salvation,
Vouchsafe that my sinking
Body may ride!

II

(*Period of Bunrokū* — 1592–96)

Who twice shall live his youth?
What flower faded blooms again?
Fugitive as dew
Is the form regretted,
Seen only
In a moment of dream.

FANTASIES

. . . Vainly does each, as he glides,
Fable and dream
Of the lands which the River of Time
Has left ere he woke on its breast,
Or shall reach when his eyes have been closed.

MATTHEW ARNOLD

NOCTILUCÆ

THE moon had not yet risen; but the vast of the
night was all seething with stars, and bridged by a
Milky Way of extraordinary brightness. There was
no wind; but the sea, far as sight could reach, was
running in ripples of fire — a vision of infernal
beauty. Only the ripplings were radiant (between
them was blackness absolute); — and the luminosity was amazing. Most of the undulations were
yellow like candle-flame; but there were crimson
lampings also — and azure, and orange, and emerald. And the sinuous flickering of all seemed, not
a pulsing of many waters, but a laboring of many
wills — a fleeting conscious and monstrous — a
writhing and a swarming incalculable, as of dragon-
life in some depth of Erebus.

And life indeed was making the sinister splendor
of that spectacle — but life infinitesimal, and of
ghostliest delicacy — life illimitable, yet ephemeral,
flaming and fading in ceaseless alternation over the
whole round of waters even to the sky-line, above
which, in the vaster abyss, other countless lights
were throbbing with other spectral colors.

Watching, I wondered and I dreamed. I thought
of the Ultimate Ghost revealed in that scintillation
tremendous of Night and Sea; — quickening above

me, in systems aglow with awful fusion of the past
dissolved, with vapor of the life again to be; —
quickening also beneath me, in meteor-gushings and
constellations and nebulosities of colder fire — till
I found myself doubting whether the million ages of
the sun-star could really signify, in the flux of perpetual dissolution, anything more than the momentary sparkle of one expiring noctiluca.

Even with the doubt, the vision changed. I saw
no longer the sea of the ancient East, with its shud-
derings of fire, but that Flood whose width and
depth and altitude are one with the Night of Eter-
nity — the shoreless and timeless Sea of Death and
Birth. And the luminous haze of a hundred millions
of suns — the Arch of the Milky Way — was a
single smouldering surge in the flow of the Infinite
Tides.

Yet again there came a change. I saw no more
that vapory surge of suns; but the living darkness
streamed and thrilled about me with infinite spar-
kling; and every sparkle was beating like a heart —
beating out colors like the tints of the sea-fires.
And the lampings of all continually flowed away,
as shivering threads of radiance, into illimitable
Mystery. . . .

Then I knew myself also a phosphor-point — one
fugitive floating sparkle of the measureless current;
— and I saw that the light which was mine shifted
tint with each changing of thought. Ruby it some-

times shone, and sometimes sapphire: now it was flame of topaz; again, it was fire of emerald. And the meaning of the changes I could not fully know. But thoughts of the earthly life seemed to make the light burn red; while thoughts of supernal being — of ghostly beauty and of ghostly bliss — seemed to kindle ineffable rhythms of azure and of violet.

But of white lights there were none in all the Visible. And I marveled.

Then a Voice said to me:

"The White are of the Altitudes. By the blending of the billions they are made. Thy part is to help to their kindling. Even as the color of thy burning, so is the worth of thee. For a moment only is thy quickening; yet the light of thy pulsing lives on: by thy thought, in that shining moment, thou becomest a Maker of Gods."

A MYSTERY OF CROWDS

Who has not at some time leaned over the parapet of a bridge to watch the wrinklings and dimplings of the current below — to wonder at the trembling permanency of surface-shapes that never change, though the substance of them is never for two successive moments the same? The mystery of the spectacle fascinates; and it is worth thinking about. Symbols of the riddle of our own being are those shuddering forms. In ourselves likewise the substance perpetually changes with the flow of the Infinite Stream; but the shapes, though ever agitated by various inter-opposing forces, remain throughout the years.

And who has not been fascinated also by the sight of the human stream that pours and pulses through the streets of some great metropolis? This, too, has its currents and counter-currents and eddyings — all strengthening or weakening according to the tide-rise or tide-ebb of the city's sea of toil. But the attraction of the greater spectacle for us is not really the mystery of motion: it is rather the mystery of man. As outside observers we are interested chiefly by the passing forms and faces — by their intimations of personality, their suggestions of sympathy or repulsion. We soon cease to think about the general flow. For the atoms of the human current are visible to our gaze: we see them walk, and deem their movements sufficiently explained by our own experience of walking. And, nevertheless, the motions of the visible individual are more mysterious than those of the always invisible molecule of water. I am not forgetting the truth that all forms of motion are ultimately incomprehensible: I am referring only to the fact that our common relative knowledge of motions, which are supposed to depend upon will, is even less than our possible relative knowledge of the behavior of the atoms of a water-current.

Every one who has lived in a great city is aware of certain laws of movement which regulate the flow of population through the more crowded thoroughfares. (We need not for present purposes concern ourselves about the complex middle-currents of the living river, with their thunder of hoofs and wheels: I shall speak of the side-currents only.) On either footpath the crowd naturally divides itself into an upward and a downward stream. All persons going in one direction take the right-hand side; all going in the other direction take the left-hand side. By moving with either one of these two streams you can proceed even quickly; but you cannot walk against it: only a drunken or insane person is likely to attempt such a thing. Between the two currents there is going on, by reason of the pressure, a continual self-displacement of individuals to left and right, alternately — such a yielding and swerving as might be represented, in a drawing of the double-current, by zigzag medial lines ascending and descending. This constant yielding alone makes progress possible: without it the contrary streams would quickly bring each other to a standstill by lateral pressure. But it is especially where two crowd-streams intersect each other, as at street-angles, that this systematic self-displacement is worthy of study. Everybody observes the phenomenon; but few persons think about it. Whoever really thinks about it will discover that there is a mystery in it — a mystery which no individual experience can fully explain.

In any thronged street of a great metropolis thousands of people are constantly turning aside to left or right in order to pass each other. Whenever two persons walking in contrary directions come face to face in such a press, one of three things is likely to happen: — Either there is a mutual yielding — or one makes room for the other — or else both, in their endeavor to be accommodating, step at once in the same direction, and as quickly repeat the blunder by trying to correct it, and so keep dancing to and fro in each other's way — until the first to perceive the absurdity of the situation stands still, or until the more irritable actually pushes his vis-à-vis to one side. But these blunders are relatively infrequent: all necessary yielding, as a rule, is done quickly and correctly.

A MYSTERY OF CROWDS

Of course there must be some general law regulating all this self-displacement — some law in accord with the universal law of motion in the direction of least resistance. You have only to watch any crowded street for half an hour to be convinced of this. But the law is not easily found or formulated: there are puzzles in the phenomenon.

If you study the crowd-movement closely, you will perceive that those encounters in which one person yields to make way for the other are much less common than those in which both parties give way. But a little reflection will convince you that, even in cases of mutual yielding, one person must of necessity yield sooner than the other — though the difference in time of the impulse-manifestation should be — as it often is — altogether inappreciable. For the sum of character, physical and pyschical, cannot be precisely the same in two human beings. No two persons can have exactly equal faculties of perception and will, nor exactly similar qualities of that experience which expresses itself in mental and physical activities. And therefore in every case of apparent mutual yielding, the yielding must really be successive, not simultaneous. Now although what we might here call the "personal equation" proves that in every case of mutual yielding one individual necessarily yields sooner than the other, it does not at all explain the mystery of the individual impulse in cases where the yielding is not mutual; — it does not explain why you feel at one time that you are about to make your vis-à-vis give place, and feel at another time that you must yourself give place. What origi-- nates the feeling?

A friend once attempted to answer this question by the ingenious theory of a sort of eye-duel between every two persons coming face to face in a street-throng; but I feel sure that his theory could account for the psychological facts in scarcely half-a-dozen of a thousand such encounters. The greater number of people hurrying by each other in a dense press rarely observe faces: only the disinterested idler has time for that. Hundreds actually pass along the street with their eyes fixed upon the pavement. Certainly it is not the man in a hurry who can guide himself by ocular snap-shot views of physiognomy; — he is usually absorbed in his own thoughts. . . . I have studied my own case repeatedly. While in a crowd I seldom look at faces; but without any con-scious observation I am always able to tell when I should give way, or when my vis-à-vis is going to save me that trouble. My knowledge is certainly intuitive — a mere knowledge of feeling; and I know not with what to compare it except that blind faculty by which, in absolute darkness, one becomes aware of the proximity of bulky objects without touching them. And my intuition is almost infallible. If I hesitate to obey it, a collision is the invariable con-sequence.

Furthermore, I find that whenever automatic,

or at least semi-conscious, action is replaced by reasoned action — in plainer words, whenever I begin to think about my movements — I always blunder. It is only while I am thinking of other matters — only while I am acting almost automatically — that I can thread a dense crowd with ease. Indeed, my personal experience has convinced me that what pilots one quickly and safely through a thick press is not conscious observation at all, but unreasoning, intuitive perception. Now intuitive action of any kind represents inherited knowledge, the experience of past lives — in this case the experience of past lives incalculable.

Utterly incalculable. . . . Why do I think so? Well, simply because this faculty of intuitive self-direction in a crowd is shared by man with very inferior forms of animal being — evolutional proof that it must be a faculty immensely older than man. Does not a herd of cattle, a herd of deer, a flock of sheep, offer us the same phenomenon of mutual yielding? Or a flock of birds — gregarious birds especially: crows, sparrows, wild pigeons? Or a shoal of fish? Even among insects — bees, ants, termites — we can study the same law of intuitive self-displacement. The yielding, in all these cases, must still represent an inherited experience unimaginably old. Could we endeavor to retrace the whole course of such inheritance, the attempt would probably lead us back, not only to the very beginnings of sentient life upon this planet, but farther — back into the history of

non-sentient substance — back even to the primal
evolution of those mysterious tendencies which are
stored up in the atoms of elements. Such atoms
we know of only as points of multiple resistance
— incomprehensible knittings of incomprehensible
forces. Even the tendencies of atoms doubtless represent accumulations of inheritance — But here
thought checks with a shock at the eternal barrier
of the Infinite Riddle.

GOTHIC HORROR

I

LONG before I had arrived at what catechisms call the age of reason, I was frequently taken, much against my will, to church. The church was very old; and I can see the interior of it at this moment just as plainly as I saw it forty years ago, when it appeared to me like an evil dream. There I first learned to know the peculiar horror that certain forms of Gothic architecture can inspire. . . . I am using the word "horror" in a classic sense — in its antique meaning of ghostly fear.

On the very first day of this experience, my child-fancy could place the source of the horror. The wizened and pointed shapes of the windows immediately terrified me. In their outline I found the form of apparitions that tormented me in sleep; — and at once I began to imagine some dreadful affinity between goblins and Gothic churches. Presently, in the tall doorways, in the archings of the aisles, in the ribbings and groinings of the roof, I discovered other and wilder suggestions of fear. Even the façade of the organ — peaking high into the shadow above its gallery — seemed to me a frightful thing. . . . Had I been then suddenly obliged to answer the question, "What are you afraid of?" I should have whispered, "*Those points!*" I could not have otherwise explained

the matter: I only knew that I was afraid of the
"points."

Of course the real enigma of what I felt in that
church could not present itself to my mind while I
continued to believe in goblins. But long after the
age of superstitious terrors, other Gothic experiences
severally revived the childish emotion in so startling
a way as to convince me that childish fancy could
not account for the feeling. Then my curiosity was
aroused; and I tried to discover some rational cause
for the horror. I read many books, and asked many
questions; but the mystery seemed only to deepen.

Books about architecture were very disappointing. I was much less impressed by what I could
find in them than by references in pure fiction to
the awfulness of Gothic art — particularly by one
writer's confession that the interior of a Gothic
church, seen at night, gave him the idea of being inside the skeleton of some monstrous animal; and by a
far-famed comparison of the windows of a cathedral
to eyes, and of its door to a great mouth, "devouring
the people." These imaginations explained little;
they could not be developed beyond the phase of
vague intimation: yet they stirred such emotional re-
sponse that I felt sure they had touched some truth.
Certainly the architecture of a Gothic cathedral
offers strange resemblances to the architecture of
bone; and the general impression that it makes upon
the mind is an impression of life. But this impression or sense of life I found to be indefinable — not

a sense of any life organic, but of a life latent and dæmonic. And the manifestation of that life I felt to be in the *pointing* of the structure.

Attempts to interpret the emotion by effects of altitude and gloom and vastness appeared to me of no worth; for buildings loftier and larger and darker than any Gothic cathedral, but of a different order of architecture — Egyptian, for instance — could not produce a like impression. I felt certain that the horror was made by something altogether peculiar to Gothic construction, and that this something haunted the tops of the arches.

"Yes, Gothic architecture is awful," said a religious friend, "because it is the visible expression of Christian faith. No other religious architecture symbolizes spiritual longing; but the Gothic embodies it. Every part climbs or leaps; every supreme detail soars and points like fire. . . ." "There may be considerable truth in what you say," I replied; — "but it does not relate to the riddle that baffles me. Why should shapes that symbolize spiritual longing create horror? Why should any expression of Christian ecstasy inspire alarm? . . ." .

Other hypotheses in multitude I tested without avail; and I returned to the simple and savage conviction that the secret of the horror somehow belonged to the points of the archings. But for years I could not find it. At last, at last, in the early hours of a certain tropical morning, it revealed itself quite unexpectedly, while I was looking at a glorious group of palms.

Then I wondered at my stupidity in not having guessed the riddle before.

II

THE characteristics of many kinds of palm have been made familiar by pictures and photographs. But the giant palms of the American tropics cannot be adequately represented by the modern methods of pictorial illustration: they must be seen. You cannot draw or photograph a palm two hundred feet high.

The first sight of a group of such forms, in their natural environment of tropical forest, is a magnificent surprise — a surprise that strikes you dumb. Nothing seen in temperate zones — not even the huger growths of the Californian slope — could have prepared your imagination for the weird solemnity of that mighty colonnade. Each stone-gray trunk is a perfect pillar — but a pillar of which the stupendous grace has no counterpart in the works of man. You must strain your head well back to follow the soaring of the prodigious column, up, up, up through abysses of green twilight, till at last — far beyond a break in that infinite interweaving of limbs and lianas which is the roof of the forest — you catch one dizzy glimpse of the capital: a parasol of emerald feathers outspread in a sky so blinding as to suggest the notion of azure electricity.

GOTHIC HORROR

Now what is the emotion that such a vision excites — an emotion too powerful to be called wonder, too weird to be called delight? Only when the first shock of it has passed — when the several elements that were combined in it have begun to set in motion widely different groups of ideas — can you comprehend how very complex it must have been. Many impressions belonging to personal experience were doubtless revived in it, but also with them a multitude of sensations more shadowy — accumulations of organic memory; possibly even vague feelings older than man — for the tropical shapes that aroused the emotion have a history more ancient than our race.

One of the first elements of the emotion to become clearly distinguishable is the æsthetic; and this, in its general mass, might be termed the sense of terrible beauty. Certainly the spectacle of that unfamiliar life — silent, tremendous, springing to the sun in colossal aspiration, striving for light against Titans, and heedless of man in the gloom beneath as of a groping beetle — thrills like the rhythm of some single marvelous verse that is learned in a glance and remembered forever. Yet the delight, even at its vividest, is shadowed by a queer disquiet. The aspect of that monstrous, pale, naked, smooth-stretching column suggests a life as conscious as the serpent's. You stare at the towering lines of the shape — vaguely fearing to discern some sign of stealthy movement, some beginning of undulation. Then sight and reason combine to correct the sus-

picion. Yes, motion is there, and life enormous —
but a life seeking only sun — life, rushing like the
jet of a geyser, straight to the giant day.

III

DURING my own experience I could perceive that
certain feelings commingled in the wave of delight —
feelings related to ideas of power and splendor and
triumph — were accompanied by a faint sense of
religious awe. Perhaps our modern æsthetic senti-
ments are so interwoven with various inherited
elements of religious emotionalism that the recognition of beauty cannot arise independently of rever-
ential feeling. Be this as it may, such a feeling de-
fined itself while I gazed; — and at once the great
gray trunks were changed to the pillars of a mighty
aisle; and from altitudes of dream there suddenly
descended upon me the old dark thrill of Gothic
horror.

Even before it died away, I recognized that it
must have been due to some old cathedral-memory
revived by the vision of those giant trunks uprising
into gloom. But neither the height nor the gloom
could account for anything beyond the memory.
Columns tall as those palms, but supporting a classic
entablature, could evoke no sense of disquiet resembling the Gothic horror. I felt sure of this — because
I was able, without any difficulty, to shape immediately the imagination of such a façade. But presently the mental picture distorted. I saw the archi-

trave elbow upward in each of the spaces between the pillars, and curve and point itself into a range of prodigious arches; — and again the sombre thrill descended upon me. Simultaneously there flashed to me the solution of the mystery. I understood that the Gothic horror was *a horror of monstrous motion* — and that it had seemed to belong to the points of the arches because the idea of such motion was chiefly suggested by the extraordinary angle at which the curves of the arching touched.

To any experienced eye, the curves of Gothic arching offer a striking resemblance to certain curves of vegetal growth; — the curves of the palm-branch being, perhaps, especially suggested. But observe that the architectural form suggests more than any vegetal comparison could illustrate! The meeting of two palm-crests would indeed form a kind of Gothic arch; yet the effect of so short an arch would be insignificant. For nature to repeat the strange impression of the real Gothic arch, it were necessary that the branches of the touching crests should vastly exceed, both in length of curve and strength of spring, anything of their kind existing in the vegetable world. The effect of the Gothic arch depends altogether upon the intimation of energy. An arch formed by the intersection of two short sprouting lines could suggest only a feeble power of growth; but the lines of the tall mediæval arch seem to express a crescent force immensely surpassing that of nature. And the horror of Gothic architecture is not in the mere suggestion of a growing life, but in the suggestion of an energy supernatural and tremendous.

Of course the child, oppressed by the strangeness of Gothic forms, is yet incapable of analyzing the impression received: he is frightened without comprehending. He cannot divine that the points and the curves are terrible to him because they represent the prodigious exaggeration of a real law of vegetal growth. He dreads the shapes because they seem alive; yet he does not know how to express this dread. Without suspecting why, he feels that this silent manifestation of power, everywhere pointing and piercing upward, is not natural. To his startled imagination, the building stretches itself like a phantasm of sleep — makes itself tall and taller with intent to frighten. Even though built by hands of men, it has ceased to be a mass of dead stone: it is infused with Something that thinks and threatens; — it has become a shadowing malevolence, a multiple goblinry, a monstrous fetish!

LEVITATION

Out of some upper-story window I was looking into a street of yellow-tinted houses — a colonial street, old-fashioned, narrow, with palm-heads showing above its roofs of tile. There were no shadows; there was no sun — only a gray soft light, as of early gloaming.

Suddenly I found myself falling from the window; and my heart gave one sickening leap of terror. But the distance from window to pavement proved to be much greater than I supposed — so great that, in spite of my fear, I began to wonder. Still I kept falling, falling — and still the dreaded shock did not come. Then the fear ceased, and a queer pleasure took its place; — for I discovered that I was not falling quickly, but only *floating* down. Moreover, I was floating feet foremost — must have turned in descending. At last I touched the stones — but very, very lightly, with only one foot; and instantly at that touch I went up again — rose to the level of the eaves. People stopped to stare at me. I felt the exultation of power superhuman; — I felt for the moment as a god.

Then softly I began to sink; and the sight of faces, gathering below me, prompted a sudden resolve to fly down the street, over the heads of the gazers. Again like a bubble I rose, and, with the same im-

157

pulse, I sailed in one grand curve to a distance that astounded me. I felt no wind; — I felt nothing but the joy of motion triumphant. Once more touching pavement, I soared at a bound for a thousand yards. Then, reaching the end of the street, I wheeled and came back by great swoops — by long slow aerial leaps of surprising altitude. In the street there was dead silence: many people were looking; but nobody spoke. I wondered what they thought of my feat, and what they would say if they knew how easily the thing was done. By the merest chance I had found out how to do it; and the only reason why it seemed a feat was that no one else had ever attempted it. Instinctively I felt that to say anything about the accident, which had led to the discovery, would be imprudent. Then the real meaning of the strange hush in the street began to dawn upon me. I said to myself:

"This silence is the Silence of Dreams; — I am quite well aware that this is a dream. I remember having dreamed the same dream before. But the discovery of this power is not a dream: *it is a revelation!* . . . Now that I have learned how to fly, I can no more forget it than a swimmer can forget how to swim. To-morrow morning I shall astonish the people, by sailing over the roofs of the town."

Morning came; and I woke with the fixed resolve to fly out of the window. But no sooner had I risen from bed than the knowledge of physical relations returned, like a sensation forgotten, and compelled

me to recognize the unwelcome truth that I had not
made any discovery at all.

This was neither the first nor the last of such
dreams; but it was particularly vivid, and I therefore selected it for narration as a good example of
its class. I still fly occasionally — sometimes over
fields and streams — sometimes through familiar
streets; and the dream is invariably accompanied by
remembrance of like dreams in the past, as well as by
the conviction that I have really found out a secret,
really acquired a new faculty. "This time, at all
events," I say to myself, "it is impossible that I can
be mistaken; — I *know* that I shall be able to fly
after I awake. Many times before, in other dreams,
I learned the secret only to forget it on awakening;
but this time I am absolutely sure that I shall not
forget." And the conviction actually stays with me
until I rise from bed, when the physical effort at once
reminds me of the formidable reality of gravitation.

The oddest part of this experience is the feeling of
buoyancy. It is much like the feeling of floating —
of rising or sinking through tepid water, for example;
— and there is no sense of real effort. It is a delight;
yet it usually leaves something to be desired. I am
a low flyer; I can proceed only like a pteromys or a
flying-fish — and far less quickly: moreover, I must
tread earth occasionally in order to obtain a fresh
impulsion. I seldom rise to a height of more than

twenty-five or thirty feet; — the greater part of the time I am merely skimming surfaces. Touching the ground only at intervals of several hundred yards is pleasant skimming; but I always feel, in a faint and watery way, the dead pull of the world beneath me.

Now the experience of most dream-flyers I find to be essentially like my own. I have met but one who claims superior powers: he says that he flies over mountains — goes sailing from peak to peak like a kite. All others whom I have questioned acknowledge that they fly low — in long parabolic curves — and this only by touching ground from time to time. Most of them also tell me that their flights usually begin with an imagined fall, or desperate leap; and no less than four say that the start is commonly taken from the top of a stairway.

For myriads of years humanity has thus been flying by night. How did the fancied motion, having so little in common with any experience of active life, become a universal experience of the life of sleep?

It may be that memory-impressions of certain kinds of aerial motion — exultant experiences of leaping or swinging, for example — are in dream-revival so magnified and prolonged as to create the illusion of flight. We know that in actual time the duration of most dreams is very brief. But in the half-life of sleep (nightmare offering some startling exceptions) there is scarcely more than a faint smouldering of consciousness by comparison with the quick flash and vivid thrill of active cerebration; — and time, to the dreaming brain, would seem to be magnified, somewhat as it must be relatively magnified to the feeble consciousness of an insect. Supposing that any memory of the sensation of falling, together with the memory of the concomitant fear, should be accidentally revived in sleep, the dream-prolongation of the sensation and the emotion — unchecked by the natural sequence of shock — might suffice to revive other and even pleasurable memories of airy motion. And these, again, might quicken other combinations of inter-related memories able to furnish all the incident and scenery of the long phantasmagoria.

But this hypothesis will not fully explain certain feelings and ideas of a character different from any experience of waking-hours — the exultation of voluntary motion without exertion — the pleasure of the utterly impossible — the ghostly delight of imponderability. Neither can it serve to explain other dream-experiences of levitation which do not begin with the sensation of leaping or falling, and are seldom of a pleasurable kind. For example, it sometimes happens during nightmare that the dreamer, deprived of all power to move or speak, actually feels his body lifted into the air and floated away by the force of the horror within him. Again, there are dreams in which the dreamer has no physical being. I have thus found myself without any body — a viewless and voiceless phantom, hovering upon a mountain-road in twilight time, and trying to frighten lonely folk by making small moaning noises. The sensation was of moving through the air by mere act of will: there was no touching of surfaces; and I seemed to glide always about a foot above the road.

Could the feeling of dream-flight be partly interpreted by organic memory of conditions of life more ancient than man — life weighty, and winged, and flying heavily, *a little above the ground?*

Or might we suppose that some all-permeating Over-Soul, dormant in other time, wakens within the brain at rare moments of our sleep-life? The limited human consciousness has been beautifully compared to the visible solar spectrum, above and below which whole zones of colors invisible await the evolution of superior senses; and mystics aver that something of the ultra-violet or infra-red rays of the vaster Mind may be momentarily glimpsed in dreams. Certainly the Cosmic Life in each of us has been all things in all forms of space and time. Perhaps you would like to believe that it may bestir, in slumber, some vague sense-memory of things more ancient than the sun — memory of vanished planets with fainter powers of gravitation, where the normal modes of voluntary motion would have been like the realization of our flying dreams? . . .

NIGHTMARE-TOUCH

I

WHAT *is* the fear of ghosts among those who believe in ghosts?

All fear is the result of experience — experience of the individual or of the race — experience either of the present life or of lives forgotten. Even the fear of the unknown can have no other origin. And the fear of ghosts must be a product of past pain.

Probably the fear of ghosts, as well as the belief in them, had its beginning in dreams. It is a peculiar fear. No other fear is so intense; yet none is so vague. Feelings thus voluminous and dim are super-individual mostly — feelings inherited — feelings made within us by the experience of the dead.

What experience?

Nowhere do I remember reading a plain statement of the reason why ghosts are feared. Ask any ten intelligent persons of your acquaintance, who remember having once been afraid of ghosts, to tell you exactly why they were afraid — to define the fancy behind the fear; — and I doubt whether even one will be able to answer the question. The literature of folk-lore — oral and written — throws no clear light upon the subject. We find, indeed, various legends of men torn asunder by phantoms; but such gross imaginings could not explain the peculiar quality of ghostly fear. It is not a fear of bodily violence. It is not even a reasoning fear — not a fear that can readily explain itself — which would not be the case if it were founded upon definite ideas of physical danger. Furthermore, although primitive ghosts may have been imagined as capable of tearing and devouring, the common idea of a ghost is certainly that of a being intangible and imponderable.[1]

Now I venture to state boldly that the common fear of ghosts is *the fear of being touched by ghosts* — or, in other words, that the imagined Supernatural is dreaded mainly because of its imagined power to touch. Only to *touch*, remember! — not to wound or to kill.

But this dread of the touch would itself be the result of experience — chiefly, I think, of prenatal experience stored up in the individual by inheritance, like the child's fear of darkness. And who can ever have had the sensation of being touched by ghosts? The answer is simple: Everybody who has been seized by phantoms in a dream.

Elements of primeval fears — fears older than humanity — doubtless enter into the child-terror of darkness. But the more definite fear of ghosts may very possibly be composed with inherited results of dream-pain — ancestral experience of nightmare.

---

[1] I may remark here that in many old Japanese legends and ballads, ghosts are represented as having power to *pull off* people's heads. But so far as the origin of the fear of ghosts is concerned, such stories explain nothing — since the experiences that evolved the fear must have been real, not imaginary, experiences.

And the intuitive terror of supernatural touch can thus be evolutionally explained.

Let me now try to illustrate my theory by relating some typical experiences.

II

WHEN about five years old I was condemned to sleep by myself in a certain isolated room, thereafter always called the Child's Room. (At that time I was scarcely ever mentioned by name, but only referred to as "the Child.") The room was narrow, but very high, and, in spite of one tall window, very gloomy. It contained a fire-place wherein no fire was ever kindled; and the Child suspected that the chimney was haunted.

A law was made that no light should be left in the Child's Room at night — simply because the Child was afraid of the dark. His fear of the dark was judged to be a mental disorder requiring severe treatment. But the treatment aggravated the disorder. Previously I had been accustomed to sleep in a well-lighted room, with a nurse to take care of me. I thought that I should die of fright when sentenced to lie alone in the dark, and — what seemed to me then abominably cruel — actually *locked* into my room, the most dismal room of the house. Night after night when I had been warmly tucked into bed, the lamp was removed; the key clicked in the lock; the protecting light and the foot-

steps of my guardian receded together. Then an
agony of fear would come upon me. Something in
the black air would seem to gather and grow (I
thought that I could even *hear* it grow) till I had to
scream. Screaming regularly brought punishment;
but it also brought back the light, which more than
consoled for the punishment. This fact being at
last found out, orders were given to pay no further
heed to the screams of the Child.

Why was I thus insanely afraid? Partly because the dark had always been peopled for me with
shapes of terror. So far back as memory extended,
I had suffered from ugly dreams; and when aroused
from them I could always *see* the forms dreamed of,
lurking in the shadows of the room. They would
soon fade out; but for several moments they would
appear like tangible realities. And they were always
the same figures. . . . Sometimes, without any pre-
face of dreams, I used to see them at twilight-time
— following me about from room to room, or reaching long dim hands after me, from story to story, up
through the interspaces of the deep stairways.

I had complained of these haunters only to be
told that I must never speak of them, and that they
did not exist. I had complained to everybody in the
house; and everybody in the house had told me the
very same thing. But there was the evidence of my
eyes! The denial of that evidence I could explain
only in two ways: Either the shapes were afraid

of big people, and showed themselves to me alone, because I was little and weak; or else the entire household had agreed, for some ghastly reason, to say what was not true. This latter theory seemed to me the more probable one, because I had several times perceived the shapes when I was not un-attended; — and the consequent appearance of secrecy frightened me scarcely less than the visions did. Why was I forbidden to talk about what I saw, and even heard — on creaking stairways — behind wavering curtains?

"Nothing will hurt you" — this was the merci-less answer to all my pleadings not to be left alone at night. But the haunters *did* hurt me. Only — they would wait until after I had fallen asleep, and so into their power — for they possessed occult means of preventing me from rising or moving or crying out.

Needless to comment upon the policy of locking me up alone with these fears in a black room. Un-utterably was I tormented in that room — for years! Therefore I felt relatively happy when sent away at last to a children's boarding-school, where the haunters very seldom ventured to show them-selves.

They were not like any people that I had ever known. They were shadowy dark-robed figures, capable of atrocious self-distortion — capable, for instance, of growing up to the ceiling, and then across it, and then lengthening themselves, head-down-wards, along the opposite wall. Only their faces were distinct; and I tried not to look at their faces. I tried also in my dreams — or thought that I tried — to awaken myself from the sight of them by pull-ing at my eyelids with my fingers; but the eyelids would remain closed, as if sealed. . . . Many years afterwards, the frightful plates in Orfila's "Traité des Exhumés," beheld for the first time, recalled to me with a sickening start the dream-terrors of childhood. But to understand the Child's experi-ence, you must imagine Orfila's drawings intensely alive, and continually elongating or distorting, as in some monstrous anamorphosis.

Nevertheless the mere sight of those nightmare-faces was not the worst of the experiences in the Child's Room. The dreams always began with a suspicion, or sensation of something heavy in the air — slowly quenching will — slowly numbing my power to move. At such times I usually found my-self alone in a large unlighted apartment; and, al-most simultaneously with the first sensation of fear, the atmosphere of the room would become suffused, halfway to the ceiling, with a sombre-yellowish glow, making objects dimly visible — though the ceiling itself remained pitch-black. This was not a true appearance of light: rather it seemed as if the black air were changing color from beneath. . . . Certain terrible aspects of sunset, on the eve of storm, offer like effects of sinister color. . . . Forth-

with I would try to escape (feeling at every step a
sensation *as of wading*), and would sometimes succeed in struggling half-way across the room; — but
there I would always find myself brought to a
standstill — paralyzed by some innominable op-
position. Happy voices I could hear in the next
room; — I could see light through the transom over
the door that I had vainly endeavored to reach; —
I knew that one loud cry would save me. But not
even by the most frantic effort could I raise my
voice above a whisper. . . . And all this signified
only that the Nameless was coming — was nearing
— was mounting the stairs. I could hear the step —
booming like the sound of a muffled drum — and I
wondered why nobody else heard it. A long, long
time the haunter would take to come — malevo-
lently pausing after each ghastly footfall. Then,
without a creak, the bolted door would open —
slowly, slowly — and the thing would enter, gibber-
ing soundlessly — and put out hands — and clutch
me — and toss me to the black ceiling — and catch
me descending to toss me up again, and again, and
again. . . . In those moments the feeling was not
fear: fear itself had been torpified by the first seizure.
It was a sensation that has no name in the language
of the living. For every touch brought a shock of
something infinitely worse than pain — something
that thrilled into the innermost secret being of me —
a sort of abominable electricity, discovering unimagined capacities of suffering in totally unfamiliar

regions of sentiency. . . . This was commonly the work of a single tormentor; but I can also remember having been caught by a group, and tossed from one to another — seemingly for a time of many minutes.

III

WHENCE the fancy of those shapes? I do not know. Possibly from some impression of fear in earliest infancy; possibly from some experience of fear in other lives than mine. That mystery is forever insoluble. But the mystery of the shock of the touch admits of a definite hypothesis.

First, allow me to observe that the experience of the sensation itself cannot be dismissed as "mere imagination." Imagination means cerebral activity: its pains and its pleasures are alike inseparable from nervous operation, and their physical importance is sufficiently proved by their physiological effects. Dream-fear may kill as well as other fear; and no emotion thus powerful can be reasonably deemed undeserving of study.

One remarkable fact in the problem to be considered is that the sensation of seizure in dreams differs totally from all sensations familiar to ordinary waking life. Why this differentiation? How interpret the extraordinary massiveness and depth of the thrill?

I have already suggested that the dreamer's fear is most probably not a reflection of relative experience, but represents the incalculable total of ancestral experience of dream-fear. If the sum of the experience of active life be transmitted by inheritance, so must likewise be transmitted the summed experience of the life of sleep. And in normal heredity either class of transmissions would probably remain distinct.

Now, granting this hypothesis, the sensation of dream-seizure would have had its beginnings in the earliest phases of dream-consciousness — long prior to the apparition of man. The first creatures capable of thought and fear must often have dreamed of being caught by their natural enemies. There could not have been much imagining of pain in these primal dreams. But higher nervous development in later forms of being would have been accompanied with larger susceptibility to dream-pain. Still later, with the growth of reasoning-power, ideas of the supernatural would have changed and intensified the character of dream-fear. Furthermore, through all the course of evolution, heredity would have been accumulating the experience of such feeling. Under those forms of imaginative pain evolved through reaction of religious beliefs, there would persist some dim survival of savage primitive fears, and again, under this, a dimmer but incomparably deeper substratum of ancient animal-terrors. In the dreams of the modern child all these latencies might quicken — one below another — unfathomably — with the coming and the growing of nightmare.

FANTASIES

It may be doubted whether the phantasms of any particular nightmare have a history older than the brain in which they move. But the shock of the touch would seem to indicate *some point of dream-contact with the total race-experience of shadowy seizure*. It may be that profundities of Self — abysses never reached by any ray from the life of sun — are strangely stirred in slumber, and that out of their blackness immediately responds a shuddering of memory, measureless even by millions of years.

READINGS FROM A DREAM-BOOK

OFTEN, in the blind dead of the night, I find myself reading a book — a big broad book — a dream-book. By "dream-book," I do not mean a book about dreams, but a book made of the stuff that dreams are made of.

I do not know the name of the book, nor the name of its author: I have not been able to see the title-page; and there is no running title. As for the back of the volume, it remains — like the back of the Moon — invisible forever.

At no time have I touched the book in any way — not even to turn a leaf. Somebody, always viewless, holds it up and open before me in the dark; and I can read it only because it is lighted by a light that comes from nowhere. Above and beneath and on either side of the book there is darkness absolute; but the pages seem to retain the yellow glow of lamps that once illuminated them.

A queer fact is that I never see the entire text of a page at once, though I see the whole page itself plainly. The text rises, or seems to rise, to the surface of the paper as I gaze, and fades out almost immediately after having been read. By a simple effort of will, I can recall the vanished sentences to the page; but they do not come back in the same form as before: they seem to have been oddly

173

revised during the interval. Never can I coax even one fugitive line to reproduce itself exactly as it read at first. But I can always force something to return; and this something remains sharply distinct during perusal. Then it turns faint gray, and appears to sink — as through thick milk — backward out of sight.

By regularly taking care to write down, immediately upon awakening, whatever I could remember reading in the dream-book, I found myself able last year to reproduce portions of the text. But the order in which I now present these fragments is not at all the order in which I recovered them. If they seem to have any inter-connection, this is only because I tried to arrange them in what I imagined to be the rational sequence. Of their original place and relation, I know scarcely anything. And, even regarding the character of the book itself, I have been able to discover only that a great part of it consists of dialogues about the Unthinkable.

FRAGMENT I

... Then the Wave prayed to remain a wave forever.

The Sea made answer:

"Nay, thou must break: there is no rest in me. Billions of billions of times thou wilt rise again to break, and break to rise again."

The Wave complained:

"I fear. Thou sayest that I shall rise again. But when did ever a wave return from the place of breaking?"

The Sea responded:

"Times countless beyond utterance thou hast broken; and yet thou art! Behold the myriads of the waves that run before thee, and the myriads that pursue behind thee! — all have been to the place of breaking times unspeakable; and thither they hasten now to break again. Into me they melt, only to swell anew. But pass they must; for there is not any rest in me."

Murmuring, the Wave replied:

"Shall I not be scattered presently to mix with the mingling of all these myriads? How should I rise again? Never, never again can I become the same."

"The same thou never art," returned the Sea, "at any two moments in thy running: perpetual change is the law of thy being. What is thine 'I'? Always thou art shaped with the substance of waves forgotten — waves numberless beyond the sands of the shores of me. In thy multiplicity what art thou? — a phantom, an impermanency!"

"Real is pain," sobbed the Wave — "and fear and hope, and the joy of the light. Whence and what are these, if I be not real?"

"Thou hast no pain," the Sea responded — "nor fear nor hope nor joy. Thou art nothing — save in me. I am thy Self, thine 'I': thy form is my dream;

175

thy motion is my will; thy breaking is my pain.
Break thou must, because there is no rest in me; but
thou wilt break only to rise again — for death is the
Rhythm of Life. Lo! I, too, die that I may live:
these my waters have passed, and will pass again,
with wrecks of innumerable worlds to the burning
of innumerable suns. I, too, am multiple unspeak-
ably: dead tides of millions of oceans revive in mine
ebb and flow. Suffice thee to learn that only because
thou wast thou art, and that because thou art thou
wilt become again."

Muttered the Wave:

"I cannot understand."

Answered the Sea:

"Thy part is to pulse and pass — never to understand. I also — even I, the great Sea — do not
understand. . . ."

FRAGMENT II

. . . "The stones and the rocks have felt; the winds
have been breath and speech; the rivers and oceans
of earth have been locked into chambers of hearts.
And the palingenesis cannot cease till every cosmic
particle shall have passed through the uttermost
possible experience of the highest possible life."

"But what of the planetary core? — has that, too,
felt and thought?"

"Even so surely as that all flesh has been sun-fire!
In the ceaseless succession of integrations and dis-
solutions, all things have shifted relation and place

176

numberless billions of times. Hearts of old moons will make the surface of future worlds. . . ."

FRAGMENT III

. . . "No regret is vain. It is sorrow that spins the thread — softer than moonshine, thinner than fragrance, stronger than death — the Gleipnirchain of the Greater Memory. . . .

"In millions of years you will meet again; — and the time will not seem long; for a million years and a moment are the same to the dead. Then you will not be all of your present self, nor she be all that she has been: both of you will at once be less, and yet incomparably more. Then, to the longing that must come upon you, body itself will seem but a barrier through which you would leap to her — or, it may be, to him; for sex will have shifted numberless times ere then. Neither will remember; but each will be filled with a feeling immeasurable of having met before. . . ."

FRAGMENT IV

. . . "So wronging the being who loves — the being blindly imagined but of yesterday — this mocker mocks the divine in the past of the Soul of the World. Then in that heart is revived the countless million sorrows buried in forgotten graves — all the old pain of Love, in its patient contest with Hate, since the beginning of Time.

"And the Gods know — the dim ones who dwell

177

beyond Space — spinning the mysteries of Shape and Name. For they sit at the roots of Life; and the pain runs back to them; and they feel that wrong — as the Spider feels in the trembling of her web that a thread is broken. . . ."

FRAGMENT V

. . . "Love at sight is the choice of the dead. But the most of them are older than ethical systems; and the decision of their majorities is rarely moral. They choose by beauty — according to their memory of physical excellence; and as bodily fitness makes the foundation of mental and of moral power, they are not apt to choose ill. Nevertheless they are sometimes strangely cheated. They have been known to want beings that could never help ghost to a body — hollow goblins. . . ."

FRAGMENT VI

. . . "The Animulæ making the Self do not fear death as dissolution. They fear death only as reintegration — recombination with the strange and the hateful of other lives: they fear the imprisonment, within another body, of that which loves together with that which loathes. . . ."

FRAGMENT VII

. . . "In other time the El-Woman sat only in waste places, and by solitary ways. But now in the shadows of cities she offers her breasts to youth; and he whom she entices, presently goes mad, and becomes, like herself, a hollowness. For the higher ghosts that entered into the making of him perish at that goblin-touch — die as the pupa dies in the cocoon, leaving only a shell and dust behind. . . ."

FRAGMENT VIII

. . . The Man said to the multitude remaining of his Souls:

"I am weary of life."

And the remnant replied to him:

"We also are weary of the shame and pain of dwelling in so vile a habitation. Continually we strive that the beams may break, and the pillars crack, and the roof fall in upon us."

"Surely there is a curse upon me," groaned the Man. "There is no justice in the Gods!"

Then the Souls tumultuously laughed in scorn — even as the leaves of a wood in the wind do chuckle all together. And they made answer to him:

"As a fool thou liest! Did any save thyself make thy vile body? Was it shapen — or misshapen — by any deeds or thoughts except thine own?"

"No deed or thought can I remember," returned the Man, "deserving that which has come upon me."

"Remember!" laughed the Souls. "No — the folly was in other lives. But we remember; and remembering, we hate."

"Ye are all one with me!" cried the Man — "how can ye hate?"

179

"One with thee," mocked the Souls — "as the wearer is one with his garment! . . . How can we hate? As the fire that devours the wood from which it is drawn by the fire-maker — even so we can hate."

"It is a cursed world!" cried the Man — "why did ye not guide me?"

The Souls replied to him:

"Thou wouldst not heed the guiding of ghosts that were wiser than we. . . . Cowards and weaklings curse the world. The strong do not blame the world: it gives them all that they desire. By power they break and take and keep. Life for them is a joy, a triumph, an exultation. But creatures without power merit nothing; and nothingness becomes their portion. Thou and we shall presently enter into nothingness."

"Do ye fear?" — asked the Man.

"There is reason for fear," the Souls answered. "Yet no one of us would wish to delay the time of what we fear by continuing to make part of such an existence as thine."

"But ye have died innumerable times?" — wonderingly said the Man.

"No, we have not," said the Souls — "not even once that we can remember; and our memory reaches back to the beginnings of this world. We die only with the race."

The Man said nothing — being afraid. The Souls resumed:

"Thy race ceases. Its continuance depended upon thy power to serve our purposes. Thou hast lost all power. What art thou but a charnel-house, a mortuary-pit? Freedom we needed, and space: here we have been compacted together, a billion to a pin-point! Doorless our chambers and blind; — and the passages are blocked and broken; — and the stairways lead to nothing. Also there are Haunters here, not of our kind — Things never to be named."

For a little time the Man thought gratefully of death and dust. But suddenly there came into his memory a vision of his enemy's face, with a wicked smile upon it. And then he wished for longer life — a hundred years of life and pain — only to see the grass grow tall above the grave of that enemy. And the Souls mocked his desire:

"Thine enemy will not waste much thought upon thee. He is no half-man — thine enemy! The ghosts in that body have room and great light. High are the ceilings of their habitation; wide and clear the passageways; luminous the courts and pure. Like a fortress excellently garrisoned is the brain of thine enemy; — and to any point thereof the defending hosts can be gathered for battle in a moment together. *His* generation will not cease — nay! that face of his will multiply throughout the centuries! Because thine enemy in every time provided for the needs of his higher ghosts: he gave heed to their warnings; he pleasured them in all just ways; he did

not fail in reverence to them. Wherefore they now
have power to help him at his need. . . . How hast
thou reverenced or pleasured us?"

The Man remained silent for a space. Then as in
horror of doubting, he questioned:

"Wherefore should ye fear — if nothingness be
the end?"

"What is nothingness?" the Souls responded.
"Only in the language of delusion is there an end.
That which thou callest the end is in truth but the
very beginning. The essence of us cannot cease. In
the burning of worlds it cannot be consumed. It
will shudder in the cores of great stars; — it will
quiver in the light of other suns. And once more, in
some future cosmos, it will reconquer knowledge —
but only after evolutions unthinkable for multitude.
Even out of the nameless beginnings of form, and
thence through every cycle of vanished being —
through all successions of exhausted pain — through
all the Abyss of the Past — it must climb again."

The Man uttered no word: the Souls spoke on:

"For millions of millions of ages must we shiver
in tempests of fire: then shall we enter anew into
some slime primordial — there to quicken, and
again writhe upward through all foul dumb blind
shapes. Innumerable the metamorphoses! — immeasurable the agonies! . . . And the fault is not
of any Gods: it is thine!"

"Good or evil," muttered the Man — "what

signifies either? The best must become as the worst in the grind of the endless change."

"Nay!" cried out the Souls; "for the strong there is a goal — the goal that thou couldst not strive to gain. They will help to the fashioning of fairer worlds; — they will win to larger light; — they will tower and soar as flame to enter the Zones of the Divine. But thou and we go back to slime! Think of the billion summers that might have been for us! — think of the joys, the loves, the triumphs cast away! — the dawns of the knowledge undreamed — the glories of sense unimagined — the exultations of illimitable power! . . . think, think, O fool, of all that thou hast lost!"

Then the Souls of the Man turned themselves into worms, and devoured him.

IN A PAIR OF EYES

THERE is one adolescent moment never to be forgotten — the moment when the boy learns that this world contains nothing more wonderful than a certain pair of eyes. At first the surprise of the discovery leaves him breathless: instinctively he turns away his gaze. That vision seemed too delicious to be true. But presently he ventures to look again — fearing with a new fear — afraid of the reality, afraid also of being observed; — and lo! his doubt dissolves in a new shock of ecstasy. Those eyes are even more wonderful than he had imagined — nay! they become more and yet more entrancing every successive time that he looks at them! Surely in all the universe there cannot be another such pair of eyes! What can lend them such enchantment? Why do they appear divine? ... He feels that he must ask somebody to explain — must propound to older and wiser heads the riddle of his new emotions. Then he makes his confession, with a faint intuitive fear of being laughed at, but with a strange, fresh sense of rapture in the telling. Laughed at he is — tenderly; but this does not embarrass him nearly so much as the fact that he can get no answer to his question — to the simple "Why?" made so interesting by his frank surprise and his timid blushes.

IN A PAIR OF EYES

No one is able to enlighten him; but all can sympathize with the bewilderment of his sudden awakening from the long soul-sleep of childhood.

Perhaps that "Why?" never can be fully answered. But the mystery that prompted it constantly tempts one to theorize; and theories may have a worth independent of immediate results. Had it not been for old theories concerning the Unknowable, what should we have been able to learn about the Knowable? Was it not while in pursuit of the Impossible that we stumbled upon the undreamed-of and infinitely marvelous Possible?

Why indeed should a pair of human eyes appear for a time to us so beautiful that, when likening their radiance to splendor of diamond or amethyst or emerald, we feel the comparison a blasphemy? Why should we find them deeper than the sea, deeper than the day — deep even as the night of Space, with its scintillant mist of suns? Certainly not because of mere wild fancy. These thoughts, these feelings, must spring from some actual perception of the marvelous — some veritable revelation of the unspeakable. There is, in very truth, one brief hour of life during which the world holds for us nothing so wonderful as a pair of eyes. And then, while looking into them, we discover a thrill of awe vibrating through our delight — awe made by a something *felt* rather than seen: a latency — a power — a shadowing of depth unfathomable as the cosmic Ether. It is as though, through some intense and sudden stimulation of vital being, we had obtained — for one supercelestial moment — the glimpse of a reality, never before imagined, and never again to be revealed.

There is, indeed, an illusion. We seem to view the divine; but this divine itself, whereby we are dazzled and duped, is a ghost. Not to actuality belongs the spell — not to anything that *is* — but to some infinite composite phantom of what has been. Wondrous the vision — but wondrous only because our mortal sight then pierces beyond the surface of the present into profundities of myriads of years — pierces beyond the mask of life into the enormous night of death. For a moment we are made aware of a beauty and a mystery and a depth unutterable: then the Veil falls again forever.

The splendor of the eyes that we worship belongs to them only as brightness to the morning-star. It is a reflex from beyond the shadow of the Now — a ghost-light of vanished suns. Unknowingly within that maiden-gaze we meet the gaze of eyes more countless than the hosts of heaven — eyes otherwhere passed into darkness and dust.

Thus, and only thus, the depth of that gaze is the depth of the Sea of Death and Birth — and its mystery is the World-Soul's vision, watching us out of the silent vast of the Abyss of Being.

Thus, and only thus, do truth and illusion mingle

IN A PAIR OF EYES

in the magic of eyes — the spectral past suffusing
with charm ineffable the apparition of the present;
— and the sudden splendor in the soul of the Seër
is but a flash — one soundless sheet-lightning of
the Infinite Memory.

A JAPANESE MISCELLANY

TO

MRS. ELIZABETH BISLAND WETMORE

A JAPANESE MISCELLANY

• •
•

STRANGE STORIES

A JAPANESE MISCELLANY

. .
.

OF A PROMISE KEPT [1]

"I shall return in the early autumn," said Akana
Soyëmon several hundred years ago — when bidding
good-bye to his brother by adoption, young Hasébé
Samon. The time was spring; and the place was the
village of Kato in the province of Harima. Akana
was an Izumo samurai; and he wanted to visit his
birthplace.

Hasébé said:

"Your Izumo — the Country of the Eight-Cloud
Rising [2] — is very distant. Perhaps it will therefore
be difficult for you to promise to return here upon
any particular day. But, if we were to know the
exact day, we should feel happier. We could then
prepare a feast of welcome and we could watch at the
gateway for your coming."

"Why, as for that," responded Akana, "I have
been so much accustomed to travel that I can usually
tell beforehand how long it will take me to reach a
place; and I can safely promise you to be here upon
a particular day. Suppose we say the day of the festival Chōyō?"

[1] Related in the *Ugétsu Monogatari*.
[2] One of the old poetical names for the province of Izumo, or Unshū.

193

"That is the ninth day of the ninth month," said Hasébé; — "then the chrysanthemums will be in bloom, and we can go together to look at them. How pleasant! . . . So you promise to come back on the ninth day of the ninth month?"

"On the ninth day of the ninth month," repeated Akana, smiling farewell. Then he strode away from the village of Kato in the province of Harima; — and Hasébé Samon and the mother of Hasébé looked after him with tears in their eyes.

"Neither the Sun nor the Moon," says an old Japanese proverb, "ever halt upon their journey." Swiftly the months went by; and the autumn came — the season of chrysanthemums. And early upon the morning of the ninth day of the ninth month Hasébé prepared to welcome his adopted brother. He made ready a feast of good things, bought wine, decorated the guest-room, and filled the vases of the alcove with chrysanthemums of two colors. Then his mother, watching him, said: "The province of Izumo, my son, is more than one hundred ri [1] from this place; and the journey thence over the mountains is difficult and weary; and you cannot be sure that Akana will be able to come to-day. Would it not be better, before you take all this trouble, to wait for his coming?" "Nay, mother!" Hasébé made answer — "Akana promised to be here to-day: he could not break a promise! And if he were to see us

[1] A ri is about equal to two and a half English miles.

194

beginning to make preparation after his arrival, he would know that we had doubted his word; and we should be put to shame."

The day was beautiful, the sky without a cloud, and the air so pure that the world seemed to be a thousand miles wider than usual. In the morning many travelers passed through the village — some of them samurai; and Hasébé, watching each as he came, more than once imagined that he saw Akana approaching. But the temple-bells sounded the hour of midday; and Akana did not appear. Through the afternoon also Hasébé watched and waited in vain. The sun set; and still there was no sign of Akana. Nevertheless Hasébé remained at the gate, gazing down the road. Later his mother went to him, and said: "The mind of a man, my son — as our proverb declares — may change as quickly as the sky of autumn. But your chrysanthemum-flowers will still be fresh to-morrow. Better now to sleep; and in the morning you can watch again for Akana, if you wish." "Rest well, mother," returned Hasébé; — "but I still believe that he will come." Then the mother went to her own room; and Hasébé lingered at the gate.

The night was pure as the day had been: all the sky throbbed with stars; and the white River of Heaven shimmered with unusual splendor. The village slept; — the silence was broken only by the noise of a little brook, and by the far-away barking

of peasants' dogs. Hasébé still waited — waited
until he saw the thin moon sink behind the neighboring hills. Then at last he began to doubt and to
fear. Just as he was about to reënter the house, he
perceived in the distance a tall man approaching —
very lightly and quickly; and in the next moment he
recognized Akana.

"Oh!" cried Hasébé, springing to meet him —
"I have been waiting for you from the morning until
now! . . . So you really did keep your promise after
all. . . . But you must be tired, poor brother! —
come in; — everything is ready for you." He guided
Akana to the place of honor in the guest-room, and
hastened to trim the lights, which were burning
low. "Mother," continued Hasébé, "felt a little
tired this evening, and she has already gone to bed;
but I shall awaken her presently." Akana shook
his head, and made a little gesture of disapproval.
"As you will, brother," said Hasébé; and he set
warm food and wine before the traveler. Akana
did not touch the food or the wine, but remained
motionless and silent for a short time. Then, speaking in a whisper — as if fearful of awakening the
mother, he said:

"Now I must tell you how it happened that I
came thus late. When I returned to Izumo I found
that the people had almost forgotten the kindness
of our former ruler, the good Lord Enya, and were
seeking the favor of the usurper Tsunéhisa, who had
possessed himself of the Tonda Castle. But I had to

visit my cousin, Akana Tanji, though he had accepted service under Tsunéhisa, and was living, as a
retainer, within the castle grounds. He persuaded
me to present myself before Tsunéhisa: I yielded
chiefly in order to observe the character of the new
ruler, whose face I had never seen. He is a skilled
soldier, and of great courage; but he is cunning and
cruel. I found it necessary to let him know that I
could never enter into his service. After I left his
presence he ordered my cousin to detain me — to
keep me confined within the house. I protested that
I had promised to return to Harima upon the ninth
day of the ninth month; but I was refused permis-
sion to go. I then hoped to escape from the castle
at night; but I was constantly watched; and until
to-day I could find no way to fulfill my promise. . . ."

"Until to-day!" exclaimed Hasébé in bewilderment; — "the castle is more than a hundred ri from
here!"

"Yes," returned Akana; "and no living man can
travel on foot a hundred ri in one day. But I felt
that, if I did not keep my promise, you could not
think well of me; and I remembered the ancient
proverb, 'Tama yoku ichi nichi ni sen ri wo yuku'
('The soul of a man can journey a thousand ri in a
day'). Fortunately I had been allowed to keep my
sword; — thus only was I able to come to you. . . .
Be good to our mother."

With these words he stood up, and in the same
instant disappeared.

Then Hasébé knew that Akana had killed himself in order to fulfill the promise.

At earliest dawn Hasébé Samon set out for the Castle Tonda, in the province of Izumo. Reaching Matsué, he there learned that, on the night of the ninth day of the ninth month, Akana Soyëmon had performed harakiri in the house of Akana Tanji, in the grounds of the castle. Then Hasébé went to the house of Akana Tanji, and reproached Akana Tanji for the treachery done, and slew him in the midst of his family, and escaped without hurt. And when the Lord Tsunéhisa had heard the story, he gave commands that Hasébé should not be pursued. For, although an unscrupulous and cruel man himself, the Lord Tsunéhisa could respect the love of truth in others, and could admire the friendship and the courage of Hasébé Samon.

OF A PROMISE BROKEN[1]

"I AM not afraid to die," said the dying wife; —
"there is only one thing that troubles me now. I
wish that I could know who will take my place in
this house."

"My dear one," answered the sorrowing husband,
"nobody shall ever take your place in my home. I
will never, never marry again."

At the time that he said this he was speaking out
of his heart; for he loved the woman whom he was
about to lose.

"On the faith of a samurai?" she questioned,
with a feeble smile.

"On the faith of a samurai," he responded —
stroking the pale thin face.

"Then, my dear one," she said, "you will let me
be buried in the garden — will you not? — near
those plum-trees that we planted at the farther end?
I wanted long ago to ask this; but I thought, that
if you were to marry again, you would not like to
have my grave so near you. Now you have promised
that no other woman shall take my place; — so I
need not hesitate to speak of my wish. . . . I want
so much to be buried in the garden! I think that in
the garden I should sometimes hear your voice, and

[1] Izumo legend.

that I should still be able to see the flowers in the spring."

"It shall be as you wish," he answered. "But do not now speak of burial: you are not so ill that we have lost all hope."

"*I* have," she returned; — "I shall die this morning. . . . But you will bury me in the garden?"

"Yes," he said — "under the shade of the plum-trees that we planted; — and you shall have a beautiful tomb there."

"And will you give me a little bell?"

"Bell — ?"

"Yes: I want you to put a little bell in the coffin — such a little bell as the Buddhist pilgrims carry. Shall I have it?"

"You shall have the little bell — and anything else that you wish."

"I do not wish for anything else," she said. . . . "My dear one, you have been very good to me always. Now I can die happy."

Then she closed her eyes and died — as easily as a tired child falls asleep. She looked beautiful when she was dead; and there was a smile upon her face.

She was buried in the garden, under the shade of the trees that she loved; and a small bell was buried with her. Above the grave was erected a handsome monument, decorated with the family crest, and bearing the kaimyō:

OF A PROMISE BROKEN

Great Elder Sister, Luminous-Shadow-of-the-Plum-Flower-Chamber, dwelling in the Mansion of the Great Sea of Compassion."

. . . .

But, within a twelve-month after the death of his wife, the relatives and friends of the samurai began to insist that he should marry again. "You are still a young man," they said, "and an only son; and you have no children. It is the duty of a samurai to marry. If you die childless, who will there be to make the offerings and to remember the ancestors?"

By many such representations he was at last persuaded to marry again. The bride was only seventeen years old; and he found that he could love her dearly, notwithstanding the dumb reproach of the tomb in the garden.

II

NOTHING took place to disturb the happiness of the young wife until the seventh day after the wedding — when her husband was ordered to undertake certain duties requiring his presence at the castle by night. On the first evening that he was obliged to leave her alone, she felt uneasy in a way that she could not explain — vaguely afraid without knowing why. When she went to bed she could not sleep. There was a strange oppression in the air — an indefinable heaviness like that which sometimes precedes the coming of a storm.

About the Hour of the Ox she heard, outside in

the night, the clanging of a bell — a Buddhist pilgrim's bell; — and she wondered what pilgrim could be passing through the samurai quarter at such a time. Presently, after a pause, the bell sounded much nearer. Evidently the pilgrim was approaching the house; — but why approaching from the rear, where no road was? . . . Suddenly the dogs began to whine and howl in an unusual and horrible way; — and a fear came upon her like the fear of dreams. . . . That ringing was certainly in the garden. . . . She tried to get up to waken a servant. But she found that she could not rise — could not move — could not call. . . . And nearer, and still more near, came the clang of the bell; — and oh! how the dogs howled! . . . Then, lightly as a shadow steals, there glided into the room a Woman — though every door stood fast, and every screen unmoved — a Woman robed in a grave-robe, and carrying a pilgrim's bell. Eyeless she came — because she had long been dead; — and her loosened hair streamed down about her face; — and she looked without eyes through the tangle of it, and spoke without a tongue:

Not in this house — not in this house shall you stay! Here I am mistress still. You shall go; and you shall tell to none the reason of your going. If you tell HIM, I will tear you into pieces!

So speaking, the haunter vanished. The bride became senseless with fear. Until the dawn she so remained.

Nevertheless, in the cheery light of day, she doubted the reality of what she had seen and heard. The memory of the warning still weighed upon her so heavily that she did not dare to speak of the vision, either to her husband or to any one else; but she was almost able to persuade herself that she had only dreamed an ugly dream, which had made her ill.

On the following night, however, she could not doubt. Again, at the Hour of the Ox, the dogs began to howl and whine; — again the bell resounded — approaching slowly from the garden; — again the listener vainly strove to rise and call; — again the dead came into the room, and hissed:

You shall go; and you shall tell to no one why you must go! If you even whisper it to HIM, I will tear you in pieces! . . .

This time the haunter came close to the couch — and bent and muttered and mowed above it. . . .

Next morning, when the samurai returned from the castle, his young wife prostrated herself before him in supplication:

"I beseech you," she said, "to pardon my ingratitude and my great rudeness in thus addressing you: but I want to go home; — I want to go away at once."

"Are you not happy here?" he asked, in sincere surprise. "Has any one dared to be unkind to you during my absence?"

"It is not that —" she answered, sobbing.

"Everybody here has been only too good to me. . . . But I cannot continue to be your wife; — I must go away. . . ."

"My dear," he exclaimed, in great astonishment, "it is very painful to know that you have had any cause for unhappiness in this house. But I cannot even imagine why you should want to go away — unless somebody has been very unkind to you. . . . Surely you do not mean that you wish for a divorce?"

She responded, trembling and weeping:

"If you do not give me a divorce, I shall die!"

He remained for a little while silent — vainly trying to think of some cause for this amazing declaration. Then, without betraying any emotion, he made answer:

"To send you back now to your people, without any fault on your part, would seem a shameful act. If you will tell me a good reason for your wish — any reason that will enable me to explain matters honorably — I can write you a divorce. But unless you give me a reason, a good reason, I will not divorce you — for the honor of our house must be kept above reproach."

And then she felt obliged to speak; and she told him everything — adding, in an agony of terror:

"Now that I have let you know, she will kill me! — she will kill me! . . ."

Although a brave man, and little inclined to believe in phantoms, the samurai was more than startled for the moment. But a simple and natural explanation of the matter soon presented itself to his mind.

"My dear," he said, "you are now very nervous; and I fear that some one has been telling you foolish stories. I cannot give you a divorce merely because you have had a bad dream in this house. But I am very sorry indeed that you should have been suffering in such a way during my absence. To-night, also, I must be at the castle; but you shall not be alone. I will order two of the retainers to keep watch in your room; and you will be able to sleep in peace. They are good men; and they will take all possible care of you."

Then he spoke to her so considerately and so affectionately that she became almost ashamed of her terrors, and resolved to remain in the house.

III

THE two retainers left in charge of the young wife were big, brave, simple-hearted men — experienced guardians of women and children. They told the bride pleasant stories to keep her cheerful. She talked with them a long time, laughed at their good-humored fun, and almost forgot her fears. When at last she lay down to sleep, the men-at-arms took their places in a corner of the room, behind a screen, and began a game of go [1] — speaking only in whis-

---

[1] A game resembling draughts, but much more complicated.

pers, that she might not be disturbed. She slept like
an infant.

But again at the Hour of the Ox she awoke with
a moan of terror — for she heard the bell! . . . It
was already near, and was coming nearer. She
started up; she screamed; — but in the room there
was no stir — only a silence as of death — a silence
growing — a silence thickening. She rushed to the
men-at-arms: they sat before their checker-table —
motionless — each staring at the other with fixed
eyes. She shrieked to them: she shook them: they remained as if frozen. . . .

Afterwards they said that they had heard the bell
— heard also the cry of the bride — even felt her
try to shake them into wakefulness; — and that,
nevertheless, they had not been able to move or
speak. From the same moment they had ceased to
hear or to see: a black sleep had seized upon them.

.   .   .   .

Entering his bridal-chamber at dawn, the samurai
beheld, by the light of a dying lamp, the headless
body of his young wife, lying in a pool of blood.
Still squatting before their unfinished game, the two
retainers slept. At their master's cry they sprang
up, and stupidly stared at the horror on the floor. . . .
The head was nowhere to be seen; — and the
hideous wound showed that it had not been cut off,
but *torn off*. A trail of blood led from the chamber
to an angle of the outer gallery, where the storm-

doors appeared to have been riven apart. The three men followed that trail into the garden — over reaches of grass — over spaces of sand — along the bank of an iris-bordered pond — under heavy shadowings of cedar and bamboo. And suddenly, at a turn, they found themselves face to face with a nightmare-thing that chippered like a bat: the figure of the long-buried woman, erect before her tomb — in one hand clutching a bell, in the other the dripping head. . . . For a moment the three stood numbed. Then one of the men-at-arms, uttering a Buddhist invocation, drew, and struck at the shape. Instantly it crumbled down upon the soil — an empty scattering of grave-rags, bones, and hair; — and the bell rolled clanking out of the ruin. But the fleshless right hand, though parted from the wrist, still writhed; — and its fingers still gripped at the bleeding head — and tore, and mangled — as the claws of the yellow crab cling fast to a fallen fruit. . . .

"That is a wicked story," I said to the friend who had related it. "The vengeance of the dead — if taken at all — should have been taken upon the man."

"Men think so," he made answer. "But that is not the way that a woman feels. . . ."

He was right.

BEFORE THE SUPREME COURT

THE great Buddhist priest, Mongaku Shōnin, says in his book "Kyō-gyō Shin-shō":

Many of those gods whom the people worship are unjust gods [*jajin*]: therefore such gods are not worshiped by persons who revere the Three Precious Things.[1] And even persons who obtain favors from those gods, in answer to prayer, usually find at a later day that such favors cause misfortune.

This truth is well exemplified by a story recorded in the book "Nihon-Rei-Iki."

' During the time of the Emperor Shōmu[2] there lived in the district called Yamadagori, in the province of Sanuki, a man named Fushiki no Shin. He had but one child, a daughter called Kinumé.[3] Kinumé was a fine-looking girl, and very strong; but, shortly after she had reached her eighteenth year, a dangerous sickness began to prevail in that part of the country, and she was attacked by it. Her parents and friends then made offerings on her behalf to a certain Pest-God, and performed great austerities in honor of the Pest-God — beseeching him to save her.

[1] Sambō (Ratnatraya) — the Buddha, the Doctrine, and the Priesthood.
[2] He reigned during the second quarter of the eighth century.
[3] "Golden Plum-Flower."

BEFORE THE SUPREME COURT

After having lain in a stupor for several days, the sick girl one evening came to herself, and told her parents a dream that she had dreamed. She had dreamed that the Pest-God appeared to her, and said: "Your people have been praying to me so earnestly for you, and have been worshiping me so devoutly, that I really wish to save you. But I cannot do so except by giving you the life of some other person. Do you happen to know of any other girl who has the same name as yours?" "I remember," answered Kinumé, "that in Utarigori there is a girl whose name is the same as mine." "Point her out to me," the God said, touching the sleeper; — and at the touch she rose into the air with him; and, in less than a second, the two were in front of the house of the other Kinumé, in Utarigori. It was night; but the family had not yet gone to bed, and the daughter was washing something in the kitchen. "That is the girl," said Kinumé of Yamadagori. The Pest-God took out of a scarlet bag at his girdle a long sharp instrument shaped like a chisel; and, entering the house, he drove the sharp instrument into the forehead of Kinumé of Utarigori. Then Kinumé of Utarigori sank to the floor in great agony; and Kinumé of Yamadagori awoke, and related the dream.

Immediately after having related it, however, she again fell into a stupor. For three days she remained without knowledge of the world; and her parents began to despair of her recovery. Then once more

209

she opened her eyes, and spoke. But almost in the same moment she rose from her bed, looked wildly about the room, and rushed out of the house, exclaiming: "This is not my home! — you are not my parents!" . . .

Something strange had happened.

Kinumé of Utarigori had died after having been stricken by the Pest-God. Her parents sorrowed greatly; and the priests of their parish-temple performed a Buddhist service for her; and her body was burned in a field outside the village. Then her spirit descended to the Meido, the world of the dead, and was summoned to the tribunal of Emma-Dai-Ō — the King and Judge of Souls. But no sooner had the Judge cast eyes upon her than he exclaimed: "This girl is the Utarigori-Kinumé: she ought not to have been brought here so soon! Send her back at once to the Shaba-world,[1] and fetch me the other Kinumé — the Yamadagori girl!" Then the spirit of Kinumé of Utarigori made moan before King Emma, and complained, saying: "Great Lord, it is more than three days since I died; and by this time my body must have been burned; and, if you now send me back to the Shaba-world, what shall I do? My body has been changed into ashes and smoke; — I shall have no body!" "Do not be anxious," the terrible King answered; — "I am going to give you

[1] The Shaba-world (Sahaloka), in common parlance, signifies the world of men — the region of human existence.

the body of Kinumé of Yamadagori — for her spirit must be brought here to me at once. You need not fret about the burning of your body: you will find the body of the other Kinumé very much better." And scarcely had he finished speaking when the spirit of Kinumé of Utarigori revived in the body of Kinumé of Yamadagori.

Now when the parents of Kinumé of Yamadagori saw their sick girl spring up and run away, exclaiming, "This is not my home!" — they imagined her to be out of her mind, and they ran after her, calling out: "Kinumé, where are you going? — wait for a moment, child! you are much too ill to run like that!" But she escaped from them, and ran on without stopping, until she came to Utarigori, and to the house of the family of the dead Kinumé. There she entered, and found the old people; and she saluted them, crying: "Oh, how pleasant to be again at home! . . . Is it well with you, dear parents?" They did not recognize her, and thought her mad; but the mother spoke to her kindly, asking: "Where have you come from, child?" "From the Meido I have come," Kinumé made answer. "I am your own child, Kinumé, returned to you from the dead. But I have now another body, mother." And she related all that had happened; and the old people wondered exceedingly, yet did not know what to believe. Presently the parents of Kinumé of Yamadagori also came to the house, looking for their daughter;

and then the two fathers and the two mothers consulted together, and made the girl repeat her story, and questioned her over and over again. But she replied to every question in such a way that the truth of her statements could not be doubted. At last the mother of the Yamadagori Kinumé, after having related the strange dream which her sick daughter had dreamed, said to the parents of the Utarigori Kinumé: "We are satisfied that the spirit of this girl is the spirit of your child. But you know that her body is the body of our child; and we think that both families ought to have a share in her. So we would ask you to agree that she be considered henceforward the daughter of both families." To this proposal the Utarigori parents joyfully consented; and it is recorded that in after-time Kinumé inherited the property of both households.

"This story," says the Japanese author of the "Bukkyō Hyakkwa Zenshō," "may be found on the left side of the twelfth sheet of the first volume of the 'Nihon-Rei-Iki.'"

THE STORY OF KWASHIN KOJI [1]

DURING the period of Tenshō [2] there lived, in one of the northern districts of Kyōto, an old man whom the people called Kwashin Koji. He wore a long white beard, and was always dressed like a Shintō priest; but he made his living by exhibiting Buddhist pictures and by preaching Buddhist doctrine. Every fine day he used to go to the grounds of the temple Gion, and there suspend to some tree a large kakemono on which were depicted the punishments of the various hells. This kakemono was so wonderfully painted that all things represented in it seemed to be real; and the old man would discourse to the people crowding to see it, and explain to them the Law of Cause and Effect — pointing out with a Buddhist staff [nyoi], which he always carried, each detail of the different torments, and exhorting everybody to follow the teachings of the Buddha. Multitudes assembled to look at the picture and to hear the old man preach about it; and sometimes the mat which he spread before him, to receive contributions, was covered out of sight by the heaping of coins thrown upon it.

Oda Nobunaga was at that time ruler of Kyōto and

---

[1] Related in the curious old book *Yasō-Kidan*.

[2] The period of Tenshō lasted from 1573 to 1591 (A.D.). The death of the great captain, Oda Nobunaga, who figures in this story, occurred in 1582.

of the surrounding provinces. One of his retainers, named Arakawa, during a visit to the temple of Gion, happened to see the picture being displayed there; and he afterwards talked about it at the palace. Nobunaga was interested by Arakawa's description, and sent orders to Kwashin Koji to come at once to the palace, and to bring the picture with him.

When Nobunaga saw the kakemono he was not able to conceal his surprise at the vividness of the work: the demons and the tortured spirits actually appeared to move before his eyes; and he heard voices crying out of the picture; and the blood there represented seemed to be really flowing — so that he could not help putting out his finger to feel if the painting was wet. But the finger was not stained — for the paper proved to be perfectly dry. More and more astonished, Nobunaga asked who had made the wonderful picture. Kwashin Koji answered that it had been painted by the famous Oguri Sōtan [1] — after he had performed the rite of self-purification every day for a hundred days, and practiced great austerities, and made earnest prayer for inspiration to the divine Kwannon of Kiyomidzu Temple.

Observing Nobunaga's evident desire to possess the kakemono, Arakawa then asked Kwashin Koji whether he would "offer it up," as a gift to the

[1] Oguri Sōtan was a great religious artist who flourished in the early part of the fifteenth century. He became a Buddhist priest in the later years of his life.

great lord. But the old man boldly answered: "This painting is the only object of value that I possess; and I am able to make a little money by showing it to the people. Were I now to present this picture to the lord, I should deprive myself of the only means which I have to make my living. However, if the lord be greatly desirous to possess it, let him pay me for it the sum of one hundred ryō of gold. With that amount of money I should be able to engage in some profitable business. Otherwise, I must refuse to give up the picture."

Nobunaga did not seem to be pleased at this reply; and he remained silent. Arakawa presently whispered something in the ear of the lord, who nodded assent; and Kwashin Koji was then dismissed, with a small present of money.

But when the old man left the palace, Arakawa secretly followed him — hoping for a chance to get the picture by foul means. The chance came; for Kwashin Koji happened to take a road leading directly to the heights beyond the town. When he reached a certain lonesome spot at the foot of the hills, where the road made a sudden turn, he was seized by Arakawa, who said to him: "Why were you so greedy as to ask a hundred ryō of gold for that picture? Instead of a hundred ryō of gold, I am now going to give you one piece of iron three feet long." Then Arakawa drew his sword, and killed the old man, and took the picture.

The next day Arakawa presented the kakemono — still wrapped up as Kwashin Koji had wrapped it before leaving the palace — to Oda Nobunaga, who ordered it to be hung up forthwith. But, when it was unrolled, both Nobunaga and his retainer were astounded to find that there was no picture at all — nothing but a blank surface. Arakawa could not explain how the original painting had disappeared; and as he had been guilty — whether willingly or unwillingly — of deceiving his master, it was decided that he should be punished. Accordingly he was sentenced to remain in confinement for a considerable time.

Scarcely had Arakawa completed his term of imprisonment, when news was brought to him that Kwashin Koji was exhibiting the famous picture in the grounds of Kitano Temple. Arakawa could hardly believe his ears; but the information inspired him with a vague hope that he might be able, in some way or other, to secure the kakemono, and thereby redeem his recent fault. So he quickly assembled some of his followers, and hurried to the temple; but when he reached it he was told that Kwashin Koji had gone away.

Several days later, word was brought to Arakawa that Kwashin Koji was exhibiting the picture at Kiyomidzu Temple, and preaching about it to an immense crowd. Arakawa made all haste to Kiyomidzu; but he arrived there only in time to see the crowd disperse — for Kwashin Koji had again disappeared.

At last one day Arakawa unexpectedly caught sight of Kwashin Koji in a wine-shop, and there captured him. The old man only laughed good-humoredly on finding himself seized, and said: "I will go with you; but please wait until I drink a little wine." To this request Arakawa made no objection; and Kwashin Koji thereupon drank, to the amazement of the bystanders, twelve bowls of wine. After drinking the twelfth he declared himself satisfied; and Arakawa ordered him to be bound with a rope, and taken to Nobunaga's residence.

In the court of the palace Kwashin Koji was examined at once by the Chief Officer, and sternly reprimanded. Finally the Chief Officer said to him: "It is evident that you have been deluding people by magical practices; and for this offense alone you deserve to be heavily punished. However, if you will now respectfully offer up that picture to the Lord Nobunaga, we shall this time overlook your fault. Otherwise we shall certainly inflict upon you a very severe punishment."

At this menace Kwashin Koji laughed in a bewildered way, and exclaimed: "It is not I who have been guilty of deluding people." Then, turning to Arakawa, he cried out: "You are the deceiver! You wanted to flatter the lord by giving him that picture; and you tried to kill me in order to steal it. Surely, if there be any such thing as crime, that was a crime!

As luck would have it, you did not succeed in killing me; but if you had succeeded, as you wished, what would you have been able to plead in excuse for such an act? You stole the picture, at all events. The picture that I now have is only a copy. And after you stole the picture, you changed your mind about giving it to Lord Nobunaga; and you devised a plan to keep it for yourself. So you gave a blank kakemono to Lord Nobunaga; and, in order to conceal your secret act and purpose, you pretended that I had deceived you by substituting a blank kakemono for the real one. Where the real picture now is, I do not know. You probably do."

At these words Arakawa became so angry that he rushed towards the prisoner, and would have struck him but for the interference of the guards. And this sudden outburst of anger caused the Chief Officer to suspect that Arakawa was not altogether innocent. He ordered Kwashin Koji to be taken to prison for the time being; and he then proceeded to question Arakawa closely. Now Arakawa was naturally slow of speech; and on this occasion, being greatly excited, he could scarcely speak at all; and he stammered, and contradicted himself, and betrayed every sign of guilt. Then the Chief Officer ordered that Arakawa should be beaten with a stick until he told the truth. But it was not possible for him even to seem to tell the truth. So he was beaten with a bamboo until his senses departed from him, and he lay as if dead.

THE STORY OF KWASHIN KOJI

Kwashin Koji was told in the prison about what had happened to Arakawa; and he laughed. But after a little while he said to the jailer: "Listen! That fellow Arakawa really behaved like a rascal; and I purposely brought this punishment upon him in order to correct his evil inclinations. But now please say to the Chief Officer that Arakawa must have been ignorant of the truth, and that I shall explain the whole matter satisfactorily."

Then Kwashin Koji was again taken before the Chief Officer, to whom he made the following declaration: "In any picture of real excellence there must be a ghost; and such a picture, having a will of its own, may refuse to be separated from the person who gave it life, or even from its rightful owner. There are many stories to prove that really great pictures have souls. It is well known that some sparrows, painted upon a sliding-screen [fusuma] by Hōgen Yenshin, once flew away, leaving blank the spaces which they had occupied upon the surface. Also it is well known that a horse, painted upon a certain kakemono, used to go out at night to eat grass. Now, in this present case, I believe the truth to be that, inasmuch as the Lord Nobunaga never became the rightful owner of my kakemono, the picture voluntarily vanished from the paper when it was unrolled in his presence. But if you will give me the price that I first asked — one hundred ryō of gold — I think that the painting will then reappear, of its own accord, upon the now blank paper. At all events, let us try! There is nothing to risk — since, if the picture does not reappear, I shall at once return the money."

On hearing of these strange assertions, Nobunaga ordered the hundred ryō to be paid, and came in person to observe the result. The kakemono was then unrolled before him; and, to the amazement of all present, the painting reappeared, with all its details. But the colors seemed to have faded a little; and the figures of the souls and the demons did not look really alive, as before. Perceiving this difference, the lord asked Kwashin Koji to explain the reason of it; and Kwashin Koji replied: "The value of the painting, as you first saw it, was the value of a painting beyond all price. But the value of the painting, as you now see it, represents exactly what you paid for it — one hundred ryō of gold. . . . How could it be otherwise?" On hearing this answer, all present felt that it would be worse than useless to oppose the old man any further. He was immediately set at liberty; and Arakawa was also liberated, as he had more than expiated his fault by the punishment which he had undergone.

Now Arakawa had a younger brother named Buichi — also a retainer in the service of Nobunaga. Buichi was furiously angry because Arakawa had been beaten and imprisoned; and he resolved to kill Kwashin Koji. Kwashin Koji no sooner found himself again at liberty than he went straight to a wineshop, and called for wine. Buichi rushed after him into the shop, struck him down, and cut off his head. Then, taking the hundred ryō that had been paid to the old man, Buichi wrapped up the head and the gold together in a cloth, and hurried home to show them to Arakawa. But when he unfastened the cloth he found, instead of the head, only an empty wine-gourd, and only a lump of filth instead of the gold. . . . And the bewilderment of the brothers was presently increased by the information that the headless body had disappeared from the wine-shop — none could say how or when.

Nothing more was heard of Kwashin Koji until about a month later, when a drunken man was found one evening asleep in the gateway of Lord Nobu-naga's palace, and snoring so loud that every snore sounded like the rumbling of distant thunder. A retainer discovered that the drunkard was Kwashin Koji. For this insolent offense, the old fellow was at once seized and thrown into the prison. But he did not awake; and in the prison he continued to sleep without interruption for ten days and ten nights — all the while snoring so that the sound could be heard to a great distance.

About this time, the Lord Nobunaga came to his death through the treachery of one of his captains, Akéchi Mitsuhidé, who thereupon usurped rule. But Mitsuhidé's power endured only for a period of twelve days.

Now when Mitsuhidé became master of Kyōto, he
was told of the case of Kwashin Koji; and he ordered
that the prisoner should be brought before him.
Accordingly Kwashin Koji was summoned into the
presence of the new lord; but Mitsuhidé spoke
to him kindly, treated him as a guest, and commanded that a good dinner should be served to him.
When the old man had eaten, Mitsuhidé said to
him: "I have heard that you are very fond of wine;
— how much wine can you drink at a single sitting?"
Kwashin Koji answered: "I do not really know how
much; I stop drinking only when I feel intoxication
coming on." Then the lord set a great wine-cup [1]
before Kwashin Koji, and told a servant to fill the
cup as often as the old man wished. And Kwashin
Koji emptied the great cup ten times in succession,
and asked for more; but the servant made answer
that the wine-vessel was exhausted. All present
were astounded by this drinking-feat; and the lord
asked Kwashin Koji, "Are you not yet satisfied,
Sir?" "Well, yes," replied Kwashin Koji, "I am
somewhat satisfied; — and now, in return for your
august kindness, I shall display a little of my art.
Be therefore so good as to observe that screen." He
pointed to a large eight-folding screen upon which
were painted the Eight Beautiful Views of the Lake

[1] The term "bowl" would better indicate the kind of vessel to which
the story-teller refers. Some of the so-called cups, used on festival occasions, were very large — shallow lacquered basins capable of holding
considerably more than a quart. To empty one of the largest size, at a
draught, was considered to be no small feat.

THE STORY OF KWASHIN KOJI

of Ōmi (Ōmi-Hakkei); and everybody looked at the screen. In one of the views the artist had represented, far away on the lake, a man rowing a boat — the boat occupying, upon the surface of the screen, a space of less than an inch in length. Kwashin Koji then waved his hand in the direction of the boat; and all saw the boat suddenly turn, and begin to move toward the foreground of the picture. It grew rapidly larger and larger as it approached; and presently the features of the boatman became clearly distinguishable. Still the boat drew nearer — always becoming larger — until it appeared to be only a short distance away. And, all of a sudden, the water of the lake seemed to overflow — out of the picture into the room; — and the room was flooded; and the spectators girded up their robes in haste, as the water rose above their knees. In the same moment the boat appeared to glide out of the screen — a real fishing-boat; — and the creaking of the single oar could be heard. Still the flood in the room continued to rise, until the spectators were standing up to their girdles in water. Then the boat came close up to Kwashin Koji; and Kwashin Koji climbed into it; and the boatman turned about, and began to row away very swiftly. And, as the boat receded, the water in the room began to lower rapidly — seeming to ebb back into the screen. No sooner had the boat passed the apparent foreground of the picture than the room was dry again! But still the painted vessel appeared to glide over the painted water — retreating farther into the distance, and ever growing smaller — till at last it dwindled to a dot in the offing. And then it disappeared altogether; and Kwashin Koji disappeared with it. He was never again seen in Japan.

THE STORY OF UMÉTSU CHŪBEI [1]

Umétsu Chūbei was a young samurai of great
strength and courage. He was in the service of the
Lord Tomura Jūdayū, whose castle stood upon a
lofty hill in the neighborhood of Yokoté, in the province of Dewa. The houses of the lord's retainers
formed a small town at the base of the hill.

Umétsu was one of those selected for night-duty
at the castle-gates. There were two night-watches;
— the first beginning at sunset and ending at midnight; the second beginning at midnight and ending
at sunrise.

Once, when Umétsu happened to be on the second
watch, he met with a strange adventure. While
ascending the hill at midnight, to take his place on
guard, he perceived a woman standing at the last
upper turn of the winding road leading to the castle.
She appeared to have a child in her arms, and to be
waiting for somebody. Only the most extraordinary
circumstances could account for the presence of a
woman in that lonesome place at so late an hour;
and Umétsu remembered that goblins were wont
to assume feminine shapes after dark, in order to
deceive and destroy men. He therefore doubted
whether the seeming woman before him was really a
human being; and when he saw her hasten towards

[1] Related in the *Bukkyō-Hyakkwa-Zenshō*.

him, as if to speak, he intended to pass her by without a word. But he was too much surprised to do so when the woman called him by name, and said, in a very sweet voice: "Good Sir Umétsu, to-night I am in great trouble, and I have a most painful duty to perform: will you not kindly help me by holding this baby for one little moment?" And she held out the child to him.

Umétsu did not recognize the woman, who appeared to be very young: he suspected the charm of the strange voice, suspected a supernatural snare, suspected everything; — but he was naturally kind; and he felt that it would be unmanly to repress a kindly impulse through fear of goblins. Without replying, he took the child. "Please hold it till I come back," said the woman: "I shall return in a very little while." "I will hold it," he answered; and immediately the woman turned from him, and, leaving the road, sprang soundlessly down the hill so lightly and so quickly that he could scarcely believe his eyes. She was out of sight in a few seconds.

Umétsu then first looked at the child. It was very small, and appeared to have been just born. It was very still in his hands; and it did not cry at all.

Suddenly it seemed to be growing larger. He looked at it again. . . . No: it was the same small creature; and it had not even moved. Why had he imagined that it was growing larger?

In another moment he knew why; — and he felt a chill strike through him. The child was not grow-

ing larger; *but it was growing heavier.* . . . At first
it had seemed to weigh only seven or eight pounds:
then its weight had gradually doubled — tripled —
quadrupled. Now it could not weigh less than
fifty pounds; — and still it was getting heavier and
heavier. . . . A hundred pounds! — a hundred and
fifty! — two hundred! . . . Umétsu knew that he
had been deluded — that he had not been speaking
with any mortal woman — that the child was not
human. But he had made a promise; and a samurai
was bound by his promise. So he kept the infant
in his arms; and it continued to grow heavier and
heavier . . . two hundred and fifty! — three hundred! — four hundred pounds! . . . What was going
to happen he could not imagine; but he resolved not
to be afraid, and not to let the child go while his
strength lasted. . . . Five hundred! — five hundred
and fifty! — six hundred pounds! All his muscles
began to quiver with the strain; — and still the
weight increased. . . . "Namu Amida Butsu!" he
groaned — "Namu Amida Butsu! — Namu Amida
Butsu!" Even as he uttered the holy invocation
for the third time, the weight passed away from him
with a shock; and he stood stupefied, with empty
hands — for the child had unaccountably disappeared. But almost in the same instant he saw the
mysterious woman returning as quickly as she had
gone. Still panting she came to him; and he then
first saw that she was very fair; — but her brow
dripped with sweat; and her sleeves were bound back

with tasuki-cords, as if she had been working hard.

"Kind Sir Umétsu," she said, "you do not know how great a service you have done me. I am the Ujigami [1] of this place; and to-night one of my Ujiko found herself in the pains of childbirth, and prayed to me for aid. But the labor proved to be very difficult; and I soon saw that, by my own power alone, I might not be able to save her: — therefore I sought for the help of your strength and courage. And the child that I laid in your hands was the child that had not yet been born; and in the time that you first felt the child becoming heavier and heavier, the danger was very great — for the Gates of Birth were closed. And when you felt the child become so heavy that you despaired of being able to bear the weight much longer — in that same moment the mother seemed to be dead, and the family wept for her. Then you three times repeated the prayer, 'Namu Amida Butsu!' — and the third time that you uttered it the power of the Lord Buddha came to our aid, and the Gates of Birth were opened. . . . And for that which you have done you shall be fitly rewarded. To a brave samurai no gift can be more serviceable than strength: therefore, not only to you, but likewise to your children and to your children's children, great strength shall be given."

---

[1] Ujigami is the title given to the tutelary Shintō divinity of a parish or district. All persons living in that parish or district, and assisting in the maintenance of the temple (miya) of the deity, are called "Ujiko."

THE STORY OF UMÉTSU CHŪBEI

And, with this promise, the divinity disappeared.

Umétsu Chūbei, wondering greatly, resumed his way to the castle. At sunrise, on being relieved from duty, he proceeded as usual to wash his face and hands before making his morning prayer. But when he began to wring the towel which had served him, he was surprised to feel the tough material snap asunder in his hands. He attempted to twist together the separated portions; and again the stuff parted — like so much wet paper. He tried to wring the four thicknesses; and the result was the same. Presently, after handling various objects of bronze and of iron which yielded to his touch like clay, he understood that he had come into full possession of the great strength promised, and that he would have to be careful thenceforward when touching things, lest they should crumble in his fingers.

On returning home, he made inquiry as to whether any child had been born in the settlement during the night. Then he learned that a birth had actually taken place at the very hour of his adventure, and that the circumstances had been exactly as related to him by the Ujigami.

The children of Umétsu Chūbei inherited their father's strength. Several of his descendants — all remarkably powerful men — were still living in the province of Dewa at the time when this story was written.

THE STORY OF KŌGI THE PRIEST [1]

NEARLY one thousand years ago there lived in the famous temple called Miidera, at Ōtsu [2] in the province of Ōmi, a learned priest named Kōgi. He was a great artist. He painted, with almost equal skill, pictures of the Buddhas, pictures of beautiful scenery, and pictures of animals or birds; but he liked best to paint fishes. Whenever the weather was fair, and religious duty permitted, he would go to Lake Biwa, and hire fishermen to catch fish for him, without injuring them in any way, so that he could paint them afterwards as they swam about in a large vessel of water. After having made pictures of them, and fed them like pets, he would set them free again — taking them back to the lake himself. His pictures of fish at last became so famous that people traveled from great distances to see them. But the most wonderful of all his drawings of fish was not drawn from life, but was made from the memory of a dream. For one day, as he sat by the lake-side to watch the fishes swimming, Kōgi had fallen into a doze, and had dreamed that he was

[1] From the collection entitled *Ugétsu Monogatari*.
[2] The town of Ōtsu stands on the shore of the great Lake of Ōmi — usually called Lake Biwa; — and the temple Miidera is situated upon a hill overlooking the water. Miidera was founded in the seventh century, but has been several times rebuilt: the present structure dates back to the latter part of the seventeenth century.

playing with the fishes under the water. After he awoke, the memory of the dream remained so clear that he was able to paint it; and this painting, which he hung up in the alcove of his own room in the temple, he called "Dream-Carp."

Kōgi could never be persuaded to sell any of his pictures of fish. He was willing to part with his drawings of landscapes, of birds, or of flowers; but he said that he would not sell a picture of living fish to any one who was cruel enough to kill or to eat fish. And as the persons who wanted to buy his paintings were all fish-eaters, their offers of money could not tempt him.

One summer Kōgi fell sick; and after a week's illness he lost all power of speech and movement, so that he seemed to be dead. But after his funeral service had been performed, his disciples discovered some warmth in the body, and decided to postpone the burial for awhile, and to keep watch by the seeming corpse. In the afternoon of the same day he suddenly revived, and questioned the watchers, asking:

"How long have I remained without knowledge of the world?"

"More than three days," an acolyte made answer. "We thought that you were dead; and this morning your friends and parishioners assembled in the temple for your funeral service. We performed the service; but afterwards, finding that your body was not altogether cold, we put off the burial; and now we are very glad that we did so."

Kōgi nodded approvingly: then he said:

"I want some one of you to go immediately to the house of Taira no Suké, where the young men are having a feast at the present moment (they are eating fish and drinking wine) and say to them: 'Our master has revived; and he begs that you will be so good as to leave your feast, and to call upon him without delay, because he has a wonderful story to tell you.' . . . At the same time" — continued Kōgi — "observe what Suké and his brothers are doing; — see whether they are not feasting as I say."

Then an acolyte went at once to the house of Taira no Suké, and was surprised to find that Suké and his brother Jūrō, with their attendant, Kamori, were having a feast, just as Kōgi had said. But, on receiving the message, all three immediately left their fish and wine, and hastened to the temple. Kōgi, lying upon the couch to which he had been removed, received them with a smile of welcome; and, after some pleasant words had been exchanged, he said to Suké:

"Now, my friend, please reply to some questions that I am going to ask you. First of all, kindly tell me whether you did not buy a fish to-day from the fisherman Bunshi."

"Why, yes," replied Suké — "but how did you know?"

"Please wait a moment," said the priest. . . . "That fisherman Bunshi to-day entered your gate, with a fish three feet long in his basket: it was early in the afternoon, just after you and Jūrō had begun a game of go; — and Kamori was watching the game, and eating a peach — was he not?"

"That is true," exclaimed Suké and Kamori together, with increasing surprise.

"And when Kamori saw that big fish," proceeded Kōgi, "he agreed to buy it at once; and, besides paying the price of the fish, he also gave Bunshi some peaches, in a dish, and three cups of wine. Then the cook was called; and he came and looked at the fish, and admired it; and then, by your order, he sliced it and prepared it for your feast. . . . Did not all this happen just as I have said?"

"Yes," responded Suké; "but we are very much astonished that you should know what happened in our house to-day. Please tell us how you learned these matters."

"Well, now for my story," said the priest. "You are aware that almost everybody believed me to be dead; — you yourselves attended my funeral service. But I did not think, three days ago, that I was at all dangerously ill: I remember only that I felt weak and very hot, and that I wanted to go out into the air to cool myself. And I thought that I got up from my bed, with a great effort, and went out — supporting myself with a stick. . . . Perhaps this may have been imagination; but you will presently

233

be able to judge the truth for yourselves: I am going to relate everything exactly as it appeared to happen. . . . As soon as I got outside of the house, into the bright air, I began to feel quite light — light as a bird flying away from the net or the basket in which it has been confined. I wandered on and on till I reached the lake; and the water looked so beautiful and blue that I felt a great desire to have a swim. I took off my clothes, and jumped in, and began to swim about; and I was astonished to find that I could swim very fast and very skillfully — although before my sickness I had always been a very poor swimmer. . . . You think that I am only telling you a foolish dream — but listen! . . . While I was wondering at this new skill of mine, I perceived many beautiful fishes swimming below me and around me; and I felt suddenly envious of their happiness — reflecting that, no matter how good a swimmer a man may become, he never can enjoy himself under the water as a fish can. Just then, a very big fish lifted its head above the surface in front of me, and spoke to me with the voice of a man, saying: 'That wish of yours can very easily be satisfied: please wait there a moment!' The fish then went down, out of sight; and I waited. After a few minutes there came up, from the bottom of the lake — riding on the back of the same big fish that had spoken to me - – a man wearing the headdress and the ceremonial robes of a prince; and the man said to me: 'I come to you with a message from the

Dragon-King, who knows of your desire to enjoy for a little time the condition of a fish. As you have saved the lives of many fish, and have always shown compassion to living creatures, the God now bestows upon you the attire of the Golden Carp, so that you will be able to enjoy the pleasures of the Water-World. But you must be very careful not to eat any fish, or any food prepared from fish — no matter how nice may be the smell of it; — and you must also take great care not to get caught by the fishermen, or to hurt your body in any way.' With these words, the messenger and his fish went below and vanished in the deep water. I looked at myself, and saw that my whole body had become covered with scales that shone like gold; — I saw that I had fins; — I found that I had actually been changed into a Golden Carp. Then I knew that I could swim wherever I pleased.

"Thereafter it seemed to me that I swam away, and visited many beautiful places. [Here, in the original narrative, are introduced some verses describing the Eight Famous Attractions of the Lake of Ōmi — "Ōmi-Hakkei."] Sometimes I was satisfied only to look at the sunlight dancing over the blue water, or to admire the beautiful reflection of hills and trees upon still surfaces sheltered from the wind. . . . I remember especially the coast of an island — either Okitsushima or Chikubushima — reflected in the water like a red wall. . . . Sometimes I would approach the shore so closely that I could

see the faces and hear the voices of people passing
by; sometimes I would sleep on the water until
startled by the sound of approaching oars. At night
there were beautiful moonlight-views; but I was
frightened more than once by the approaching
torchfires of the fishing-boats of Katasé. When the
weather was bad, I would go below — far down —
even a thousand feet — and play at the bottom of
the lake. But after two or three days of this wandering pleasure, I began to feel very hungry; and I
returned to this neighborhood in the hope of finding
something to eat. Just at that time the fisherman
Bunshi happened to be fishing; and I approached
the hook which he had let down into the water.
There was some fish-food upon it that was good to
smell. I remembered in the same moment the warning of the Dragon-King, and swam away, saying to
myself: 'In any event I must not eat food containing fish; — I am a disciple of the Buddha.' Yet
after a little while my hunger became so intense that
I could not resist the temptation; and I swam back
again to the hook, thinking, 'Even if Bunshi should
catch me, he would not hurt me; — he is my old
friend.' I was not able to loosen the bait from the
hook; and the pleasant smell of the food was too
much for my patience; and I swallowed the whole
thing at a gulp. Immediately after I did so, Bunshi
pulled in his line, and caught me. I cried out to
him, 'What are you doing? — you hurt me!' — but
he did not seem to hear me, and he quickly put a

string through my jaws. Then he threw me into his basket, and took me to your house. When the basket was opened there, I saw you and Jūrō playing go in the south room, and Kamori watching you — eating a peach the while. All of you presently came out upon the veranda to look at me; and you were delighted to see such a big fish. I called out to you as loud as I could: 'I am not a fish! — I am Kōgi — Kōgi the priest! please let me go back to my temple!' But you clapped your hands for gladness, and paid no attention to my words. Then your cook carried me into the kitchen, and threw me down violently upon a cutting-board, where a terribly sharp knife was lying. With his left hand he pressed me down, and with his right hand he took up that knife — and I screamed to him: 'How can you kill me so cruelly! I am a disciple of the Buddha! — help! help!' But in the same instant I felt his knife dividing me — a frightful pain! — and then I suddenly awoke, and found myself here in the temple."

When the priest had thus finished his story, the brothers wondered at it; and Suké said to him: "I now remember noticing that the jaws of the fish were moving all the time that we were looking at it; but we did not hear any voice. . . . Now I must send a servant to the house with orders to throw the remainder of that fish into the lake."

Kōgi soon recovered from his illness, and lived to

paint many more pictures. It is related that, long after his death, some of his fish-pictures once happened to fall into the lake, and that the figures of the fish immediately detached themselves from the silk or the paper upon which they had been painted, and swam away!

FOLK–LORE GLEANINGS

DRAGON-FLIES

I

ONE of the old names of Japan is Akitsushima, meaning "The Island of the Dragon-Fly," and written with the character representing a dragon-fly — which insect, now called "tombō," was anciently called "akitsu." Perhaps this name Akitsushima, "Island of the Dragon-Fly," was phonetically suggested by a still older name for Japan, also pronounced "Akitsushima," but written with different characters, and signifying "The Land of Rich Harvests." However this may be, there is a tradition that the Emperor Jimmu, some twenty-six hundred years ago, ascended a mountain to gaze over the province of Yamato, and observed to those who accompanied him that the configuration of the land was like a dragon-fly licking its tail. Because of this august observation the province of Yamato came to be known as the Land of the Dragon-Fly; and eventually the name was extended to the whole island. And the Dragon-Fly remains an emblem of the Empire even to this day.

In a literal sense, Japan well deserves to be called the Land of the Dragon-Fly; for, as Rein poetically declared, it is "a true Eldorado to the neuroptera-fancier." Probably no other country of either temperate zone possesses so many kinds of dragon-flies; and I doubt whether even the tropics can produce any dragon-flies more curiously beautiful than some of the Japanese species. The most wonderful dragon-fly that I ever saw was a Japanese *Calepteryx*, which I captured last summer in Shidzuoka. It was what the country-folk call a "black dragon-fly"; but the color was really a rich deep purple. The long narrow wings, velvety purple, seemed — even to touch — like the petals of some marvelous flower. The purple body, slender as a darning-needle, was decorated with dotted lines of dead gold. The head and thorax were vivid gold-green; but the eyes were pure globes of burnished gold. The legs were fringed on the inner side with indescribably delicate spines, set at right angles to the limb, like the teeth of a fairy-comb. So exquisite was the creature that I felt a kind of remorse for having disturbed it — felt as if I had been meddling with something belonging to the gods; — and I quickly returned it to the shrub on which it had been reposing. . . . This particular kind of dragon-fly is said to haunt only the neighborhood of a clear stream near the town of Yaidzu. It is, however, but one of many lovely varieties.

But the more exquisite dragon-flies are infrequently seen; and they seldom figure in Japanese literature; — and I can attempt to interest my reader only in the poetry and the folk-lore of dragon-flies. I propose to discourse of dragon-flies in the old-fashioned Japanese way; and the little that I have been able to learn upon the subject — with the help of quaint books and of long-forgotten drawings — mostly relates to the commoner species.

But before treating of dragon-fly literature, it will be necessary to say something regarding dragon-fly nomenclature. Old Japanese books profess to name about fifty kinds; and the "Chūfu-Zusétsu" actually contains colored pictures of nearly that number of dragon-flies. But in these volumes several insects resembling dragon-flies are improperly classed with dragon-flies; and in more than one case it would seem that different names have been given to the male and female of the same species. On the other hand I find as many as four different varieties of dragon-fly bearing the same folk-name! And in view of these facts I venture to think that the following list will be found sufficiently complete:

1. Mugiwara-tombō, or simply, tombō (barley-straw dragon-fly) — so called because its body somewhat resembles in shape and color a barley-straw. This is perhaps the most common of all the dragon-flies, and the first to make its appearance.

2. Shiokara-tombō, or Shio-tombō (salt-fish dragon-fly, or salt dragon-fly) — so called because the end of its tail looks as if it had been dipped in salt. Shiokara is the name given to a preparation of fish preserved in salt.

3. Kino-tombō (yellow dragon-fly). It is not all yellow, but reddish, with yellow stripes and bands.

4. Ao-tombō. Ao means either blue or green; and two

different kinds of dragon-fly — one green, and one metal-lic-blue — are called by this name.

5. Koshiaki-tombō (shining loins). The insect usually so called is black and yellow.

6. Tono-Sama-tombō (august-lord dragon-fly). Many different kinds of dragon-fly are called by this name — probably on account of their beautiful colors. The name "Koshiaki," or "Shining Loins," is likewise given to several varieties.

7. Ko-mugi-tombō (wheat-straw dragon-fly). Some-what smaller than the barley-straw dragon-fly.

8. Tsumaguro-tombō (black-skirted, or black-hemmed dragon-fly). Several kinds of dragon-flies are thus called, because the edges of the wings are black or dark-red.

9. Kuro-tombō (black dragon-fly). As the word "kuro" means either dark in color or black, it is not sur-prising to find this name given both to deep red and to deep purple insects.

10. Karakasa-tombō (umbrella dragon-fly). The body of this creature is said to resemble, both in form and color, a closed umbrella of the kind known as "karakasa," made of split bamboo covered with thick oil-paper.

11. Chō-tombō (butterfly dragon-fly). Several varie-ties of dragon-fly are thus called — apparently because of wing-markings like those of moths or butterflies.

12. Shōjō-tombō. A bright-red dragon-fly is so named, simply because of its tint. In the zoölogical mythology of China and Japan, the Shōjō figures as a being less than human, but more than animal — in appearance resem-bling a stout boy with long crimson hair. From this crim-son hair it was alleged that a wonderful red dye could be extracted. The Shōjō was supposed to be very fond of saké; and in Japanese art the creature is commonly repre-sented as dancing about a saké-vessel.

13. Haguro-tombō (black-winged dragon-fly).

14. Oni-yamma (demon dragon-fly). This is the larg-

est of all the Japanese dragon-flies. It is rather unpleas-
antly colored; the body being black, with bright yellow
bands and stripes.

15. Ki-yamma (goblin dragon-fly). Also called "Ki-
Emma" — "Emma," or "Yemma," being the name of
the King of Death and Judge of Souls.

16. Shōryō-tombō (the dragon-fly of the ancestral
spirits). This appellation, as well as another of kindred
meaning — Shōrai-tombō (dragon-fly of the dead) —
would appear, so far as I could learn, to be given to many
kinds of dragon-fly.

17. Yurei-tombō (ghost dragon-fly). Various creatures are called by this name — which I thought especially appropriate in the case of one beautiful *Calepteryx*, whose soundless black flitting might well be mistaken for the motion of a shadow — the shadow of a
dragon-fly. Indeed this appellation for the black insect
must have been intended to suggest the primitive idea of
shadow as ghost.

18. Kané-tsuké-tombō, or O-haguro-tombō. Either
name refers to the preparation formerly used to blacken
the teeth of married women, and might be freely
rendered as "tooth-blackening dragon-fly." O-haguro
("honorable tooth-blackening") or kané, were the terms
by which the tooth-staining infusion was commonly
known. Kané wo tsukéru signified to apply, or, more literally, *to wear* the stuff: thus the appellation kané-tsuké-
tombō might be interpreted as "the kané-stained dragon-
fly." The wings of the insect are half-black, and look as if
they had been partly dipped in ink. Another and equally
picturesque name for the creature is Kōya, "the dyer."

19. Ta-no-Kami-tombō (dragon-fly of the God of
Rice-Fields). This appellation has been given to an insect
variegated with red and yellow.

20. Yanagi-jorō (the lady of the weeping-willow).
A beautiful, but ghostly name; for the Yanagi-jorō is the

Spirit of the Willow-Tree. I find that two very graceful species of dragon-fly are thus called.

21. Seki-i-Shisha (red-robed messenger).

22. Yamma-tombō. The name is a sort of doublet; yamma signifying a large dragon-fly, and tombō any sort of dragon-fly. This is the name for a black-and-green insect, called Onjō in Izumo.

23. Kuruma-yamma (wagon dragon-fly). Probably so named from the disk-like appendages of the tail.

24. Aka-tombō (red dragon-fly). The name is now given to various species; but the insect especially referred to as Aka-tombō by the old poets is a small dragon-fly, which is often seen in flocks.

25. Tōsumi-tombō (lamp-wick dragon-fly). A very small creature — thus named because of the resemblance of its body to the slender pith-wick used in the old-fashioned Japanese lamp.

26. Mono-sashi-tombō (foot-measure dragon-fly). This also is a very small insect. The form of its body, with the ten joint-markings, suggested this name; — the ordinary Japanese foot-measure, usually made of bamboo, being very narrow, and divided into only ten sun, or inches.

27. Beni-tombō. This is the name given to a beautiful pink dragon-fly, on account of its color. Beni is a kind of rouge, with which the Japanese girl tints her lips and cheeks on certain occasions.

28. Mékura-tombō (blind dragon-fly). The creature thus called is not blind at all; but it dashes its large body in so clumsy a way against objects in a room that it was at one time supposed to be sightless.

29. Ka-tombō (mosquito dragon-fly). Perhaps in the same sense as the American term "mosquito-hawk."

30. Kuro-yama-tombō (black mountain dragon-fly) — so called to distinguish it from the Yama-tombō, or "mountain dragon-fly," which is mostly green.

31. Ko-yama-tombō (little mountain dragon-fly) —
the name of a small insect resembling the Yama-tombō in
form and color.

32. Tsukété-dan. The word "dan" is a general term
for variegated woven stuffs; and the name "tsukété-dan"
might be freely rendered as "The Wearer of the Many-
Colored Robe."

I believe that in the foregoing list the only name
requiring further explanation is the name "Shōrai-
tombō," or "Shōryō-tombō," in its meaning of
"the dragon-fly of the dead." Unlike the equally
weird name "Yurei-tombō," or "ghost dragon-fly,"
the term "Shōrai-tombō" does not refer to the
appearance of the insect, but to the strange belief
that certain dragon-flies *are ridden by the dead* —
used as winged steeds. From the morning of the
thirteenth to the midnight of the fifteenth day of the
old seventh month — the time of the Festival of the
Bon — the dragon-flies are said to carry the Hotoké-
Sama, the August Spirits of the Ancestors, who then
revisit their former homes. Therefore during this
Buddhist "All-Souls," children are forbidden to
molest any dragon-flies — especially dragon-flies
that may then happen to enter the family dwelling.
This supposed relation of dragon-flies to the supernatural world helps to explain an old folk saying, still
current in some provinces, to the effect that the
child who catches dragon-flies will never "obtain
knowledge." Another curious belief is that certain
dragon-flies "carry the image of Kwannon-Sama

(Âvalokitesvara)" — because the markings upon the backs of the insects bear some faint resemblance to the form of a Buddhist icon.

II

DIFFERENT kinds of dragon-fly show themselves at different periods; and the more beautiful species, with few exceptions, are the latest to appear. All Japanese dragon-flies have been grouped by old writers into four classes, according to the predominant color of each variety — the yellow, green (or blue), black (or dark), and red dragon-flies. It is said that the yellow-marked insects are the earliest to appear; that the green, blue, and black varieties first show themselves in the Period of Greatest Heat; and that the red kinds are the last to come and the last to go—vanishing only with the close of autumn. In a vague and general way, these statements can be accepted as results of observation. Nevertheless, the dragon-fly is popularly spoken of as a creature of autumn: indeed one of its many names, Akitsu-mushi, signifies "autumn insect." And the appellation is really appropriate; for it is not until the autumn that dragon-flies appear in such multitude as to compel attention. For the poet, however, the true dragon-fly of autumn is the red dragon-fly:

Aki no ki no
Aka-tombō ni
Sadamarinu.

That the autumn season has begun is decided by the [appearance of the] red dragon-fly.

248

DRAGON–FLIES

Onoga mi ni
Aki wo soménuku
Tombō kana!

O the dragon-fly! — he has dyed his own body with [the color of] autumn!

Aki no hi no
Sométa iro nari
Aka-tombō!

Dyed he is with the color of autumn days — O the red dragon-fly!

"Spring," says a Japanese poet, "is the Season of the Eyes; Autumn is the Season of the Ears" — meaning that in spring the blossoming of the trees and the magic of morning haze make delight for the eyes, and that in autumn the ears are charmed by the music of countless insects. But he goes on to say that this pleasure of autumn is toned with melancholy. Those plaintive voices evoke the memory of vanished years and of vanished faces, and so to Buddhist thought recall the doctrine of impermanency. Spring is the period of promise and of hope; autumn, the time of remembrance and of regret. And the coming of autumn's special insect, the soundless dragon-fly — voiceless in the season of voices — only makes weirder the aspects of change. Everywhere you see a silent play of fairy lightnings — flashes of color continually intercrossing, like a weaving of interminable enchantment over the face of the land. Thus an old poet describes it:

FOLK-LORE GLEANINGS

Kurénai no
Kagerō hashiru,
Tombō kana!

Like a fleeting of crimson gossamer-threads, the flashing of the dragon-flies.

III

For more than ten centuries the Japanese have been making verses about dragon-flies; and the subject remains a favorite one even with the younger poets of to-day. The oldest extant poem about a dragon-fly is said to have been composed, fourteen hundred and forty years ago, by the Emperor Yūriaku. One day while this Emperor was hunting, say the ancient records, a gadfly came and bit his arm. Therewith a dragon-fly pounced upon that gadfly, and devoured it. Then the Emperor commanded his ministers to make an ode in praise of that dragon-fly. But as they hesitated how to begin, he himself composed a poem in praise of the insect, ending with words:

Even a creeping insect
Waits upon the Great Lord:
Thy form it will bear,
O Yamato, land of the dragon-fly!

And in honor of the loyal dragon-fly, the place of the incident was called "Akitsuno," or the "Moor of the Dragon-Fly."

The poem attributed to the Emperor Yūriaku is written in the form called "naga-uta," or "long-poetry"; but the later poems on dragon-flies are mostly composed in the briefer forms of Japanese verse. There are three brief forms — the ancient tanka, consisting of thirty-one syllables; the popular dodoitsu, consisting of twenty-six syllables; and the hokku, consisting of only seventeen. The vast majority of dragon-fly poems are in hokku. There are scarcely any poems upon the subject in dodoitsu, and — strange to say! — but very few in the classical tanka. The friend who collected for me all the verses quoted in this essay, and many hundreds more, declares that he read through *fifty-two volumes* of thirty-one-syllable poetry in the Imperial Library before he succeeded in finding a single composition about dragon-flies; and eventually, after much further research, he was able to discover only about a dozen such poems in tanka.

The reason for this must be sought in the old poetical conventions. Japanese thirty-one-syllable poetry is composed according to rules that have been fixed for hundreds of years. These rules require that almost every subject treated shall be considered in some relation to one of the seasons. And this should be done in accordance with certain laws of grouping — long-established conventions of association, recognized both in painting and in poetry: for example, the nightingale should be mentioned, or portrayed, together with the plum-tree; the sparrow, with the bamboo; the cuckoo, with the moon; frogs, with rain; the butterfly, with flowers; the bat, with the willow-tree. Every Japanese child knows something about these regulations. Now, it so happens that no such relations have been clearly fixed for the dragon-fly in tanka-poetry — though in pictures we often see it perched on the edge of a water-bucket, or upon an ear of ripened rice. Moreover, in the classification of subject-groupings for poetry, the dragon-fly is not placed among mushi ("insects" — by which word the poet nearly always means a musical insect of some sort), but among zō — a term of very wide signification; for it includes the horse, cat, dog, monkey, crow, sparrow, tortoise, snake, frog — almost all fauna, in short.

Thus the rarity of tanka-poems about dragon-flies may be explained. But why should dragon-flies be almost ignored in dodoitsu? Probably for the reason that this form of verse is usually devoted to the subject of love. The voiceless dragon-fly can suggest to the love-poet no such fancies as those inspired by the singing-insects — especially by those night-crickets whose music lingers in the memory of some evening tryst. Out of several hundred dragon-fly poems collected for me, I find only seven relating, directly or indirectly, to the subject of love; and not one of the seven is in twenty-six-syllable verse.

But in the form hokku — limited to seventeen syllables — the poems on dragon-flies are almost as numerous as are the dragon-flies themselves in the early autumn. For in this measure there are few restraints placed upon the composer, either as to theme or method. Almost the only rule about hokku — not at all a rigid one — is that the poem shall be a little word-picture — that it shall revive the memory of something seen or felt — that it shall appeal to some experience of sense. The greater number of the poems that I am going to quote certainly fulfill this requirement: the reader will find that they are really pictures — tiny color-prints in the manner of the Ukiyo-yé school. Indeed almost any of the following could be delightfully imaged, with a few touches of the brush, by some Japanese master:

PICTURE-POEMS ABOUT DRAGON-FLIES

Iné no ho no
Tombō tomari
Tarénikéri.

An ear of rice has bent because a dragon-fly perched upon it.

Tombō no
Éda ni tsuitari
Wasuré-guwa.

See the dragon-fly resting on the handle of the forgotten mattock. [1]

Tombō no
Kaidé yukikéri
Suté waraji.

Dragon-flies have gone to sniff at a pair of cast-off sandals of straw.

---

[1] The kuwa is shaped like a hoe, but is a much heavier tool. When left with the heavy blade resting flat upon the ground, as suggested in this little word-picture, the handle remains almost perpendicular.

FOLK–LORE GLEANINGS

Sodé ni tsuku
Sumi ka? — obana ni
Kané-tombō!

Is it an ink-stain upon a sleeve? — no: it is only the black dragon-fly resting upon the obana. [1]

Hi wa nanamé
Sékiya no yari ni
Tombō kana!

See the dragon-fly perching on the blade of the spear leaning against the rampart-wall!

Tombō no
Kusa ni undéya,
Ushi no tsuno!

O dragon-fly! how have you wearied of the grass that you should thus perch upon the horn of a cow!

Kaki-daké no
Ippon nagaki —
Tombō kana!

One of the bamboo-stakes in that fence seems to be higher than the others — but no! there is a dragon-fly upon it!

Kaki-daké to
Tombō to utsuru
Shōji kana!

The shadow of the bamboo-fence, with a dragon-fly at rest upon it, is thrown upon my paper-window!

Tsurigané ni
Hito-toki yasumi
Tombō kana!

See! the dragon-fly is resting awhile upon the temple-bell!

---

[1] Obana is another name for the beautiful flowering grass usually called "susuki," and known to botanists as *Eularia Japonica.*

DRAGON-FLIES

O wo motté
Kané ni mukaëru —
Tombō kana!

Only with his tail he thinks to oppose [the weight of] the great temple-bell — O silly dragon-fly!

Naki-hito no
Shirushi no také ni
Tombō kana!

Lo! a dragon-fly rèsts upon the bamboo that marks the grave!

Itté wa kité
Tombō taëzu
Funé no tsuna.

About the ropes of the ship the dragon-flies cease not to come and go.

Tombō ya
Funé wa nagarété
Todomarazu.

The dragon-fly ceases not to flit about the vessel drifting down the stream.

Tombō ya!
Hobashira até ni
Tōku yuku.

O the dragon-fly! — keeping an eye upon the mast, he ventures far!

Tombō ya!
Hi no kagé dékité,
Nami no uë.

Poor dragon-fly! — now that the sun has become obscured, he wanders over the waves.

Wata-tori no
Kasa ya tombō no
Hitotsu-zutsu.

Look at the bamboo-hats of the cotton-pickers! — there is a dragon-fly perched on each of them!

FOLK-LORE GLEANINGS

Nagaré-yuku
Awa ni yumé miru
Tombō kana!

Lo! the dragon-fly dreams a dream above the flowing of the foam-bubbles!

Uki-kusa no
Hana ni asobu ya,
Aka-tombō!

See the red dragon-fly sporting about the blossoms of the water-weed!

Tombō no
Hitoshio akashi
Fuchi no uë.

Much more red seems the red dragon-fly when hovering above the pool.

Tsuri-béta no
Sao ni kité néru
Tombō kana!

See! the dragon-fly settles down to sleep on the rod of the unskillful angler!

Tombō no
Ha-ura ni sabishi —
Aki-shiguré.

Lonesomely clings the dragon-fly to the underside of the leaf — Ah! the autumn rains!

Tombō no
Tō bakari tsuku
Kara-é kana!

Only ten dragon-flies — all clinging to the same withered spray!

Yosogoto no
Naruko ni nigéru,
Tombō kana!

Poor dragon-fly! scared away by the clapper [1] that never was intended for you!

---

[1] Naruko. This clapper, used to frighten away birds from the crops,

DRAGON-FLIES

Ao-zora ya,
Ka hodo muré-tobu
Aka-tombō.

High in the azure sky the gathering of red dragon-flies looks like a swarming of mosquitoes.

Furu-haka ya;
Aka-tombō tobu;
Karé shikimi.

Old tomb! — [only] a flitting of red dragon-flies; — some withered [offerings of] shikimi [1] [before the grave]!

Sabishisa wo!
Tombō tobu nari
Haka no uë.

Desolation! — dragon-flies flitting above the graves!

Tombō tondé,
Koto-naki mura no
Hi go nari.

Dragon-flies are flitting, and the noon-sun is shining, above the village where nothing eventful ever happens.

Yūzuki hi
Usuki tombō no
Ha-kagé kana!

O the thin shadow of the dragon-fly's wings in the light of sunset!

Tombō no
Kabé wo kakayuru
Nishi-hi kana!

O that sunlight from the West, and the dragon-fly clinging to the wall!

---

consists of a number of pieces of bamboo, or hard wood, fastened to a rope extended across the field or garden. When the end of the rope is pulled, the pieces of wood rattle loudly.

[1] It is the custom to set sprays of shikimi in bamboo vases before the graves of Buddhist dead. This shikimi is a kind of anise, botanically known as *Illicium religiosum*.

FOLK–LORE GLEANINGS

Tombō toru
Iri-hi ni tori no
Métsuki kana!

O the expression of that cock's eyes in the sunset-light —
trying to catch a dragon-fly!

Tombō no
Mō ya iri-hi no
Issékai.

Dance, O dragon-flies, in your world of the setting sun!

Nama-kabé ni
Yū-hi sasunari
Aka-tombō.

To the freshly plastered wall a red dragon-fly clings in the
light of the setting-sun. [1]

Déru tsuki to
Iri-hi no ai ya —
Aka-tombō.

In the time between the setting of the sun and the rising of
the moon — red dragon-flies.

Yū-kagé ya,
Nagaré ni hitasu
Tombō no o!

The dragon-fly at dusk dips her tail into the running stream.

IV

THE foregoing compositions are by old authors
mostly: few modern hokku on the subject have the
same naïve quality of picturesqueness. The older
poets seem to have watched the ways of the dragon-
fly with a patience and a freshness of curiosity
impossible to this busier generation. They made

---

[1] This is a tiny color-study. The tint of the freshly plastered wall is
supposed to be a warm gray.

verses about all its habits and peculiarities — even
about such matters as the queer propensity of the
creature to return many times in succession to any
spot once chosen for a perch. Sometimes they
praised the beauty of its wings, and compared them
to the wings of devas or Buddhist angels; sometimes they celebrated the imponderable grace of its
hovering — the ghostly stillness and lightness of its
motion; and sometimes they jested about its waspish
appearance of anger, or about the goblin oddity of
its stare. They noticed the wonderful way in which
it can change the direction of its course, or reverse
the play of its wings with the sudden turn that suggested the modern Japanese word for a somersault
— tombogaëri (dragon-fly-turning).[1] In the dazzling
rapidity of its flight — invisible but as a needle-
gleam of darting color — they found a similitude
for impermanency. But they perceived that this
lightning flight was of short duration, and that the
dragon-fly seldom travels far, unless pursued, pre-
ferring to flit about one spot all day long. Some
thought it worth while to record in verse that at
sunset all the dragon-flies flock towards the glow, and
that they rise high in air when the sun sinks below
the horizon — as if they hoped to obtain from the
altitudes one last sight of the vanishing splendor.
They remarked that the dragon-fly cares nothing
for flowers, and is apt to light upon stakes or stones

---

[1] Tombogaëri wo utsu (to throw a dragon-fly-turning) is the Japanese
expression corresponding with our phrase, "to turn a somersault."

rather than upon blossoms; and they wondered what pleasure it could find in resting on the rail of a fence or upon the horn of a cow. Also they marveled at its stupidity when attacked with sticks or stones — as often flying toward the danger as away from it. But they sympathized with its struggles in the spider's net, and rejoiced to see it burst through the meshes. The following examples, selected from hundreds of compositions, will serve to suggest the wide range of these curious studies:

Dragon-Flies and Sunshine

Tombō ya,
Hi no sasu kataë
Taté-yuku!

O dragon-fly! ever towards the sun you rise and soar!

Hiatari no
Doté ya hinémosu
Tombō tobu.

Over the sunlit bank, all day long, the dragon-flies flit to and fro.

Go-roku shaku
Onoga kumoi no
Tombō kana!

Poor dragon-fly! — the [blue] space of five or six feet [above him] he thinks to be his own sky!

Tombō no
Muki wo soroëru
Nishi-hi kana!

Ah, the sunset glow! Now all the dragon-flies are shooting in the same direction.

DRAGON–FLIES

Tombō ya!
Sora é hanarété
Kurékakari.

Dusk approaches: see! the dragon-flies have risen toward the sky!

Hoshi hitotsu
Miru madé asobu
Tombō kana!

O dragon-fly! you continue to sport until the first star appears!

FLIGHT OF DRAGON-FLIES

Tō yama ya,
Tombō tsui-yuki,
Tsui-kaëru.

Quickly the dragon-fly starts for the distant mountain, but as quickly returns.

Yukiōté,
Dochiramo soréru
Tombō kana!

Meeting in flight, how wonderfully do the dragon-flies glance away from each other!

Narabu ka to
Miété wa soréru
Tombō kana!

Lo! the dragon-flies that seemed to fly in line all scatter away from each other.

MENTIONED IN LOVE-SONGS

Kagérō no
Kagé tomo waré wa
Nari ni kéri
Aruka nakika no
Kimi ga nasaké ni.

Even as the shadow of a dragon-fly [1] I have become, by reason of the slightness of your love.

---

[1] The word "kagérō" here means "dragon-fly." There is another

FOLK-LORE GLEANINGS

> Obotsu kana!
> Yumé ka? utsusu ka?
> Kagerō no
> Honoméku yori mo
> Hakanakarishi wa!

O my doubt! Is it a dream or a reality? — more fugitive than even the dim flitting of a dragon-fly! [1]

> Tombō ya!
> Mi wo mo kogasazu,
> Naki mo sézu!

Happy dragon-fly! — never self-consumed by longing — never even uttering a cry!

STRANGENESS AND BEAUTY

> Tombō no
> Kao wa ōkata
> Médama kana!

O the face of the dragon-fly! — almost nothing but eyes!

> Koë naki wo,
> Tombō munen ni
> Miyuru kana!

O dragon-fly! you appear to be always angry because you have no voice!

> Sémi ni makénu
> Hagoromo mochishi,
> Tombō kana!

O dragon-fly! the celestial raiment [2] you possess is nowise inferior to that of the cicada!

---

word "kagérō" meaning "gossamer." Though written alike in Romaji, these two terms are represented in Japanese by very different characters.

[1] The thought suggested is — "Can it be true that we were ever united, even for a moment?"

[2] Literally: "feather-robe" (hagoromo); — this is the name given to the raiment supposed to be worn by the "Sky-People" — angelic inhabitants of the Buddhist heaven. The hagoromo enables its wearer to soar through space; and the poet compares the wings of the beautiful insect to such a fairy robe.

DRAGON-FLIES

LIGHTNESS OF DRAGON-FLIES

Tsubamé yori
Tombō wa mono mo
Ugokasazu.

More lightly even than the swallow does the dragon-fly touch things without moving them.

Tombō ya,
Tori no fumarénu
Éda no saki!

O dragon-fly, you perch on the tip of the spray where never a bird can tread!

STUPIDITY OF DRAGON-FLIES

Utsu-tsuë no
Saki ni tomarishi,
Tombō kana!

O dragon-fly! you light upon the end of the very stick with which one tries to strike you down!

Tachi-kaëru
Tombō tomaru
Tsubuté kana!

See! the dragon-fly returns to perch upon the pebble that was thrown at it!

DRAGON-FLIES AND SPIDERS

Kumonosu no
Atari ni asobu
Tombō kana!

Ah! the poor dragon-fly, sporting beside the spider's web!

Sasagami no
Ami no hazurété,
Tombō kana!

Good dragon-fly! — he has extricated himself from the net of the spider!

FOLK–LORE GLEANINGS

Kumo gaki mo
Yaburu kihoi ya,
Oni-tombō!

Through even the spider's fence he has force to burst his way!
— C the demon dragon-fly!

HEEDLESS OF FLOWERS

Tombō ya!
Hana-no ni mo mé wa
Hosorasézu.

Ah, the dragon-fly! even in the flower-field he never half-shuts his eyes! [1]

Tombō ya!
Hana ni wa yoradé,
Ishi no uë.

O the dragon-fly! — heedless of the flowers, he lights upon a stone!

Tombō ya!
Hana naki kui ni
Sumi-narai.

Ah, the dragon-fly! content to dwell upon a flowerless stake!

Néta ushi no
Tsuno ni hararénu,
Yamma kana!

O great dragon-fly! will you never leave the horn of the sleeping ox?

Kui no saki
Nanika ajiwō
Tombō kana?

O dragon-fly! what can you be tasting on the top of that fence-stake?

---

[1] Alluding to the fact that one half-closes one's eyes — in order to shadow them, and so to see more distinctly — when looking at some beautiful object. Perhaps the rendering, "never makes his eyes narrower," would better express the exact sense of the original.

DRAGON-FLIES

Of course these compositions make but slight appeal to æsthetic sentiment: they are merely curious, for the most part. But they help us to understand something of the soul of the elder Japan. The people who could find delight, century after century, in watching the ways of insects, and in making such verses about them, must have comprehended, better than we, the simple pleasure of existence. They could not, indeed, describe the magic of nature as our great Western poets have done; but they could feel the beauty of the world without its sorrow, and rejoice in that beauty, much after the manner of inquisitive and happy children.

If they could have seen the dragon-fly as we can see it — if they could have looked at that elfish head with its jeweled ocelli, its marvelous compound eyes, its astonishing mouth, under the microscope — how much more extraordinary would the creature have seemed to them! ... And yet, though wise enough to have lost that fresh naïve pleasure in natural observation which colors the work of these quaint poets, we are not so very much wiser than they were in regard to the real wonder of the insect. We are able only to estimate more accurately the immensity of our ignorance concerning it. Can we ever hope for a Natural History with colored plates that will show us how the world appears to the faceted eyes of a dragon-fly?

FOLK-LORE GLEANINGS

V

CATCHING dragon-flies has been for hundreds of years a favorite amusement of Japanese children. It begins with the hot season, and lasts during the greater part of the autumn. There are many old poems about it — describing the recklessness of the little hunters. To-day, just as in other centuries, the excitement of the chase leads them into all sorts of trouble: they tumble down embankments, and fall into ditches, and scratch and dirty themselves most fearfully—heedless of thorns or mud-holes or quag-mires — heedless of heat — heedless even of the dinner-hour:

> Méshi-doki mo
> Modori wasurété,
> Tombō-tsuri!

Even at the hour of the noon-day meal they forget to return home — the children catching dragon-flies!

> Hadaka-go no
> Tombō tsuri-kéri
> Hiru no tsuji!

The naked child has been catching dragon-flies at the road-crossing — heedless of the noon-sun!

But the most celebrated poem in relation to this amusement is of a touching character. It was writ-ten by the famous female poet, Chiyo of Kaga, after the death of her little boy:

266

DRAGON-FLIES

Tombō-tsuri! —
Kyō wa doko madé
Itta yara!

"Catching dragon-flies! . . . I wonder where *he* has gone to-day!"

The verse is intended to suggest, not to express, the emotion of the mother. She sees children running after dragon-flies, and thinks of her own dead boy who used to join in the sport — and so finds herself wondering, in presence of the infinite Mystery, what has become of the little soul. Whither has it gone? — in what shadowy play does it now find delight?

Dragon-flies are captured sometimes with nets, sometimes by means of bamboo rods smeared at the end with birdlime, sometimes even by striking them down with a light stick or switch. The use of a switch, however, is not commonly approved; for the insect is thereby maimed, and to injure it unnecessarily is thought to be unlucky — by reason, perhaps, of its supposed relation to the dead. A very successful method of dragon-fly-catching — practiced chiefly in the western provinces — is to use a captured female dragon-fly as a decoy. One end of a long thread is fastened to the insect's tail, and the other end of the thread to a flexible rod. By moving the rod in a particular way the female can be kept circling on her wings at the full length of the thread; and a male is soon attracted. As soon as he clings to the female, a slight jerk of the rod will

267

bring both insects into the angler's hand. With a single female for lure, it is easy to capture eight or ten males in succession.

During these dragon-fly hunts the children usually sing little songs, inviting the insect to approach. There are many such dragon-fly songs; and they differ according to province. An Izumo song of this class [1] contains a curious allusion to the traditional conquest of Korea in the third century by the armies of the Empress Jingō; the male dragon-fly being thus addressed: "Thou, the male, King of Korea, art not ashamed to flee from the Queen of the East?" In Tōkyō to-day the little dragon-fly hunters usually sing the following:

> Tombō! tombō!
> O-tomari! —
> Ashita no ichi ni,
> Shiōkara kōté,
> Néburashō!

Dragon-fly! dragon-fly! honorably wait! — to-morrow at the market I will buy some shiōkara and let you lick it!

Children also find amusement in catching the larva of the dragon-fly. This larva has many popular names; but is usually called in Tōkyō taiko-mushi, or "drum-insect," because it moves its forelegs in the water somewhat as a man moves his arms while playing upon a drum.

A most extraordinary device for catching dragon-

[1] Cited in *Glimpses of Unfamiliar Japan*, vol. II, p. 36. (Vol. VI of this edition.)

flies is used by the children of the province of Kii. They get a long hair — a woman's hair — and attach a very small pebble to each end of it, so as to form a miniature "bolas"; and this they sling high into the air. A dragon-fly pounces upon the passing object; but the moment that he seizes it, the hair twists round his body, and the weight of the pebbles brings him to the ground. I wonder whether this method of bolassing dragon-flies is known anywhere outside of Japan.

BUDDHIST NAMES OF PLANTS AND ANIMALS

AT one time I hoped to compile a glossary of the Buddhist names given to Japanese animals and plants; and I began to collect material for the work. But I then knew very little about the real difficulties of such an undertaking. To mention only one, I may observe that in almost every province of Japan the folk-speech is different; and the difference appears even in the names given to certain plants, insects, reptiles, fishes, and birds. Such names must be learned, of course, from the lips of peasants and of fishermen; and that which I wished to do could never be well done except through the patient labors of a folk-lore society. And now I find that, instead of being able to prepare the glossary intended, I must content myself with a few general notes upon the subject.

But perhaps these notes — relics of an undertaking for which I possessed neither the requisite scholarship nor the means — will have at least a suggestive worth to future explorers in this unfamiliar region of Far-Eastern folk-lore.

The name Buddha appears in the appellations of several trees and plants. Marubushukan (round-fingers-of-Buddha) is the name of a kind of lemontree — so called from the very remarkable shape of its fruit. The Chinese hibiscus is called Bussōgé (Buddha's mulberry); and a variety of rock-moss is popularly known by the picturesque names of Hotoké-no-tsumé and Bukkōsō — both signifying "finger-nails of Buddha." A kind of yam is called Tsukuné-imo — which appellation, as written with the proper Chinese characters, signifies "Buddha's-hand potato"; and a variety of clover is honored by the name Hotoké-no-za (Buddha's Throne).

Names of Bodhisattvas and of other Buddhist divinities are also to be found in the appellations of plants and animals. The name of Kwannon (Âvalokitesvara) appears in the term Kwannon-chiku (bamboo of Kwannon); and several different plants are known, in different provinces, by the name Kwannon-sō (herb of Kwannon). The name of Fugen (Samantabhadra) has been given to a variety of cherry-tree — the Fugen-zakura (Fugen's cherry-tree). The name of Dai-Mokukenren (Mahamaudgalyâyana) — shortened by popular usage into Mokuren — figures both in the common appellation of the *Ficus pumila*, known as Mokuren, and in that of the *Magnolia conspicua*, usually called Haku-mokuren (white Mokuren). The name of Brahma — known to Japanese Buddhism as Bonten — appears in the designation of a kind of upland rice, Bonten-mai. The memory of Bōdai-Daruma (Bôdhidharma) is preserved in the popular appellation of the *Aster spatufolium*,

271

called Daruma-giku (Daruma's chrysanthemum) —
as well as in the name of the swamp-cabbage, Dar-
uma-sō (Daruma's plant). Two fishes also have been
named after this patriarch: the *Priacanthus nipho-
nius*, which is called Daruma-dai (Daruma's sea-
bream); and the *Synanceia erosa*, popularly known
as Daruma-kasago — "kasago" being properly the
name of the fish scientifically called *Sebastes inermis*.
More curious than any of the above terms, however,
is the popular name for a species of grain weevil, Kokuzō — "Kokuzō" being the Japanese appellation
of the great Bodhisattva Âkâsapratishthita.

The term Bosatsu (Bodhisattva) also appears in
some plant-names. A variety of rose is known as the
Bosatsu-ibara (thorny-rose of the Bodhisattva); and
a kind of rice is called Bosatsu.

The term Rakan (Arhat) forms a prefix to several
plant-names. Rakan-haku (Arhat's oak) is the popular name of the *Thuya dolobrata*. Rakan-shō
(Arhat's pine) is the common appellation of the *Podocarpus macrophylla*; and the name Rakan-maki
(Arhat's maki, "maki" being the Japanese name for
the *Podocarpus chinensis*) has been given to the
umbrella-pine. And the fruit of a tree, of which I cannot find the scientific name, is called in several provinces Rakan, or "the Arhat," because it curiously
resembles in shape the rude stone images of Arhats
set up in temple-gardens.

Kukai, or Kōbōdaishi, the great Japanese patriarch of the Shingon sect, also has a place in this no-

menclature. Kōbō-mugi (wheat of Kōbōdaishi) is a common name for the *Carex macrocephala;* and a variety of chestnut is called Kōbōdaishi-kawazu-no-kuri (the chestnut that Kōbōdaishi did not eat).

Many names of plants or living creatures refer to Buddhist customs, legends, rites, or beliefs. The word "bōzu," "priest" (the origin of our word "bonze") has been attached to several plant-names. No less than three different herbs are known, in different parts of the country, by the name of Bōzugusa (priest-grass). In the dialect of Chikuzen a kind of turtle is called Umi-bōzu (priest of the sea) — a name, by the way, also given to a mythical marine-monster, often represented in Japanese picture-books. The name of the famous Bo-tree of Buddhist tradition has been given in Japan, not only to the *Ficus religiosa,* but also to the *Tilia miqueliana,* popularly called Bōdaijū (Bodhidruma). The great Buddhist festival of the spring equinox, the festival of the Higan (farther shore) has furnished names for two plants which blossom about that time — the Higan-zakura (Higan cherry-tree) (*Prunus miqueliana*), and the Higan-bana, or "Flower of Higan" (*Lycoris radiata*). What we term "Job's Tears" are in Japan called Zuzudama, or Buddhist rosary-beads; and a kind of dove is known — probably because of its markings — as the Zuzukaké-bato (rosary-bearing dove). The *Allium victoriale* is called Gyoja-ninniku (hermit's garlic — "gyōja" being the Bud-

273

dhist term for hermit); and the popular Japanese name for the bleeding-heart is Keman-sō, or "Ke-man-herb" — an appellation probably due to the resemblance of the flower to the Keman, or decoration, placed upon the head of the statue of Buddha. Perhaps the water-arum has the most curious of all such Buddhist appellations: its Japanese name, Kokuzen-sō literally signifies the "small-sitting-in-Dhyâna-meditation-plant."

The word sennin (commonly translated as "genius" or "fairy," but originally meaning Rishi — a being who has acquired supernatural power and unlimited life by force of ascetic practices) occasionally appears in plant-names. A variety of clematis is known as Sennin-sō (fairy-weed); and a kind of cactus has received the grotesque appellation of Sennin-shō (Sennin's palm) — the palm of the hand being referred to.

The Sanscrit term Yaksha, signifying a man-devouring demon, appears in several plant-names under its Japanese form — Yasha. The cone of the *Aldus firma* is picturesquely called Yasha-bushi (Yaksha's joint); and a water-plant is known by the curious name of Yasha-bishaku (Yaksha's ladle).

Very many Japanese names of vegetables, birds, fishes, and insects, have attached to them as a prefix the word "Oni," a Buddhist term for "demon" or "devil" — just as in English folk-speech we have such names for plants and insects as devil's-apron, devil-wood, devil's-fingers, devil's-horse, and devil's-darning-needle. The tiger-lily is known in Japan by the equally fantastic name of Oni-yuri (devil-lily). A species of coix is called Oni-zuzudama (devil's rosary-beads). The bur-marigold is called Oni-bari (devil's needle); and a water-weed, injurious to lotus-cultivation, is popularly termed the Oni-basu (demon-lotus). This prefix of Oni is probably attached to hundreds of folk-names of flora and fauna: I have myself collected no less than seventy-one examples. Nevertheless, few of them are interesting.

The word Kijin, or Kishin, signifying a kind of goblin recognized by Japanese Buddhism, is similarly used as a prefix; — for example, a sort of needle-grass is known as Kishin-sō (goblin-weed). Kijo, another Buddhist word signifying a kind of female goblin, appears in the common name of an orchid — Kijoran (goblin-orchid). Also there is a prefix, Ki — abbreviation of a term for demon or goblin — which sometimes figures in plant-names: the *Pardanthus chinensis*, for instance, is called in Japan Kisen, meaning "goblin-fan." It is worthy of remark that these devilish names are given to vegetables or to animals, not merely because of some ugly or extraordinary shape, but even because of remarkable size. Thus a species of lark is called Oni-hibari (demon-lark) because it happens to be a much larger bird than the common field-lark; and a very large kind of dragon-fly is designated for the same reason Oni-yamma (demon-dragon-fly).

Many Buddhist names, both of creatures and of plants, are ghostly. A pretty green grasshopper is called Hotoké-uma (Buddha-horse); — the head of the insect curiously resembling the head of a horse in shape. But the word "hotoké" also means the spirit of a dead person — all good persons being supposed by popular faith to become Buddhas; — and the real meaning of the name Hotoké-uma is "the horse of the dead." Now during the great three-days' Festival of the Dead in the seventh month, it is believed that many spirits revisit their homes, or their former friends, either with the help of insects or actually in the form of insects. The name of this grasshopper really implies that it is used as a horse by the shadowy visitors. . . . Again, we find the word "shōryō" — a general term for the spirits of ancestors worshiped according to Buddhist rite — coupled with the name of a dragon-fly: Shōryō-yamma (the dragon-fly of the ancestral spirits). Shōrai-tombō (ghost dragon-fly), and Ki-yamma, a term of similar meaning, are names likewise intended to suggest the relation of the insect to the invisible world. Equally weird is the name by which the mole-cricket is known in the dialect of Kyōto — a name probably suggested by the creature's underground life — Shōrai-mushi (ghost-insect). Among appellations of plants one finds also such terms as Yurei-daké (ghost-bamboo), and Yurei-bana (ghost-flower) — the latter name being not inappropriately given to a species of delicate mushroom.

Some of the Buddhist names, although highly interesting in themselves, could not be understood by the Western reader without the help of pictorial illustration, because they have reference to the furniture of temples, or to particular articles used in Buddhist religious service. Such, for example, is the name of a tree popularly known as sankō-matsu (sankō-pine); — the term "sankō" (Sanscrit, vadjra) signifying a brass object — shaped much like the classic representation of a thunderbolt, with prongs at either end — which priests use in certain rites as a symbol of supernatural power. Such also is the name hossugai (hossu-shell), given to the beautiful glass-sponge, *Hyalonema sieboldii*, because of its resemblance to the hossu — a brush or duster of long white hair used in Buddhist religious service. And such, again, is the excellent name of a little insect called the koromo-sémi (priest's robe cicada), because the general form and color of the creature, when resting with closed wings, really suggest the figure of a priest in his "koromo." But unless you had seen the insect, and the kind of "koromo" thus referred to, you could not appreciate the graphic worth of the appellation.

Very remarkable Buddhist names have been given to some species of birds. There is a bird, known to ornithologists as *Eurysotmus orientalis,* which is called "buppōsō," because its cry resembles the sound of the word "buppōsō." This word is a Japanese equivalent for the Sanscrit term "triratna" or "ratnatraya" (three jewels); — the syllable "bu" standing for Butsu (the Buddha); "pō," for hō (the Law); and "sō" for the priesthood. The bird is also called sambōchō (the sambō-bird); — the word "sambō" being a literal translation of triratna. Another bird, of which I do not know the scientific appellation, is called the Jihishinchō (Compassionate-Mind-Bird) — because its call resembles the utterance of the phrase Jihi-shin (Compassionate Mind) which forms one of the epithets of the Buddha. "This bird," my informant writes, "lives only in the neighborhood of Nikkō, where in the summer it may be heard continually crying out, 'O thou Compassionate Mind! — O thou Compassionate Mind!'" ... Almost equally interesting is the common Buddhist name for the hototogisu (*Cuculus poliocephalus*), a species of cuckoo much celebrated by Japanese poets. It is called mujō-dori (the bird of impermanency). This name would not appear to be derived from the bird's note, which is popularly interpreted as "Honzon kakétaka?" — meaning, "Has the honzon yet been suspended?" (The "honzon" is the sacred picture displayed in temples upon the eighth day of the fourth month — a little before the

278

time at which the bird makes its annual appearance.) It seems to me more probable that the name
was given in the signification, "bird of death"; — for
the word "mujō" has also the meaning of death as
change; and this meaning is strongly suggested by
the strange fact that the hototogisu is supposed to
come from the spirit-world. It is also called Tama-
mukaë-dori (the ghost-welcoming bird) because it
is said to meet and to greet the spirits of the dead on
their journey over the Mountain of Shidé to the
River of Souls. There are many ghostly legends and
fancies about the hototogisu; and this weird folk-
lore sufficiently explains why the bird is known in
the provinces by no less than fifty-two different
names!

The uguisu, a variety of nightingale, and the
sweetest-voiced of all Japanese singers, does not
appear to have any popular Buddhist name; but its
flute-like call is said to be an utterance of the word
"Hokkékyō," which is the popular name for the
Saddharma-Pundarîka-Sutra — the grand scripture
of the Nichiren or Hokké sect. And Buddhist piety
asserts that the bird passes its life in chanting the
praise of the Sutra of the Lotus of the Good Law.
So that the uguisu is really regarded as a Buddhist
bird. Another bird which seems to have some relation to Buddhism is the snowy heron, to which the
extraordinary appellation of bonnō-sagi (Bonnō-
heron) has been given. "Bonnō" is a Buddhist
term for worldly desire, lust, passion; and I am

not able to say why it appears in the name of the bird.

The difficulty of guessing at the origin of these Buddhist names cannot even be imagined without the help of examples. The literal meaning, in many cases, serves only to mislead investigation. For instance, the hammer-headed shark is known on parts of the Kyūshū coast by the extraordinary appellation, Nembutsu-bō (Nembutsu-priest). The word "Nembutsu" is the name of the invocation, "Namu Amida Butsu!" (Salutation to the Buddha Amitâbha!) uttered by the pious of many sects as a prayer, and *especially as a prayer for the dead*. The grim suggestiveness of the name Nembutsu-bō reminded me that the modern French word for shark is, according to Littré, only a corruption of "requiem" — the appellation originally implying (as stated by Père Dutertre in 1667) that for the man caught by a shark there was nothing to be done except to chant his requiem. But I was wrong in imagining that the Buddhist name Nembutsu-bō implied something of the same kind. The real meaning of the term is proved by another Buddhist name for the same monster — shumoku-zamé (shumoku-shark). The word "shumoku" signifies a peculiar "T"-shaped mallet with which the priest strikes a gong during the repetition of the Nembutsu and of other prayers. (I may observe that the same kind of mallet is used to sound a gong during the chanting of the Nembutsu, in some pious households, before the family shrine.) It was this use of the mallet and gong, during the repetition of the invocation, that suggested the term Nembutsu-bō as an alternate name for the shumoku-zamé (mallet-shark); — and the true signification of Nembutsu-bō is not "the Nembutsu-priest," but "the priest with the mallet."

SONGS OF JAPANESE CHILDREN

UNDER the influence of twenty-seven thousand public schools the old folk-literature of Japan, the
unwritten literature of song and tradition, is rapidly
passing out of memory. Even within my own recol-
lection one variety of this oral literature, partly
corresponding to our own literature of the nursery,
has been greatly affected by the new order of things.
When I first came to Japan the children were singing
the old songs which they had been taught by their
grandfathers and grandmothers — the home-teach-
ing being usually left to the grandparents. But
to-day the little folk, at play in the streets or in the
temple-courts, are singing new songs learned in the
class-room — songs set to music written according
to the Western scale; — and the far more interesting
pre-Meiji songs are now but seldom heard.

As yet, however, they are not entirely forgotten
— partly because many of them are inseparably
connected with games that cannot be suddenly
superseded — partly because there are still alive
some millions of delightful grandfathers and grandmothers who never studied under organ-playing
schoolmasters, and who like to hear the children
repeat the ditties of long ago. But I suppose that
after these charming old people have been gathered
to their ancestors, most of the songs which they

taught will cease to be sung. Happily the Japanese folk-lorists have been exerting themselves to pre-serve such unwritten literature; and their labors have enabled me to attempt the present paper.

Out of a great number of the old-time child-songs and nonsense-verses, carefully copied and translated for me, I have endeavored to make a fairly represent-ative selection — grouping all the examples under six subject-titles, in the following order:

1. Songs of Weather and Sky.
2. Songs about Animals.
3. Miscellaneous Play-Songs.
4. Narrative Songs.
5. Battledoor and Ball Songs.
6. Lullabies.

The classification is very loose, especially as regards the third group; but I think that it is justified by the strangely indefinite character of many composi-tions.

Of course the plain English renderings can give an idea of the Japanese verses only as flowers pressed and dried between the leaves of a book can represent the living blossoms in their natural environment. The queer rhythm of the rhymeless lines, the naïveté of the Japanese words, the curious little airs — difficult to memorize as bird-warblings — and the sweet freshness of many child-voices chanting in unison: these help to make the true charm of the original song, and all are equally irreproducible.

FOLK–LORE GLEANINGS

A good deal of the exotic may be discovered in these cullings; but the reader will occasionally find something to remind him of familiar nursery-rhymes. Children, all the world over, think and feel in nearly the same way on certain subjects, and sing of like experiences. In almost every country they sing about the sun and the moon — about wind and rain — about birds and beasts — about flowers and trees and brooks; — also about such daily household duties as drawing water, making fire, cooking and washing. Yet I believe that, even within these limits, the differences between Japanese child-literature and other child-literature will be found more interesting than the resemblances.

I

SONGS OF WEATHER AND SKY
(Tōkyō Sunset-song)

Yu-yaké!
Ko-yaké!
Ashita wa tenki ni naré.

Evening-burning!
Little burning!
Weather, be fair to-morrow! [1]

(Kite-flying song — Province of Iga)

engu San,
Kazé okuré!
Kazé ga nakéra
Zéni okuré!

---

[1] This little song is still sung by the children in my neighborhood whenever a beautiful sunset occurs.

SONGS OF JAPANESE CHILDREN

Tengu San [Lord Mountain-Spirit],
Please to give me some wind!
If there be no wind,
Please give some money! [1]

(Rain-song — Province of Tosa)
Amé, amé, furi-yamé!
O-tera no maë no
Kaki no ki no moto dé
Kiji no ko ga nakuzo!

Rain, rain! stop falling! — At the foot of the kaki-tree in
front of the temple, the young of the pheasant is crying!

(Snow-song — Province of Iga)
Yuki wa chira-chira!
Kumo wa hai-daraké!

Snow is fluttering — chira-chira!
The clouds are full of ashes! [2]

(Province of Izumo)
Yuki ya!
Konko ya!
Araré ya!
Konko ya!
Omaë no sédo dé
Dango mo niéru,
Azuki mo niéru,

---

[1] In Tōkyō the little kite-flyers usually sing:
Kazé no kami wa
Yowai na!
("Ah! the God of the Wind is weak to-day!")
In Izumo they sing:
Daisen no yama kara
O-Kazé fuété!
Koi yo!
("Come, August-Wind, and blow from the mountain Daisen!")
[2] White ashes of wood are referred to.

285

FOLK-LORE GLEANINGS

Yamado wa modoru,
Akago wa hoëru,
Shakushi wa miézu,
Yaré isogashiya nā!

Snow-grains! hail-grains! — In your kitchen dumplings are boiling; beans too are boiling; the huntsman is returning; the baby is squalling; the ladle is missing! — O what a flurry and worry!

(Star-song — Province of Iga)

— Hoshi San, Hoshi San!
Hitori-boshi dé dénu monja;
Sen mo, man mo déru monja.

— Mr. Star, Mr. Star!
For a single star to rise alone is not right;
Even a thousand, even ten thousand should rise together! [1]

(Moon-song — Province of Shinano)

O-Tsuki Sama,
Kwannon-dō orité,
Mamma agaré!
— Mamma wa iya-iya:
Ammo nara mitsu kuryō!

— O Lady Moon,
Come down from over the Temple of Kwannon,
And help yourself to some boiled rice!
— Rice? no! I do not like rice.
But if you have ammochi,[2] let me have three!

(Province of Kii)

— O-Tsuki Sama, ikutsu?
— Jiu-san hitotsu.
— Sorya mada wakai:
Waka-buné é notté,
Kara madé wataré!

---

[1] Sung when the first stars begin to twinkle after sundown.
[2] Rice-cakes stuffed with a mixture of sugar and bean-flour.

SONGS OF JAPANESE CHILDREN

— Lady Moon, how old are you?
— Thirteen and one.
— That is still young:
In the Ship of Youth embarking,
Cross over the sea to China!

(Province of Tosa)

— O-Tsuki Sama
Momo-iro!
— Daré ga iuta?
— Ama ga iuta.
— Ama no kuchi wo
Hikisaké!

— O Lady Moon, your face is the color of a peach! — Who
said so? — A nun said so. — Pinch and tear the mouth of that
nun!

(Province of Suwō)

O-Tsuki Sama,
O-Tsuki Sama,
Mōshi! mōshi! —
Néko to nézumi ga,
Isshō-daru sagèté,
Fuji-no-yama wo
Ima koëta!

O Lady Moon!
O Lady Moon!
I say! I say!
A cat and a rat,
Carrying a one-shō barrel [of saké],
The Mountain of Fuji
Just now crossed over! [1]

---

[1] Sung when a cloud passes over the Moon. The cat and the rat are
playful goblins, of course — such as figure in children's picture-books.
The purpose of the song is to make the Moon peep out again.

An Izumo moon-song, more interesting than any of these, will be
found in my *Kokoro*, p. 321, vol. VII of this edition.

FOLK–LORE GLEANINGS

II

SONGS ABOUT ANIMALS [1]

Of child-songs about insects and reptiles, birds and beasts, the number is surprising — almost every Japanese village having one or two songs of its own belonging to this class. The great majority are brief compositions of from two to eight lines. Some of the better ones recall English nursery-rhymes on kindred topics — such nursery-rhymes, for example, as, "Bat, bat, come under my hat!" — "Lady-bird, lady-bird, fly away home!" — "Cuckoo, cuckoo, what do you do?" — "A pie sat on a pear-tree," etc., etc. Very probably several of the following selections are older than most of our nursery-rhymes. Variants of nearly all exist in multitude.

(*Dove-song — Tōkyō*)

Hato
Poppō!
Mamé ga tabétai.[2]

"*Poppō*," says the dove — "I want to eat some beans."

(*Crow-song — Tōkyō*)

Karasu!
Karasu!
Kanzaburō!
Oya no on wo wasuréna yo!

O crow! O crow! Kanzaburō! [3] — never forget the goodness of your parents!

---

[1] See also, for a small collection of Izumo songs relating to natural history, the chapter "In a Japanese Garden," in my *Glimpses of Unfamiliar Japan*, vol. II, vol. VI of this edition.

[2] Or kuétai.

[3] Kanzaburō is a very common form of masculine proper name —

288

SONGS OF JAPANESE CHILDREN

(*Owl-song — Tōkyō*)

Gorosuké-hōkō
Muda-bōkō!

Gorosuké's service, useless service!

(*Bird-song — Province of Isé*)

Suzumé wa, Chū-Chū-Chūzaburō!
Karasu wa, Ka-Ka-Kanzaburō!
Tombi wa, Toyama no kanétataki!
Ichi nichi tataité; —
Komé isshō!
Awa isshō!

As for the sparrow — Chū-Chū-Chūzaburō,
As for the crow — Ka-Ka-Kanzaburō;
As for the kite [1] — the Bell-Ringer of Toyama:
All day he taps his bell,
[Crying] Rice, one shō! [2]
Millet, one shō!

The personal names Kanzaburō, Chūzaburō, and Gorosuké, are common names of men. No doubt that the sparrow's sharp cry, resembling the sound "chū," first suggested the use of the name Chūzaburō in the foregoing nursery-rhyme; and the crow was probably called Kanzaburō because its caw sounds like the syllable "Ka." [3] But there is a

here probably given to the bird merely for the sake of the sound. — The song was no doubt suggested by the old proverb, "Karasu ni hampo no kō ari": "The filial duty of feeding one's parents is known even to the crow." It is said that the old crows, unable to forage for themselves, are fed by their offspring. Children sing this song when they see the crows flying home at sundown.

[1] Another version reads, "Tobi wa, Tō-Tō-Tōzaburō." Tōzaburō, like Chūzaburō and Kanzaburō, is a real name.

[2] One shō is equal to about a quart and a half.

[3] I may observe also that the crow is popularly said to cry, Kawa!

curious legend about the name given to the owl — Gorosuké. A long time ago, in the house of some great samurai, there was a retainer called Gorosuké. This Gorosuké was naturally dull; and the very first time that a duty of importance was confided to him, he made such a blunder that serious mischief resulted. Therefore everybody laughed at him, and put him to shame; and at last he killed himself. Then his spirit took the form of the little owl which now bears his name; and all night long this owl cries out, in a tone of utter despair:

"Gorosuké's service!
Useless service!"

(*Hare-song — Tōkyō*)

"Usagi, usagi,
Nani wo mité hanéru?"
"Jiu-go-ya no O-Tsuki Sama
Mité hanéru!
Hyoi!
Hyoi!"

— "Hare, hare! what do you see that makes you jump?" — "Seeing the Lady-Moon of the fifteenth night, I jump! — Hyoi! hyoi!" [1]

(*Sparrow-song — Tōkyō*)

Suzumé no atsumari:
Chi-ī, chi-ī — pappa!
Daré ni atattémo
Okoruna yo!

---

kawa! (River! river!) — meaning, "Let us go to the river!" The sound of the cawing really resembles the sound of the word "Kawa."

[1] At the words "hyoi! hyoi!" all the singers jump together.

SONGS OF JAPANESE CHILDREN

Okorunara hajimé kara
Yoran ga yoi.

Hear the gathering of the sparrows! — chi-ī, chi-ī, — pappa! [1]
— Be not so angry with everybody who happens to touch you!
Better in the beginning not to have come at all, than to get
angry thus!

(Song about the white heron — Province of Isé)

Shirosagi, shirosagi,
Nazé kubi ga nagai?
— Hidaruté nagai.
— Hidarukya ta uté.
— Ta ucha, doro ga tsuᴋu.
— Doro ga tsukya, haraë.
— Haraya, itai.

— White-heron, white-heron! why is your neck so long? —
Because of hunger it became long. — If you are hungry, go and
till the rice-field. — I should get muddy if I were to till the
rice-field. — If you get muddy, you can brush the mud off. —
If I should brush myself, it would hurt me!

(Toad-song — Province of Tosa)

Hiki-San, Hiki San, dété gonsé
Denya mogusa suéru-zo!

Toad, toad, come out of your hole! If you don't come out I
shall give you a moxa!

(Kite-song — Province of Izumo)

Tobi! tobi! mauté misé!
Ashita no ban ni,
Karasu ni kakushité,
Nezumi yaru!

Kite! kite! let me see you dance! To-morrow evening, without letting the crows see it, I shall give you a rat!

---

[1] Chi-ī is an onomatope invented to describe the angry chirping of
the sparrow; pappa signifies the sound of the quick flapping of its wings.

FOLK–LORE GLEANINGS

(Bat-song — Province of Izumo)

Komori, koi! saké nomashō!
Saké ga nakya, taru furashō.

Bat, come hither, and you will drink some saké! If there be no saké [ready], I will pour out some from the barrel.

(Firefly-song — Province of Izumo)

Hotaru koi midzu nomashō:
Achi no midzu wa nigai zo;
Kochi no midzu wa amai zo;
Amai hō é tondé koi!

Firefly, come hither, and you shall have water to drink! Yonder the water is bitter; — here the water is sweet! Come, fly this way, to the sweet side!

(Firefly song — Province of Isé)

Hotaru, koi!
Tsuchi-mushi, koi!
Onoga hikari dé
Jō mottékoi!

Firefly, come hither!
Earth-insect,[1] come!
By your own light
Bring me a letter!

(Tōkyō)

O-wata, koi! koi!
Mamé kuwashō!
O-mamma ga iyanara,
Toto kuwashō!

Come here, o-wata![2] come here! I will give you beans to eat. If there be no boiled rice, then I will give you some fish.

---

[1] Tsuchi-mushi, literally, is "earth-insect" or "earth-worm"; but in this little song it probably means "glow-worm."

[2] The name "o-wata" (honorable cotton) is given to a small purplish fly having a fluffy white protuberance on its tail, resembling a tuft of cotton.

SONGS OF JAPANESE CHILDREN

(Butterfly-song)

Chōchō! chōchō!
Na no ha ni tomaré!
Na no ha ga iyénara,
Té ni tomaré!

Butterfly! butterfly! light upon the na-leaf![1] If you do not like the na-leaf, perch upon my hand!

(Tōkyō song)

Chōchō, tombō mo,
Tori no uchi,
Yama saëzuru no wa,
Matsumushi,
Suzumushi,
Kutsuwamushi,
Ō-chōko choï no choï!

The butterfly, and the dragon-fly, too, at the house of the bird. Oh, the twittering in the mountains! The pine-insect, the bell-insect, the bridle-bit-insect all together — Ō-chōko choï no choï!

(Sung by children chasing dragon-flies)

Achi é yuku to,
Yemma ga niramu;
Kochi é kuru to,
Yurushité yaru zo.

— If you go that way,[2] Yemma [*or* Emma] will glare at you! — if you come this way, I promise to forgive you!

---

[1] The name "na" is given to several different kinds of vegetables; but the Japanese turnip is probably here referred to. This song is sung in nearly all parts of Japan.
[2] Yama, King of Death.

FOLK-LORE GLEANINGS

(Dragon-fly-song — Tōkyō)

Shio ya!
Kané ya!
Yamma kaësé! [1]

Salt dragon-fly! — Black dragon-fly! — give us back the big dragon-fly!

(Snail-song — Tōkyō)

Maimaitsubura!
O-yuya no maë ni
Kenkwa ga aru kara
Tsuno dasé, yari dasé!

O snail! there is a fight in front of the bath-house: so put out your horns, put out your spears!

(Frog-song — Tōkyō)

Kaëru ga
Naku kara kaërō!

Since the frogs are crying, I shall take leave.[2]

(Snail-song — Province of Shinano)

Tsubu, tsubu, yama é yuké.
— Orya iya da! — waré yuké!
Kyonen no haru mo ittaréba,
Karasu to mōsu kurodori ga,
Achi é tsutsuki tsun-mawashi,
Kochi é tsutsuki tsun-mawashi; —
Ni-do to yukumai ano yama é!

— River-snail, river-snail, go to the mountain! — I? not I! Go yourself if you want to! When I went there in the spring of last year, the black bird that is called "crow" pecked me and turned me over on one side, and then pecked me again and

---

[1] This song is very old. Some account of the insects referred to will be found in the preceding paper on dragon-flies!

[2] In this little song there is a play on the word "kaëru," which, as pronounced, might mean either "to return" or "frog." Kaërō is a future form of the verb.

294

turned me over on the other side. Not twice do I go to that mountain!

(*Song about the cicada called Tsuku-tsuku-bōshi* [1] — *Province of Chikuzen*)

> Tsuku-tsuku-bō-San na,
> Nanyu naku ka? —
> Oya ga nai ka?
> Ko ga nai ka?
> — Oya mo gozaru,
> Ko mo gozaru;
> Oitoshi tonogo wo
> Mottaréba,
> Takajo ni torarété;
> Kyō nanuka.
> Nanuka to omoëba —
> Shijiu-ku nichi!
> Shijiu-ku nichi no
> Zeni-kané wo
> Dōshité tsukōtana
> Yokarō ka?
> Takai komé kōté,
> Funé ni tsumu;
> Yasui komé kōté,
> Funé ni tsumu.
> Funé wa, doko funé?
> Ōsaka-buné.
> Ōsaka-buné koso
> Né ga yokéré.

— Tsuku-tsuku-bō-San, wherefore do you cry? Have you no parents? — have you no children? — Parents I have, children also I have; but my good husband was snatched away from me by a falconer; and to-day is the seventh day since his death. Nay — I thought it was the seventh day, — it is already the forty-ninth! [2] What will be the best way to spend the money

---

[1] See article "Sémi" in my *Shadowings, ante,* p. 45, for some account of this curious insect.

[2] There is a reference here to the Buddhist services for the dead held on the seventh and forty-ninth days after interment.

of the forty-ninth day? — Buying dear rice, to freight a ship; — buying cheap rice, to freight a ship. — As for the ship, where is it from? — It is an Ōsaka ship. — Ah! the cost of an Ōsaka ship is indeed very high!

III

MISCELLANEOUS PLAY-SONGS

OF play-songs — songs to be sung with various out-door or in-door games — the number is very great: my own collection includes upwards of two hundred pieces. Some take the form of stories; others, of dialogues; others belong to that class which the French call "chanson énumérative," or "randonnée": a few are impossible to classify. And some of the most remarkable are so very queer — so utterly unlike anything sung by Western children — that any translation of them would remain, even with the aid of a multitude of notes, unintelligible to readers unfamiliar with Japanese life. But I think that the following series of examples will sufficiently serve to indicate the oddity and the variety of this category of child-songs.

(*Sung to a crying child*)

Naki-mushi! ké-mushi!
Hasandé sutérō!

Cry-insect! — hairy-insect! [i.e., caterpillar] — with a pair of chop-sticks we will throw you out of doors! [1]

---

[1] Alluding to the Japanese method of catching and removing a centipede, caterpillar, or other unpleasant visitor, with a pair of iron chop-sticks, or fire-tongs.

296

SONGS OF JAPANESE CHILDREN

(Sung to a child afraid of being away from home)

Inoru! inoru!
Inagasaki ni oni ga iru!
Ato miriya ja ga iru!

Wants to go home! — wants to go home! On the going-home way [1] a demon is waiting; and if you look behind you will see a dragon!

(Dance-song)

Rengé no hana hiraita,
Hiraita, hiraita!
Hiraita to omōtara
Yatokosa to tsubonda!

The lotus-flower has opened, has opened, has opened! — Even as I thought that it had opened — lo! yatokosa! — it has closed up again! [2]

(Play-song)

Uméboshi-San
To iu hito wa,
Ashi kara kao madé
Shiwa-yotté —
　　　　Shiwa-yotté!
Aré wa sui,
Koré wa sui, —
　　　　Sui, sui, sui!

The person called Mr. Pickled-Plum is wrinkled all over from feet to face — wrinkled all over! Sour on that side! sour on this side! — sour, sour, sour!

(Play-song)

Chinkan-chinkara!
Kajiya no ko;

---

[1] There is a play upon words here not possible to render in English.

[2] This Song of the Lotus is sung by a company of children who form a circle, or dancing-round, all holding hands, and facing inwards. As the song begins the circle is slowly widened; but at the word "yatokosa" all run in together — closing up the round with a simultaneous pull.

FOLK-LORE GLEANINGS

Hadaka dé tobidasu,
Furoya no ko [1] . . .

Clink! clank! — the child of the blacksmith!
Jumping out naked — the child of the bath house!

(Play-song)

"Kaji-don! Kaji-don!
Hi hitotsu gosharé!"
"Hi wa nai, nai ya!
Ano yama koëté,
Kono yama koëté,
Hi wa koko, koko ni aru!"

"Sir Smith! Sir Smith!
Please give us a little fire."
"Fire I have none, none at all.
Crossing over that mountain,
Crossing over this mountain,
Fire then you will find here." [2]

(Dance-song)

Naka no, naka no
Kobotoké wa,
Nazé mata kaganda?
Oya no hi ni
Ébi tabété,
Soré de mata
Kaganda.

— The little Buddha in the middle [of the dancing-circle], the little Buddha in the middle — why does he remain thus always bent? — On the anniversary of his parents' death, he ate shrimps: [3] therefore he remains thus always bent.

---

[1] This appears to be a fragment of some "enumerative song," in which different trades and occupations are referred to.

[2] This song is sung in accompaniment to an ingenious and difficult finger-play — not altogether unlike our nursery-game of "Dance, Thumbkin, dance!" — but much more complicated; both hands being used.

[3] On the anniversary of a parent's death, and during the Festival of the Dead, no good Buddhist should eat fish of any kind.

SONGS OF JAPANESE CHILDREN

(Another version)

Mawari, mawari no
Kobotoké wa,
Nazé sé ga hikui?
Oya no hi ni
Toto kutté,
Soré dé sé ga
Hikui sō na.

— The little Buddha in the middle of the dancing-round, the little Buddha in the middle — why is his stature thus low? — Having eaten fish upon the anniversary of his parents' death, therefrom his stature remains low.

(Centipede-dance — Province of Kii)

Yurasu ya mukadé!
Atama wa cha-usu;
O wa hiko-hiko yo!

The centipede moves — shivery-shaky! The head is like a rice-mortar; — the tail goes *hiko-hiko* [wiggle-waggle]! [1]

(Dance-song — Izumo)

Jizō-San! Jizō-San!
Omaë no mizu-wo
Dondo to kundé,
Matsu-ba ni irété,
Makkuri-kaëta! [2]

Jizō-San, Jizō-San! plentifully drawing the water of your well, round and round we stir it with pine-leaves, until it spills over.

---

[1] This Centipede-Dance is performed by a number of children in line — each grasping the girdle of the one before him; while the leader holds in his hand some object shaped like a tea-mortar, to represent the centipede's head. The real tea-mortar would probably prove much too heavy for the sport.

[2] This is usually sung by little girls. The singers at first stand face to face, in couples, holding hands as they sing. At the words "makkuri-kaëta," they turn about, without loosing the clasp, so as to come back to back.

FOLK-LORE GLEANINGS

Ichi ga saita,
Ni ga saita,
San ga saita,
Shi ga saita,
Go ga saita,
Roku ga saita,
Shichi ga saita,
Hachi ga saita,
Kumabachi ga saita,
Tōkagé ga saita!

One stings! [here one child lays his right hand upon the right hand of a playfellow] — *two* stings! [left hand upon the right] — *three* stings! [left hand upon the left] —*four* stings! [undermost right hand brought up and laid on] —*five* stings! [same manœuvre by the other player] — *six* stings! — *seven* stings! — the BEE [1] stings! [here the one whose hand is uppermost pinches the other's hand] — the WASP stings! [retaliation] — the LIZARD bites! [a very hard pinch.]

(Game-song)

"Koko wa doko no hoso-michi ja?"
"Tenjin-San no hoso-michi ja."
"Chotto tōshité kudanshansé!"
"Goyō no nai mono tōshimasénu."
"Tenjin-San é gwan-kakété,
  Ofuda osamé ni mairimasu."
"Omaë no uchi wa doko jaina?"
"Hakoné no o-séki degozarimas."
"Sonnara tōyaré, tōyaré!
  Yuki wa yoi-yoi
  Kaëri wa kowai!"

"This narrow road, where does it go?" — "This narrow road is the Road of the God Tenjin." — "I pray you, allow me to pass for a moment." — "No one must pass who has no business to pass." — "Having made a vow to the God Tenjin, I want to

---

[1] Hachi, as pronounced, may mean either "eight" or "bee."

pass to present an *ofuda*." [1] — "Where is your house?" —
"My house is at the barrier [2] of Hokoné." — "Pass, then! pass!
Going, all will be well for you; but coming back you will have
reason to be afraid."

(*Game-song — Izumo*)

"Kona ko yoi ko da!
Doko no ko da?"
"Tonya Hachibei no otomusumé."
"Nanto yoi ko da!
Kiyō na ko da!
Kiyō ni sodatété
Kita hodo ni
Oya ni jikkwan,
Ko ni go kwan,
Semété O-Baba ni
Shijiu-go kwan."
"Shijiu-go kwan no o-kané wo
Nani ni suru?"
"Yasui komé kōté,
Funé ni tsumi:
Funé wa shirokané,
Ro wa kogané.
Saasā osé-osé
Miyako madé."
"Miyako modori ni
Nani morota?"
"Ichi-ni kōgai,
Ni-ni kagami,
San-ni sarasa no
Obi morota."
"Kukété kudasaré,
O-Baba San!"
"Kukyō — kukyō,
To omoëdomo,

---

[1] Ofuda, a holy text, either written on paper, or stamped upon wood.
[2] Hakoné no seki. There used to be a military guard-house at
Hakoné, where all travelers had to give an account of themselves
before proceeding farther.

FOLK-LORE GLEANINGS

Obi ni michikashi,
Tasuki ni nagashi."
"Yamada Yakushi no
Kané no o ni."

— "This child is a fine child! — whose child is she?" —
"She is the youngest daughter of Hachibei, the wholesale merchant." — "O what a fine child! O what a clever child! Because she has been so well brought up, I shall give to the parents
ten kwan,[1] and to the child five kwan, and to the grandmamma
not less than forty-five kwan." — "With so much money as
forty-five kwan, what will you do?" — "Cheap rice I will buy,
and load it on a boat. The boat is of silver; the oar is of gold. . . .
Saasā! [Hearty now!] — row hard till we get to the Capital!"
— "What presents have you brought us on your return from
the Capital?" — "Firstly, a hair-pin of tortoise-shell. Secondly,
a mirror. Thirdly, a girdle of sarasa." [2] — "Please sew it,
grandmamma." — "Though I thought to sew it — though I
thought to sew it, it is too short for a girdle; it is too long for a
tasuki [3]-cord." — "Then I will offer it up as a bell-rope for the
bell of [the temple of] Yakushi [4] at Yamada."

(Game-song)

"Kozō, kozō!
Ko hitori gosharé!"
"Dono ko ga hoshikéra?"
"Ano ko ga hoshii wa."
"Nani soété yashinau?"
"Tai soété yashinau."

---

[1] One kwan was equal to a thousand copper-cash in old times. The
value of the present given to the grandmother reminds one of the fact
that, in a Japanese family, the early training of the children is usually
left to the grandparents, and especially to the grandmother.

[2] Sarasa is a kind of calico, or chintz.

[3] Tasuki, a cord used to tie back the long sleeves of the Japanese
robe during working-hours.

[4] Yakushi is the Japanese form of the name Bhaishagyaraga. (Bhaishagyaraga literally signifies "The Medical King.") Yakushi, or
Yakushi-Nyōrai, is a very popular Buddhist divinity in Japan — and
is especially prayed to as a healing Buddha.

"Soré wa honé ga atté ikénu."
"Sonnara tai ga honé nara,
 Ika soété yashinau."
"Soré wa mushi no dai-doku."
"Sonnara Tono-San no nikai dé
 Mōsén shiite ténarai sashozō."
"Té ga yogorété ikénu."
"Sonnara Tono-San no nikai dé
 Mōsén shiité satō mochi."
"Sonnara yaruzō!"

"Acolyte, acolyte, please give me one child!" — "Which child do you wish to have?" — "That child I want to have." — "With what kind of food will you feed the child?" — "With tai-fish I will feed the child." — "That will not do — there are too many bones." — "Then, as there are too many bones in tai-fish, I will feed the child with cuttle-fish." — "That would be very bad for the stomach of the child." — "Then, in the house of the lord, upstairs, I will spread a rug, and teach the child to write." — "That will not do: it would make the child's hands dirty." — "Then in the house of the lord, upstairs, I will spread a rug, and give sugar-cakes to the child." — "Very well, I will let you have the child."

(New-Year song)

Senzō ya! manzō!
O-funé ya gichiri ko,
Gichiri, gichiri, kogéba,
O-Ébisu ka? Daikoku ka?
Kocha fuku no kami!

A thousand ships! ten thousand ships! Hear the August [Treasure-] Ship coming — gichiri, gichiri, gichiri, as they row! Is it the God Ebisu? is it the God Daikoku? — Hither come the Gods of Good Fortune.

(Old Tōkyō Songs of the Bon-Festival)

I

Bon no jiu-roku nichi
A-sobasénu oya wa,

FOLK-LORE GLEANINGS

Ki-Butsu, Kana-Butsu,
Ishi-Botoké!
Ishi-Botoké!

The parents who will not let their children play on the sixteenth day of the [month of the] Bon-Festival — they are
wooden Buddhas — they are metal Buddhas — they are Buddhas of stone, Buddhas of stone!

II

Bon, Bon, Bon no
Jiu-roku nichi,
O-Emma Sama yé
Maërō to shitara,
Zuzu no o ga kirété,
Hanao ga kirété,
Namu Shaka Nyōrai!
Té dé ogamu,
Té dé ogamu!

If we go to [visit the temple of] the August Lord Emma,[1] on
the sixteenth day of the Bon, Bon, Bon, the string of the praying beads having been broken, and the thong of the sandal
having been burst, Namu Shaka Nyōrai![2] [we cry] — and pray
with hands joined, and pray with hands joined.

III

"O-Bon ga kita kara
Kamiyuté okuré."
"Shimada ga yoi ka?
Karako ga yoi ka?"
"Shimada mo iya yo!
Karako mo iya yo!

---

[1] Yama, the King of Death. His festival is held on the sixteenth day
of the seventh month, after the three days' Festival of the Dead —
usually called the "Bon."

[2] "Hail to the Tathâgata, Sakyamuni!" — an invocation uttered, by
the members of certain Buddhist sects, on all occasions of distress. It
is believed to be a bad omen for the thong of one's sandal to break.

SONGS OF JAPANESE CHILDREN

O-Édo dé hayaru
O-sagé-gami!"

"Now that the Bon-festival has come, please to dress my hair." — "Will the Shimada-style [1] suit you? — or will the Karako [2] style suit you?" — "No, I will not have my hair dressed in the Shimada-style, nor will I have it dressed in the Karako style. The honorable sagé-gami [3] style is now the fashion in the noble city of Yedo."

IV

Ichi no maru koëté,
Ni no maru koëté,
San no maru saki yé
Hori-ido hotté,
Hori wa, hori-ido:
Tsurubé wa kogané;
Kogané no saki yé
Tombō ga tomatté;
Yaré, soré tombō!
Soré, soré tombō!
Tobanakya hané wo
Kirigirisu!
Kiriko ga tōrō,
Kiriko ga tōrō!
Kiriko ga tōrō wa,
Donata no saiku?
O-Akashi Sama no
O-té zaiku,
O-té zaiku!

Crossing the innermost line of fortification [4] — crossing the

---

[1] The Shimada-style is the fashion in which a bride's hair is dressed.

[2] The Karakowagé was an old-fashioned style of coiffure — probably as the name implies, of Chinese origin; the literal meaning of the term being "Chinese-child-coiffure."

[3] The term sagé-gami means loose-flowing hair. Anciently noble ladies wore their hair thus.

[4] The lines of defense about a Japanese castle are counted from within outwards.

305

second line of fortification — at the end of the third line of fortification dug a well, a moat and a well. The well-bucket is of gold. On the top of the golden bucket a dragon-fly alighted. Oh! that dragon-fly! that dragon-fly! If it does not fly, its wings shall be cut off.[1] — O the kiriko-lanterns! [2] — O the kiriko-lanterns — who made the kiriko-lanterns? Our august Lord Akashi made them with his own august hand, with his own august hand.

v

> Nagai, nagai,
> Ryōgoku-bashi nagai!
> Nagai Ryōgoku-bashi
> Suzumi ni détara,
> O-ko-sama-gata ga
> Yakata no funé dé,
> Hikuya, kataruya,
> Yaré omoshiroya,
> Yaré omoshiroya!
> Bon-odori!

Long, long — the Ryōgoku Bridge is long. Had you gone there to get cool, on the long Ryōgoku Bridge, oh! to see the honorable children in the pleasure-boats, and to hear the musicians, and the reciters! — how pleasant it was, how pleasant! — and the festival dance, too — the Bon-Odori!

vi

> Yanagi no shita no
> Oshidori-Sama wa
> Asahi ni terarété,
> O-iro ga kuroi; —
> O-iro ga kurokirya
> Ganguri-gasa o-sashi.
> Ganguri-gasa iya yo!

---

[1] There is here an untranslatable play of words — the term "kiri-girisu," which is the name of a cricket, being used for the verb "kiri," to cut.

[2] This is given to a kind of four-sided or polygonal lantern.

SONGS OF JAPANESE CHILDREN

Ganguri-gasa iya yo!
O-Édo dé hayaru
Ja-no-mé gasa,
Ja-no-mé-gasa!

Under the willow-tree
Sir Mandarin-Duck
Being shone upon by the morning sun,
His honorable color is dark.
If the honorable complexion be dark,
Spread a ganguri-umbrella. [1]
A ganguri-umbrella I will not have!
A ganguri-umbrella I will not have!
Now in the honorable city of Yedo, is fashionable
The Serpent's-Eye umbrella,[2]
The Serpent's-Eye umbrella.

VII

Konata no yashiki wa
Kirei na yashiki —
Oku no ma dé samisen,
Naka no ma dé odori wo,
Daidoko ma demo
Fué taiko! fué taiko!

This residence of yours is a fine residence — with a samisen
playing in the best back-room, and dancing going on in the
middle-room, and even in the kitchen a flute and drum, a flute
and drum!

(*Tōkyō play-song*)

"Ōyama no,
Ōyama no
O-Kon San wa
Doko ittaka?"

---

[1] Ganguri-gasa. I do not know what kind of umbrella was thus called.
[2] A paper umbrella painted black, all but a band some four or five
inches from the top, so that when the umbrella is opened, this white
ring with the black space which it encloses, resembles in form a serpent's
eye.

FOLK-LORE GLEANINGS

"Tonari é
O-imo tabéni ikimashita."
"Ō-okashii! ō-okashii!"

"O-Kon San of Oyama — where has she gone?" — "She went next door, to eat some potatoes." — "How very, very strange! — how very, very strange!" [1]

(Tōkyō play-song)
Mukō no yama no
Sumotori-bana wa
Enyaraya to hikéba,
O-té-té ga kiréru —
O-té-té no kiréta
O-kusuri nai ka?
Aka no mo aru,
Shiroi no mo aru.
Onaji-ku naréba
Akai no ni shō yo!

When [with a cry of] Enyaraya! we pull the violets [2] of yonder mountain, our hands get torn. Is there no medicine for the torn hand? Red medicine there is, and also white. — If the two medicines are equally good, then I shall certainly take the red.

(Dialogue song — Province of Izumo)
"Mūkō no yama no
Kawazu ga naku ga!
Nashité naku ka?
Samuté naku ka?
Himoji té naku-ka?
Himojikya ta tsukuré."

---

[1] This song belongs to a game of hide-and-seek, played by girls.

[2] Literally, the "wrestler's-flower" — so called because of a game played with violet-flowers. Two children each take a violet, twist the heads of their flowers together, and pull the stalks in opposite directions until one of them breaks. The player whose violet breaks first is the loser. Perhaps the reader will be reminded of our "wishing-bone" sport; but in the Japanese play the flowers are supposed to represent wrestlers.

SONGS OF JAPANESE CHILDREN

"Ta tsukuriya kitanai."
"Kitanakya araë."
"Arauya tsumétai."
"Tsumétakya ataré."
"Atarya atsui."
"Atsukya shizaré."
"Shizara nomi ga kū."
"Nomi ga kūya korosé."
"Korosha kawai!"
"Kawaikya daitèné."
"Daiténérya nomi ga kū."
"Nomi ga kūya korosé." . . .
Etc., etc.

"The frogs of yonder mountain cry. Why do they cry? Is it for cold that they cry? Is it for hunger that they cry? If you are hungry, till the rice-field." — "It is dirty work, to till the rice-field." — "If it be dirty work, wash." — "It is cold, to wash." — "If it be cold, warm yourselves by the fire." — "It is too hot by the fire." — "If it be too hot, go farther away." — "If we go farther away, the fleas will bite us." — "If the fleas bite you, kill them." — "It is too pitiful to kill the poor things." — "If you pity them so much, embrace them, and sleep with them." — "If we embrace the fleas and sleep with them, they will bite us." — "If the fleas bite you, kill them," etc., etc.

By far the strangest thing in this part of my collection is a kind of metaphysical dialogue, chanted by children as a play-song! It probably survives from the period when the teaching of children was chiefly intrusted to the Buddhist priesthood, and when almost every Buddhist temple was also a school, or had some kind of a school attached to it. There is nothing very remarkable about the composition itself: it is only the choice of subject — an astonishing subject for a play-song — that makes the thing seem strange to a Western mind.

FOLK-LORE GLEANINGS

This subject is the infinity of Jizō Bosatsu (the Bodhisattva Kshitigarbha), whose smiling images may be seen by almost every roadside, and in countless Buddhist cemeteries. Often at cross-roads, and still more often in graveyards, you will find, instead of a single statue of Jizō, six images in a row — each figure bearing a different mystical emblem. These Six Jizō, or Roku-Jizō, symbolize the teaching that Jizō Bosatsu, self-multiplied, at once exercises his saving pity in all the Six Spheres of Sentient Existence — that is to say throughout the entire Universe of Forms. But, according to the higher Buddhism, "there is no being besides Buddha, and no Buddha besides being." All the Buddhas and the Bodhisattvas are veritably but One; — all substance, all life, all mind is but One. And Jizō of the Six States of Existence is not only a multiple manifestation of the Absolute: he also *is* the Absolute. . . . To find these conceptions embodied in a child's play-song is somewhat startling; but there are many things quite as startling to be met with in the old popular literature of Buddhism:

(Province of Matsu)

Hashi no shita ni Roku-Jizō
Nezumi ni atama wo kajirarété,
— Nezumi koso Jizō da!
— Nezumi Jizō dara,
Nanishini neko ni torarébéna?
— Neko koso Jizō yo!
— Neko wa Jizō dara,
Nanishini inu ni torarébéna?

SONGS OF JAPANESE CHILDREN

— Inu koso Jizō yo!
— Inu wa Jizō dara,
Nanishini ōkami ni torarébéna?
— Ōkami koso Jizō yo!
— Ōkami Jizō dara,
Nanishini hi ni makarébéna?
— Hi koso Jizō yo!
— Hi wa Jizō dara,
Nanishini mizu ni késarébéna?
— Mizu koso Jizō yo!
— Mizu wa Jizō dara,
Nanishini hito ni nomarébéna?
— Hito koso Jizō yo!
— Hito wa Jizō dara,
Nanishini Jizō ogamubéna?
— Hon no Jizō wa Roku-Jizō.

—The heads of the Six Jizō under the bridge have been gnawed by some rat. — But that rat itself is really Jizō. — If the rat be Jizō, how comes it that the rat is caught by a cat? —The cat itself is really Jizō. — If the cat be Jizō, how does it happen that the cat is worried by a dog? — Truly the dog itself is also Jizō. — If the dog be Jizō, how explain the fact that it is captured by a wolf? — The wolf itself is certainly Jizō. — If the wolf be Jizō, why should it be overcome by fire? — The fire indeed is also Jizō. — If the fire be Jizō, why should it be extinguished by water? — The water also is really Jizō. — If the water be Jizō, how explain the fact that it is drunk by mankind? — Mankind is really Jizō. — If mankind be Jizō, why should mankind pray to Jizō? — The true Jizō is the Jizō of the Six States of Existence (literally: "the true Jizō is the Six-Jizō").

IV

NARRATIVE–SONGS

(Province of Chōshi)

Ora ga tonari no Semmatsu wa,
Ōmi no ikusa ni tanomarété,
Ichi-nen tatté mo mada komai,

311

FOLK-LORE GLEANINGS

Ni-nen tatté mo mada konai,
San-nen tattara kubi ga kita.

As for my neighbor Semmatsu,
Having been engaged for the war in Ōmi,
Though one year passed, still he did not come back;
Though two years passed, still he did not come back:
When three years had passed, his head came back.[1]

(Province of Izumo)

Mukō no yama ni
Saru ga sambiki tōmatté;
Maë no saru wa mono shirazu;
Ato no saru mo mono shirazu;
Naka no ko-zaru yō mono shitté.
Gozaré tomodachi, hana-mi ni yuko ya?
Hana wa doko bana?
Jizō no maë no sakura-bana.
Hito-éda oréba, patto chiru;
Futa-éda oréba, patto chiru;
Mi-éda ga saki ni hi ga kurété.
Dochi no kōya é yado toroka?
Higashi no kōya é yado toroka?
Minami no kōya é yado toroka?
Tonosan no kōya é yado totté,
Tatami wa mijikashi, yo wa nagashi.
Akazuki okité sora mitara
Gikko no bakko no kiisengo.
Funédomo saraëté ho wo kakétsu.
Hokakébuné no tsuri-mono wa,
Shiro-ori, aka-ori, aka-ji no
Majitta tsuba-katana.

In yonder mountain three monkeys dwell. The first monkey knows nothing. The last monkey also knows nothing. But the midmost little monkey knows everything well. — Come, friends, let us go to see the flowers. — Flowers? where are the flowers? — Before the statue of Jizō the cherry-flowers are blooming. As

---

[1] Cut off, we must suppose.

SONGS OF JAPANESE CHILDREN

I break one branch, the cherry-flowers fall scattering. As I break a second branch the cherry-flowers fall scattering. Before I can break a third, the darkness comes. — In what dye-house shall I find lodging? Shall I take lodging in the eastern dye-house? Shall I take lodging in the southern dye-house? — Lodging in the dye-house of the Tono-Sama (*lord*), the mats I find short, and the night long. — Awaking at dawn, if I see the sky . . . [1], cleaning out the ships, hoisting the sails. The sails of this sailing-ship are of white cloth and red; the rigging is of red silk cord from the variegated hilts of swords.[2]

(Province of I·umo)

Yaré haratatsu! — tatsu naraba;
Suzuri to fudé to o-té ni motté,
Omou koto wo kaki-oïté,
Murasaki-ga é mi wo nagéta.
Shita kara zako ga tsutsuku yara,
Uë kara karasu ga tsutsuku yara.
Tsutsuita karasu wa doko yukita?
Mori-ki no shita é mugi maki ni.
Nan-goku, nan-goku maité kita?
Ni-sen-goku maité kita.
Ni-sen-goku no nō ni wa
Téra no maë dé ko wo unda.
Jūji no koromo é chi ga tsuité,
Amé-taré-mizu dé aratté,
Kōro no hi dé abutté;
Kōro no hi ga taraidé,
Abura-hi dé abutté;
Abura-hi ga taraidé,
Kudo no hi dé abutté;
Kudo no hi ga taraidé,
Kotatsu no hi dé abutté.

---

[1] Here is a line of which I could not obtain a translation — gikko no bakko no kiisengo. Perhaps the text is corrupt.

[2] This is not quite literal ; but it is certainly the original meaning of the description. There are a great many songs of the same kind. Might not the kind be described as an imperfect form of randonnée — a randonnée in the first stage of evolution?

FOLK-LORE GLEANINGS

What! you are angry? Ah! if you be angry, taking inkstone and writing-brush in your honorable hand, think of what you wish to write and to leave behind you![1] When you have cast your body into the Purple River [Murasaki-gawa] small fishes will nibble it from below; crows will pick it from above. — The crow that picked, where is it gone? — It has gone under a forest-tree, to sow wheat. — How many koku,[2] how many koku have been sown? — Two thousand koku have been sown. — By reason of the sowing of two thousand koku, a child is born in front of the temple. — The upper robe of the chief priest having been sprinkled with blood, he washed it in rainwater, and dried it by·the fire of a censer. The fire in the censer being insufficient, he dried it by fire of oil. The fire of oil being insufficient, he dried it by the fire of a cooking-range. The fire of the cooking-range being insufficient, he dried it by the fire of a kotatsu.[3]

(Province of Isé)

Néko ga Kuwana é mairutoté;
Kuwana no michi dé hi ga kiété,
Toboshitémo, toboshitémo, toboraidé.
Chaya no en éto koshikakété,
— Mizu wo ippai okurenka?
— Mizu wo yaru no wa yasui kédo,
Tsurubé no soko ga nukémashita.
— Yaré, yaré! kitsui ané-san ja!
O-cha wo ippuku okurenka?
— O-cha wo yaru no wa yasui kédo,

---

[1] Alluding to the custom of writing a letter to explain one's motives before suicide.

[2] One koku is equal to about 5.13 bushels.

[3] A kotatsu is a square structure; the sides and top being formed by wooden bars; and the lower part containing a metal brasier, or warming-pan, in which a charcoal fire is lighted. Over this structure heavy quilts are thrown; and a number of persons can keep themselves warm by sitting round the kotatsu with their knees under the quilts. The size of the kotatsu varies from about one foot to two feet square. Dictionaries absurdly describe the thing as "a kind of hearth." It is not a hearth; but in Western Japan it occupies a place in the home like that of the hearth with us — for the family assemble about it of winter evenings.

SONGS OF JAPANESE CHILDREN

Chagama no soko ga nukémashita.
— Yaré, yaré! kitsui ané-san ja!
Tabako wo ippuku okurenka?
— Tabako yaru no wa yasui kédo,
Kiséru no kubi ga nukémashita.
—Yaré, yaré! kitsui ané-san ja! ...
Hi — fu — mi — yo — itsu — mu — nana — ya — kono — to!

A cat set out for Kuwana., On the road to Kuwana her light went out. Though she tried and tried to relight it, she could not. Then, having seated herself on the veranda of a tea-house, she asked: — "One cup of water will you not kindly give me?" — "It would be very easy to give you water; but the bottom of the well-bucket has been taken out." — "Oh! oh! how harshly speaks this Elder Sister![1] Then will you not kindly give me a cup of tea?" — "To give you some tea were an easy matter; but the bottom of the tea-kettle has been taken out." — "Oh! oh! how merciless this Elder Sister! Then will you not let me have one pipeful of tobacco?" — "To give you some tobacco were an easy matter; but the bowl of the pipe has fallen off." — "Oh! oh! what a merciless Elder Sister!"
— *One — two — three — four — five — six — seven — eight — nine — ten![2]*

Of course the cat, in the foregoing narration, is a goblin-cat — a cat having power to assume divers shapes. She travels in human form; but this disguise is penetrated by the eye of the tea-house servant, who answers her as goblins are answered. ... If any goblin or ghost ask you for a bucket or other vessel, it is better not to refuse directly; but you must be careful to knock the bottom out of the

---

[1] "Elder Sister" is still the title of courtesy by which the maid-servant of an inn is addressed; but the form Nésan, a contraction of Ané-san, is more frequently used.

[2] The numbers here refer to a game played to the accompaniment of the song.

315

vessel asked for before yielding it up — otherwise the consequences might be fatal.

This reminds me of a superficial criticism sometimes made in regard to those European fairy-tales which recount the wooing of beautiful maidens by frogs or birds, and the intermarriage of different species of animals. It has been said that the monstrous absurdity of such stories unfits them for the perusal of children, and, furthermore, deprives them of all artistic merit. But most of these fairy-tales can be traced back to Oriental sources; and to the Oriental mind there is nothing absurd in the idea of marriage between human and non-human beings — since it is believed that many animals can assume human shapes at will. To Far-Eastern faith all life is One; and the forms that enclose it but temporary conditions. Without some knowledge of Far-Eastern beliefs,[1] the real charm of the old Japanese fairy-tales cannot be understood. In any event they should be read in translation only when illustrated by Japanese artists. The illustrations will explain much that the bare text leaves in mystery.

In the next song we have the story of a serpent assuming the shape of a certain man's daughter. Stories of serpent-women and dragon-women

[1] The beliefs are older than Buddhism; but Buddhism gave them considerable recognition. One of the questions formerly to be asked of any one desiring to enter the Buddhist Order, according to the Vinaya texts, was this: " Are you a human being?"

316

abound in Japanese literature. Probably both this song and the preceding one were inspired by the memory of some old romance or drama:

(*Province of Shinano*)

Mukō no ozawa ni ja ga tatté —
Hachiman-Chōja no oto-musumé.
Yoku mo tattari takundari,
Té ni wa nihon no tama wo mochi,
Ashi ni wa kogané no kutsu wo haki,
Ā yobé, kŏ yobé, to iinagara,
Yama kuré no kuré ittaréba,
Kusakari tonogo ni yukiatte,
— Obi wo kudasaré, tonogo-sama.
— Obi mo kasa mo yasui koto,
Oré no nyōbo ni naru-naraba:
Asa wa okité kami-yūté.
— Hana no saku madé nété machi yo!

From the swamp beyond there rose up a serpent, in the likeness of the youngest daughter of the wealthy Hachiman. Well did it assume that form, skillfully standing. Holding in its hands two gems, and wearing upon its feet shoes of gold, it traversed mountains and fields, crying out the while: "Call there! — Call here!" Then did it meet a grass-cutter, and say to him: "Fair husband, deign to give me a girdle!" — "To give you [he answered] both a girdle and a hat will be easily done, if you become my wife. Then every morning, early rising, I will arrange your hair." — "Wait then [she said] — patiently wait until the season of the blooming of flowers."

V

BATTLEDORE-SONGS AND BALL-SONGS

IN the time of the New-Year holidays the streets are made beautiful by groups of young girls playing at battledore-and-shuttlecock, or at various games of

317

hand-ball. It were difficult to imagine anything more charming than some of these little maids in their long-sleeved and many-colored holiday-costume: only the most radiant of moths or butterflies might serve for a comparison. Very skillful are the Tōkyō artists in portraying the grace and the daintiness of them; and every year these artists delight us with new colored prints of bevies of ball-players (showing the fashions of the season) or pictures of some fairy-damsel with upturned smiling face and shining eyes, and flower-lips half-parted, as she watches, battledore in hand, the feathery missile in its course. Yet the reality may often be much more lovely than the picture. And, oh! what wonderful battledores are sometimes to be seen! — cushioned at the back with silk mosaic-work, making the dream of a landscape, a garden, a princess of ancient days!

Yet the charm is not visual only; — these fairies, in their play, sing little songs of strange rhythm and melody, very sweet to hear, and (for the Western listener) impossible to remember.

Many of these queer little songs are so constructed that the first syllable of each successive line or phrase corresponds with the first syllable of a numeral noting the ordinal place of the line or phrase. Most commonly the Japanese numerals are used: hitotsu, futatsu, mitsu, yotsu, itsutsu, mutsu, nanatsu, yatsu, kokonotsu, and tō. But in various examples the Chinese numerals are used — ichi, ni, san, shi, go, roku, shichi, hachi, ku, jiu. And in sundry compositions the two sets of numerals are mixed together. With the utterance of each line or phrase the shuttlecock or the ball ought to be struck once. The term "chō" (even number) seems usually to signify ten strokes; — but this meaning is not always evident.

(*Tōkyō battledore-song*)

*Hito*ri kina,
*Futa*ri kina,
Mité yukina,
Yotté yukina;
Itsu kité
*Muzu*kashi;
Nana Yakushi,
Koko no ma dé
To yo!

Come, one! come, two! — After seeing, go! — After entering, go! — Whenever I come to see you, your face is gloomy. — Seven for Yakushi![1] — There you are! — ten with the stroke of nine!

(*Kyōto battledore-song*)

*Hito*ri kina,
*Futa*ri kina,
Mité yukita,
Yotté yukina;
Itsu kité mitémo
*Nana*ko obi wo
*Ya*kuruma ni shimété.
Kokono yo dé itchō yo!

Come, one! Come, two! — After seeing, departed; — after entering, go! Whenever I come to see you, you put on your

---

[1] Yakushi-Nyōrai (*Bhaishagyarâga*), the Healing Buddha.

319

FOLK-LORE GLEANINGS

Nanako [1] girdle, tying it in the mode called "Eight Wheels."
With this ninth stroke, one chō is completed.

(Kyōto battledore-song)

Hitomé,
Futamé,
Miyakashi,
Yomégo,
Itsuya no
Musashi,
Nanaya no
Yatsushi —
Kokono ya!
To!

One eye-glance! — two glances! — the August Lights [of the Gods]! — the Daughter-in-Law! — the Chequer-game [sold at the shop] Itsuya! — the dandy [-clerk] of the shop Nanaya! — Nine there are! — And ten!

(Battledore-song — Province of Shinano)

Hi-yara Hikobé;
Nakané no O-Toyo;
Sando-mé ni makété,
Abékobé chinchikurin,
Chinchikurin no chinchikurin;
Hitoko ni futago,
Miwatasu yomégo,
Itsu kité mitémo,[2]
Nanako no obi wo
Ya no ji ni shimété,
Kono ya wo íoru.

There goes one, Hikobé! — O-Toyo of Nakané; — three times defeated; — upside-down now, chinchikurin! — chinchikurin! and chinchikurin! — one child and twins; — bride

---

[1] Nanako is the name given to a kind of heavy twilled silk with a wavy lustre.

[2] The syllable "mi" of mitémo is here considered to be an equivalent for "mu," the first syllable of mutsu (six).

320

seen far away; whenever I go to see her, she puts on her Nanako-obi (taffeta girdle), tying it in the form of the character Ya [1] — and so she passes before this house.

Sometimes the names of ten celebrated temples, or the names of ten divinities, or even the names of the months, are used for the same enumerative purpose — as in the following examples:

(Tōkyō bail-song) [2]

Ichi ni Ichibata O-Yakushi Sama yo!
Ni-niwa Nihon no Nikkō-Sama yo!
San-ni Sanuki no Kompira-Sama yo!
Shi-ni wa Shinano no Zenkōji-Sama yo!
Itsutsu Enoshima Benten-Sama yo!
Roku-ni Rokkakudō no Kwannon-Sama yo!
Nanatsu Nana-ura no Tenjin-Sama yo!
Yatsu Yawata no Hachiman-Sama yo!
Kokonotsu Kōya no Kōbō-Sama yo!
Tō dé tokoro no Ujigami-Sama yo!
Kakéta gwan nara tokanéba naranu!

The first time for the August Lord Yakushi of Ichibata;
The second, for the Lord Deity of Nikkō in Japan;
The third, for the Lord Kompira of Sanuki;
The fourth, for the Lord Buddha of Zenkōji in Shinano;
The fifth, for the deity Benten of Enoshima;
The sixth, for the deity Kwannon of the Rokkakudō;
The seventh, for the August Lord Tenjin, of Nana-ura;
The eighth, for the August Lord Hachiman, of Yawata;
The ninth, for the Lord Kōbōdaishi of Kōya;
The tenth, for the tutelary Gods of this place.
The vow that has been made must always be kept!

---

[1] The Hiragana character "ya" is here referred to. This way of tying the girdle is still in fashion, and is still called the "Ya-no-ji" manner.
[2] Variants of this composition seem to be known in almost every part of Japan.

FOLK-LORE GLEANINGS

(*Kyōto battledore-song*)

Shōgwatsu —
    Kadomatsu;
Nigwatsu —
    Hatsu-uma;
Sangwatsu —
    Sekku;
Shigwatsu —
    O-Shaka;
Gogwatsu —
    Nobori;
Rokugwatsu —
    Tennō;
Shichigwatsu —
    Tanabata;
Hachigwatsu —
    Hassaku;
Kugwatsu —
    Kiku-tsuki;
Jiugwatsu —
    Ebisu-kō;
Shimotsuki;
    Shiwasu;
Kokono yo dé
    Itchō yo!

First Month, Gate-Pine-Tree; [1] — Second Month, First Day-of-the-Horse; [2] — Third Month, Girls' Festival; [3] — Fourth Month, the August Sâkyamuni; [4] — Fifth Month, Flags; [5] —

---

[1] The Kadomatsu, or "Gate-Pine," is planted before the main entrance of a house on the first day of the new year.

[2] This is the great festival of the Rice-God; — the term "Hatsu-uma," or "First Horse-Day," signifies only seventh day, each day of the old month being named after one of the twelve Signs of the Zodiac.

[3] Also called the Festival of Dolls.

[4] The Birthday of the Buddha is celebrated on the eighth day of the fourth month.

[5] This is the Boys' Festival. Nobori are flags, bearing symbolic designs, and are hoisted in celebration of the birth of a son. In Tōkyō paper or cotton figures of carp-fish are used in lieu of nobori.

SONGS OF JAPANESE CHILDREN

Sixth Month, Festival of the tutelar God; [1] — Seventh Month, Festival of the Weaver; [2] — Eighth Month, Festival of the First Day; — Ninth Month, the Month of Chrysanthemums; — Tenth Month, Festival of Ebisu; [3] — The Frost Month; — The Last Month; — Nine strokes given — now one chō is now completed.

(Ball-song — Province of Shinano)

Daikoku-Sama, to iu hito wa —
Ichi-ni, tawara wo funmaëté;
Ni-ni, nikkori warōté;
San-ni, sakazuki itadaité;
Yotsu dé, yo no naka yoi yō ni;
Itsutsu dé, izumi no waku yō ni;
Mutsu, mubyō sokusai ni;
Nanatsu, nanigoto nai yō ni;
Yatsu dé, yashiki wo tairagété;
Kokonotsu, ko-kura wo oshitatété;
Tō dé, tokkuri osamatta.

[Praying to] the person called Daikoku-Sama — firstly, as he treads upon the rice-bales; secondly, as he laughs with pleasant countenance; thirdly, taking the saké-cup respectfully in hand; fourthly, [we beseech him] that all the world may prosper; fifthly, that the springs may purely flow; sixthly, that the people may be free from all sickness and calamity; seventhly, that all evils may cease; eighthly, that our house may be victorious [in war]; ninthly, that treasure-houses may be erected; tenthly, that universal peace may continue to prevail.

This last is a curious example of a prayer transformed into a ball-song. Excepting the first four lines the text is almost, word-for-word, the text of an old samurai-prayer — the household prayer which every warrior repeated daily. . . . Some of the

---

[1] Tennō is the name usually given to the guardian-deity of a city or district.
[2] The Weaver is the Star Vega.
[3] Patron-God of Labor.

following, on the other hand, are little more than nonsense-verses:

(Battledore-song — Province of Echizen)

> Hi ya!
> Fu ya!
> O-Koma San!
> Tabako no
> Kemuri wa,
> Jōhattsan!

One struck! — two struck! O-Komo San! Smoke of tobacco — Jōhattsan.[1]

(Battledore-song — Province of Shinano)

> Ichigwatsu;
> Nigwatsu;
> Sangwatsu,
> Sakura;
> Yanagi no
> Shita dé,
> Keshō
> Shité; —
> Tō
> Yo!

The first month; the second month; the third month, cherry-flowers! Under the willow-tree, making my toilet — there goes ten!

(Battledore-song — Province of Shinano)

> Hi ya!
> Hikobé!
> Hagétaka,
> Jirobé?

---

[1] Jōhattsan, familiar abbreviation of Jōhachi San (Mr. Jōhachi). The song alludes to the popular drama entitled "O-Koma-Saiza." O-Koma, the heroine of this play, is a beautiful girl who comes to an unhappy end through the rascality of Jōhachi, a trusted servant in her father's house. Jōhachi appears on the stage, in various scenes of the drama, squatting before a hibachi, and smoking furiously.

SONGS OF JAPANESE CHILDREN

Jirobé no
Atama wa,
Nazé hagéta?
Oya ga
Jakendé,
Hi é kubéta.

One for Hikobé! How did you get bald, Jirobé? As for Jirobé's head — how did it become bald? His parents, being
cruel, put his head in the fire.

(Kyōto ball-song)

Hi, fu, mi, yo,
Yomo no keshiki wo
Haru to nagamété; —
Umé ni uguisu
"Hō-Hō-Hōkékyō" to saëzuru.
Asu wa Gion no
Niken chaya dé,
Koto ya samisen
Hayashi tenten
Témari-uta,
"Uta no Nakayama"
Chiyo go ni go-jiu dé
Chiyo roku — roku — roku,
Chiyo shichi — shichi — shichi,
Chiyo hachi — hachi — hachi,
Chiyo ku ni ku-jiu dé
Chotto hyaku tsuita.

One, two, three, four! — in each of the four directions gazing,
everywhere the signs of spring are seen. On the plum-tree the
nightingale sings "Hō-Hō-Hōkékyō." [1] To-morrow in the two
tea-houses of Gion-street, with accompaniment of koto and
samisen — ting-ting! — will be sung the hand-ball songs, and
the song called "Uta no Nakayama." . . . Thus making fifty
and five chiyo. [2] . . . Chiyo, six — six — six! Chiyo, seven —

---

[1] With regard to the cry of the uguisu, see the preceding paper on
Buddhist nomenclature.

[2] Chiyo is here the same as cho, meaning the even number, or full ten.

325

seven — seven! Chiyo, eight — eight — eight! Chiyo, nine and ninety now! . . . Even so a hundred have been struck!

(City of Shidzuoka)

Uguisu ya! uguisu ya!
Tama-tama miyako é noboru toki,
Umé no ko-éda ni hiruné shité,
O-Chiyo ni nani-nani kisété yaru?
Uwagi wa kon-kon-kon-chirimen,
Shitagi wa chin-chin-chirimen; —
Soré wo kisété yattaréba
Michi dé korobu ka? — té wo tsuku ka?
Tono-San ga tōtara, o-jigi wo séyo;
Omma [1] kitaraba, waki ni yoré;
Té-narai kodomo wo kamō-nayo;
Kamōto sōshi dé butaréruzo!
Mazu, mazu ikkwan okashimōshita!

— O Nightingale, Nightingale! when some time you go to the capital, sleeping by day on a plum-tree bough, what will you give O-Chiyo to wear? — An upper dress of dark-blue, dark-blue, dark-blue crêpe-silk; an under-dress of rare, rare, rare crêpe-silk. So dressed, when I send her out, I shall warn her not to stumble, or to dirty her hands. "If a Lord passes on the road, [I shall say to her,] make the honorable reverence. If an honorable horse approaches, keep well to one side of the road. Do not vex the children on their way to the writing-school; — if you vex them, you will certainly be beaten with copy-books." Now, now I have lent you one kwan [i.e., I have struck the ball one hundred times!] [2]

(Province of Echizen)

Hitotsu, hiita mamé —
     Ko ni shita mamé;
Futatsu, funda mamé —
     Tsuburéta mamé;

---

[1] Omma is a corruption of O-uma, "honorable horse."

[2] The ancient kwan was worth one thousand cash — or mon. Its value was therefore about the same as that of the dollar of one hundred cents.

SONGS OF JAPANESE CHILDREN

Mitsu, miso-mamé —
    Fukuréta mamé;
Yotsu, yotta mamé —
    Kirei na mamé;
Itsutsu, itta mamé —
    Hara-kitta mamé;
Mutsu, murōta mamé —
    Tokushita mamé;
Nanatsu, natta mamé —
    Saya-tsuki mamé;
Yatsu, yatta mamé —
    Son-shita mamé;
Kokonotsu, kōta mamé —
    Zéni-dashita mamé;
To dé totta mamé —
    Nushito-shita mamé.

One — for ground peas —
    the peas made into flour;
Two — for trampled peas —
    the peas which were crushed;
Three — the peas made into miso-sauce —
    fermented peas;
Four — the selected peas —
    the beautiful peas;
Five — for parched peas —
    the belly-cut peas;
Six — for peas given to us —
    the peas which we gained;
Seven — for growing peas —
    the peas in the pod;
Eight — the peas given away —
    the peas that are lost;
Nine — the peas which we paid for —
    the money-bought peas;
And *Ten* — for the peas that we took —
    the stolen peas!

The interest of the next selection — best of all

the ball-songs — is of quite another kind. The scheme of the composition is not unlike that of our celebrated nursery-game, " I love my love with an A "; and the narration can be extended or varied indefinitely according to the imaginative wit of the players:

(Tōkyō hand-ball song)

FIRST PLAYER:

O-Kan — Kan — Kan —
Kaga-Sama yashiki ja,
O-Késa kométsuku,
Konuka ga ochiru.
— Nantoté ochiru?
Sasa! shichiku-daké!
Sasa! hachiku-daké!
— Mukō no mukō no
Kōshi-zukuri no
Shirakabé-zukuri no
Akai-noren no kakatta,
O-Himé-Sama madé
O-watashi —
Mōsu-su-su no su!

SECOND PLAYER:

Ukétotta! ukétotta!
Ukétotta!
Daiji no o-mari wo ukétotta!
Aa! ukétotta!
Chō ya, hana ya to
O-sodatémōshité;
O-kaëshimōshité
Konya no ban kara:
Kami mo irazumi,
Suzuri mo irazumi;
Hari sambon —
Kinu-ito mi-suji ni —

SONGS OF JAPANESE CHILDREN

Omma ga sambiki —
O-kago ga sanchō.
Norikaë-hik'kaë,
Mukō no mukō no
Kōshi-zukuri no
Kaki no noren no
? —— Sama madé
O-watashi —
Mōsu-su-su no su!

FIRST PLAYER:

In the residence of the Lord of Ka — Ka — Kaga, the maid
O-Késa is cleaning rice, and the rice-bran falls. With what
sound does it fall? — With the sound of *Sasa! shichiku-daké!* —
sasa! hachiku-daké![1] . . . Now to the maiden-princess dwelling
far, far away [2] — in the house with the lattice-work — in the
house with the white walls — in the house with the red curtains
hung up — I do now most worshipfully this ball pas-s-s-ss!

[Here the ball is thrown to another girl, who catches it, and
sings:]

SECOND PLAYER:

I have caught it! I have caught it! I have received the precious
ball. Ah! I have received it! Like a butterfly, like a blossom,
even so tenderly shall it be honorably cared for; and by this
night shall it worshipfully be returned. [To return it] neither
paper nor inkstone will be needed [3] — but three needles, and

---

[1] These words are all names of bamboo. The sasa is a small variety
of bamboo: the shichiku-daké is a black bamboo; and the hachiku-daké
is a purplish bamboo. But in this song the words are used only as onomatopes. The syllables "sasa" represent the creaking of the great
wooden mallet, when lifted by the feet of the rice-pounder; and the
syllables "shichiku-daké, hachiku-daké," are intended to imitate the
noise of the mallet falling, and the dull thud of the blow.

[2] Mukō no mukō (literally: "in front of in front") might better be
rendered by our colloquial phrase, "at the back of beyond."

[3] Because the ball will not be returned merely by a messenger bearing
a letter of thanks.

three lines of silken thread,[1] — and three honorable horses, and three honorable palanquins. . . . Changing horses, and again changing horses [I myself shall carry this ball] to the Lady ——[2] who dwells far, far away from here — in the building with the lattice-work, in the building with the persimmon-colored curtains hung up. To her I now do worshipfully [this ball] pas-s-s-ss!

VI

LULLABIES

A PARTICULAR psychological interest attaches to the literature of the lullaby, independently of country or race. Being the natural utterance of mother-love, the lullaby may be said to express the most ancient form of tender experience; and in almost every time and place the essential character of this variety of folk-song has been little affected by social changes of any sort. Whether narrative or jingle, sense or nonsense, the verses usually contain some reference to those familiar things in which the child-mind discovers cause for wonder: horses or cows, trees or flowers, the moon and the stars, birds or butterflies, sights of the street or garden. Often the lullaby represents the reiteration of one term of caress, alternated with promises of reward for docility, and hints of danger as a result of fretfulness. The promises commonly refer to food or toys; and the threatened penalties are not to be inflicted by the mother, but by some bogey or goblin having power to punish

---

[1] Because it will be respectfully enclosed in a silken wrapper or bag.
[2] Here the real name of the girl, to whom the ball is next to be thrown, may be mentioned.

naughty children. To such general rules the Japanese lullabies do not offer any remarkable exceptions; but they abound in queer fancies, and have a distinctly Oriental quality.

Perhaps the European reader will be startled by the apparition of the syllables "nenné" and "nennéko" at the beginning of these little songs; for many of the French berceuses also begin with the syllables "néné," having nearly the same sound. (The French word "néné" — pronounced in some dialects "nenna" and "nono" — is commonly used by mothers in southern France; "dodo" being the Northern equivalent.[1]) But of course there is no real etymological relation between the French "néné" and the Japanese "nenné." The Japanese phrase, "nennéko," is compounded with a syllable of the verb "neru," signifying to sleep; a syllable of the word "nenné" or "nennéï," meaning baby; and the word "ko," meaning child. "Sleep, baby-child!" is the real meaning of the expression.

(Province of Isé)

Nenné, nenné-to!
Neru-ko wa kawai;
Okité-naku-ko wa
Tsura-nikui.

Sleep, little one, sleep! Sweet is the face of the sleeping child; — ugly the face of the wakeful child that cries!

---

[1] See, for examples, M. Tiersot's *Histoire de la Chanson Populaire en France*, pp. 136–37, *et seq.*

FOLK-LORE GLEANINGS

Nennéko, nennéko, nennéko ya!
Netara o-kaka é tsurété ina!
Okitara gagama ga totté kama!

Sleep, sleep, O sleep, my child! If you sleep I will go home to fetch your mother! If you stay awake, the Gagama [1] will catch and bite you!

(*Kyōto lullaby*)

Nétaka? nénandaka?
Makura ni toëba,
Makura mono iuta,
Néta to iuta.

Gone to sleep? — not yet sleeping? When I questioned the pillow, the pillow spoke words: "Already asleep" — so it said.

(*Province of Musashi*)

Nennéko! nennéko!
Nennéko yō!
Oraga akabo wa
Itsu dékita?
San-gwatsu, sakura no
Saku toki ni:
Dōri dé o-kao ga
Sakura-iro.

Sleep, sleep, sleep, my child! When was my baby made? In the third month, in the time of the blooming of cherry-flowers. Therefore the color of the honorable face of my child is the color of the cherry-blossom.

(*Province of Sanuki*)

Nennen, nennen,
Nennen yō! —

---

[1] This is an Izumo name for some kind of goblin. I wonder if the term is not a corruption of the ancient word "Gogomé" — a name given to certain phantoms of the primitive Shintō cult — the Ugly Women of the Underworld.

SONGS OF JAPANESE CHILDREN

Nennéshita ko ni
Hanéita to hané to;
Nenné-sen ko ni
Hané bakari. . . .

Sleep, sleep, sleep! — For the little one who goes to sleep, a battledoor and shuttlecock! For the child who does not sleep, only a shuttlecock!

(Province of Shinano)

Nennen-yō!
Korokoro yō!
Nennen-Koyama [1] no
Kiji no ko wa,
Nakuto o-taka ni
Toraréru yō!

Sleep! happily sleep! The young of the kiji in the Hill of Nennen — if it cries it is sure to be taken by the hawk.

(Province of Izumo)

Nennéko, nennéko, nennéko ya!
Achira muitémo yama yama;
Kochira muitémo yama yama.
Yama no naka ni nani ga aru?
Shii ya donguri kaya no mi.

Sleep, sleep, little one, sleep! I turn that way; but I see only mountains. I turn this way; but I see only mountains. In the midst of those mountains what can there be? There are shii [2]-nuts and acorns and seeds of kaya.[3]

(Province of Izumo)

Nennéko sé, nennéko sé!
Nenné no omori wa doko é itta?

---

[1] Perhaps the name Nennen-Koyama might be translated, "The Hills of the Land of Nod." The Kiji, a beautiful green pheasant, often betrays itself to the hunter by its cry; — hence the proverb, "Kiji mo nakazuba utaré wa shimai": "If the Kiji did not cry, it would not be shot."

[2] The shii-tree is a variety of live-oak.

[3] The kaya is a kind of yew.

333

FOLK-LORE GLEANINGS

Yama wo koëté sato, é itta.
Sato no miyagé ni nani morota?
Denden-taiko ni furi-tsuzumi,
Okiagarikoboshi ni inu-hariko.

Sleep, little one, sleep! Where is the sleep-nurse, the girl-nurse gone? Over the hills to her own village-home. When she comes back, what presents will she bring you? A round drum to beat and a hand-drum [1] to shake; an okiagarikoboshi,[2] and a paper dog.

(Province of Isé)

Nenné sansé yō!
Kyō wa ni-jiu-go nichi;
Asu wa kono ko no
Miya-mairi.
Miya é mairaba
Dō iuté ogamu?
Kono ko ichi-dai
Mamé na yo ni.

Sleep, child! sleep! To-day is the twenty-fifth day. To-morrow morning this child will make his first visit to the [Shintō] parish-temple. When I go with him to the temple, what shall I pray for? I will pray that through all his life this child may be healthy and strong.

(Province of Musashi)

Nennéko, nennéko,
Nennéko yō!
Oraga akabō no
Néta rusu ni,
Azuki wo yonagété,
Komé toïdé,
Aka no mamma é
Toto soëté,

---

[1] The round shallow drum is called a "dendem-taiko." The tsuzumi is a hand-drum of a very peculiar shape. Of course the toy-drums here referred to are considerably smaller than the real instrument.

[2] The okiagarikoboshi is a little figure of a wrestler which is so weighted as to assume an erect posture, no matter how thrown down.

SONGS OF JAPANESE CHILDREN

Aka no ii-ko ni
Kūréru-zo!

Sleep, sleep, sleep, little one! While my baby sleeps I will wash some red beans and clean some rice; — then adding some fish to the red rice, I will serve it up to this best of little babies.

(Province of Echizen)

Uchi no kono ko no
Makura no moyō,
Umé ni uguisu,
Matsu ni tsuru:
Umé ni narétémo,
Sakura wa iyaya; —
Onaji hana demo,
Chiri yasui.

The designs upon the pillow of this child of the house are nightingales and plum-trees, storks and pines. I am used to the plum-tree design; but I would not have the cherry-flower design. Though the cherry-tree be equal in beauty to the plum-tree, its blossoms too easily fall.[1]

(Matsŭ — Province of Izumo)

Nennéko, nennéko nennéko ya!
Kono ko nashité naku-yara?
O-chichi ga taranuka? — o-mama ga taranuka?
Ima ni ototsan no ōtono no o-kaëri ni
Amé ya, o-kwashi ya, hii-hii ya,
Gara-gara, naguréba fuito tatsu
Okiagarikoboshi! —
Nennéko, nennéko, nennéko ya!

---

[1] Therefore the design is unlucky. Some local bit of folk-lore is suggested by this composition; — usually the cherry-flower is thought to be a happy symbol. In this connection I may observe that the lotus-flower design is held to be unlucky. It is never to be seen in patterns for children's clothing; and even pictures of the flower are scarcely ever suspended in a room. The reason is that the lotus, being the symbolic flower of Buddhism, is sculptured upon tombstones, and is borne as an emblem in funeral processions.

FOLK–LORE GLEANINGS

Sleep, sleep, sleep, little one! Why does the child continue to cry? Is the honorable milk deficient? — is the honorable rice deficient? Presently when father returns from the great Lord's palace, amé will be given you, and also cake, and a hii-hii likewise, and a rattle as well, and an okiagarikoboshi that will stand up immediately after being thrown down.

(Shidzuoka City)

Yoi-ko da!
San-ko da!
Mamé na ko da!
Mamé dé sodatéta
O-ko ja mono!
Néruto nérimochi
Kurétéyaru;
Damaruto dango wo
Kurétéyaru;
Nakuto nagamochi
Showaséru zō;
Okoruto okorimushi ni
Kurétéyaru.

Good child, genteel child — what a healthy child it is! For it is a child that has been nourished with peas. Kneaded rice-cakes I will give you if you sleep. Dumplings I will give you if you hush. If you cry I will make you carry a nagamochi [quilt-chest]. If you get angry I will give you to the Anger-Insect.[1]

(Province of Suruga)

Bō ya wa iiko da!
Nennéshina!
Kono ko no kawaisa
Kagiri nai —

---

[1] The chief interest of this composition is the curiously alliterative structure of the phrases. There are several queer plays upon words; Mamé, as pronounced, may mean either "peas" or "healthy." In the same way okori might mean either "to be angry" or "ague." Oko-rimushi properly signifies the "ague-insect," and is the popular name of a large moth, believed to cause chills and fever.

SONGS OF JAPANESE CHILDREN

Yama de no ki no kazu,
Kaya no kazu,
Ten é nobotté
Hoshi no kazu,
Numadzu é kudaréba
Senbon matsu —
Senbon-matsubara,
Ko-matsubara,
Matsuba no kazu yori
Mada kawai!

Oh! how good a child this boy is! Sleep, my child! — My
love of this child is incalculable as the number of the trees in the
mountain-forest — as the number of the fruits of the kaya —
as the number of the stars in the sky above — as the thousands
of the pines of Numadzu below — as the myriad great pines
of the pine-forest — as the myriad little pines of the young pine-
wood: more incalculable even than the leaves of those pine-trees,
is my love of this little one!

(Lullaby sung to the child of a Daimyō — Province of Izumo) [1]

O-nenné, o-nenné, o-nenné ya!
Yoi ni wa tōkara gyōshin nari.
Asama wa tōkara omézamété,
Omézamé no ohōbi ni nani, nani?
O-chichi no débana wo agémashozo,
O-chichi no débana ga o-iya nara,
Niwatori-kéawasé o-mé ni kakyō;
Niwatori-kéawasé o-iya nara,
O-kwashi wa takusan o-agarika!

Augustly rest, augustly rest! Soon this evening augustly
sleep! Early at daybreak, at the august awakening, what,
what honorable gift shall be presented at the august awakening?
Flower of honorable milk shall be presented. If the flower of
honorable milk be augustly disliked, then the fighting of the
cocks will be honorably displayed. If the fighting of the cocks

---

[1] Obtained from dictation at Matsuĕ, Izumo. The original interest
of this piece lies in the curious and really untranslatable honorifics.

be augustly disliked, then will not honorable cake be augustly accepted?

(*Tōkyō*)

Nennen yō!
Korokoro yō!
Nennen-Koyama no
Usagi wa,
Nazé ni o-mimi ga
O-nagai né?
Okkasan no
O-naka ni,
Ita toki ni,
Biwa no mi,
Sasa no mi,
Tabémashité; —
Soré dé o-mimi ga
O-nagai yo! [1]

Sleep, little one! — pleasantly sleep! — Why are the ears of the hare of the Hill of Nennen so honorably long? When he was in his mother's honorable womb, she ate the fruits of the loquat, the seeds of the small bamboo: therefore his honorable ears are thus honorably long!

(*Province of Settsu*)

Nenné! Koro ïchi! —
Temma no ichi yo!
Daikon soroëté,
Funé ni tsumu,
Funé ni tsundara
Doko-madé ikiyaru?
Kizu ya Namba no
Hashi no shita.
Hashi no shita ni wa
O-kamé ga iyaru;

---

[1] An Izumo version of this lullaby will be found in *Glimpses of Unfamiliar Japan*, vol. VI, p. 306. The Izumo version is more interesting. There are several Tōkyō versions.

SONGS OF JAPANESE CHILDREN

O-kamé toritaya,
Také hoshiya!
Také ga hoshikérya,
Takéya é ikiyaré;
Také wa nandémo
Gozarimasu!

Sleep, child! Fair-time is coming. Oh! the fair of Temma! —
The ends of the radishes having been evenly trimmed, the ship
is loaded. Having been laden, where will the ship go? — Under
the Bridge of Kizu, and under the Bridge of Namba. — Under
those bridges live many honorable tortoises. Honorable tortoises I want to catch! — I want a bamboo-pole. — If you wish
for a bamboo-pole, go to the bamboo-shop. In that bamboo-
shop all kinds of bamboos augustly exist.

(*Tōkyō*)

O-Tsuki Sama, ikutsu?
Jiu-san, nanatsu.
Mada toshi waka yé!
Ano ko wo undé,
Kono ko wo undé,
Daré ni dakashō?
O-Man ni dakashō.
O-Man doko itta?
Abura-kaë, cha-kaë.
Aburaya no maë dë
Subité korondé;
Abura isshō koboshita.
Sono abura doshita?
Tarō-Don no inu to,
Jirō-Don no inu to,
Mina namété shimatta.
Sono inu doshita?
Taiko ni hatté,
Achi no hō démo,
Don-doko-don!
Kochi no hō démo,
Don-doko-don!
Tataita-to-sa!

339

FOLK-LORE GLEANINGS

Lady Moon, how old are you? — Thirteen, seven. — That is
still young. — That child being born, this child being born, to
whom shall the child be given to carry? — To O-Man it shall
be given to carry. — Where is O-Man gone? — She has gone to
buy oil; she has gone to buy tea. — Slipping and falling, in
front of the oil-shop, one whole shō [1] of oil she spilled. — What
was done with that oil? — The dog of Master Tarō, and the dog
of Master Jirō, licked it all up. — What was done with those
dogs? — Their skins were stretched and made into drums.
There you can hear [the drum] even now — *don-doko-don!*
Here you can hear [the drum] even now — *don-doko-don!* So
they beat the drums!

(Province of Gifu)

Nenné ya! korokoro ya!
Nenné no umaréta
Sono hi ni wa,
Akai o-mamma ni
Toto soëté,
Toto-sama no o-hashi dé
Agémashōka?
Toto-sama no o-hashi wa
Toto kusai.
Haha-sama no o-hashi dé
Agémashōka?
Haha-sama no o-hashi wa
Chichi kusai.
Ané-sama no o-hashi dé
Agémashō.
Nennen! korokoro
Nenné-shō!

Sleep, little one! happily sleep! On your next birthday I will
give you red rice cooked with fish. Shall I then feed you with
the honorable chopsticks of your father? — The honorable
chopsticks of father smell of fish. — Shall I feed you with the
honorable chopsticks of your mother? — Mother's honorable
chopsticks smell of milk. — Then I shall feed you with the

---

[1] One shō is a little more than a quart and a half.

honorable chopsticks of your elder sister. — Sleep! pleasantly go to sleep!

(Province of Settsu)

> Nennéko, sannéko, sakaya no ko!
> Sakaya wo iyanara yomé ni yarō.
> Yomé no dōgu wa, nani-nani zo?
> Tansu, nagamochi, hitsu, todana;
> Ryūkyū-zutsumi ga rokka aru;
> Furoshiki-zutsumi wa kazu shirézu
> Soréhodo koshiraë yaru-kara-nya,
> Isshō sararété modoruna yo!
> —Sorya mata okkasan dōyoku na!
> Sengoku tsundaru funé saëmo,
> Kazé ga kawaréba modoru mono!

Sleep, sleep, my child — child of the saké-dealer! If you do not like this saké-house, I will send you away as a bride. What are the bridal-gifts that will be given? A tansu (chest of drawers), a nagamochi (quilt-chest), one hitsu (clothes-chest), one todana (cupboard). Of Ryūkyū [1] goods the packages are six; — as for the presents wrapped in furoshiki, [2] their number cannot be told. So much having been done for you, when you are given as a bride, remember that if you be divorced, you must never in your life come back to this house! — Ah, mother! that is too cruel of you! Even the ship that is freighted with a thousand koku of rice returns to port if the fair wind changes.

(Tōkyō lullaby)

> Senjō zashiki no
> Karakami sodachi!
> Botchama mo yoi ko ni
> Naru toki wa,

---

[1] Rykūyū is the Japanese name of the Loochoo Islands. Various textile and other fabrics, made in the Loochoo Islands, are greatly prized in Japan.

[2] Small presents are usually wrapped in a square piece of cotton or silk before being sent; and this wrapper, much resembling a large handkerchief, is called a furoshiki.

Jimen wo fuyashité,
Kura tatété,
Kura no tonari ni
Matsu uëté,
Matsu no tonari ni
Také uëté,
Také no tonari ni
Umé uëté,
Umé no ko-éda ni
Suzu sagété —
Sono suzu chara-chara
Naru toki wa,
Botchama mo sazo-sazo
Uréshikarō!

[Big and beautiful] as the sliding-screens of a thousand-mat room — so Sir Baby-Boy is growing! When he becomes a good boy likewise, then I will make larger the grounds about our dwelling, and there build for him a treasure-house. Next to the treasure-house I will plant pine-trees. Next to the pine-trees I will plant bamboos. Next to the bamboos I will plant plum-trees. To the little branches of those plum-trees shall be hung little bells. When those little bells sound chara-chara — O Sir Baby-Boy, how happy you will be!

(City of Hakata)

Kinkan, mikan, nambō tabéta?
O-tera no nikai dé mitsu tabéta.
Sono o-tera wa daré ga tatéta?
Hachiman-Chōja no oto-musumé.
Oto ga yomé-iri suru toki nya
Nangai-teramachi shara-shara to,
Mijikai-teramachi shara-shara to.
Shara-shara setta no o ga kiréta:
— Anésan, tatété kurénkana?
— Tatété yarō kota yarokendo
Hari mo nakaréba, ito mo nai.
— Hari wa hariya dé kōté-yaru,
Ito wa itoya dé kōté-yaru.
— Hari wa hariya no kusaré-bari,

SONGS OF JAPANESE CHILDREN

Ito wa itoya no kusaré-ito!
— Anésan, setta ni chi ga tsuita!
— Soré wa chi ja nai — béni ja mono!
Ōsaka béni koso iro yokéré;
Iro no yoi hodo né ga takai.

— Citrons, oranges — how many did you eat?
— Upstairs in the honorable temple I ate three.
— As for that honorable temple — by whom was it built?
By the youngest daughter of the wealthy Hachiman.
On the day when that youngest daughter went out to be married,
Down the long Street-of-Temples she walked — shara-shara,
Down the short Street-of-Temples she walked — shara-shara:
Then was broken a thong of the sandals [1] that sounded shara-shara.
"Elder sister, will you not kindly mend it?"
"The thong I would mend for you;
But I have neither a needle nor thread."
"A needle from the needle-shop I will buy for you;
Thread from the threadshop I will buy for you."
"Ah, this needle of the needle-shop is a rotten needle!
This thread of the thread-shop is rotten thread."
"Elder Sister! there is blood upon my sandals!"
"That is not blood, it is only béni (rouge). [2]
The rouge of Ōsaka has indeed a fine color:
Very fine is the color — therefore the price is dear."

. . . .

And now, by way of conclusion, let me state that in preparing this rather lengthy paper I could only hope to furnish the reader with a new experience — an experience somewhat like that of passing, for the first time, through Japanese streets.

The first general impression of a Japanese street

[1] The setta is a light but very strong sandal, of which the leather sole is strengthened with plates of thin metal.
[2] Béni is used chiefly to color the lips.

343

must be, for most people, even more vague than strange. Unless you happen to have senses of superlative delicacy — unless you possess a visual faculty like that of Pierre Loti, for example — you can remember very little, and understand almost nothing, of what you looked at while passing through that street. Nevertheless you will find yourself surprised and pleased; — you will feel, without knowing why, the sensation of the elfish and the odd — the charm of the unexpected.

Well, in all the child-songs which I have quoted, perhaps less than half-a-dozen fairly arrested your attention; and of the rest you probably remember scarcely anything. But if you have read through the series, even hastily and superficially, you should have obtained a general impression, or vague sensation, not unlike the sensation that follows upon the first vision of Japanese streets: — dim surmise of another and inscrutable humanity — another race-soul, strangely alluring, yet forever alien to your own.

STUDIES HERE AND THERE

ON A BRIDGE

My old kurumaya, Heishichi, was taking me to a famous temple in the neighborhood of Kumamoto.

We came to a humped and venerable bridge over the Shirakawa; and I told Heishichi to halt on the bridge, so that I could enjoy the view for a moment. Under the summer sky, and steeped in a flood of sunshine electrically white, the colors of the land seemed almost unreally beautiful. Below us the shallow river laughed and gurgled over its bed of gray stones, overshadowed by verdure of a hundred tints. Before us the reddish-white road alternately vanished and reappeared as it wound away, through grove or hamlet, toward the high blue ring of peaks encircling the vast Plain of Higo. Behind us lay Kumamoto — a far bluish confusion of myriad roofs; — only the fine gray lines of its castle showing sharp against the green of farther wooded hills. . . . Seen from within, Kumamoto is a shabby place; but seen as I beheld it that summer day, it is a fairy-city, built out of mist and dreams. . . .

"Twenty-two years ago," said Heishichi, wiping his forehead — "no, twenty-three years ago — I stood here, and saw the city burn."

"At night?" I queried.

"No," said the old man, "it was in the afternoon

— a wet day. . . . They were fighting; and the city was on fire."

"Who were fighting?"

"The soldiers in the castle were fighting with the Satsuma men. We dug holes in the ground and sat in them, to escape the balls. The Satsuma men had cannons on the hill; and the soldiers in the castle were shooting at them over our heads. The whole city was burned."

"But how did you happen to be here?"

"I ran away. I ran as far as this bridge — all by myself. I thought that I could get to my brother's farm — about seven miles from here. But they stopped me."

"Who stopped you?"

"Satsuma men — I don't know who they were. As I got to the bridge I saw three peasants — I thought they were peasants — leaning over the railing: men wearing big straw hats and straw rain-cloaks and straw sandals. I spoke to them politely; and one of them turned his head round, and said to me, 'You stay here!' That was all he said: the others did not say anything. Then I saw that they were not peasants; and I was afraid."

"How did you know that they were not peasants?"

"They had long swords hidden under their rain-cloaks — very long swords. They were very tall men. They leaned over the bridge, looking down into the river. I stood beside them — just there, by the third post to the left, and did as they did. I knew that they would kill me if I moved from there. None of them spoke. And we four stood leaning over the railing for a long time."

"How long?"

"I do not know exactly — it must have been a long time. I saw the city burning. All that while none of the men spoke to me or looked at me: they kept their eyes upon the water. Then I heard a horse; and I saw a cavalry officer coming at a trot— looking all about him as he came. . . ."

"From the city?"

"Yes — along that road behind you. . . . The three men watched him from under their big straw hats; but they did not turn their heads; — they pretended to be looking down into the river. But, the moment that the horse got on the bridge, the three men turned and leaped; — and one caught the horse's bridle; and another gripped the officer's arm; and the third cut off his head — all in a moment. . . ."

"The officer's head?"

"Yes — he did not even have time to shout before his head was off. . . . I never saw anything done so quickly. Not one of the three men uttered a word."

"And then?"

"Then they pitched the body over the railing into the river; and one of them struck the horse — hard; and the horse ran away. . . ."

"Back to the town?"

349

"No — the horse was driven straight out over the bridge, into the country. . . . The head was not thrown into the river: one of the Satsuma men kept it — under his straw cloak. . . . Then all of us leaned over the railing, as before — looking down. My knees were shaking. The three samurai did not speak a single word. I could not even hear them breathing. I was afraid to look at their faces; — I kept looking down into the river. . . . After a little while I heard another horse — and my heart jumped so that I felt sick; — and I looked up, and saw a cavalry-soldier coming along the road, riding very fast. No one stirred till he was on the bridge: then — in one second — his head was off! The body was thrown into the river, and the horse driven away — exactly as before. Three men were killed like that. Then the samurai left the bridge."

"Did you go with them?"

"No: they left immediately after having killed the third man — taking the heads with them; — and they paid no attention to me. I stayed on the bridge, afraid to move, until they were very far away. Then I ran back to the burning town; — I ran quick, quick! There I was told that the Satsuma troops were retreating. Soon afterwards, the army came from Tōkyō; and I was given some work: I carried straw sandals for the soldiers."

"Who were the men that you saw killed on the bridge?"

"I don't know."

ON A BRIDGE

"Did you never try to find out?"

"No," said Heishichi, again mopping his forehead: "I said nothing about the matter until many years after the war."

"But why?" I persisted.

Heishichi gave me one astonished look, smiled in a pitying way, and answered:

"Because it would have been wrong; — it would have been ungrateful."

I felt properly rebuked.

And we resumed our journey.

THE CASE OF O-DAI

Honor thy father and thy mother. (*Deut.* v, 16.)
Hear the instruction of thy father, and forsake
not the law of thy mother. (*Proverbs* 1, 8.)

I

O-DAI pushed aside the lamplet and the incense-cup and the water vessel on the Buddha-shelf, and opened the little shrine before which they had been placed. Within were the ihai, the mortuary tablets of her people — five in all; and a gilded figure of the Bodhisattva Kwannon stood smiling behind them. The ihai of the grandparents occupied the left side; those of the parents the right; and between them was a smaller tablet, bearing the kaimyo of a child-brother with whom she used to play and quarrel, to laugh and cry, in other and happier years. Also the shrine contained a makēmono, or scroll, inscribed with the spirit-names of many ancestors. Before that shrine, from her infancy, O-Dai had been wont to pray.

The tablets and the scroll signified more to her faith in former time — very much more — than remembrance of a father's affection and a mother's caress; — more than any remembrance of the ever-loving, ever-patient, ever-smiling elders who had fostered her babyhood, carried her pickaback to every temple-festival, invented her pleasures, con-soled her small sorrows, and soothed her fretfulness

352.

with song; — more than the memory of the laughter and the tears, the cooing and the calling and the running of the dear and mischievous little brother; —more than all the traditions of the ancestors.

For those objects signified the actual viewless presence of the lost — the haunting of invisible sympathy and tenderness — the gladness and the grief of the dead in the joy and the sorrow of the living. When, in other time, at evening dusk, she was wont to kindle the lamplet before them, how often had she seen the tiny flame astir with a motion not its own!

Yet the ihai is even more than a token to pious fancy. Strange possibilities of transmutation, transubstantiation, belong to it. It serves as temporary body for the spirit between death and birth: each fibre of its incense-penetrated wood lives with a viewless life-potential. The will of the ghost may quicken it. Sometimes, through power of love, it changes to flesh and blood. By help of the ihai the buried mother returns to suckle her babe in the dark. By help of the ihai, the maid consumed upon the funeral pyre may return to wed her betrothed — even to bless him with a son. By power of the ihai, the dead servant may come back from the dust of his rest to save his lord from ruin. Then, after love or loyalty has wrought its will, the personality vanishes; — the body again becomes, to outward seeming, only a tablet.

All this O-Dai ought to have known and remembered. Maybe she did; for she wept as she took the tablets and the scroll out of the shrine, and dropped them from a window into the river below. She did not dare to look after them, as the current whirled them away.

II

O-Dai had done this by order of two English missionary-women who, by various acts of seeming kindness, had persuaded her to become a Christian. (Converts are always commanded to bury or to cast away their ancestral tablets.) These missionary-women — the first ever seen in the province — had promised O-Dai, their only convert, an allowance of three yen a month, as assistant — because she could read and write. By the toil of her hands she had never been able to earn more than two yen a month; and out of that sum she had to pay a rent of twenty-five sen for the use of the upper floor of a little house, belonging to a dealer in second-hand goods. Thither, after the death of her parents, she had taken her loom, and the ancestral tablets. She had been obliged to work very hard indeed in order to live. But with three yen a month she could live very well; and the missionary-women had a room for her. She did not think that the people would mind her change of religion.

As a matter of fact they did not much care. They did not know anything about Christianity, and did

354

not want to know: they only laughed at the girl for being so foolish as to follow the ways of the foreign women. They regarded her as a dupe, and mocked her without malice. And they continued to laugh at her good-humoredly enough, until the day when she was seen to throw the tablets into the river. Then they stopped laughing. They judged the act in itself, without discussing its motives. Their judgment was instantaneous, unanimous, and voiceless. They said no word of reproach to O-Dai. They merely ignored her existence.

The moral resentment of a Japanese community is not always a hot resentment — not the kind that quickly burns itself out. It may be cold. In the case of O-Dai it was cold and silent and heavy like a thickening of ice. No one uttered it. It was altogether spontaneous, instinctive. But the universal feeling might have been thus translated into speech:

Human society, in this most eastern East, has been held together from immemorial time by virtue of that cult which exacts the gratitude of the present to the past, the reverence of the living for the dead, the affection of the descendant for the ancestor. Far beyond the visible world extends the duty of the child to the parent, of the servant to the master, of the subject to the sovereign. Therefore do the dead preside in the family council, in the communal assembly, in the high seats of judgment, in the governing of cities, in the ruling of the land. Against the Virtue Supreme of Filial Piety — against the religion of the Ancestors — against all faith and grat-

itude and reverence and duty — against the total moral
experience of her race — O-Dai has sinned the sin that
cannot be forgiven. Therefore shall the people account
her a creature impure — less deserving of fellowship than
the Éta — less worthy of kindness than the dog in the
street or the cat upon the roof; since even these, according to their feebler light, observe the common law of duty
and affection.

O-Dai has refused to her dead the word of thankfulness,
the whisper of love, the reverence of a daughter. Therefore, now and forever, the living shall refuse to her the
word of greeting, the common salutation, the kindly
answer.

O-Dai has mocked the memory of the father who begot
her, the memory of the mother whose breasts she sucked,
the memory of the elders who cherished her childhood, the
memory of the little one who called her Sister. She has
mocked at love: therefore all love shall be denied her, all
offices of affection.

To the spirit of the father who begot her, to the spirit
of the mother who bore her, O-Dai has refused the shadow
of a roof, and the vapor of food, and the offering of water.
Even so to her shall be denied the shelter of a roof, and the
gift of food, and the cup of refreshment.

And even as she cast out the dead, the living shall cast
her out. As a carcass shall she be in the way — as the
small carrion that none will turn to look upon, that none
will bury, that none will pity, that none will speak for in
prayer to the Gods and the Buddhas. As a Gaki [1] she
shall be — as a Shōjiki-Gaki — seeking sustenance in
refuse-heaps. Alive into hell shall she enter; — yet shall
her hell remain the single hell, the solitary hell, the hell
Kodoku, that spheres the spirit accurst in solitude of
fire. . . .

[1] Prêt

356

THE CASE OF O-DAI

UNEXPECTEDLY the missionary-women informed O-Dai that she would have to take care of herself. Perhaps she had done her best; but she certainly had not been to them of any use whatever, and they required a capable assistant. Moreover, they were going away for some time, and could not take her with them. Surely she could not have been so foolish as to think that they were going to give her three yen per month merely for being a Christian! . . .

O-Dai cried; and they advised her to be brave, and to walk in the paths of virtue. She said that she could not find employment: they told her that no industrious and honest person need ever want for work in this busy world. Then, in desperate terror, she told them truths which they could not understand, and energetically refused to believe. She spoke of a danger imminent; and they answered her with all the harshness of which they were capable — believing that she had confessed herself utterly depraved. In this they were wrong. There was no atom of vice in the girl: an amiable weakness and a childish trustfulness were the worst of her faults. Really she needed help — needed it quickly — needed it terribly. But they could understand only that she wanted money; and that she had threatened to commit sin if she did not get it. They owed her nothing, as she had always been paid in advance;

357

STUDIES HERE AND THERE

and they imagined excellent reasons for denying her
further aid of any sort. :

So they put her into the street. Already she had
sold her loom. She had nothing more to sell except
the single robe upon her back, and a few pair of useless tabi, or cleft stockings, which the missionary-
women had obliged her to buy, because they thought
that it was immodest for a young girl to be seen
with naked feet. (They had also obliged her to
twist her hair into a hideous back-knot, because the
Japanese style of wearing the hair seemed to them
ungodly.)

What becomes of the Japanese girl publicly convicted of offending against filial piety? What becomes of the English girl publicly convicted of
unchastity? . . .

Of course, had she been strong, O-Dai might have
filled her sleeves with stones, and thrown herself into
the river — which would have been an excellent
thing to do under the circumstances. Or she might
have cut her throat — which is more respectable, as
the act requires both nerve and skill. But, like most
converts of her class, O-Dai was weak: the courage of
the race had failed in her. She wanted still to see the
sun; and she was not of the sturdy type able to
wrestle with the earth for that privilege. Even after
fully abjuring her errors, there was left but one road
for her to travel.

THE CASE OF O-DAI

Said the person who bought the body of O-Dai at a third of the price prayed for:

"My business is an exceedingly shameful business. But even into this business no woman can be received who is known to have done the thing that you have done. If I were to take you into my house, no visitors would come; and the people would probably make trouble. Therefore to Ōsaka, where you are not known, you shall be sent; and the house in Ōsaka will pay the money. . . ."

So vanished forever O-Dai — flung into the furnace of a city's lust. . . . Perhaps she existed only to furnish one example of facts that every foreign missionary ought to try to understand.

BESIDE THE SEA

I

THE Buddhist priests had announced that a ségaki-service, in behalf of all the drowned folk of Yaidzu, would be held on the shore at two o'clock in the afternoon. Yaidzu is an ancient place (it is mentioned, under the name of "Yakidzu," in the oldest chronicles of Japan); — and for thousands of years the fishers of Yaidzu have been regularly paying their toll of life to the great deep. And the announcement of the priests reminded me of something very much older than Buddhism — the fancy that the spirits of the drowned move with the waters forever. According to this belief, the sea off Yaidzu must be thick with souls. . . .

Early in the afternoon I went to the shore to observe preparations; and I found a multitude of people already there assembled. It was a burning July day — not a speck of cloud visible; and the coarse shingle of the slope, under the blaze of sun, was radiating heat like slag just raked from a furnace. But those fisher-folk, tanned to all tints of bronze, did not mind the sun: they sat on the scorching stones, and waited. The sea was at ebb, and gentle — moving in slow, long, lazy ripples.

Upon the beach there had been erected a kind of

rude altar, about four feet high; and on this had been placed an immense ihai, or mortuary tablet, of unpainted wood — the back of the tablet being turned to the sea. The ihai bore, in large Chinese characters, the inscription, "Sangai-Ban-Rei-I — signifying, "Resting-place [or, seat] of the myriad [innumerable] spirits of the Three States of Existence." Various food-offerings had been set before this tablet — including a bowl of cooked rice; rice-cakes; eggplants; pears; and, piled upon a fresh lotus leaf, a quantity of what is called "hyaku-mi-no-onjiki." It is really a mixture of rice and sliced eggplant, though the name implies one hundred different kinds of nourishment. In the bowl of boiled rice tiny sticks were fixed, with cuttings of colored paper attached to them. I also observed candles, a censer, some bundles of incense-rods, a vessel of water, and a pair of bamboo cups containing sprays of the sacred plant shikimi.[1] Beside the water-vessel there had been laid a bunch of miso-hagi,[2] with which to sprinkle water upon the food-offerings, according to the prescriptions of the rite.

To each of the four posts supporting the altar a freshly cut bamboo had been attached; and other bamboos had been planted in the beach, to right and left of the structure; and to every bamboo was fastened a little banner inscribed with Chinese characters. The banners of the bamboos at the four corners of the altar bore the names and attributes

[1] *Illicium religiosum.* [2] A kind of bush-clover.

of the Four Deva Kings — Zōchō Tennō, guardian of the West; Jikoku Tennō, guardian of the East; Tamon Tennō, guardian of the North; and Kōmoku Tennō, guardian of the South.

In front of the altar straw-mattings had been laid, so as to cover a space of beach about thirty feet long by fifteen wide; and above this matted space awnings of blue cotton had been rigged up, to shelter the priests from the sun. I squatted down awhile under the awnings to make a rough drawing (afterwards corrected and elaborated by a Japanese friend) of the altar and the offerings.

The service was not held at the appointed time: it must have been nearly three o'clock when the priests made their appearance. There were seven of them, in vestments of great ceremony; and they were accompanied by acolytes carrying bells, books, stools, reading-stands, and other necessary furniture. Priests and acolytes took their places under the blue awning; the spectators standing outside, in the sun. Only one of the priests — the chief officiant — sat facing the altar; the others, with their acolytes, seated themselves to right and left of him — so as to form two ranks, facing each other.

II

AFTER some preliminary rearrangment of the offerings upon the altar, and the kindling of some incense-rods, the ceremony proper began with a Buddhist hymn, or gâthâ, which was chanted to the accompaniment of hyōshigi[1] and of bells. There were two bells — a large deep-sounding bell; and a small bell of very sweet tone — in charge of a little boy. The big bell was tapped slowly; the little bell was sounded rapidly; and the hyōshigi rattled almost like a pair of castanets. And the effect of the gâthâ as chanted by all the officiants in unison, with this extraordinary instrumentation, was not less impressive than strange:

> Biku Bikuni
> Hosshin hōji
> Ikki jō-jiki,
> Fusé jippō,
> Kyū-jin kokū,
> Shūhen hōkai,
> Mijin setchū
> Sho-u kokudo,
> Issai gaki;
> Senbō kyūmétsu,
> Sansen chishu,
> Naishi koya,
> Shō-kijin to,
> Shōrai shushi....

This brief sonorous metre seemed to me particularly well adapted for invocatory or incantatory chanting; and the gâthâ of the ségaki-service was indeed a veritable incantation — as the following free translation will make manifest:

---

[1] Hyōshigi are small blocks of hard wood, which are used, either for signalling or for musical purposes, by striking them quickly together so as to produce a succession of sharp dry sounds.

STUDIES HERE AND THERE

We, Bhikshus and Bhikunis, devoutly presenting this vessel of pure food, do offer the same to all, without exception, of the Pretas dwelling in the Ten Directions of Space, in the surrounding Dharma-worlds, and in every part of the Earth — not excepting the smallest atom of dust within a temple. And also to the spirits of those long dead and passed away — and likewise unto the Lord-Spirits of mountain and river and soil, and of waste places. Hither deign therefore to approach and to gather, all ye goblins! — we now, out of our pity and compassion, desire to give you food. We wish that each and all of you may enjoy this our food-gift. And moreover we shall pray, doing homage to all the Buddhas and to all the Heavenly Ones who dwell within the Zones of Formlessness, that you, and that all beings having desire, may be enabled to obtain contentment. We shall pray that all of you, by virtue of the utterance of the dhâranîs, and by the enjoyment of this food-offering, may find the higher knowledge, and be freed from every pain, and soon obtain rebirth in the Zone Celestial — there to know every bliss, moving freely in all the Ten Directions, and finding everywhere delight. Awaken within yourselves the Bodhi-Mind! — follow the Way of Enlightenment! Rise to Buddhahood! Turn ye no more backward! — neither linger on the path! Let such among you as first obtain the Way vow each to lead up the rest, and so become free! — Also we beseech you now to watch over us and to guard us, by night and by day. And help us even now to obtain our desire in bestowing this food upon you — that the merit produced by this action may be extended to all beings dwelling within the Dharma-worlds, and that the power of this merit may help to spread the Truth through all those Dharma-worlds, and help all beings therein to find the Supreme Enlightenment, and to obtain all wisdom. And we now pray that all your acts hereafter may serve to gain for you the merit that will help you to Buddhahood. And thus we desire that you quickly become Buddhas."

Then began the most curious part of the service — namely, the sprinkling and the presentation of the food-offerings, with recitation of certain dhâranîs, or magical verses, composed of talismanic Sanscrit words. This portion of the rite was brief; but to recount all its details would require much space — every utterance or gesture of the officiant being made according to rule. For example, the hands and fingers of the priest, during the recital of any dhâranî, must be held in a position prescribed for that particular dhâranî. But the principal incidents of this complicated ritual are about as follows:

First of all is recited, seven times, the Dhâranî of Invitation, to summon the spirits from the Ten Directions of Space. During its recitation the officiant must hold out his right hand, with the tip of the middle finger touching the tip of the thumb, and the rest of the fingers extended. Then is recited, with a different, but equally weird gesture, the Dhâranî of the Breaking of the Gates of Hell. Next is repeated the Se-Kanrô verse, or Dhâranî of the Bestowal of the Amrita, — by virtue of which it is supposed that the food-offerings are transformed, for the sake of the ghosts, into heavenly nectar and ambrosia. And thereafter is chanted, three times, an invocation to the Five Tathâgatas:

Salutation to Hōshō Nyōrai — hereby besought to

relive [the Pretas] from the karma of all desire, and to fill them with bliss!

Salutation to Myō-Shikishin-Nyōrai — besought to take away from them every imperfection of form!

Salutation to Kanrō-Ō-Nyōrai — besought to purify their bodies and their minds, and to give them peace of heart!

Salutation to Kobaku-Shin-Nyōrai — besought to favor them with the delight of excellent taste!

Salutation to Rifui-Nyōrai — besought to free them from all their fears, and to deliver them out of the World of Hungry Spirits!

The book "Bongyō Ségaki-Monben" says:

When the officiants have thus recited the names of the Five Tathâgatas, then, by the grace of the power of those Buddhas, all the Pretas shall be liberated from the karma of their former errors — shall experience immeasurable bliss — shall receive excellent features and complete bodies — shall be rid of all their terrors — and, after having partaken of the food-offerings which have been changed for them into amrita of delightful taste, shall soon be reborn into the Pure Land [Jōdo].

After the invocation of the Five Tathâgatas, other verses are recited; and during this recitation the food-offerings are removed, one by one. (There is a mysterious regulation that, after having been taken from the altar, they must not be placed under a willow-tree, a peach-tree, or a pomegranate-tree.) Last of all is recited the Dhâranî of Dismissal, seven times — the priest each time snapping his fingers as a signal to the ghosts that they are free to return. This is called the "Hakken," or Sending-Away.

366

III

THE sea never ebbs far on this steep coast — though it often rises tremendously, breaking into the town; and its gentler moods are not to be trusted. By way of precaution the posts of the ihai-stand had been driven deeply into the beach. The event proved that this precaution had not been taken in vain; for the rite began, owing to the delay of the priests, only with the turn of the tide. Even while the gâthâ was being chanted, the sea roughened and darkened; and then — as if the outer deep responded — the thunder-roll of a great breaker suddenly smothered the voices of the singers and the clanging of the bells. Soon another heavy surge boomed along the shore — then another; and during the reciting of the dhâranîs the service could be heard only in the intervals of wave-bursts — while the foam sheeted up the slope, whirling and hissing even to within a few paces of the altar. . . .

And again I found myself thinking of the old belief in some dim relation between the dead and the sea. In that moment the primitive fancy appeared to me much more reasonable and more humane than the ghastly doctrine of a Preta-world, with its thirty-six orders of hideous misery, — its swarms of goblins hungering and burning! . . . Nay, the poor dead! — why should they be thus deformed and doomed by human judgment? Wiser

and kindlier to dream of them as mingling with
flood and wind and cloud — or quickening the
heart of the flower — or flushing the cheek of the
fruit — or shrilling with the cicadæ in forest-
solitudes, — or thinly humming in summer-dusk
with the gathering of the gnats. . . . I do not believe
— I do not wish to believe in hungry ghosts. . . .
Ghosts break up, I suppose, into soul-dust at the
touch of death — though their atoms, doubtless,
thereafter recombine with other dust for the making
of other ghosts. . . . Still, I cannot convince myself
that even the grosser substance of vanished being
ever completely dies, however dissolved or scattered
— fleeting in the gale — floating in the mists —
shuddering in the leaf — flickering in the light of
waters — or tossed on some desolate coast in a
thunder of surf, to whiten and writhe in the clatter
of shingle. . . .

As the ceremony ended, a fisherman mounted
lightly to the top of one of the awning-posts: and
there, gymnastically poised, he began to shower
down upon the crowd a quantity of very small rice-
cakes, which the young folks scrambled for, with
shouts of laughter. After the uncanny solemnity of
that rite, the outburst of merriment was almost
startling; but I found it also very natural, and
pleasant, and human. Meanwhile the seven priests
departed in many-colored procession — their acolytes trudging wearily behind them, under much

weight of stands and stools and bells. Soon the assembly scattered — all the rice-cakes having been distributed and appropriated; — then the altar, the awnings, the mattings were removed; — and in a surprisingly short time every trace of the strange ceremony had disappeared. . . . I looked about me; — I was alone upon the beach. . . . There was no sound but the sound of the returning tide: a muttering enormous, appalling — as of some Life innominable, that had been at peace, awakened to immeasurable pain. . . .

DRIFTING

A TYPHOON was coming; and I sat on the sea-wall in a great wind to look at the breakers; and old Amano Jinsuké sat beside me. Southeast all was black-blue gloom, except the sea, which had a strange and tawny color. Enormous surges were already towering in. A hundred yards away they crumbled over with thunder and earthquake, and sent their foam leaping and sheeting up the slope, to spring at our faces. After each long crash, the sound of the shingle retreating was exactly like the roar of a railway train at full speed. I told Amano Jinsuké that it made me afraid; and he smiled.

"I swam for two nights and two days," he said, "in a sea worse than this. I was nineteen years old at the time. Out of a crew of eight, I was the only man saved.

"Our ship was called the Fukuju Maru;[1] — she was owned by Mayéda Jingorō, of this town. All of the crew but one were Yaidzu men. The captain was Saito Kichiyĕmon — a man more than sixty years of age: he lived in Jō-no-Koshi — the street just behind us. There was another old man on board, called Nito Shōshichi, who lived in the Araya quarter. Then there was Terao Kankichi, forty-two

[1] The word "Fukuju" signifies "fortunate longevity."

370

years old: his brother Minosuké, a lad of sixteen, was also with us. The Terao folk lived in Araya. Then there was Saito Heikichi, thirty years old; and there was a man called Matsushirō; — he came from Suō, but had settled in Yaidzu. Washino Otokichi was another of the crew: he lived in Jō-no-Koshi, and was only twenty-one. I was the youngest on board — excepting Terao Minosuké.

"We sailed from Yaidzu on the morning of the tenth day of the seventh month of Manyen Gwannen [1] — the Year of the Ape — bound for Sanuki. On the night of the eleventh, in the Kishū offing, we were caught by a typhoon from the southeast. A little before midnight, the ship capsized. As I felt her going over, I caught a plank, and threw it out, and jumped. It was blowing fearfully at the time; and the night was so dark that I could see only a few feet away; but I was lucky enough to find that plank, and put it under me. In another moment the ship was gone. Near me in the water were Washino Otokichi and the Terao brothers and the man Matsushirō — all swimming. There was no sign of the rest: they probably went down with the ship. We five kept calling to each other as we went up and down with the great seas; and I found that every one except Terao Kankichi had a plank or a timber of some sort. I cried to Kankichi: 'Elder brother, you have children, and I am very young; — let me

---

[1] That is to say the first, or coronation-year, of the Period Manyen — 1860–61.

371

give you this plank!' He shouted back: 'In this sea
a plank is dangerous! — keep away from timber,
Jinyō! — you may get hurt!' Before I could answer him, a wave like a black mountain burst over
us. I was a long time under; and when I came up
again, there was no sign of Kankichi. The younger
men were still swimming; but they had been swept
away to the left of me; — I could not see them: we
shouted to each other. I tried to keep with the
waves — the others called to me: 'Jinyō! Jinyō! —
come this way — this way!' But I knew that to go
in their direction would be very dangerous; for every
time that a wave struck me sideways, I was taken
under. So I called back to them, 'Keep with the
tide! — keep with the current!' But they did not
seem to understand; — and they still called to me,
'Kocchi é koi! — kocchi é koi!' [1] — and their voices
each time sounded more and more far away. I became afraid to answer. . . . The drowned call to you
like that when they want company: Kocchi é koi! —
kocchi é koi! . . .

"After a little time the calling ceased; and I
heard only the sea and the wind and the rain. It
was so dark that one could see the waves only at
the moment they went by — high black shadows —
each with a great pull. By the pull of them I guessed
how to direct myself. The rain kept them from
breaking much; — had it not been for the rain, no
man could have lived long in such a sea. And hour

---

[1] "Come this way!"

after hour the wind became worse, and the swells grew higher; — and I prayed for help to Jizō-Sama of Ogawa all that night. . . . Lights? — yes, there were lights in the water, but not many: the large kind, that shine like candles. . . .

"At dawn the sea looked ugly — a muddy green; and the waves were like hills; and the wind was terrible. Rain and spray made a fog over the water; and there was no horizon. But even if there had been land in sight I could have done nothing except try to keep afloat. I felt hungry — very hungry; and the pain of the hunger soon became hard to bear. All that day I went up and down with the great waves — drifting under the wind and the rain; and there was no sign of land. I did not know where I was going: under that sky one could not tell east from west.

"After dark the wind lulled; but the rain still poured, and all was black. The pain of the hunger passed; but I felt weak — so weak that I thought I must go under. Then I heard the voices calling me — just as they had called me the night before: 'Kocchi é koi! — kocchi é koi!' . . . And, all at once, I saw the four men of the Fukuju Maru — not swimming, but standing by me — Terao Kankichi, and Terao Minosuké, and Washino Otokichi, and the man Matsushirō. All looked at me with angry faces; and the boy Minosuké cried out, as in reproach: 'Here I have to fix the helm; and you, Jinsuké, do nothing but sleep!' Then Terao Kankichi

373

— the one to whom I had offered the plank — bent over me with a kakemono in his hands, and half-unrolled it, and said: 'Jinyō! here I have a picture of Amida Buddha — see! Now indeed you must repeat the Nembutsu!' He spoke strangely, in a way that made me afraid: I looked at the figure of the Buddha; and I repeated the prayer in great fear — 'Namu Amida Butsu! — namu Amida Butsu!' [1] In the same moment a pain, like the pain of fire, stung through my thighs and hips; and I found that I had rolled off the plank into the sea. The pain had been caused by a great katsuo-no-éboshi. . . . You never saw a katsuo-no-éboshi? It is a jelly-fish shaped like the éboshi, or cap, of a Shintō priest; and we call it the katsuo-no-éboshi because the katsuo-fish [bonito] feed upon it. When that thing appears anywhere, the fishermen expect to catch many katsuo. The body is clear like glass; but underneath there is a kind of purple fringe, and long purple strings; and when those strings touch you, the pain is very great, and lasts for a long time. . . . That pain revived me; if I had not been stung I might never have awakened. I got on the plank again, and prayed to Jizō-Sama of Ogawa, and to Kompira-Sama; and I was able to keep awake until morning.

"Before daylight the rain stopped, and the sky began to clear; for I could see some stars. At dawn I got drowsy again; and I was awakened by a blow on

[1] This invocation, signifying "Salutation to the Buddha Amitâbha," is commonly repeated as a prayer for the dead.

the head. A large sea-bird had struck me. The sun
was rising behind clouds; and the waves had become
gentle. Presently a small brown bird flew by my
face — a coast-bird (I do not know its real name);
and I thought that there must be land in sight. I
looked behind me, and I saw mountains. I did not
recognize the shapes of them: they were blue —
seemed to be nine or ten ri distant. I made up my
mind to paddle toward them — though I had little
hope of getting to shore. I was feeling hungry again
— terribly hungry!

"I paddled toward the mountains, hour after hour.
Once more I fell asleep; and once again a sea-bird
struck me. All day I paddled. Toward evening I
could tell, from the look of the mountains, that I was
approaching them; but I knew that it would take me
two days to reach the shore. I had almost ceased to
hope when I caught sight of a ship — a big junk.
She was sailing toward me; but I saw that, unless I
could swim faster, she would pass me at a great distance. It was my last chance: so I dropped the plank,
and swam as fast as I could. I did get within about
two chō of her: then I shouted. But I could see nobody on deck; and I got no answer. In another min-
ute she had passed beyond me. The sun was setting;
and I despaired. All of a sudden a man came on
deck, and shouted to me: 'Don't try to swim! don't
tire yourself! — we are going to send a boat!' I saw
the sail lowered at the same time; and I felt so glad
that new strength seemed to come to me; — I swam

375

on fast. Then the junk dropped a little boat; and as the boat came toward me, a man called out: 'Is there anybody else? — have you dropped anything?' I answered: 'I had nothing but a plank.' ... In the same instant all my strength was gone: I felt the men in the boat pulling me up; but I could neither speak nor move, and everything became dark.

"After a time I heard the voices again — the voices of the men of the Fukuju Maru: — 'Jinyō! Jinyō!' — and I was frightened. Then somebody shook me, and said: 'Oi! oi![1] it is only a dream!' — and I saw that I as lying in the junk, under a hanging lantern (for it was night); — and beside me an old man, a stranger, was kneeling, with a cup of boiled rice in his hand. 'Try to eat a little,' he said, very kindly. I wanted to sit up, but could not: then he fed me himself, out of the cup. When it was empty I asked for more; but the old man answered: 'Not now; — you must sleep first.' I heard him say to some one else: 'Give him nothing more until I tell you: if you let him eat much, he will die.' I slept again; and twice more that night I was given rice — soft-boiled rice — one small cupful at a time.

"In the morning I felt much better; and the old man, who had brought me the rice, came and questioned me. When he heard about the loss of our ship, and the time that I had been in the water, he expressed great pity for me. He told me that I had drifted, in those two nights and days, more than

[1] As we should say, "Hey! hey!" — to call attention.

twenty-five ri.[1] 'We went after your plank,' he said, 'and picked it up. Perhaps you would like to present it some day to the temple of Kompira-Sama.' I thanked him, but answered that I wanted to offer it to the temple of Jizō-Sama of Ogawa, at Yaidzu; for it was to Jizō-Sama of Ogawa that I had most often prayed for help.

"The kind old man was the captain, and also the owner, of the junk. She was a Banshū ship, and was bound for the port of Kuki, in Kishū. . . . You write the name, Ku-ki, with the character for 'demon' — so that it means the Nine Demons. . . . All the men of the ship were very good to me. I was naked, except for a loin-cloth, when I came on board; and they found clothes for me. One gave me an under-robe, and another an upper-robe, and another a girdle; — several gave me towels and sandals; — and all of them together made up a gift of money for me, amounting to between six and seven ryō.

"When we reached Kuki — a nice little place, though it has a queer name — the captain took me to a good inn; and after a few days' rest I got strong again. Then the Governor of the district — the Jitō, as we called him in those days — sent for me, and heard my story, and had it written down. He told me that he would have to send a report of the matter to the Jitō of the Yaidzu district, after which he would find means to send me home. But the Banshū captain, who had saved me, offered to take

[1] That is to say, about sixty-three English miles.

me home in his own ship, and also to act as messenger for the Jitō; and there was much argument between the two. At that time we had no telegraph and no post; and to send a special messenger (hi-kyaku), from Kuki to Yaidzu,[1] would have cost at least fifty ryō. But, on the other hand, there were particular laws and customs about such matters — laws very different from those of to-day. Meanwhile a Yaidzu ship came to the neighboring port of Arasha; and a woman of Kuki, who happened to be at Arasha, told the Yaidzu captain that I was at Kuki. The Yaidzu ship then came to Kuki; and the Jitō decided to send me home in charge of the Yaidzu captain — giving him a written order.

"Altogether, it was about a month from the time of the loss of the Fukuju Maru when I returned to Yaidzu. We reached the harbor at night; and I did not go home at once: it would have frightened my people. Although no certain news of the loss of our ship had then been received at Yaidzu, several things belonging to her had been picked up by fishing-craft; and as the typhoon had come very suddenly, with a terrible sea, it was generally believed that the Fukuju Maru had gone down, and that all of us had been drowned. . . . None of the other men were ever heard of again. . . . I went that night to the house of a friend; and in the morning I sent word to my parents and brother; and they came for me. . . .

[1] The distance is more than one hundred and fifty miles.

DRIFTING

"Once every year I go to the temple of Kompira in Sanuki: all who have been saved from shipwreck go there to give thanks. And I often go to the temple of Jizō-Sama of Ogawa. If you will come with me there to-morrow, I will show you that plank."

OTOKICHI'S DARUMA

I

THE young folks are delighted, because last night a heavy fall of snow made for us what the Japanese poets so prettily call "a silver world." . . . Really these poets have been guilty of no extravagance in their charming praises of winter. For in Japan winter is beautiful — fantastically beautiful. It bestirs no melancholy imaginings about "the death of Nature" — inasmuch as Nature remains most visibly alive during even the Period of Greatest Cold.

It does not afflict the æsthetic eye with the spectacle of "skeleton-woods" — for the woods largely consist of evergreens. And the snow — heaping softly upon the needles of the pines, or forcing the bamboos to display their bending grace under its momentary weight — never suggests to Far-Eastern poet the dismal fancy of a winding-sheet. Indeed the singular charm of Japanese winter is made by this snow — lumping itself into grostesqueries unimaginable above the constant verdure of woods and gardens.

This morning my two students, Aki and Niimi, have been amusing themselves and the children by making a Yuki-Daruma; and I have been amusing myself by watching them. The rules for making a Yuki-Daruma are ancient and simple. You first compose a huge snowball — between three and four feet in diameter, if possible — which is to represent the squatting body of Daruma. Then you make a smaller snowball, about two feet in diameter, to represent his head; and you put this smaller ball on top of the other — packing snow around the under-parts of both, so as to fix them in place. Two round lumps of charcoal serve to make eyes for Daruma; and some irregular fragments of the same material will suffice to indicate his nose and mouth. Finally, you must scoop out a hollow in the great belly of him, to represent a navel, and stick a lighted candle inside. The warmth of the candle gradually enlarges the opening. . . .

But I forgot to explain the term Yuki-Daruma, or Snow-Daruma. "Daruma" is an abbreviation of the name Bodài-Daruma — Japanese rendering of the Sanscrit "Bodhidharma." And who was Bodhidharma?

Bodhidharma, or Bodhitara, was the twenty-eighth patriarch of Buddhism, by succession from the great Kâsyapa. He went to China as a Buddhist missionary in the first year of the Ryō dynasty [520 A.D.]; and in China he founded the great Zen (Dhyâna) sect — whose doctrine is called "The Doctrine of Thought transmitted by Thought":

that is to say, transmitted without words, either written or spoken. Says Professor Bunyiu Nanjio, in his "History of the Twelve Buddhist Sects": "Besides all the doctrines of the Mahâyâna and Hînayâna, there is one distinct line of transmission of a secret doctrine, which is not subject to any utterance at all. According to this doctrine, one is to see the so-called key to the thought of Buddha, or the nature of Buddha, directly by his own thought."

The tradition of the Zen doctrine is curious. When the Buddha was preaching upon the Vulture Peak, there suddenly appeared before him the great Brahma, who presented a gold-colored flower to the Blessed One, and therewith besought him to preach the Law. The Blessed One accepted the heavenly flower, and held it in his hand, but spoke no word. Then the great assembly wondered at the silence of the Blessed One. But the venerable Kâsyapa smiled. And the Blessed One said to the venerable Kâsyapa: "I have the wonderful thought of Nirvâna, the Eye of the True Law, which I now shall give you." . . . So by thought alone the doctrine was transmitted to Kâsyapa; and by thought alone Kâsyapa transmitted it to Ananda; and thereafter by thought alone it was transmitted from patriarch to patriarch even to the time of Bodhidharma, who communicated it to his successor, the second Chinese patriarch of the sect. By some writers it is said that Bodhidharma visited Japan;

but this statement appears to have little foundation. At all events, the Zen doctrine was not introduced into Japan before the eighth century.

Now of the many legends about Daruma, the most famous is the story that he once remained for nine years in uninterrupted meditation, during which time his legs fell off. Wherefore images of him are made without legs.

Certainly Daruma has large claims to respect. But the artists and the toymakers of the Far East have never allowed these claims to interfere with the indulgence of their sense of humor — originally bestirred, no doubt, by the story of the loss of his legs. For centuries this legendary mishap has been made the subject of comical drawings and comical carvings; and generations of Japanese children have amused themselves with a certain toy-image of Daruma so contrived that, however the little figure be thrown down, it will always bob up again into a squatting posture. This still popular toy, called "Okiagari-koboshi" (The Getting-up Little Priest) may have been originally modeled, or remodeled, after a Chinese toy made upon the same principle, and called "Puh-Tau-Ung" (The Not-falling-down Old Man). Mention is made of the Okiagari-Koboshi in a Japanese play called "Manjū-Kui," known to have been composed in the fourteenth century. But the earlier forms of the toy do not seem to have been representations of Daruma.

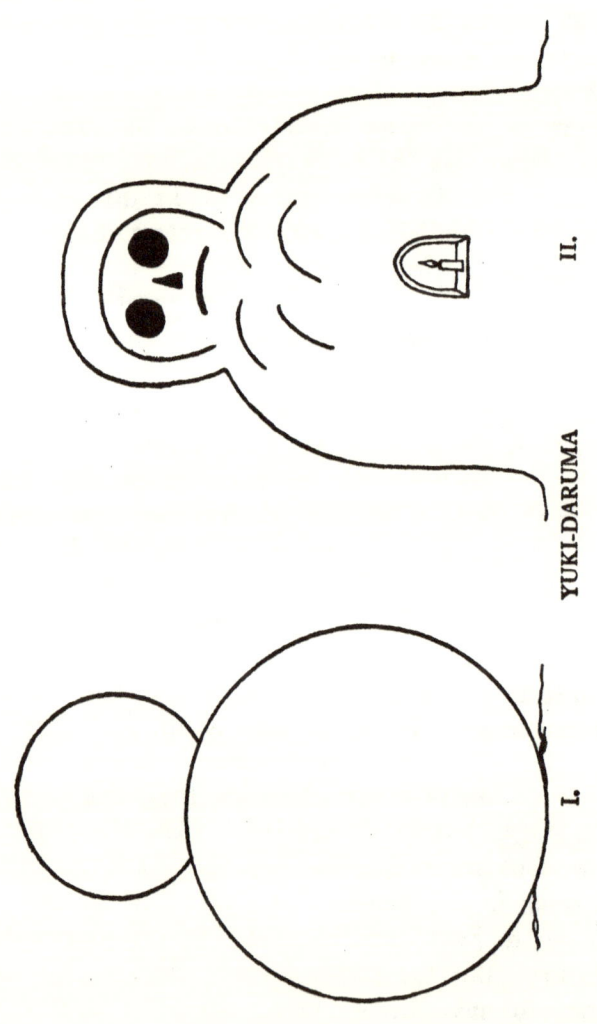

YUKI-DARUMA

I.   II.

OTOKICHI'S DARUMA

There is, however, a children's-song, dating from the seventeenth century, which proves that the Daruma-toy was popular more than two hundred years ago:

> Hi ni! fu ni!
> Fundan Daruma ga
> Akai zukin kaburi sunmaita!

[Once! twice!... Ever the red-hooded Daruma heedlessly sits up again!]

From this little song it would seem that the form of the toy has not been much changed since the seventeenth century; Daruma still wears his hood, and is still painted red — all of him except his face.

Besides the Snow-Daruma already described, and the toy-Daruma (usually made of papier-mâché), there are countless comical varieties of Daruma: figures moulded or carved in almost every kind of material, and ranging in size from the tiny metal Daruma, half-an-inch long, designed for a pouch-clasp, to the big wooden Daruma, TOY-DARUMA two or three feet high, which the Japanese tobacconist has adopted for a shop-sign.... Thus profanely does popular art deride the holy legend of the nine years' meditation.

II

Now that Yuki-Daruma in my garden reminds me of a very peculiar Daruma which I discovered several years ago, at a certain fishing-village on the eastern coast where I passed a happy summer. There was no hotel in the place; but a good man called Otokichi, who kept a fish-shop, used to let me

occupy the upper part of his house, and fed me with fish cooked in a wonderful variety of ways.

One morning he called me into his shop to show me a very fine hōbō. . . . I wonder if you ever saw anything resembling a hōbō. It looks so much like a gigantic butterfly or moth, that you must examine it closely to make sure that it is not an insect, but a fish—a sort of gurnard. It has four fins arranged like pairs of wings — the upper pair dark, with bright spots of sky-blue; the lower pair deep red. It seems also to have legs like a butterfly — slender legs upon which it runs about quickly. . . .

"Is it good to eat?" I asked.

"Hé!" answered Otokichi: "this shall be prepared for the Honorable Dinner."

[To any question asked of him — even a question requiring answer in the negative — Otokichi would begin his reply with the exclamation "Hé" (Yes) — uttered in such a tone of sympathy and good-will as to make the hearer immediately forget all the tribulations of existence.]

Then I wandered back into the shop, looking at things. On one side were rows of shelves supporting boxes of dried fish, and packages of edible seaweed, and bundles of straw sandals, and gourds for holding saké, and bottles of lemonade! On the opposite side, high up, I perceived the kamidana — the Shelf of the Gods; and I noticed, under the kamidana, a smaller shelf occupied by a red image of Daruma. Evidently the image was not a toy: there were offerings in front of it. I was not surprised to find Daruma accepted as a household divinity — because I knew that in many parts of Japan prayers were addressed to him on behalf of children attacked by smallpox. But I was rather startled by the peculiar aspect of Otokichi's Daruma, which had only one eye — a large and formidable eye that seemed to glare through the dusk of the shop like the eye of a

great owl. It was the right eye, and was made of
glazed paper. The socket of the left eye was a white
void.

Therefore I called to Otokichi:

"Otokichi San! — did the children knock out the
left eye of Daruma Sama?"

"Hé, hé!" sympathetically chuckled Otokichi —

lifting a superb katsuo to the cutting-bench — "he
never had a left eye."

"Was he made that way?" I asked.

"Hé!" responded Otokichi — as he swept his long
knife soundlessly through the argent body — "the
folk here make only blind Darumas. When I got
that Daruma, he had no eyes at all. I made the right
eye for him last year — after a day of great fishing."

"But why not have given him both eyes?" I
queried; "he looks so unhappy with only one eye!"

OTOKICHI'S DARUMA

"Hé, hé!" replied Otokichi — skillfully ranging the slices of pink-and-silver flesh upon a little mat of glass rods [1] — "when we have another day of great good fortune, then he shall be given the other eye."

Then I walked about the streets of the village, peeping into the houses and shops; and I discovered various other Darumas in different stages of development — some without eyes, some with only one, and some with two. I remembered that in Izumo it was especially Hotei — the big-bellied God of Comfort — who used to be practically rewarded for his favors. As soon as the worshiper found reason for gratitude, Hotei's recumbent image was put upon a soft cushion; and for each additional grace bestowed the god would be given an additional cushion. But it occurred to me that Daruma could not be given more than two eyes: three would change him into the sort of goblin called "Mitsumé-Kozō." . . . I learned, upon inquiry, that when a Daruma has been presented with a pair of eyes, and with sundry small offerings, he is put away to make room for an eyeless successor. The blind Daruma can be expected to do wonderful things, because he has to work for his eyes.

There are many such funny little deities in Japan — so many that it would need a very big book to describe them; and I have found that the people

1 Such a little glass mat is called sudaré.

who worship these queer little gods are, for the most part, pathetically honest. Indeed my own experience would almost justify the belief that the more artless the god, the more honest the man — though I do not want my reader to make any hasty deductions. I do not wish to imply, for example, that the superlative point of honesty might begin at the vanishing point of the god. Only this much I would venture: Faith in very small gods — toy-gods — belongs to that simplicity of heart which, in this wicked world, makes the nearest possible approach to pure goodness.

On the evening before I left the village, Otokichi brought me his bill — representing the cost of two months' good cheer; — and the amount proved to be unreasonably small. Of course a present was expected, according to the kindly Japanese custom; but, even taking that fact into consideration, the bill was absurdly honest. The least that I could do to show my appreciation of many things was to double the payment requested; and Otokichi's satisfaction, because perfectly natural and at the same time properly dignified, was something beautiful to see.

I was up and dressed by half-past three the next morning, in order to take an early express-train; but even at that ghostly hour I found a warm breakfast awaiting me downstairs, and Otokichi's little brown daughter ready to serve me. . . . As I swallowed the final bowl of warm tea, my gaze involuntarily wandered in the direction of the household gods, whose tiny lamps were still glowing. Then I noticed that a light was burning also in front of Daruma; and almost in the same instant I perceived that Daruma was looking straight at me — WITH TWO EYES! . . .

IN A JAPANESE HOSPITAL

I

... THE last patient of the evening — a boy less than four years old — is received by nurses and surgeons with smiles and gentle flatteries, to which he does not at all respond. . . . He is both afraid and angry — especially angry — at finding himself in an hospital to-night: some indiscreet person assured him that he was being taken to the theatre; — and he sang for joy on the way, forgetting the pain of his arm; — and this is not the theater! There are doctors here — doctors that hurt people. . . . He lets himself be stripped, and bears the examination without wincing; but when told that he must lie down upon a certain low table, under an electric lamp, he utters a very emphatic "Iya!"[1] . . . The experience inherited from his ancestors has assured him that to lie down in the presence of a possible enemy is not good; and by the same ghostly wisdom he has divined that the smile of the surgeon was intended to deceive. . . . "But it will be so nice upon the table!" — coaxingly observes a young nurse; — "see the pretty red cloth!" "Iya!" repeats the little man — made only more wary by this appeal to æsthetic sentiment. . . . So they lay hands upon him — two surgeons and two nurses —

[1] "No!"

lift him deftly — bear him to the table with the red cloth. Then he shouts his small cry of war — for he comes of good fighting stock — and, to the general alarm, battles most valiantly, in spite of that broken arm. But lo! a white wet cloth descends upon his eyes and mouth — and he cannot cry — and there is a strange sweet smell in his nostrils — and the voices and the lights have floated very, very far away — and he is sinking, sinking, sinking into wavy darkness. . . . The slight limbs relax; — for a moment the breast heaves quickly, in the last fight of the lungs against the paralyzing anæsthetic: then all motion stops. . . . Now the cloth is removed; and the face reappears — all the anger and pain gone out of it. So smile the little gods that watch the sleep of the dead. . . . Quickly the ends of the fractured bone are brought into place with a clear snap; — bandages and cotton and plaster-of-Paris, and yet more bandages, are rapidly applied by expert hands; — the face and little hands are sponged. Then the patient, still insensible, is wrapped in a blanket and taken away. . . . Interval, between entrance and exit: twelve minutes and a half.

Nothing is commonplace as seen for the first time; and the really painless details of the incident — the stifling of the cry, the sudden numbing of will, the subsequent pallid calm of the little face — so simulated tragedy as to set imagination wandering

393

in darksome ways. . . . A single wicked blow would have produced exactly the same results of silence and smiling rest. Countless times in the countless ages of the past it must have done so; — countless times passion must have discerned, in the sudden passionless beauty of the stricken, the eternal consequence of the act. . . . Till the heavens be no more they shall not awake, nor be roused out of their sleep. "Till the heavens be no more" — but after? Thereafter — perhaps: yet never again the same. . . .

But I felt that I had been startled more than touched by that sudden suppression of the personality, the Self — because of the mystery thereby made manifest. In one moment — under the vapor of a chemical — voice, motion, will, thought, all pleasure and pain and memory, had ceased to be; — the whole life of the budding senses — the delicate machinery of the little brain, with its possible priceless inheritance from countless generations — had been stilled and stopped as by the very touch of death. And there remained, to all outward seeming, only the form, the simulacrum — a doll of plastic flesh, with the faint unconscious smile of an icon. . . .

The faces of the little stone Buddhas, who dream by roadsides or above the graves, have the soft charm of Japanese infancy. They resemble the faces of children asleep; — and you must have seen Japanese children asleep to know the curious beauty of the immature features — the vague sweetness of the lines of lids and lips. In the art of the Buddhist image-maker, the peace of the divine condition is suggested by the same shadowy smile that makes beautiful the slumber of the child.

II

THE memory of icons naturally evoked remembrance of those powers which icons do but symbolize; and presently I found myself thinking that, to the vision of a God, the entire course of a human life would appear much like the incident which I had just witnessed — a coming, a crying and struggling, and a sudden vanishing of personality under the resistless anæsthetic of death. (I am not speaking of a cosmic divinity, to whom the interval between the kindling and the extinction of a sun would seem as brief as seems to us the flash of a firefly in the night: I mean an anthropomorphic God.) According to Herbert Spencer, the tiny consciousness of a gnat can distinguish intervals of time representing something between the ten-thousandth and the fifteen-thousandth part of a second. For a being as mentally superior to man as man to the gnat, would not the time of a generation appear but an instant? Would such a being perceive our human existence at all, except as a budding and a withering — a ceaseless swift succession of apparitions and disparitions — a mere phenomenon of fermentation peculiar to the surface of a cooling planet? Of course, were he

395

to study that phenomenon in detail, somewhat as we study ferments under the lens, he would not see the smile of the babe change instantaneously to the laughter of the skull; — but I fancy that whatever might psychologically happen, between the first smile of rosy flesh and the last dull grin of bone, would remain for him as indistinguishable as the gnat's ten or fifteen thousand wing-beats per second remain for us. I doubt whether the God of a system, or even of a single world, could sympathize with our emotions any more than we ourselves can sympathize with the life that thrills in a droplet of putrid water. . . .

But what is this human creature that, in the sight of a God, might seem to rise from earth merely to weep and laugh one moment in the light, ere crumbling back to clay again? A form evolved, in the course of a hundred million years, from out some shapeless speck of primordial slime. But this knowledge of the evolution nowise illuminates the secret of the life in itself — the secret of the sentiency struggling against destruction through all those million centuries — ever contriving and building, to baffle death, more and more astounding complexities of substance, more and yet more marvelous complexities of mind — and able at last to prolong the term of its being from the primal duration of an instant to the possible human age of a hundred years. The sentiency is the riddle of riddles.

IN A JAPANESE HOSPITAL

Thought has been proved a compounding of sensation. But the simplest sensation perceptible is itself a compound or the result of a compounding — perhaps the shock of a fusion — the flash of a blending; — and the mystery of life remains the most inscrutable, the most tremendous, the most appalling of enigmas.

From the terror of that mystery our fathers sought to save their world by uttering the black decree:

On pain of sword and fire — on peril of the Everlasting Death — THOU SHALT NOT THINK!

But the elder wisdom of the East proclaimed:

Fear not to think, O child of the Abyss, upon the Depth that gave thee birth! Divining that Formless out of which thou hast come, into which thou must dissolve again, thou shalt know thy Being timeless, and infinitely One! . . .

www.ingramcontent.com/pod-product-compliance
Lightning Source LLC
Chambersburg PA
CBHW020833030726
47496CB00001B/222